PRAISE FOR MADDIE DAWSON

"Dawson (*The Opposite of Maybe*, 2014, etc.) is a generous storyteller, creating characters who are both complex and unexpected while being wholly relatable."

—*Kirkus Reviews*

"In this heartfelt novel, Dawson (*The Opposite of Maybe*, 2014) weaves together the stories of three very different women who are bound by blood, delving deeply into the true meaning of family."

—*Booklist*

"In Nina, Dawson (*The Opposite of Maybe*) introduces a lovable, flawed character challenged by day-to-day life and searching for love and a feeling of belonging . . . Nina is delightful and spirited, and her engaging, charming story illustrates the humor and quirkiness of life."

—*Library Journal*

"Engaging writing and compelling characters seize readers from the first chapter of Dawson's latest novel. The examination of family—in all its forms and fashions—makes this an ideal book club read."

—RT Book Reviews

"Maddie Dawson writes a charming story about family in her new novel, *The Survivor's Guide to Family Happiness* . . . an endearing story of love and loss."

—Associated Press

"Maddie Dawson has been a longtime favorite writer of mine because she has the gift of tapping into the emotions and complexities of a woman's heart and effortlessly combining tension with joy. She's done it again with *The Survivor's Guide to Family Happiness*. Put it on your list of not-to-be-missed fiction."

—Marybeth Mayhew Whalen, cofounder of She Reads and author of *The Things We Wish Were True* and *When We Were Worthy*

"Like authors Liane Moriarty and JoJo Moyes, Maddie Dawson is one of those gifted writers who spins seemingly comic, romantic tales that tackle our most universal longings for love, connection, and family. In her newest book, she delivers the story of two sisters given up for adoption. Their journey to discover each other and the mother who gave them up is by turns heart-wrenching and laugh-out-loud hilarious. I loved every witty sentence."

—Holly Robinson, author of *Chance Harbor* and *Beach Plum Island*

"Maddie Dawson has done it again. Witty, warm, and full of insights into life's maddening complexities, her novels should come with a warning label: May cause tears, laughter, or all of the above."

—Sarah Knight, bestselling author of *The Life-Changing Magic of Not Giving a F*ck*

MATCHMAKING for BEGINNERS

ALSO BY MADDIE DAWSON

The Survivor's Guide to Family Happiness
The Opposite of Maybe
The Stuff That Never Happened
Kissing Games of the World
A Piece of Normal

MATCH MAKING for BEGINNERS

A Novel

MADDIE DAWSON

LAKE UNION
PUBLISHING

Published by Lake Union Publishing, Seattle

www.apub.com

ISBN-13: 9781503900684 (hardcover)
ISBN-10: 1503900681 (hardcover)
ISBN-13: 9781503901209 (paperback)
ISBN-10: 1503901203 (paperback)

Cover design by David Drummond

Printed in the United States of America

First edition

MATCH MAKING for BEGINNERS

ONE

BLIX

I shouldn't have come, and that's the truth of it. It's not even five o'clock in the afternoon, and I'm already fantasizing about a swift, painless coma. Something dramatic, involving a nice collapse to the floor, with my eyes rolling back in their sockets and my limbs shaking.

It's my niece's annual post-Christmas tea, you see, when people who are barely crawling out from underneath weeks of holiday shopping, parties, and hangovers find themselves required by Wendy Spinnaker to don their red sweaters and pleated slacks *one more time* and go stand for hours in her living room so they can admire her expensive Christmas decorations and her refurbished mansion and drink a ridiculous red cocktail that a high school student in a waitress uniform delivers on a tray.

As near as I can tell, the purpose of this gathering is simply so my niece can remind the good people of Fairlane, Virginia, that she is a Very Important Person, and wealthy besides—a force to be reckoned with. A giver to charity. A chairwoman of most things. I can't keep track of it all, to tell you the truth.

I'm tempted to stand up and ask for a show of hands. *How many of y'all have souls that have withered in just the last few hours? How many would like to join me in a conga line right out the front door?* I know I'd have some takers. My niece would also have me murdered in my bed.

I live far away, and I'm old as dirt, so I wouldn't have even come to this thing—most years I have enough sense to avoid it—but Houndy said I had to. He said I'd regret not seeing the family for the last time if I didn't. Houndy worries about things like deathbed regrets. I think he imagines the end of life like the finish of a satisfying novel: something that should be wrapped up with a nice bow, all the sins forgiven. Like that would ever happen.

"I'll go," I said to him finally, "but I am not telling them I'm sick."

"They'll know when they look at you," he said. And then of course they *didn't.*

Worse, this year *would* be the time when my grandnephew, Noah, has just gotten himself engaged, and so the party has stretched on into infinity because we're all waiting for him and his fiancée to arrive from California so she can be shown the high society she is marrying into.

"She's just some flibbertigibbet he met at a conference, and somehow she figured out how to snag him," Wendy told me over the phone. "Probably doesn't have a functioning brain cell in her head. A nursery school aide, if you can stand it. Family isn't anybody to speak of—the father's in insurance, and the mother doesn't do anything for anybody, as near as I can tell. They're from *Flah-rida.* That's how she says it. *Flah-rida.*"

I was still processing the word *flibbertigibbet* and wondering what that might mean in Wendy's universe. No doubt I'd be described as something equally dismissive. I'm still considered the family misfit, you see, the one who has to be carefully watched. Blix the Outrage. They hate that I took my inheritance and moved to Brooklyn—which anyone knows is unacceptable, populated, as it is, by Northerners.

I look around this room in the house that was once our family homestead, passed down through the generations from favorite daughter to favorite daughter (missing me, of course), and it takes everything I can muster to block all the negative energy that slithers along the baseboards. The ten-foot-tall artificial Christmas tree with its glass Christopher Radko ornaments and the twinkling fairy lights is trying to insist that everything here is just dandy, thank you very much, but I know better.

This is a family that is rotten at its core, no matter what the decor tells you.

I see things as they are, right through the fakery and pretense. I can still remember when this place really was authentically grand, before Wendy Spinnaker decided to throw thousands of dollars into some kind of fake restoration of its façade.

But that sums up this family's philosophy of life perfectly: plaster over the real stuff, and slap a veneer on the top. Nobody will know.

But I know.

A slightly drunk old gentleman with bad breath comes over and starts telling me about bank mergers he's merged and some acquisitions he's acquired, and also that he thinks my niece is the only person who can make Welsh rarebit taste like a potload of old socks. I'm about to agree with him when I realize with a start that he didn't really say that last bit. It's too loud and hot in this room, so I vaporize him with my mind, and sure enough, he toddles off.

I have my talents.

Then, miracle of miracles, just as we're all about to succumb to despair and heavy drinking, the front door opens with a whoosh, and the party suddenly takes on energy, like somebody plugged it back in and we're allowed to come back to life.

The young couple is here!

Wendy hurries over to the entryway and claps her hands and says, "Everyone! Everyone! Of course y'all all know my darling, brilliant Noah—and now *this* is his lovely fiancée, Marnie MacGraw, soon to be our *exquisite* daughter-in-law! Welcome to you, dahlin'!"

The little quartet in the corner of the living room strikes up "Here Comes the Bride," and everyone flocks around, shaking hands with the couple, blocking my view. I can hear Noah, heir to the family's bluster and bravado, booming as he talks about the flight and the traffic, while his fiancée is being manhandled and hugged as though she's a commodity who now belongs to everybody. If I crane my neck over to the right, I can see that she's truly lovely—tall and thin, red-cheeked and golden, and wearing a blue beret tipped askew with a jauntiness you don't normally see at Wendy's parties.

And then I notice something else about her, too, something about the way she peeks out from under her long blonde bangs. And—*pow!*—from across the room, her eyes meet mine and I swear something passes in a flash from her to me.

I had been about to get up from my place on the love seat, but now I fall back into it, close my eyes, and squeeze my fingers.

I *know* her. Oh my God, I actually feel like I *know her*.

It takes me a minute to regroup. Maybe I'm mistaken after all. How could it be? But no. It's true. Marnie MacGraw is just like the old glorious me, standing there, facing this onslaught of Southern gentility, and I see her both young and old, and feel my own old heart pounding like it used to.

Come over here, sweetheart, I beam toward her.

So this—*this*—is why I'm here. It wasn't to give some closure to years of family strife. It wasn't to drink these absurd cocktails or even to revisit my roots.

I was meant to meet Marnie MacGraw.

I put my hand against my abdomen, against the ball of tumor that's been growing there since last winter, the hard, solid mass that I already know is going to kill me outright before summer comes.

Come over here, Marnie MacGraw. I have so much I need to tell you.

Not yet. Not yet. She does not come.

Ah yes. Of course. There are duties to be performed when you're being shown off to polite Southern society, when you're the heir apparent's intended. And under the strain of it all, Marnie MacGraw has turned fluttery, nervous—and then she makes a dreadful faux pas, one that's so delightfully horrendous it alone would have stood her in good stead with me for a lifetime, even if I didn't already know her. She *declines* to take a portion of Wendy's Welsh rarebit. At first she simply shakes her head politely when it is thrust in her direction. She tries to claim she isn't hungry, but that's clearly untrue, as Wendy points out with her laser-like eyes flashing, because Marnie's been traveling with Noah for hours, and Wendy happens to know that they missed both breakfast and lunch and have tried to survive on airline peanuts.

"Why, honey, you *must* eat!" Wendy exclaims. "You don't have a single extra calorie on those bones, bless your heart!"

I close my eyes. She's been here only a few minutes and has already earned herself a deadly "bless your heart." Marnie, wobbly now, reaches out and takes a scone and a single red grape, but this is not the right thing either.

"No, no, my dear, have some rarebit," urges Wendy. I know the edge in the voice. Somehow Noah has failed to explain to his true love that family law here *requires* that guests take some of the rarebit, and then they must practically fall to the ground writhing in their rapture over its wonderfulness, always *so* much more wonderful than last year.

And then Marnie says the thing that seals her fate. She stammers out the words, "I-I am so sorry, but I'm really not comfortable with eating rabbits."

I put my hand over my mouth so people can't see how hard I am smiling.

Aha! My niece's eyes flash and she laughs her brittle, scary laugh and says in a loud voice that makes everyone stop and look: "My dear, wher*ever* did you get the notion that *rarebit* has anything to *do* with *rabbits*? For heaven's sake! Is it because they both start with *R*? *Please* don't tell me that's what you think!"

"I'm sorry, I didn't—oh, I'm so sorry—"

But that is that. What's done is done. The dish is withdrawn, and Wendy sweeps away, shaking her head. People turn back to their conversations. Wendy the Wronged. *Kids today. No manners at all.*

And where is Noah, Marnie's savior and protector, during this little scene? I crane my neck to see. Ah yes, he's gone off with Simon Whipple, his best friend, of course. I see him laughing at something Whipple is saying, in the adjacent poolroom, two colts stamping their hooves in delight over some incomprehensible, meaningless joke.

So I get to my feet and go fetch her. Marnie has two bright spots of color on her cheeks, and without the beret now, her blonde hair is loose and possibly the slightest bit tangled, and might have already been deemed beyond redemption by Wendy. Beach hair. Not society hair. Definitely not hair that the movers and shakers of Fairlane, Virginia, should have to see at their annual post-Christmas tea.

I bring her over to where I had camped out, and I pat the love seat next to me, and she sits down, pressing her fingertips into her temples. "I'm so sorry," she says. "I'm such an idiot, aren't I?"

"Please," I say. "No more apologies, my love."

I can see in her eyes that it's dawning on her precisely how many things she's already done wrong. Not counting the rarebit, she's also wearing the wrong kind of clothing for this little soiree. Black skinny pants! A tunic top! In the sea of the de rigueur red cashmere sweaters and coiffed, sprayed hairdos and Santa Claus earrings, Marnie MacGraw with her lanky, bangs-in-the-eyes, tangled yellow hair dares to wear a gray shirt—without even one sparkly piece of jewelry to acknowledge that Christmas is the holiest of holidays and the post-Christmas tea is the best part of Christmas! And her shoes: turquoise leather cowboy boots! Fantastic, of course. But not high-society boots.

I take her hand in mine to soothe her and also to surreptitiously check her lifeline. When you're an old woman, you can reach over and touch people since you're harmless and invisible most of the time.

"Pay no attention to Wendy," I whisper to her. "She missed the class on manners because she was attending two extra courses on personal intimidation."

Marnie looks down at her hands. "No, I was the awful one. I should have just taken the rarebit."

"The fuck you were," I whisper back, and that makes her laugh. People find it hilarious when an old woman says *fuck*; it must break every law of nature when we swear. "You were trying to politely decline eating a cute, furry animal and got embarrassed for your trouble."

She looks at me. "But—but it's not made of rabbits. I guess."

"Well, it sounds like it is. Some people still call it *Welsh rabbit*. And what? You're supposed to research all the dishes of Northern Europe in preparation for coming to a Christmas *tea*? Give me a break!"

"I should have known."

"Look, whose side are you on? Yours or Our Lady of the Hoity-Toity Mansion?"

"What?"

I pat her hand. "You're delightful," I say. "And the truth is that my niece is a bit of a stick. In fact, look around at this whole crowd. Normally I don't like to bring down the forces of evil on myself by being critical, but just look at all the fake smiles and sour faces around here. I'm going to have to take a bath with a wire brush to get all this negativity off me when I leave. And I suggest you do the same. Bunch of damn hypocrites eating the Welsh rarebit whether they like it or not. And you know what else?"

"What?"

I lean toward her and stage-whisper, "It could be made of Welsh rabbit *turds* and they would still eat it. Because Wendy Spinnaker is their overlord and leader."

She laughs. I love her laugh. We sit in a companionable silence—to anyone else's eye, we're nothing more than two strangers who find themselves making polite small talk because they'll soon be related. But I am bursting with the need to tell her everything. Of course I begin badly because I am so out of practice when it comes to small talk.

"So, tell me about you," I say in a rush. "Are you doing everything you want as an unmarried person before you hook your life up to this guy's life?"

She raises her eyebrows slightly. "Well, yes, I have a good job, and I've . . . done stuff. Gone places. You know. I'm nearly thirty, so it's time I got ready to be a real adult. Somebody who is settled down."

"*Settled down.* That sounds god-awful, doesn't it?"

"I think it sounds . . . rather nice. I mean, if you're in love with the person, then it's a good thing that you get to stop all the running around and make a home together." She looks around the room, probably searching for anything else we could talk about, and then her eyes land back on me. "By the way, I love what you're wearing tonight."

What I'm wearing is a purple velvet vintage evening gown that I bought at a thrift shop in Brooklyn. It has little glass beads sewn in circles all over it, and it shows actual, certifiable, measurable *cleavage*. Not that my cleavage is anything great; truthfully, it looks like a sack of peach pits.

"It's my showstopper dress," I tell her, and then I lean over and whisper, "I am ridiculously proud of the girls tonight. The fact is, I had to tie them up in this wired-up bra to get them to stand up enough for this, but I figure they could give me a last hurrah. After this—no more bras ever. I promised them."

"I love the colors. I didn't know what to wear, so I put on this gray shirt that I thought would go with anything, but it looks so boring compared to everybody else." She leans over and laughs. "I do *not* think I've ever seen so many red sweaters in one room."

"It's the Christmas uniform here in Fairlane, Virginia. I'm surprised they didn't issue you one at the town line."

Just then a high school student bearing a tray of drinks comes by, and Marnie and I both select a red concoction. It's my fourth, but who's counting? I clink my glass into hers, and she smiles. I can't stop looking at her eyes, which seem so much like my own that it's disconcerting. My hairline is tingling just a little.

"So," I say, "when you get married, do you think you'll get to keep on being your wonderful free-spirit self?"

Her eyes widen. "My *free-spirit* self?" she says and laughs. "No, no, no. You've got me all wrong. I'm actually looking forward to settling down. Buying a house, having kids." She smiles. "I think a person needs to have a life plan."

I take a moment, sigh a bit, and reach into my neckline to give the girls a gentle readjustment. "Maybe that's where I went wrong. I don't think I ever followed a life plan for even one minute. Tell me this: Is it worth giving up your own free spirit for?"

"A life plan is just security. Commitment."

"Ah," I say. "That stuff. Now I see why I didn't go in for it. Anytime anybody mentions security like it's a good thing, I get the willies. And *commitment*. Ugh!"

"Huh. Well, did *you* ever get married?"

"Oh God yes. Twice. Almost three times, actually. First time was to a professor with the illustrious name of Wallace Elderberry, if you please." I bend over closer to Marnie and put my hand on hers and smile. "He spent *his* one wild, precious life on Earth researching the life cycle of a certain kind of green-headed insect, and we traveled to Africa and collected specimens of hard-shelled things so bizarre you wouldn't even want to think about them for longer than twenty seconds. Can you imagine? And when we got home, I realized I'd had enough of bugs to last me my whole life." I drop my voice to a whisper. "And, if you want to know the truth of it, Wallace Elderberry himself was starting to look like a big cockroach to me. So we got a divorce."

"Wow. Husband turned into a cockroach. Sounds like Kafka."

"God, don't you just love it when people manage to bring up Kafka in a routine post-Christmas conversation?"

"Well, you started it," she says. "What happened to the second husband? What did he turn into?"

"The second time I got married against my better judgment—which you should never, ever do, by the way, just in case you're contemplating it—"

"I'm not," she says.

"Of course *you're* not, but it's an easy mistake a lot of people make. Anyway, that marriage was to Rufus Halloran, a legal aid lawyer, and we set up shop in Brooklyn in a little storefront office in the 1970s. Brooklyn was a mess then. So we did a lot of work for runaways and homeless people. That sort of thing."

"And what happened? Did he turn into a cockroach, too?"

"No. He didn't have the imagination to turn into anything, I'm afraid. He turned out to be a horribly boring human who only saw the dark side of everything. I'd look over at him, and it was as though there was a gray haze around him that I couldn't penetrate. All the well-meaningness in the world, but nothing coming off him. No genuine pleasure. Just walls of boring, long-winded words. So—divorce. Had to happen."

"Seriously?" She tilts her head, smiling, as she considers this. "You divorced a man because he was boring? I didn't know that was legal grounds."

"I had to. It was *killing* me how boring he was. It was like he had died before his life ended, and he was going to take me down with him."

"Yeah, but life can't be fascinating all the time."

"Oh, honey. Mine is. If it gets boring for longer than two weeks, I make adjustments." I smile right into her eyes. "And it's paid off because now I live with Houndy, who is a lobsterman, and the thing about him is that he could talk to me for four days straight without stopping about lobsters and their shells and the different tides and the sky, and nothing he ever said would bore me because the language that Houndy is *really* speaking in is all about love and life and death and appreciation and gratitude and funny moments."

Her eyes flicker, and I see in her face that she knows exactly what I mean.

"I feel like that when I'm at work," she says softly. "I work in a nursery school, so I get to spend my days sitting on the floor with three- and four-year-olds, talking. People think it must be the most boring thing in the world, but oh my God! They tell me about the most astonishing things. They get into philosophical discussions about their boo-boos and about how worms on the sidewalk get their feelings hurt sometimes, and why the yellow crayon is the meanest one but the purple one is nice. Can you believe it? They know the personalities of crayons."

She laughs and sticks her legs out in front of her. "I was telling my dad about this the other day, and he didn't understand it at all. Of course he thinks I should be doing something a little bit more . . . *grown up*. He'd *really* like it if I was interested in business." She stops, looks embarrassed, and then adds, "My dad is actually very nice, but he paid for me to go to a really expensive college, you see, and all I've done is become a teacher's aide. My sister—now she did him proud. Became a research chemist. But me—meh. So I told him: 'Look, Dad, you have one amazing daughter and one ordinary daughter, and one out of two isn't that bad.'"

"Listen," I say. I've been swept off my feet by all this. "Come outside with me. I want to get out of here. Do you see how all the negative energy is pooling over there by the piano? See? The air is darker over there. I think we need to go outside and get some real air."

She looks uncertain. "Maybe I should find Noah. Where is he?"

We both are suddenly aware of the party going on around us, the little knots of people talking to each other, Wendy holding court in the dining room, laughing her brayish laugh.

Noah's gone off somewhere with his friend Whipple, I tell her. They're inseparable. She might as well know that about him right now.

"Oh, yes. I've heard a lot about Whipple," she says. "Maybe I should go talk to them. Reassure Whipple that I'm not going to be the kind of wife who, you know, keeps dude friends away."

"I say you should come outside with me. Whipple can wait. Of course you're the guest of honor here, so we'll have to time our exit just right so nobody decides to stop us. Are you good at sneaking? Just follow me, and for God's sake, don't make eye contact with anyone." I grab her hand, and we set off, heads down, scurrying along the back hallway and out through the kitchen.

The maids are washing some of the trays, and one of them—Mavis, who I noticed is in love with the UPS guy who came today—calls to me, "It's cold out there, Ms. Holliday," and I say we'll come back in for tea soon.

And then finally we've made it outside, and the night air is so cold and sharp that we have to take deep breaths. It's wonderful here, in the vast expanse of the backyard, a yard that stretches out as far as a golf course, with hedges and a rose garden down to the pond. The yellow light from the party spills out onto the patio, and the garden is lit by dozens of luminaries—white paper bags glowing with electronic candles.

The night is so perfect that I'm not surprised when it starts to snow very lightly, as if someone had turned on a switch for our benefit.

"Oh my goodness!" Marnie says, holding out her hands. "Look at this! I never get to see snow! It's wonderful!"

"The first snow of the year," I say. "Always a crowd-pleaser."

"Noah told me you grew up here. Do you ever miss it?"

"No," I say. "Not when I have Brooklyn."

I tell her then about my crazy house and my crazy little community of people—a hodgepodge of kids and parents and old people, everybody coming in and out of each other's apartments and telling their stories and giving each other advice and bossing everybody around. I tell her about Lola, my best friend next door who lost her husband twenty years ago, and about Jessica and her sweet, quirky boy, and how it is with all of them needing love so much, and yet how fearful they are whenever love comes anywhere close—and then, because Marnie needs to know this, I explain that I've got this whole matchmaking thing going on with them, simply because I can't help but see who they need to belong with. I think I will tell her about Patrick, too, but then I stop because her eyes have widened and she says, "You do matchmaking?"

And bingo! Here we are, right where I needed us to land.

"Yes. I've got this little spidey-sense thing going when I see people who need to be together. You have it, too, don't you?"

She stares at me. "How did you know? I've gone around my whole life thinking about this stuff. I'll see two people, and I just know they have to be together, but I don't know how I know. I just . . . know it."

"Yes, it's the same for me."

I'm silent, willing her to talk.

"My best thing ever was when I found my sister a husband," she says at last. "He was my roommate's brother, and I met him when he came to pick up my roommate for Christmas break, and at that very moment, I *knew* he was going to be right for Natalie. I couldn't think of anything else. It was like my heart *hurt* until I could introduce them. And then, sure enough—when they met—fireworks. They fell for each other almost immediately. I don't know how I knew, but I did."

"Of course you did," I say softly.

I look out at the gardens and the trees, so shadowy against the white, snowy sky, and I want to fall down in gratitude. Here I am; I'm at the end of my life, and the universe has sent her to me. At last.

"You have many gifts," I say when I can speak again.

"You think that's a gift? The way I see it is that I'm just this person who sits around and thinks, 'Wow, my coworker Melinda might want to hang out with the guy who teaches soccer in the after-school program, because they kind of match each other.' Meanwhile, my sister is inventing things that are going to save the world, and what's taking up space in my brain most days is who in my vicinity looks like they could fall in love. Big deal."

I feel my heart pounding so loudly I have to squeeze my fingers to ground myself. "Please," I say. "The subversive truth about love is that it really *is* the big deal everyone makes it out to be, and it's not some form of security or an insurance policy against loneliness. It's *everything*, love is. It runs the whole universe!"

"Well. It's not more important than the work of curing cancer," she says.

"Yes. It is. It's the life force. It's all there is, in fact."

She hugs herself, and I watch her as snowflakes land gently on her arms.

"Sometimes," she says, "I see colors around people. And little lights. My family would be horrified if they knew. They'd see it as some kind of neurological condition, I think. But I see—little showers of sparks coming from nowhere."

"I know. It's just thought energy," I tell her. And then I bite my lip and decide to plunge right in. "Do you ever use thoughts to make things happen? Just for fun?"

"What do you mean?"

"Well, watch. Turn around and let's look in the window there. See—um, let's choose the woman in the red sweater."

She laughs. "Which one? They all have red sweaters."

"The one with the red hair. Let's just beam some thoughts over to her. Send her some white light. Go ahead, and watch what happens."

We're both silent. I bathe the woman in a glow with white light, the way I do. And sure enough, after about thirty seconds, she puts down her drink and looks around the room, as though she's heard her name being called. Marnie laughs in delight.

"See? We did that! We sent her a little hit of something good, and she got it," I say.

"Wait a minute. That's energy? Does it always work?"

"Not always. Sometimes you get resistance. I only do it for fun. The matchmaking stuff—that seems to come from somewhere else. It's like I get *shown* which people should be together."

She looks at me with interest. The red spots on her cheeks are glowing brighter. "So did you figure out a way to make a living by being a matchmaker, then? That's maybe what I need to figure out."

"Ah, honey. I make a living being me. What I've learned is that the same intuition that lets me know which people need to be together also leads me to exactly what I need. Ever since I made up my mind to live the way I wanted to live, I've been provided for."

"Wow," she says and laughs. "I'm picturing myself trying to explain that to my dad." Then she grabs my hand. "Hey! Will you come to our wedding? I really, really want you to be there."

"Of course I will," I tell her. *If I'm still around. If I can.*

And that's when the universe evidently decides that enough is enough, and Noah appears, coming out of the back door and striding toward us. Like a man on a slightly annoying mission.

"I've been looking for you everywhere," he says. "Oh my God, it's snowing out here! And you guys don't even have coats on."

"I don't need one. It's wonderful," says Marnie. "Look how it sparkles in the light. I had no idea it did that."

"It's just flurries," he says and comes over and puts his arm across her shoulders. *He's such a handsome man,* I think, *with his dark hair and eyes, but it's so sad how he carries around him an aura of cloudy beige.*

Marnie turns a bright, lovely pink and she looks at him so fondly, it's like there's a spray of stars all around her.

"I've just been having the most delightful conversation with your fiancée," I tell him.

"Well, that's great, but we've got to get going," he says without looking at me. "Good to see you, Aunt Blix, and I'm sorry it's so short, but we've got another party to get to."

I'm sure he doesn't remember that he once adored me, that we used to walk in the woods together and stomp in puddles in our rain boots or bare feet, and that one summer we caught fireflies and minnows and then blessed them and let them go. But that was a long time ago, and sometime along the way, he seems to have adopted his mother's position that I am not worth bothering about.

I'm over it—really I am. I'd hoped for so much more, but now I'm so used to my family's indifference that I don't even mind the way they roll their eyes when they think I don't notice, and how they're always saying, *"Oh, Blix!"*

Marnie links her arm in Noah's and kisses him on the cheek, and tells me, in case I didn't know, that he's the *best* third-grade teacher there is, and that all the kids in his class and their mothers just love him to death. I look at him and smile.

Noah shifts uncomfortably. "Marnie, I'm afraid we really have to go. Traffic is building as we speak."

"Of course you do," I say. "I'd get out of this party, too, if I could think of a plausible excuse."

His expression stays the same, but she turns and grins at me. "So . . . ," he says to her. "I'll go get your coat for you. Is it in the den?"

"I'll get it," she says, but I touch her arm and when she looks at me, I shake my head just slightly. *Let him go.* And as soon as he's gone, I say, "Listen, I've got to tell you this. You're amazing and powerful, and you're in line for a big, big life. There are lots of surprises in store for you. The universe is going to take you to such heights."

She laughs. "Uh-oh. I don't think I really like surprises."

"These will be good ones, I'm sure," I say. "This is the important thing. Don't settle for anything you don't want. That's the main thing."

I close my eyes. I want to tell her that she is all golden and Noah is all beige, and that there's an unfortunate muddiness in the air when he looks at her—and if I could, if I didn't know that she'd decide I was crazy, I'd tell her that she and I are linked somehow, that I've been looking for her.

But now Noah's back with the coat and the purse and the instruction that she needs to go inside and tell his family good-bye.

She turns to him. "Your Aunt Blix says she'll come to the wedding, isn't that great?"

He helps her on with her coat, saying, "Yeah, well, tell my mom to add her to the list," and then he pecks me on the cheek. "Take care of yourself," he says.

It's time to go. He strides away in that manly, impatient way, motioning for her to follow.

"Here! Take this! Some color for you." I pull off my scarf, my favorite one with the blue silk burnouts and the straggly fringe, and I put it around her neck, and she smiles and blows me a kiss.

As they go inside, I see her tilt her face up to his, pink and gold and scarlet with love, a shower of sparks.

Once they're gone, the air slowly settles down around me. The sparks quiet themselves and burn away, like those Fourth of July sparklers once they've used up their fuel and are about to turn back into sharp metal sticks.

I close my eyes, feeling suddenly drained and tired. And then I know something I didn't know before, a truth as insistent as anything I've ever felt: Marnie MacGraw and Noah are not going to marry.

In fact, it's already over.

TWO
MARNIE

"Oh my God, that was an epic fail," says Noah in the car. "Epic! And Whipple, you freak, could you possibly drive like you're even slightly sober? Like you're not *trying* to get a DUI? We're hoping to stay alive back here."

Whipple's car—a brand-new BMW convertible—does seem to be taking the corners on two wheels, I swear, and he appears to have perfected the art of driving with two fingers of his left hand as he holds a cocktail glass in his right hand. A glass that keeps sloshing red alcohol onto the seats and into the center console.

I had automatically gotten into the backseat, and then, to my surprise, Noah had jumped in beside me, leaving Whipple alone in the front, which means he has to crane his neck around backward so he can keep up with the conversation. And every time he moves his head, the car swerves off course, and he mashes his foot even harder on the gas pedal.

Oh, so much of tonight has been a disappointment. I do *not* want to start off married life with mother-in-law problems. My boss, Sylvie, says that's just the worst thing you can do. And now that I'm in the car, I can also hear my mother's voice in my ear: "That was so rude of you, to sit there all night talking to one old lady! You should have gone and mingled with all the other guests! That's what that party was for, for you to meet your fiancé's family and friends."

And now this, the biggest disappointment of all—the great Simon Whipple, whom I have heard such fantastic things about, turns out to be nothing more than your standard-issue, red-faced, laughing, overgrown frat boy. And in his presence, Noah seems to be regressing more by the minute.

Apparently we're heading to the home of one of their other friends that Noah says I've got to meet. It's the Hometown Tour, Noah told me. Meet the freaks. He pulls me over to him, roughly, and starts sucking on my neck like he's going to give me a hickey. Like he thinks we're in high school just because we're in the backseat. "Holy shit, I am so, so sorry for what I did to you back there," he says in my ear, way too loudly. "Leaving you in the clutches of my Aunt Blix."

"You owe her big-time," says Whipple.

"Right? She's like the old woman in the forest who eats children."

"That's because she's a witch," says Whipple. "Marnie, you're lucky there's anything left of you. I told him, 'Dude, you gotta go get your girlfriend, man. Between your mom and your great-aunt, she's gonna run for the hills.'"

"Not this one," says Noah. "I've got this one in the bag."

I pull away from him. His beard is scratching me, and his breath smells like a brewery. I finger the scarf she gave me. It's amazing, with lots of shades of blue, and holes that look like they were burned out on purpose. "For real she's a witch?" I say, and that makes them both laugh. "No, no, tell me. Does she, like, practice witchcraft? Is she in a coven or something?"

"I don't know about a coven," says Whipple, "but she totally does spells, doesn't she, dude?"

"Spells and potions and all that shit," says Noah. "She's got the whole thing down. It's all over-the-top drama, if you ask me."

"She seems really nice," I say. "I liked her."

Noah leans forward between the seats and takes the drink out of Whipple's right hand and gulps down the rest of it.

Whipple laughs. "Hey! That was *mine*. I earned that, dude."

"I need it more, man, and besides, you're driving."

"Tell me," I say. "What has she done? I can't believe you really think she's a witch."

But they have moved on by this time, talking about whether or not some girls they knew in high school are going to be at the party we're all going to. Somebody named Layla is going to *shit* when she finds out that Noah is engaged without checking with her.

I look out the window at all the passing houses—big mansion-type things with huge lawns decorated with white twinkly lights wrapped around the tree trunks, and Christmas trees illuminating the windows. Boughs of holly, fa la la la la. So genteel, so rich.

I wonder if I'll ever really fit in here.

Funny, I think later, how you can meet a random handsome guy in California at a party, and he tells you he once wrote movie scripts and one almost got accepted but then didn't, and he tells you that he's now teaching school, and he loves kids and he loves to go snowboarding in the mountains in the winter and later, in bed, after he's managed to do amazing things to you, he tells you just how much he wants to help people in the world, and you can't believe how moved you are at the way his eyes change when he tells you that, how much depth he has, and you find yourself falling in love with these pieces of him that he shows you—and then later, much later, after he's moved in with you and bought you a deluxe garlic press and a pair of amazing turquoise boots and has written a song for you that he plays on his guitar, you go back to his hometown with him and find out that, oh my God, he's the somewhat spoiled son of *rich* people who let him get away with murder and who don't seem to automatically care about you, except for one ancient aunt no one else seems to like.

You see that he contains so many contradictions. And that you will have to make peace—and you will—with these people who are going to be your in-laws, and you will learn to please them. But you also know that after that night, you will look at him completely differently, and that one of the new things you'll know about him is that it's a miracle he survived his childhood and arrived intact at your heart.

And yet you still love him to pieces.

But in the days that follow your return home, you wonder why he won't answer your questions about his Aunt Blix without rolling his eyes, and why he's slightly disgruntled that you invited her to the wedding without checking with his mom first. He changes the subject, and you change it back, and he sighs and says, "Oh, she didn't get the money she wanted, and so she moved up north, and got weird. She looks at everybody like she can see straight through them, down to all the layers of bad stuff."

And you say something about how she maybe admires the so-called bad stuff (you make air quotes for this), and *he* wonders why you're so obsessed with his Aunt Blix, and you say that you're not obsessed. And you're not.

But you do wonder why in your spare time, when you're not thinking of anything else, you're having a conversation with Blix in your head. You're wondering if she's right that love is the true expression of everything in the universe, and if the sparkles you see are real. You're telling her that she's wrong about you—that you're *not* up for a big life and surprises; you just want ordinary love and happiness with her grandnephew. A house in the suburbs and three children.

And somehow, in a way you can't explain, you know she's not convinced in the least. And that just by knowing her, you're walking into something that's bigger than you are, that might even turn out to be some kind of mystical crazy thing you're never going to be able to explain to anyone. Like the time you went to the planetarium show and looking up at the stars that represented billions of light-years, you felt like a little point of pulsating light, a flicker in the universe, but something that was meant to exist.

And maybe *that's* why I have a headache.

THREE
MARNIE

Five months later—after weeks and weeks of wedding preparations, dress buying, invitation writing, venue selecting, all of it mostly orchestrated by my mom and okayed by me via telephone and Skype—I sit in the little room off the side of my parents' hometown church in Jacksonville, Florida, the room where in the normal universe the beautiful bride is to wait with her happy attendants, and I watch while everything in my life falls apart in slow motion.

Noah has not shown up for the wedding.

He is now forty-seven and a half minutes late, which, as I keep explaining to anyone who will listen, is still going to be okay. He will come strolling in. *He will.*

He could even send a text message that says something like *Hey! I'm at the Episcopal church! Where is everyone?* And then I'll say, *Ha ha ha! Wait! Not the Episcopal church! We're getting married at the Methodist church a block away!* And we'll both type in a smiley emoji, then he'll speed over, and it will all be fine.

But so far nothing like that has happened.

So far what *is* happening is that I am sweating my head off in this torture chamber with my sister, Natalie, and my two childhood friends, Ellen and Sophronia, and I am wearing a dress my mother picked out for me, a dress that I now see makes me look like a gigantic white upholstered chair, and my tongue has become this dried-out, fat piece of meat sitting in my mouth, and my hair is pulled so tightly back in a bun that it actually *hurts* my forehead, and my feet are swelling to twice their normal size, *and* it is approximately ninety-seven thousand degrees in this windowless room, and my sister and my two attendants will mercifully not look at me because they are so embarrassed for me that all they can think to do is stare into their phones until the world ends.

From the sanctuary, I hear the organist playing the same three chords over and over again. I wonder how many hours she would go on playing those chords, and how she'll know when to stop. Whose job is it to call off the wedding anyway? Maybe it's like a death, and the minister and my father—and probably *me*—will all look at our watches and one of us will say, "Well, this is it. I'm calling it. Four thirty-four. Wedding's not going to happen, folks."

Ohgodohgodohgodohgod. Noah is never late to anything unless an airline is involved, and so this means that he's either dead, or else he and Whipple are now on their way to some fabulous adventure that girls can't be part of. In which case I will have to hunt down my supposed-to-be husband and kill him.

What if he's dead? What if any moment now a police officer shows up and leads me down to the hospital, and I have to stand there in my wedding dress, hysterically weeping, while I identify his body?

I unpin the veil and start clawing my pulled-back hair out of its restraints.

"No," says Natalie. "Don't do that." She comes over and sits next to me, her eyes damp and luminous. She is six months pregnant, and maybe because she's carrying the future in her body, she is lately a bit hyperconcerned that the world might not turn out to be a predictable, rational place. She always looks like she's about to cry. Two days ago she picked me up from the airport when I came in from California for the wedding, and when a Prince song came on the radio, honest to God, she had to pull the car over because she was crying too hard to see. All because Prince shouldn't have had to die, she said.

"There's going to turn out to be a reasonable explanation for this," she says now in a high, wavery voice. "Maybe the bridge is out. Or maybe the tux shop was closed. Text him again."

I laugh. "Seriously, Nat? The *bridge*? The tux shop? Seriously?"

"Text him again."

So I do.

Hi my luv monkey . . . how's it going?

Nothing.

Can't wait to see U! #marriedtoday!!!!!

Crickets. Five minutes later, I write: *You up? LOL!*

Unbeknownst to Natalie, I make a deal with the universe: if I put down my phone and don't look at it while I count to one thousand, then when I pick it up again, he will be typing. The three little dots will be blinking at me, and he'll say he was on his way, but he just had to save somebody's life, or there was a hurt dog in the street and he had to find the owner, and he is so, so sorry, but who could leave a dog who was hurt?

I count to eight hundred and forty-eight, and then I say, "Forget this," and I write in rapid succession:

WTF?? R U OK?

Noah Spinnaker, if you don't get here soon, I am going to FREAK OUT AND PROBABLY DIE!!!!!!!!

Pleasepleasepleasepleaseplease.

Just please.

My father, all dolled up in his father-of-the-bride tuxedo, peeks in the door.

"How are you holding up, Ducky?" he asks. He hasn't called me that since I was ten and begged him to stop, so I know he is losing it.

"She's *coping*, okay?" says Natalie. "Maybe somebody needs to go and look for this son of a bitch and bring him here."

We're all stunned into silence.

I can see my dad thinking, *Uh-oh, pregnancy hormones,* and then he looks at me and says, "Um, Noah's great-aunt is out here, and she wants to know if she can have a word with you."

"Sure, send her in," I say, swallowing.

And then there's Blix, striding in, looking like she got dressed from the bargain bin at a 1970s clothing consignment shop, but in a good, fun way. She's wearing a long pink tulle skirt and some kind of silvery, shimmery shirt with a bunch of lacy scarves all tied up in loopy knots, long turquoise earrings, and about a hundred beaded bracelets. Nothing goes together, and yet somehow she makes it look like an art project. Her crazy white Einstein hair is moussed up into little points, and she's wearing bright red lipstick, and her eyes are extra beady and sharp today—X-ray eyes, Noah calls them, the better to see deep into your soul.

I have to admit I feel a little flicker of hope that maybe she really *is* a witch. Maybe she's like the fairy godmother in *Cinderella* and she'll say, *Bibbity bobbity boo* and conjure Noah up right in front of me—and then my life, which seems to have curled up into the fetal position, will somehow stand up and stretch and crank itself back up into normalcy.

Yes. I am precisely *that* far gone.

Ellen, Sophronia, and Natalie look shocked. I raise my hand in a listless wave.

"Well, what the actual *hell*?" Blix says, and we all laugh weakly. "The life force is *running* out of this room! I've been at *funerals* that had better vibrations than this." She puts her hands on her hips and looks around at us, taking in our wedding finery, and for a moment I think she might be about to dispense some fashion advice. Perhaps we need more of something. That's what's gone wrong: not even one floaty scarf among the four of us.

But instead, she comes over and takes my damp hands in her cool, bony ones, and says, dryly, her eyes shining with trouble and mischief: "I'm not here to make you feel worse, but I just want to tell you that I hope we don't have to kill him today. But if we do, we do. I want you to know I'm up for it. You girls with me?"

I see Natalie start to blink very rapidly.

"I don't think we'll have to *kill* him," I say quietly, although I had, of course, been thinking the same thing. I wouldn't be surprised if Blix knows that.

"Yeah, well, he's pushing his luck," she says and pulls up a chair like somebody who's settling in for the duration. "But we've got to take care of you. The important thing is: Are you *breathing* consciously? You're not, are you?"

I try to breathe, to make her happy.

"You know, what we need here is to raise the vibe. We need the Breath of Joy. It's a yoga thing. I'll show you how to do it." And to my surprise, she stands up and throws her arms up over her head and then swings them down fast by her sides while she bends her knees and collapses her middle. When her head is almost down to her knees, she lets out a loud "ARRRRRRRGH!"

She rights herself and looks at us. "Five times! Fast! Come on, ladies. Yell it out. Arrrgh! Arrrrgh!"

We all do it, except for Natalie. The rest of us are scared not to.

Blix claps her hands when we're finished. "Excellent, excellent! Oh my God. You young women are so beautiful, you know that? And men are—well, I like men just fine, but if we're honest, we have to admit that most of them are just smelly, sweaty, grunting ball scratchers. Somehow we're supposed to love 'em anyway." She shakes her head. "Gotta love it. Nature's joke. Can't live with 'em, can't shoot 'em."

And with that, she leans over and plants a soft, dry kiss on my cheek and stares into my eyes. She smells like powder and chai tea and something herbal, possibly marijuana. "I like you," she says. "Take it from me. He's my grandnephew, but like so many men out there, particularly the ones from my family, I'm sorry to say, he's not worth a poot. I think now's as good a time as any to ask yourself if you really do want him after all. Because, I'm just saying, we *could* all leave now and go to the beach. Skinny-dip or something."

She stands back upright and laughs again. "You're welcome," she says, "for that image I just put in your heads of me skinny-dipping."

Then she reaches into her massive bra and whips out some bottle of essential-oil that she says I need to inhale because it will calm me down, bring on the positive vibes, center my aura. She puts it under my nose. It smells like roses and lavender. She's chanting something I can't quite hear, closing her eyes, and she presses her forehead up against mine in a mind meld and says, "For the good of all and the free will of all, so mote it be," and then she opens her eyes and looks around at us. "Look, sweetie, I've got to get back to the family. The natives are getting restless out there. Trying to figure out what's come over the prodigal son, figure out if this is all their fault. Raising him so entitled and all." She wrinkles her nose. "I'm sorry he's putting you through this. I really do think there might be something wrong with that boy."

"Maybe he just overslept," I say. "Or maybe the bridge is stuck in the up position and he can't get across. Or maybe he misplaced part of his tux, and he didn't realize which tux shop my dad was using so he's lost, and his phone isn't charged."

Blix laughs. "Yeah, and maybe Mercury is in retrograde, too, or he's got jet lag or there are sunspots. Who knows? But *you* are going to be fine. Big life. Remember that. I told you that. A big, big life for you."

She blows kisses to all of us and sashays out. And that's when I hear it: the roar of Whipple's BMW out in the parking lot. They're here. Fifty-eight minutes late, but they're here, and oxygen flows back into the room like somebody turned on the valve once again.

I stand up, still shaking.

We hear pounding footsteps, and then the door bursts open, and there is Noah, standing there looking more like he's arriving to film a battle scene than to get married. His hair is sticking up all over the place, and he didn't shave, and his eyes are like little black dots in a sea of bloodshot white space—and—and—oh my God, he is wearing his tuxedo shirt with his pair of blue jeans.

I put my hand over my mouth. I may be making a little sound. Something a pigeon would say.

"Marnie," he says. "Marnie, I have to talk to you."

He leads me outside. *Outside* outside—not to the parking lot, or the little sidewalk area in front where all the nice people gather after church to talk. No, he takes me by the hand to the meadow off to the side of the church, where the church school holds picnics. Where I got my first kiss when I was in seventh grade. Steve Peacock. His parents are right now in that church waiting to watch me get married.

"Marnie," he says, and his mouth is so dry it makes a clacking sound when he talks. I want him to stop saying my name. I want him to look normal and happy and groom-like, but none of that is going to happen. "Marnie," he says, "baby, I am so, so sorry, but I'm afraid there is no way I can do this."

And the world—the big, vast, beautiful world—vanishes, shrinking down to a little point right in front of me. The only thing left is the blood roaring through my ears, and some deep feeling that nothing—nothing—is ever going to make sense again.

FOUR
MARNIE

This kind of thing has actually happened to me before.

In third grade, I was chosen to be Mary in the Christmas Eve pageant. I was to wear my mother's blue filmy bathrobe, and I made a foil halo that tied to my plastic headband. Being Mary was the high point of my life up to that time—a life in which I was already realizing that my older sister, Natalie, was going to walk away with all the best prizes, things she didn't even seem to strive for: good grades, teachers' admiration, boyfriends, the plastic diamond ring in the Cracker Jack box.

But Natalie couldn't be Mary because she had already been Mary two years ago, and so she had to be a shepherd. It was all me, and I would be propped up there by the manger, holding the Smiths' eight-week-old baby, who was playing the part of Baby Jesus. Mrs. Smith had taught me how to support the baby's head and everything.

But when we went to the church for the pageant, it turned out there was a terrible mix-up; according to the rules, Janie Hopkins, a fourth grader, was *really* the next in line to be Mary. There was a list, you see. And even though Janie hadn't been to Sunday school in *months*, now she was here, and besides, she was going to move away in the spring and was sad about it, so the Sunday school director knelt down to my level, and looking at me with her eyes all full of feeling, she told me she hoped I'd understand but we really did have to be Christian about it and let Janie be Mary. My throat closed up but I managed to say of course, fine. I took off the halo and the bathrobe, and I sat in the audience because by then there wasn't even a shepherd costume for me.

And then in ninth grade, Todd Yellin called the house, and when I answered the phone he asked me to go to the movies with him, and I said yes, and the next day at school when I went over to him at lunchtime, it turned out that he had thought he was talking to *Natalie* instead of me, and that's who he wanted to take. Natalie! She wasn't even in his grade. I was. And then in twelfth grade, the worst thing of all happened: my boyfriend, Brad Whitaker, the coolest guy in the whole senior class, somehow *forgot* we were boyfriend and girlfriend and asked someone else to the prom.

And here I am, the same old Marnie, only now it's so much worse because it's my *wedding day*, damn it, the day I get to have it be about me and the man who said he loved me, only the light is too bright, the bees too loud, and Noah's hands are shoved in his jeans pockets, and he is walking in circles, looking down at the ground.

And it's all so unfair because he loved me first, damn it. *He* was the one who thought it was time we moved in together, a guy who is so adventurous and amazing that he proposed to me on an ultralight plane he'd rented just for that purpose—not realizing it would be so loud up there that he'd have to shout, and that the gusting wind was going to send the engagement ring sailing into the sky and that he'd have to buy a new one.

Also, he wrote an actual song to sing at the wedding, a song about our love. And he tells me he loves me all the time. He brings me a bag of chocolate almonds every Friday afternoon. He polishes my toenails, and . . . and he lights candles around the bathtub for me. And whenever

I start feeling low about missing my family, he declares we're having a Play Hooky Day, and we stay in the house in our pajamas, eating ice cream out of the carton and drinking beer.

And now he has gone out of his mind.

It's a panic attack, that's all this is. I take a deep breath and reach out and take his hand. "Noah," I hear myself say. "It's okay, honey. Take a deep breath. Here, sit down. Let's take deep breaths together," I say.

"Marnie, listen, I love you too much to do this to you. It's not going to work. We're not going to make it. I see that now. I am so, so sorry, baby, but I can't."

"Of course we're going to make it," I hear myself say. "We love each other, and that's—"

"No! No, it's not. It's not enough to love each other. You think I want to do this to you? Marnie, I'm fucked up. I'm not ready to do the husband thing. I thought I could, but I have stuff I still need to do. I can't, baby."

My mouth goes dry. "Is there someone else? Do you have another woman?"

"No," he says. His eyes dart away. "God, *no*! No one. It's not that."

"Then. What. Is. It."

"I can't put it into words. I just can't say those vows. I can't settle down yet, be some man with a lawn mower."

"A *lawn mower*? What the hell does a lawn mower have to do with it?"

He's quiet.

"It's the permanence? That's what the lawn mower means? Just what the hell is it about the lawn mower, Noah?"

He puts his hands over his face and sits down in the tall grass.

I start laughing. "Ohhh, I know what this is! You and Whipple stayed up all night, didn't you? And now you're hungover and sleep deprived, and you're probably dehydrated. You need to eat every few hours, and you need at least six hours of sleep, or you go crazy."

He doesn't answer me, just keeps his head in his hands.

"Damn it, Noah Spinnaker. People are waiting for us, and all you need is a nap, some ibuprofen, and about a gallon of ice water, maybe a Bloody Mary and maybe a cheeseburger with onion rings, and you'll be fine."

It's suddenly crystal clear even in its craziness.

I plop myself down on the ground next to him. I am the only one who can save him, and the only way to save him is to marry him, and yes, there will be grass stains and possibly mud on my dress, but I don't care. I rub his back, his fine muscled back that I have rubbed a thousand times and want to spend at least the next fifty years rubbing.

"Noah, darling, it's all right. Listen, I love you more than life itself, and I know that we are meant to be together, and that we are going to have a happy marriage."

"No," he says into his arm. "It won't work."

"It will work, trust me. And if it doesn't—so what? We'll get divorced. People do it all the time."

There's a silence and then he says, "Divorce is terrible."

I explain then how much more terrible it would be if one of us has to walk into that church and break the hearts of my parents and all the people sitting there by announcing there will not be a wedding because of lawn mowers.

After a moment, he says, "What if we're making a huge mistake?"

"It's not a mistake," I say, and I realize I believe that with all my heart. "Anyway, let's make a mistake if we have to! So what? That's what living *is*, Noah. Failing and making mistakes and figuring it out as you go along, for next time. At least we're *alive* and trying things. Listen—let's just do this. If we have to get a divorce tomorrow, we will. But today we'll go in there and say those words out loud and everybody will clap for us, and then we'll dance a waltz and eat some wedding cake, and we'll go on the honeymoon because windsurfing in Costa Rica sounds pretty good, doesn't it? And then we'll come back, and if we want to, we'll get a divorce."

"Oh my God, you're insane," he says. "You're actually fucking crazy!"

"It would be hard at this moment to say for sure who is more insane," I say in a low voice. "Come on. Let's go drink to a big mistake!"

I have him. I see with some surprise that I am stronger than he is and that I always have been.

"Let me put this another way," I say amicably. My hands are on my hips. "I *am* marrying you today. I just am. So get up. Suck it up and come with me."

And he does. He actually does it. I am not even surprised when he gets up. I knew he would.

We don't touch each other on the way into the church. We walk in quickly, with our heads down, and we stride down the aisle together—him in his jeans and me in my grass-stained wedding dress—and people actually stand up and clap for us. They do. They clap so hard it's as though we're Prince and Michael Jackson and possibly even Elvis *and* the Three Stooges, all returned from the dead.

I keep smiling. I don't know what he's doing because I can't bring myself to look at him, but when we get to the altar and the ceremony starts, we say the words we're supposed to say, like all this never happened. I'm just there, getting married like so many women before me, and maybe when I stop to unpack all my emotions, I'll figure out how I really feel. But for now, I just keep moving forward, and so does he, and finally we hear the words, "I now pronounce you husband and wife," and Noah kisses me and together we run down the aisle, and everything is just like I thought it would be, except for the feeling in the pit of my stomach, like I've just come down a mile-high hill on a roller coaster and realized the track ahead of me is broken.

The reception, held at my parents' country club, is lovely even if I spend a lot of it knocking back more cocktails than is medically advisable and dancing with anyone who will dance with me, getting more and more raucous as the night wears on. For some reason, Noah goes ahead and sings the song he wrote to me, which has all the right sentiments since he wrote it back when he still wanted to marry me, and when he sings it, people go "Awww." Then he sings another and another, like he can't stop himself; he just needs the attention.

Some people ask me what the holdup was all about, and I tell them, "Oh, it was just some mix-up with the time and the tuxedo shop." I wave my arms as though it's all nothing to us now; the wedding went forward, and we're married. And, ha ha, every wedding needs *some* little drama to make it memorable, right? A bridegroom in jeans, arriving late with his nostrils flaring like a wild stallion who's been spooked. What of it?

My new in-laws stay at their table, looking dismayed and judgmental. My parents' country club perhaps does not live up to the standards they like to see in polite society, so they keep to themselves. Or perhaps, given what's happened already today, they're thinking this marriage will only be temporary, so why should they make the effort? But Blix—I see Blix off to the side dancing with everyone, even the groomsmen, even *Whipple* at one point. When she comes over and pulls me out onto the floor with her, we close our eyes and smile and fling ourselves around with abandon, like maybe we're communicating something in our own perfect, unseen world.

It's my wedding day, and I am married and doomed and half drunk, flying on the outskirts of crazy, with the world tilting under my feet and the whole night opening up in the middle of my head.

Later, after I have danced myself into a whirling frenzy, I go outside alone to get some air. I'm hanging over the railing of the deck, looking out at the moon shining on the swamp, and I'm soaking up the Florida humidity and wondering if I'd feel better if I let myself go ahead and throw up, when I hear a voice behind me.

It's Blix. "Well, you've certainly got yourself an interesting wedding story to tell, don't you, my love?" She lowers her voice. "Are you doing okay?"

I stand up straighter, put on my public happy-bride face. "Hi! Yeah. I'm fine. Just danced too much, is all."

She gets busy taking off her shoes, and loosening her blouse, flapping her skirt up and down, humming something. I look over at her.

"I'm trying to cool off my legs," she says. "Do your legs get hot when you dance?"

"I don't know. I guess so." I am suddenly so very tired. I don't want her to see me this way, on the verge of tears. A gecko runs across the top of the deck and stops to look at me, then hurries off, on a mission to catch mosquitoes. I give him my blessing and try to pull myself together.

"Whoo! God, what a time this has been!" Blix is saying. "I think I've danced with everything on two legs tonight. And if there'd been some cats and dogs around, I probably would have danced with them as well." She comes over and stands next to me, yawning and stretching her arms up in the air.

"Oh fuck it," she says. "Can't we just be honest, you and me? You don't have to answer that, because I'm going to tell you anyway. My grandnephew is a major dick. There. We probably should have done him in right when he arrived and we found out he was still breathing."

"Maybe so." I scrape the railing with my manicured fingernail. The insects are screeching from the swamp below.

"He's got some work to do on himself. Some work on his auras, that's for sure."

I don't want to look at her; it already feels like her eyes are boring right through me. But when I do finally turn toward her, the kindness in her face almost levels me.

"I think what happened is that he just had a really bad panic attack today," I tell her, "and that was probably because he didn't drink enough water. Anyway, he's said he's sorry, so I think we're going to be okay."

"Do you now?" she says. Her eyes are twinkling. "Well! Let's go with that as the official version, then."

"We've talked it out in the meadow and we're going on the honeymoon, which will be nice. We're really good when we're traveling together, and then when we come back, it'll just be our same life, living together like we've been doing already, and we'll settle down—" I stop, remembering how she hates the settling-down concept.

She puts her hand on my arm. "Well, it *is* going to be all right, darling, but maybe not for the reasons you think. I hope you'll listen to me because I don't have a lot of time. You need to forget what society has told you about life and expectations, and don't let anybody make you pretend. You are enough, just the way you are—do you hear me? You have many gifts. Many, many gifts."

To my horror, I burst into tears. "Oh yeah. I'm just fantastic. You have to be a special kind of fantastic for a guy to decide on the wedding day that he's not going to go through with it."

She smiles and pats my cheek. "Now, now. Don't turn on yourself because of him acting like a jerk. Your life is going to be so big, Marnie. Such a big, inclusive, loving heart song of a life you've got in store! You're not going to give a shit about this guy. Trust me."

"I don't think I want a big life," I blubber at her, and she says, "Oh, my, my, my," and folds me into her massive, soft bosom and we sway back and forth, kind of to the music that's playing inside but kind of not. "I just want to be ordinary," I say into her scarves and beads. "Can't I be ordinary?"

"Oh, my sweet girl. Oh my goodness. No, you can't be ordinary. Oh heavens no. I feel like I'm standing in front of a magnificent giraffe, and she's saying to me, 'Why do I have to be a giraffe? I don't think I'm going to go around giraffing anymore.' But that's just the way it is:

you're a wonderful, incredible giraffe, and you've got a life to lead that's going to take you to amazing places." She squeezes me and then lets me go. "You know, sometimes I wish I wasn't at the end of life, because I just want to stick around and watch your creations. All of them."

"Wait. What do you mean, the end of life? Are you dying?" I dab at my eyes with a handkerchief she produces.

She gets a funny look on her face, and I'm sorry I asked the question. Of course. Noah told me she's eighty-five. Any way you look at it, that's got to be pretty near the end of life.

"Hey, so listen, Ms. Giraffe, I came out here to tell you good-bye because I've got to go back to the hotel now," she says. "My plane leaves early in the morning, and Houndy called me to say that he's invited about twenty people over for lobsters tomorrow night. He can't help himself." Then she smiles at me. The wind blows some sparkles around.

"And you," she says. "You've got some miracles to perform, honey child. Please try to remember that for me, okay? The world needs your miracles."

"I don't know how to perform miracles," I tell her.

"Well, then you better start practicing. Words are a good first step. They have a lot of power. You can summon things by believing in them. First you visualize them being true, and then they come true. You'll see." She kisses me on both cheeks and then she heads through the door, but when she gets there she turns around and says, "Oh, I meant to tell you. You need a mantra to help you. You can borrow mine, if you want: 'Whatever happens, love that.'"

When I get back inside, Noah comes over to me and holds out his arms, and we finally dance.

I put my head on his shoulder, and I say, "Are you feeling a little better? Did you get something to eat?" This is probably a very wifely thing to say, and I realize he's probably resenting the hell out of it.

"Yes," he says in a weary voice. "Yes, I'm better. I ate some protein."

I feel so careful around him. "Good. And you were singing a lot, you and Whipple. That must have been okay, right?"

Then who knows what makes me brave enough to say this—maybe it's all the alcohol I've had, or Blix's words, or the fact that I'm feeling disconnected from reality—but I say the scary thing: "What's next, do you think?"

"I dunno. The honeymoon?"

"Okay," I say. "What about tonight?"

"What do you mean? Tonight we're going to the hotel and we're going to have great sex and sleep late. Like newlyweds."

There are some other things I want to know. Like, is he going to be my husband? And am I really his wife? Are those words we can use? He puts his arms around me and we slow dance to another song, and then they turn the lights on, and I see that Noah's eyes have no light in them. The air around him is a muddy beige I've never noticed before.

So I guess my first miracle will have to be to try to light him back up.

FIVE
BLIX

It's a week after the wedding and I'm back home now. My tumor wakes me up before sunrise. It is thrumming right below the surface of my skin, like something alive, running under its own power.

Hi, love, it says. *What shall we do today?*

"Sweetheart," I say to it. "I was hoping for just a little more sleep this morning. Would you very much mind if we did that—and then later we can talk and do whatever you want."

The tumor hardly ever goes for this kind of reasoning. And why should it? It knows I'm at its mercy. I've made friends with it because I don't believe in that whole battle metaphor for disease. You always read about that in obituaries, you know—*"So and so battled cancer for five years"* or worse, *"He lost his battle with cancer."* I do not believe cancer appreciates that kind of thinking. And anyway, I've made nice with trouble my whole life, and I've noticed that what happens is that problems just curl right up like declawed kittens and nestle at your feet and fall asleep. Later, you look down, and they've wandered off somewhere.

You bid them a fond farewell and get back to what you wanted to do in the first place.

In the interest of friendliness, I have given my tumor a name: Cassandra. She was the prophet nobody believed.

I turn over in the bed and listen to Houndy softly snoring beside me, his grizzled, beautiful face tipped toward mine. I lie there in the grayness of dawn and watch him breathe in and out and feel the magic of the city waking up. After a long time, the sun comes up for real, and a long time after that, the 6:43 bus comes wheeling around the corner and hits the pothole at its usual breakneck speed, causing the metal chassis to complain and screech as it always does. The windowpanes shudder. Somewhere, if I listen, there's a siren starting up.

An early summer morning in Brooklyn. The heat is already pressing against the window. I close my eyes and stretch. Cassandra, satisfied that I'm awake, goes back to whatever she was doing before she felt the call to wake me up. Sometimes she is as silent and worn out as time, and sometimes she's a rascally kindergartener wanting only to thump against something living.

I place my hand against her, and sing her a little song in my head.

Call me crazy, but the day I named her Cassandra, I also started giving her nice things to wear. Some days, when she is fierce and hot, I picture her in a hard hat, and other days—like maybe today—I think of her in a lacy dress and invite her for tea. I tell her to imagine she has been given the most delicate and beautiful of my china cups, the one I hang on the hook over the stove.

"I will not forsake you," I say to Cassandra. "I know you came for a reason, even though I'll be goddamned if I can figure out what that is."

Last week, when I got back from the wedding, on a day when I was nearly doubled over in pain, I gave myself a huge reward for making it through and to celebrate meeting Marnie. I told Houndy and Lola that I'd found the person I'd been waiting for all my life, the someone I probably knew from many other lifetimes, and who was my spiritual daughter. And then I painted the refrigerator bright turquoise. I was so proud of myself for not letting anyone in my family know that I am dying that I had to paint the refrigerator as my own little reward.

Houndy—sweet old family-oriented Houndy—thinks I should just tell my family about the mass. "Why not?" he says. "Don't they deserve to know? Maybe they'd want to be nicer to you."

Ha! My family wouldn't want to be nicer to me. They'd want me locked up in some hospital, treating Cassandra with needles and knives and making me talk to doctors, people who would speak to me in that condescending, medical way, people with clipboards and appointment books and computers. Office assistants who would speak too loudly in my presence, as if Cassandra had somehow interfered with my ability to hear.

No thank you. I went to the doctor and got my diagnosis, which I will not dignify by using its medical terminology, because to say the words makes it feel fatal and incurable, and I refuse to go with that. Except I will say this: I got up from the examination table, and put my clothes back on, thank you very much, and I tore up the pieces of paper they gave me—the *treatment plan*—and I walked out. And I will not go back.

If Cassandra leaves my body—and she may, it could still happen—it will be of her own volition, and this will be the reason: our work together is done. I don't want to die, but neither am I afraid. I won't use chemotherapy or put poison into my body. I won't suffer. Instead, I have taken energy drinks and done chants; I have consulted a shaman in an African village online; I have buried talismans and sowed seeds and performed yoga poses at midnight under a full moon. I have danced and primal screamed and practiced laughing out loud and had massages and acupuncture. And Reiki.

And by the look of things, Cassandra is thriving. So you know what that means? It means it's the way things are supposed to be.

So I am going to die. Most natural thing in the world to have happen. Life ends.

And I'm okay with that. It's just a change of address, really. It doesn't have to be awful.

I sigh, kick off the sheets because I'm suddenly hot, and then I close my eyes and tune in to the conversation the pigeons are having on the windowsill. They always sound like they're on the verge of figuring everything out.

Later, I get up and go to what Houndy calls my crazy-ass kitchen to make tea. Funny, these old Brooklyn brownstones. This one has a parquet floor that once was probably grand but which now slopes down to the outside wall. It's a floor with personality, all pocked and scarred from a century of footsteps and bootheels and water leaks and even worse grievances than those. And a high tin ceiling with a glaring fluorescent ring of light in its yellowed center—a light I never turn on because it's harsh. It promotes ugliness, that light. Instead, I've put lamps all around. Warm, yellowish light to give softness.

Houndy says we could get the floor made level and maybe have the stairs replaced in the front of the house, get the roof fixed. He's a do-something kind of guy, not one to sit around and watch the metal rust. Finally I had to say to him that I am all about slowing down all that striving. I just want to enjoy the sun coming through the cracks near the windows. I am tired of making so much effort.

He doesn't take much convincing to see the point of things I say, and that's why I let him come and live here and sleep in my bed next to me. We never got married because I've finally learned that if you have to bring the law into your personal relationships, then you're doing it wrong. And both Houndy and I have done it wrong plenty of times before. So we've just been skating along together for twenty-plus years.

We met right after his son died, when Houndy was in such a bad way, in such grief he couldn't even catch himself any lobsters anymore. Lobsters just walked on by his traps and got in other people's traps, and Houndy was so battered by life he didn't even care all that much except he was going to starve to death. So somebody told him to come see me, and I chanted some words of power summoning the forces of plenty, and put my hands on his heart—and after that lobsters started standing in line to get in his traps.

He brought me some one night to show me my spell had worked, and we stayed up late and ate lobsters and drank some homemade wine I had, and then—I don't know how it got started—we found ourselves dancing, and of course, dancing is the gateway drug to kissing, and somehow that night Houndy brought the laughter back into my eyes. And maybe I did us a little love spell that has always stood me in good stead when I've needed it. So here we are, two decades later: me doing my words of power and finding love for people when I can and him bringing me his old craggy Brooklyn self and his scratchy chin and his happy snoring. And lobsters.

And in the mornings I fix him poached eggs and salmon and make him smoothies that have plenty of antioxidants, and bread that I've baked, filled with seeds and sprouts. And then we sit outside in the sun on the roof and listen to the city moving beneath us and feel the energy of life. Well, I do. Houndy sits next to me and smiles like he's the Buddha or something, even though I don't think he has a spiritual cell in his body. Maybe that's why the universe sent him to me: we're counterbalanced. The universe always likes things to have a balance to them.

A door slams upstairs, and the building's day begins.

Voices on the stairs: "Did you get your lunch from the countertop . . . and did you get a pencil? And since it's the last day of school, you won't have aftercare, so you'll come home on the bus, and then . . . well, you and I will call each other. Right?"

"I'll call you every week."

"No, every day. Sammy, promise me. Every day!"

And then, there are two sets of footsteps clomping downstairs—Jessica's sandals carefully slapping on the wood and Sammy's exuberant sneakers—and Sammy knocks his scooter against my door as he passes just like he always does. It's supposedly an accident, and Jessica says she tries to get him not to do it, but I always tell her I don't mind. It's our ritual. Sammy is leaving for the day, and he wants me to see him out.

I jump up and go to the back door and throw it open, and there he is in the hall, the sweetest boy, ten years old with his yellow hair sticking up, and his pale, fair skin practically see-through in the light from my kitchen windows, peering at the world through those adorable giant round glasses he loves. And he's grinning at me.

"SamMEE!" I say, and we do a fist bump, which is hard because of the scooter he's carrying and the outsized New York Mets backpack he's wearing. Jessica's next to him with her harried morning face, and as usual she's juggling her cup of coffee, her bag, the car keys, and her one thousand worries, and at any moment she could drop any of it except the worries.

But today she also looks like she's about to burst into tears. Not only is it Sammy's last day of school—but for the very first time, his dad, whom Jessica hates in the way you can only hate somebody you once loved beyond reason, is going to take Sammy upstate to stay with him and his mysterious new girlfriend—whom Jessica had never even seen—for a whole month. The court said this had to happen, and Jessica fought it for as long as humanly possible, but now today is the day. When she got the news, she asked me if there was any way Houndy and I could hand Sammy over to the ex, since she didn't think she could do it without falling apart. So we're going to.

Sammy says, "Blix! Blix! Guess what! Did you know that when I come back from my dad's I'm gonna know how to play the drums?"

"What? You're going to be even more amazing than you already are?" I say, high-fiving him three more times. "You're going to play the *drums*?"

He rocks back on his heels and grins at me and nods. "I'm going to drummer camp."

Jessica rolls her eyes. "Yeah, well, we'll see. Andrew makes a lot of promises he can't keep."

"Moooommmm," says Sammy. "He's gonna do it!"

"Let's hope so," says Jessica grimly. Poor thing, she is a woman who has been given more than she thought she could handle, including a cheating husband and a boy who is sort of quirky. She's always twisting her rings around and around on her hands and looking worried. I'm always beaming love toward her, and watching as she gets bombarded with all the little love particles, but so far none of them seem to have landed in a permanent way. I think she's kind of enjoying being furious with her ex for now, if you want to know the truth. It's hard to make room for love when anger still feels so good.

"So, Sammy my boy," I say, "Houndy and I will meet you at the bus stop outside and then we'll all hang out here to wait for your dad."

"Wait. Mama's not going to stay with me?"

"No, babycakes. Today you get me and Houndy and some chocolate chip cookies."

He turns to Jessica with his tiny, serious eyes. "Is it because you're too sad to say good-bye to me?"

She has one of those faces that shows every single one of her thoughts marching across, and now she has about fifty-seven thoughts at once, most of them tragic. "I-I have to work late today, so I thought Blix could meet up with your daddy instead." She fiddles with her keys, wipes at her eyes, gets busy shuffling her bag over to her other shoulder.

"It's okay," says Sammy. He tucks his hand into hers. "I know. You're too sad to see my daddy take me. But it's going to be okay, Mama."

You see? This is when I want to rush in, slather them with love.

"I just—I want you to go off and be happy," she says. "But—"

No, I think. I send her a STOP message. *Don't say the next part, that you don't want him to love his daddy and the new girlfriend more than he loves you.*

She clears her throat, and our eyes meet. She's about to cry. So I go over and hug her and him both, mostly so I can block her from saying that she's terrified that Sammy's not going to want to come back to her. That the drum lessons and the novelty of attention from his father and his dad's girlfriend are going to make him want to stay away forever. That she's afraid her world with him, the world of homework and sadness and the grind of school, can never measure up to a month in the Berkshires. With a lake and a drum camp.

Ah, love. Why does it have to get all convoluted? I've been eighty-five years on this planet, and I still think the universe could have worked out a better system than this stumbling mess we find ourselves in.

I kiss Sammy on the top of his delicious little head and tell him I'll see him later; I squeeze Jessica's arm—and then they're off, but first she turns and gives me a look, a tearful look that says all is lost.

All is not lost, I beam to her.

I'm always beaming love messages and light over to Jessica, but Lola, next door, who is keeping score, says that Jessica's negative vibes are so far winning against my efforts. Lola jokingly claims to have an Excel spreadsheet on what she calls my Human Being Projects and that she can tell me just how all of them are going on any given date. The numbers would show, she says, that my Jessica Project might be a little bit lacking in success, which doesn't mean a thing, of course, because, as I've explained to Lola, everything can reverse in an instant when the vibes change.

And if you want to know the truth, my Lola Project might need some tending, too. She's been a widow forever, which she claims is *fine*, but I happen to know that, with just a tiny bit of courage, she could be having the time of her life and could love again. I keep calling for the universe to send her love, doing little love spells here and there when I think of them. But Lola—she can't see it.

So I have Jessica and Lola . . . and now I also have Marnie.

And oh yes, then there's Patrick.

Houndy comes into the kitchen, scratching his huge, round belly and smiling. "Is that our boy off to school already?"

"Yep, and today's the day he's going away for a month to see his dad."

"Oh, no! I've got to tell him good-bye!"

"You'll see him later. We're—"

But Houndy's already bounding off, going out the back door and down the stairs, and I hear him reach Sammy and Jessica, and hear them all talking at once. And then after a bit, he comes clomping back up the stairs, winded as hell, with Lola following him, wearing her lavender housedress and carrying a cardboard tray of cups filled with iced coffee that she goes and buys every morning even though it makes no sense at all. We can make our own coffee. But that's Lola; she's been my best friend forever, in this life and probably about five lives before this one, if you believe in that sort of thing and I *do*, so I don't question her. I start throwing fruit into the blender to make us our daily kale-strawberry smoothies, and Lola gets out the frying pan to fix the eggs for the mushroom omelet that we'll take up onto the roof. We all have our jobs to do to get breakfast going.

"By the way," says Houndy while he's collecting the plates and silverware. "I told Jessica she might as well come up after work. Have a glass of wine so she just doesn't go home and cry herself to sleep. That girl—she always looks like she's going to fall apart."

The phone rings just then, and it's Patrick. The phone seems to ring in an altogether different tone when it's him.

He lives in the basement apartment—the one that's almost completely underground, which he claims suits him perfectly—and he's calling to find out if a package was delivered for him yesterday. I tell him no but invite him up for eggs and mushrooms anyway. He's an introvert of the highest order, and so he hesitates and says he *might* come, only first he's got to write all the symptoms of all the diseases that have ever been recorded and invent a computer program that will cure Alzheimer's, so he'll probably be busy for a while getting that done.

I laugh. "Get on up here, you big galoot. You can save the world from illness after breakfast," I tell him, and he sighs.

Which means he's not coming.

"Come on," I say. "We'll sit up on the roof, just the four of us."

"Um, I'd have to take a shower first."

"No, you don't. We'll be on the roof. The fresh air will blow the stink off you."

"My hair isn't good. I should at least wash that."

"Put on your hat. You're always wearing a hat." I get out the cloth napkins and put them on the tray. I'm distracted suddenly by a dust mote that seems lit up in a sunbeam. My hairline is tingling just a little.

"And I should cut my toenails maybe."

"Now you're just toying with me."

"Get up here!" yells Houndy from across the room. "We need more representation by testosterone. Don't make me cope with these women by myself!"

Patrick says something about how he's already eaten breakfast, and he really does have a lot of work to do. And also he's waiting on a package. He's lobbing excuses like they're pebbles and he's laughing while he does it, knowing that I understand that he *can't* come. It's not one of the days when Patrick can do stuff.

If I squint, I suddenly see little points of light everywhere. My head feels funny, like something is trying to signal me.

"I have to sit down," I whisper to Lola, and she gives me an odd look. Houndy has taken the tray and gone on upstairs to the roof, and I hear the door slam behind him, feel how the whole building shakes, like it's answering him.

"Are you dizzy?" she says.

"No . . ."

"Maybe you need some water instead of coffee. Here." She turns to the sink and runs the tap.

"That's . . . not . . ."

And then I know what it is.

Marnie. Patrick needs Marnie.

They are a match.

So much clicks into place—why it was essential for me to go to my niece's Christmas party in Virginia even though my family drives me nuts, why I needed to meet Marnie, and why Noah hooked up with a woman that he isn't going to keep loving . . . oh my God. As though we've all come together in some kind of elaborate dance. For Patrick and Marnie.

Patrick and Marnie. Old souls who need to find each other.

I love when it happens this way. Even now I feel my body, tired and creaky as it is, running with energy.

Lola is looking at me closely. "Oh boy," she says. "I know what it means when you look like this. Something is *happening*."

"Later I'll tell you," I say. "Right now I need to think."

And she and I go up to the roof, and we look out over the city and soak up the early summer morning light while we eat. It is so beautiful here, and life is so full of possibilities, even though I'm not going to be here for much longer.

How can I bear to leave knowing there is so much undone? I have to trust the universe to make it all work out for them.

I watch the doorway, but Patrick does not come upstairs to the rooftop. He's downstairs pounding away on his computer keyboard, trapped by his own demons. And Marnie—Marnie's heart is being broken somewhere far away. I can feel it.

You are going to be okay, I beam to her. And then to them both: *Be brave. Be brave.*

There is so much fear to wade through before you get to love.

SIX
MARNIE

Natalie texts me two days into my honeymoon: *Is honeymoon Noah behaving better than wedding Noah?*

MUCH BETTER, I write back. *#ALLGOOD. WHEW! THANK GOODNESS.*

And then I look across the table at my handsome, tousled husband, who is sipping his Bloody Mary and gazing out through his Ray-Ban sunglasses at the turquoise sea just beyond the jungle. He looks like an ad for the tropics. We are having a perfectly normal late breakfast on the hotel restaurant's deck after having perfectly normal honeymoon sex last night, and I'm glad to report that Noah looks tanned and well rested and not anxious at all. There is just one tiny little thing: underneath the table, his knee is bouncing up and down like it's connected to an unseen metronome.

He feels me concentrating on him and looks at me. We both smile, and I turn back to my eggs quickly before I have to see his smile fading.

Jesus.

He is going to break up with me. He's just waiting for the right moment.

Which is probably why I've had a headache practically the entire time we've been here. I feel that my smile must look like a rictus grin, something you'd see on a skeleton. No wonder the waiter put our food on the table and backed away fast.

"Noah," I say, and then can't quite recall what I meant to say after that.

"What?" he says.

Do you love me? And do you remember when you first started spending the night at my apartment how sometimes my old bed frame would crash onto the floor when we made love? We started having to drag the mattress to the living room before sex. You joked that moving the mattress was the most exciting foreplay you'd ever had, and I knew I wanted to keep you forever.

"Nothing, never mind."

"Do you want to go on a hike this afternoon?" he says grimly.

So we do. We walk through the little town and out into the jungle. He walks along quietly, like a man walking to his doom, stopping every once in a while to look at birds through his pair of binoculars, or to solemnly hand me the bottled water he put in the backpack. When his long, lovely fingers brush mine, I have to squeeze my eyes tight so that I don't cry.

I am stumbling along the path behind him, tears blinding me, when I hear a voice in my head saying, *You're going to be okay. Be brave.*

That's when I take a deep breath and I say to his back, "Noah. Tell me what's the matter."

And he turns and looks at me, and I see that my week-old marriage is about to die right there on a path in the Costa Rican jungle.

It isn't that he's gone crazy or is suffering from anxiety, or any of the things I have tried to tell myself. It's worse than that. It really does turn out to be lawn mowers.

"Lawn mowers," I say blankly.

Ahead of us on the path is a middle-aged couple in matching Bermuda shorts and powder-blue T-shirts. When she passed us, the woman told me that if you wear light blue, butterflies might land on you. She said this giggling, and the man had laughed, too, and then they'd set out on the path, arm in arm. I watch their retreating backs. She is oblivious to the fact that there is a butterfly riding on her back.

"Excuse me, sir," I say in a low voice, only for Noah's benefit, once they are out of earshot. "Sir, I know this may sound strange, but could I ask you your deepest feelings about the lawn mower in your garage? Are you in any way afraid of it, sir?"

"Shut up, Marnie," Noah says.

"No, please, Noah. Tell me these fears you have, the ones you've just discovered in yourself on the day you got married to me."

He scowls. "It's the *tyranny* of lawn mowers, not the things themselves," he says. "And it's not just the lawn mowers. I don't want any of it: the lawn, the household budgets, the electric bill, the daily conversation that goes: 'How was your day, no, how was *your* day? Did you have a good day?' I can't do it."

"The tyranny of lawn mowers and being asked, 'How was your day,'" I say slowly. "You can't do 'How was your day.'" The sky is full of birds. Parrots are screaming around us.

You are going to be okay, Marnie.

He shrugs and looks off into the distance, ruggedly handsome and bored with me.

A memory swims up in my head of the time last year when he went with me to Florida to meet my parents. My mother, a firm believer in the Getting to a Man's Heart through His Stomach theory of romance, insisted on cooking us dinner. We all sat there in my mom's little suburban kitchen with the rooster wallpaper and the rooster salt-and-pepper shakers, and she made us her signature dish, which my father nicknamed Millie's Magnificent Masterpiece Meatloaf, so named because she melts whole chunks of *two different kinds of cheese* into the meat, and then she serves it, glistening with ketchup poured over the top. Ketchup! Only the finest for the MacGraws.

For as long as I can remember, Thursday has always been meatloaf night, and every single week my father would rub his hands together in great anticipation and exclaim as though it were Thanksgiving and Christmas and the Fourth of July all at once. And here they were, *sharing* this with my new boyfriend. And they were so happy about it! It broke my heart, all this optimism they had for us, when I could see, with paralyzing shame, that this handsome, bright-eyed boyfriend of mine, sitting there in their modest little three-bedroom ranch, was watching them with a little dazed half smile on his face. I knew that look: he was fashioning this whole incident into a comedy routine he'd entertain people with later. *Like, really, dude, ketchup on the top?* he'd say. *Please* tell *me you're not really going to use* two *kinds of cheese inside! It's too, too extravagant for words!*

He doesn't get domestic life, the way you can be glad for such stupid, simple things. That you can bicker and fight your way through marriage, and then Thursday night meatloaf comes to save you.

I should have known then. I should have broken up with him right then.

I wish to hell I had.

"Okay, look, I've done something kind of awful," he says finally. He puts his hand up to shade his eyes. "I didn't tell you, but on a lark I applied for a fellowship to go to Africa with Whipple. I never thought I'd get it, and to tell you the truth, I forgot all about it. But then, lo and behold, it came through. I found out a week before the wedding." He picks up a stick and pokes at the ground, drawing circles in the soft dirt. My ears are ringing from all the jungle noises around us.

"'Lo and behold,'" I say, mocking him. "Lo and behold, you happened to apply for a fellowship. On a lark."

He stabs the dirt with the end of the stick.

"What the fuck, Noah?"

"I know. I shouldn't have done it."

"No! If this is something you really wanted, then of course you should have done it. That's when you're supposed to talk about it. That's when you say to your *fiancée*, the person you're going to share your *life* with, 'Hey, there's something I might like to do. What do you think?' You're supposed to *communicate* with me."

"We shouldn't have gotten married."

"Why does it mean we can't be married? You think celibacy is a requirement for going to Africa?"

It hits me then, the true meaning of what he's saying: that the fact that he would on impulse apply for a fellowship without even telling me means that I am completely peripheral to his life. *That's* what this is. He was always so proud of the way we never fight. But maybe if you never fight, it only means you don't care enough.

I try again. "What if—what if I come and join you? What if we both do this together? You'll see," I say. "I can be adventurous, too." Oh God, I'm being so pathetic. A monkey swings down from a vine and I think he's going to smack me, but he only wants my granola bar, so I let him take it.

Noah clears his throat and tells me he doesn't want any of the life we'd planned: not the house in the suburbs, the three children, our teaching careers. None of it.

"I thought I could do it," he says. "Really I did. I love you, but—"

"Just shut up, please. If there is any worse sentence than the one that starts, 'I love you, *but*—' then I don't know what it is."

"You're right," he says. "I'm sorry."

"And *stop* saying you're sorry! God! Don't say you love me, and don't say you're sorry. You fucking betrayed me, and you know it! How long *have* you known this? How long, Noah? You knew all along through all the wedding planning that you didn't want to do this, and yet you just stood by and let the whole wedding thing happen! You let me invite all those people and you kept us all waiting even though you'd known for weeks you couldn't do this! What is *wrong* with you?"

"I wanted—"

"Don't you dare talk to me about anything you wanted! You lied to me, and embarrassed me, and now you're leaving me to go off on some fantasy trip that just came up! And when I say I love you and I'll support you, you turn me away! Like I'm just some object you're tossing out of the window! Some useless extra baggage!"

"You're not just some—"

"I said, *shut up!* You don't have the right to talk to me about what I am or what I'm not. Listen, you idiot, I'm willing to give my whole heart and soul to you, and work *together* on our dreams! We have to sacrifice! Nobody's happy all the time! Look at my parents. They have a very successful, long marriage, but do you think they were happy every single day? No one is happy every single day. And work is called *work* because that's what it is. That's what you do!"

"No," he says, and his eyes are shiny with sadness. "No, your parents definitely aren't happy, and neither are mine. And that's just the point. I'm not going to do that."

"Fuck you," I say.

He gives me a sad, knowing smile, and then he lifts his hand in farewell and walks away. Our surroundings have gone berserk, the heavy wet air filled with screeching and hollering, animals taking sides, flinging leaves and nuts at each other, raucously arguing, probably over the meaning of work versus love. I abruptly turn off the trail and go a different way down the mountain, and I walk furiously with my head down, not caring if I ever see the hotel again, or him, or the airplane that's going to take me back to California.

I want to throw myself off the cliff into the ocean.

Oh, stop already. You're going to be okay, a voice says.

I say back to it, *I am* never *again going to be okay.*

But it laughs and says again, *No, you're absolutely going to be okay. You have a big life coming. A big, gigantic heart song of a life.*

And I say back to it: *What the hell does that even* mean*?*

He moves out as soon as we get back to our apartment in Burlingame, the place we have shared for six months. He feels it's best that he stays with a friend because—get this—he feels too *guilty* to look at me across the room. He needs to *punish* himself for hurting me this way. I hate the way he's almost getting off on all this suffering—how it makes him seem so heroic in his own head, the villain with the hangdog look, the guy who bows down and closes his eyes out of such sweet sorrow with his own bad self.

Before he leaves me for good, backpack and suitcases overflowing, he tells me about all the decisions he's made without me. The one about how he and Whipple are flying to Africa in another month. Then the one about how he's not going back to teaching. Ever.

He looks at me with his new tragic expression and says he'll be in touch if I want him to be, which makes me laugh a high-pitched, maniacal laugh and fling the butter dish across the room. I think of how proud Natalie will be when she hears that I'm not putting up with being treated this way, that I am actually throwing crockery.

And then I start to cry, because I know that I am supremely unlovable in a very deep, unfixable way.

With great sadness, he picks up the pieces of the butter dish, sweeps up the shards, drops it all in the trash can. He tells me he's paid his portion of the rent for the next three months so I can keep the apartment without having to take in a roommate. He even leaves me the recipe for his secret six-layer dip—the one with four kinds of melted cheese, red onion, and avocado, the dip that he never, ever would tell me how to prepare. I rip it up in front of him while making hyena noises. He flinches, and I get louder.

So this, *this* is what I've come to: being thrilled I can screech loudly enough to possibly scare him out of his mind.

SEVEN
MARNIE

Three weeks later, I come home from work to find a letter from an online divorce site. I drink two glasses of wine, turn our engagement picture toward the wall, and then I sign the papers that say I promise not to love him anymore.

Soon after comes a copy of the decree.

And just like that, I'm divorced.

I say things to myself that get me through each day: I loved him for two years; we got married in an ill-advised ceremony; we broke up; I am still sad. I will fold my laundry and get around to sending back the wedding gifts. I will buy coffee and cream and eat oatmeal and cranberries for breakfast.

I say: This is the poster on the wall. This is my kitchen table. This is my car key. I like coffee. It is Thursday.

Then I do what MacGraws do in times of great personal upheaval and grief: I go into full denial mode. I tell my emotions that they are now on stage-four lockdown, forbidden to show up in public.

I am, in fact, a denial warrior-queen, bouncing into the nursery school where I work every day, playing the part of the happy little fulfilled bride with a big smile on her face. I don't tell anyone what has happened. I go in early and stay late. I smile so hard my face hurts sometimes. I think up approximately seven art projects for the children *per day*, projects that necessitate cutting up hundreds of little construction-paper shapes. As an added flourish, I make little books—one for each child, with stories in them of laughing cats and turtles that talk.

I could tell my boss, Sylvie, what happened, I suppose. Sylvie would be outraged for me, and she'd take me home with her, and she'd tell her husband, and they would comfort me, and I could sleep in their guest room until I'm healed up. Sylvie is the most motherly person I know. I could fall apart around her, and she would know how to put me back together again.

But I don't tell her the first day, and that makes it harder to mention on the second day, and then impossible after that. Maybe if I don't talk about it out loud, it will cease to be true.

But because the universe is in the mood to test and toy with me, the bride talk at work increases exponentially. My life becomes a hilarious succession of Bride Stories: the ones I am begged for by the women I work with (Meatloaf for dinner tonight! Noah just loves it! Yes, we eat by candlelight! And then early to bed! You know how it is!)—and the ones the four-year-old girls insist on hearing. They are obsessed with weddings and need to know every detail.

"Were you like a princess that day?" they want to know, their eyes shining. *Oh yes, I was!* In honor of my wedding, they wear white paper napkins on their heads at snack time, and walk through the reading corner wearing the nap room blankets like long trains.

"We are your Bride Girls," they tell me solemnly, and I laugh and help them toss bridal bouquets.

It's only at night that the bitterness comes for me, laying bare all my failures and misfit-itude. The bitterness has been at home all day long, pacing and waiting impatiently for me, and now it sits on the side of the bed filing its nails and smoking cigarettes. *Ready now, sweetheart?* it says. *My turn!*

That's when I see who I really am, when I know that I will never be all right, that the person who said he loved me and wanted to spend his whole life with me came to his senses at the last freaking minute, and then like some kind of idiot, I still made him go through with the charade of a ceremony.

I'm a misfit who can't pretend any longer. A dandelion in the lawn. An ugly duckling out paddling among the swans, hoping they don't notice.

Then after one sleepless night during which I think I will lose my mind, I jump out of bed at five in the morning and find myself punching in Blix's number on my phone. I can't believe I didn't think of this earlier. She is probably the one person in the world who could get him back for me. It's 8:00 a.m. in Brooklyn, and I somehow just know she'll be up. And sure enough, she answers the phone with, "Hi, Marnie, my love. I was waiting for you to call."

I'm taken aback a little. "You were?"

"Of course. I've been thinking about you."

So I just blurt it out. "Blix, it's awful. I-I need your help. I know you can do things, and so I want you to bring Noah back to me."

She's silent, and it occurs to me that maybe she didn't get the news from his family that he left me. So I back up, tell her about the honeymoon, the fatal hike, Africa, the fellowship he applied for without telling me, Whipple, all of it—even the online divorce.

She says, "Aw, sweetie. I know this feels awful to you right now, but I need to tell you, honey, that this sounds to me like it could be the start of your big life."

"My big life? *Big* life? My life has shrunk! I'm here in Burlingame, where I cannot afford to stay, and I'm working at my job, and I'm going crazy, Blix. I just miss him so much, and I know you have insight and connections somewhere, and so I thought that maybe you could help me get him back." She doesn't say anything so I see that I need to keep going, to convince her. "Because I've thought about everything you said, and I really do need him! He's the best thing that ever happened to me, and something went wrong, but I want to fix it. *That's* going to be the big life, as you call it."

"You should come to Brooklyn," she says.

Brooklyn? "I can't possibly do that," I tell her. Frankly, nothing sounds less appealing than going somewhere new, heading across the country to a city I've never been to. Being a houseguest. Ugh.

"So then tell me what you need."

"Can you look at whatever it is you look at and see if he's coming back to me?" My voice cracks. "Would you do a spell for me? To make me less ordinary, or to make him not mind how ordinary I am?"

"Oh, honey. You don't want him back! Trust me on this. There's so much—"

"Please. Give me a spell. How desperate does a man have to be to break up with somebody *on their honeymoon*? How am I supposed to get over that?"

She's silent for a moment, and then she says in a quiet voice, "Listen to me, sweet pea. Change is hard. And Noah is a high-level entitled brat who forgot to grow up, and I'm very sorry for the pain he's put you through. But trust me, there's something so much better waiting for you. You'll get through this and move on. It'll take time, but you will. So much better is waiting for you."

"No," I tell her. "It isn't. We were meant for each other. I know it, just the way I knew that Natalie and Brian were meant for each other. You said yourself that I'm a matchmaker, and I *know* he's the one for me."

"No one can read their own stuff that way," she says. "Otherwise I wouldn't have had to go through the cockroach and the dead-on-the-inside man. Think about it. And by the way, you are not ordinary, *and* you need to come to Brooklyn."

"I'm ridiculously ordinary. I lose my keys all the damn time, and I am opinionated and I get impatient, and I don't have any ambition, and I don't make enough money and I couldn't care less about it, and—and when I was little, I dressed up cats in costumes and I didn't care when they got mad about it."

She sighs and says, "Okay, listen. I have to tell you something. When I was eighteen, my father died, and the family homestead I'd counted on inheriting was given to his sister instead. And that's when I realized that I could either live under my bed and be passive for my whole life or I could do something that scared me every single day. So, being intelligent, I picked being passive. Which was a great decision. Brilliant, in fact."

She laughs a little. "So I kept living with my aunt and trying to please her by doing everything she said, and smiling nicely to everybody. And then one day my aunt told me that I was like my father, that I was a loser and I was never going to amount to anything, and for the first time all that anger I'd been pushing down simply erupted out of me. I was livid! Beyond livid. So I scraped together the little bit of money that my father had left to me, and I went to Brooklyn, a place I picked on the map just because it scared the hell out of me. I had no idea what I was doing. I was out of my mind terrified."

She is quiet for a moment, and I can hear her breathing. "But it turned out to be divine intervention or something that I came here. Because after I arrived, everything changed. I made friends with the fear. I married a scientist I barely knew, and I went with him to Africa and studied bugs—I hated bugs! And I hated heat and snakes and traveling without knowing what to expect—but after that, I went all over the world. I chanted in India; I sailed on schooners that looked like they wouldn't float for five more minutes; I climbed mountains; I studied different religions. Whenever anything scared the living daylights out of me, that was a sign to me that I needed to throw myself into it. And you know what else? That's how I've lived my whole life, doing whatever scares me."

I don't want to tell her that that sounds like the worst possible life I could imagine. So I just say, "I'm always scared."

"Good! My sweet Marnie, you really should come see me."

"But I'm working," I say.

"Ah yes, building up security and employment credits."

"Well, I have to support myself," I point out. "No one else is going to do it for me."

She's silent for a long time, and I'm sure I've insulted her. But then she says very quietly, "I want you to look very carefully around you. Because everything is about to change. Your whole life, all of it. You need to notice it just the way it is right now. Will you do that?"

She says some words I can't really hear.

"Is that the spell?" I say.

"I'm sending you my best words of power," she says. "But yes. It's your spell."

"I wish you'd come back home," says Natalie one night on the telephone. She means back to Jacksonville. To live there. "Mom and Dad aren't getting any younger, you know. And I miss you. The baby misses you."

"The baby isn't even born yet."

"I know, but I tell her about you, how you defected to California, and she's very upset about it. She wants me to tell you that you're going to lose out on a lot of family experiences if you insist on remaining there."

I look out the window at the mountains and the park and the yellow brick library building. I've loved living here, walking to the perfect little nursery school where I work, then walking home through the town, window-shopping in all the cool stores I can't afford. But now this town seems like a place that was never meant for me. Everybody I know here is already a member of a couple. I wave to them in the elevator of my posh little apartment building: smiling at each other, making their evening plans, with no interest in me whatsoever. Noah and I were like that, too, just keeping to ourselves.

It's the same pang I always feel when I talk to Natalie—she and Brian always have music playing, and they're always fooling around, laughing like I guess happily married people do, and I wish Noah and I had settled down near my family, like I'd kind of thought we'd do at some point down the road. You know, meet them for dinner sometime, run into each other at the grocery store . . . have a big old extended family right there.

But I don't want to go back to Florida alone, as the *failed* sister, the person who never figured out how to make it in the world. Besides, if Noah were to ever come looking for me . . . well, I'm just saying. This is where he would think to look: right here in Burlingame. He liked how upscale it was, said he always wanted to live in the kind of town where the weekly police blotter reports were dominated by stories of residents bothered by squirrels tossing acorns too boisterously.

Natalie reads my mind, which she is good at, having known me and my shenanigans for my whole life. "How is staying there a good idea for you? You need to get over him and move on, not stay at the scene of the crime," she is saying.

"Costa Rica was the 'scene of the crime,' as you call it."

"Come home, come home, come home," she says. And then Brian gets close to the phone, and they both start chanting. "Come! Home! Come! Home!"

One morning, after a week in which the Bride Girls have begged for us to put on pretend weddings at the preschool, I wake up with a fantastic idea. Probably the best idea I've ever had! I jump out of bed, jiggety jig, and race around the apartment, pack up my wedding dress, the veil, the something blue, the somethings old and new, as well as the corsage and the bouquet, and I put them all in a giant trash bag. But I'm not throwing it all away! I'm not *crazy* or anything. I'm taking it to school! The most dazzling show-and-tell EVER.

I get there before the sun is even up, and I set out the dress lovingly on the art table. It looks so beautiful laid out like that, so I put the veil across the chair. Noah was supposed to lift it off my face, so lovingly, smiling into my eyes.

But, well, we didn't get to that part.

I hear myself laugh out loud at the idea that things might have been altogether different if we'd done things the right way, lifting the veil for the kiss, having our first dance, tossing the bouquet, all of it. You can go insane that way—what if Whipple hadn't been the best man, what if there hadn't been a trip to Africa waiting, what if Noah hadn't realized all the stupid, conventional things about me just before he was supposed to say "I do"?

Conventional. That's what I forgot to tell Blix is my main flaw. I'm not simply ordinary—I'm *conventional.* Maybe I should call her back. I'll do that—today! Later.

But first, this.

This.

As soon as the Bride Girls arrive, I lead them over to the art table, where I take the scissors and make a nice, clean, long cut into the skirt of the wedding dress. I cut through the lace and the netting and the satin underpart. All the Bride Girls can have pieces of the dress to wear, I tell them. Their own little slice of the dress!

I hear somebody say, "Marnie?" and it's the kindest, softest voice I've ever heard.

"Thank you," I say to the voice. It's the voice of kindness, of the universe ready to apologize to me for what happened.

Only the voice has a person attached to it, and that person turns out to be my boss, Sylvie.

She says, "Marnie, honey, are you cutting up your wedding dress?"

And I try to say to her, "Yes, but it's okay," although it comes out crazy because what's happening is that I'm suddenly crying too hard.

And then she says, "Oh, honey, what's wrong? What are you doing? Let me get you a tissue. What has happened?"

"We're going to make wedding dresses for the Bride Girls!" I explain. "Because I don't need—"

And that's when I look down and see that I'm wearing my bathrobe and my bedroom slippers, and Sylvie, who is in her work clothes, says something like we should disappear into the back office while Melinda takes the children outside, and she gathers up the wedding dress pieces and the veil, and then she drives me home even though it is still early in the day. We sit in my car outside my apartment, listening to the engine making that clicking noise it does after you turn it off, and after a long time she says, "Marnie, sweetheart, I think you need to get some help."

"Just because I went to work in my bathrobe?" I say idiotically. "I was in a hurry." Even I know how stupid this sounds.

Then very quietly Sylvie reaches over and touches my hand and tells me that they've all known the whole time. Everybody. They all knew about the honeymoon and the divorce. People tried to talk to me about it, which I do not remember. Everybody has been sad for me. Nobody knew what to say. "That makes all of us!" I tell her, laughing, but she doesn't laugh.

Later in the week, there's a meeting, and the upshot is that I'm not supposed to come back anymore. In the write-up they give me, they say that they've "decided to go in a different direction" with the nursery school—by which maybe they mean they've decided not to let crazy people teach the children anymore—and they write me a check, which if I cash it, means that I won't sue them or anything.

My cheeks are numb from trying to smile through the meeting, from trying to insist that I really am okay.

Sylvie walks me out to my car when it's all over. "This is going to turn out to be a good thing," she says. "Right now, you're just in shock. But it's time for you to move on with your life, and this is the push you needed."

I hate that so much that I can't even.

So much for the big life I'm supposed to be getting. So much for the love spell.

And I just wish to hell that people would stop telling me that all my sucky tragedies are going to turn out to be good things.

EIGHT

BLIX

I am going to die very soon, and I want a big Irish wake, even though I am not Irish. And even though you're supposed to be dead when they hold a wake for you, I say you don't have to be dead. There aren't any rules about wakes, not as far as I know. And if there are, there shouldn't be. I am here to change the rules on wakes.

And anyway, I have so many people I've loved, and I yearn to have them all together so I can hug them and kiss them and tell them goodbye. I can give them little presents, and tell them my wishes for them, and we will eat barbecue and big old salads and drink whiskey, and we will talk and laugh and dance and cry. I want paper lanterns and twinkly lights and candles. I want a little séance maybe, and loud music, and Jessica to play her lute, and Sammy to play the drums. We'll light the fire pit and I'll burn things I don't need anymore, the things I want to offer up to the universe.

I want us all to hold each other's hands and dance in a conga line. It's been too long since I've had a conga line. And when Cassandra has used up the best of me, it's going to mean so much if I can just remember that conga-line moment, the moment I looked up and saw everyone I love all together—maybe it would make the leaving hurt less.

I'll try to talk Patrick into coming upstairs, even though he won't want to. But maybe he'll come because it's the end for me and then he'll see that people are kind, and he'll change his life, start to be among the living again. Maybe I can find a way to tell him that there is love coming for him, that I know something surprising and miraculous and magical is lining up in the unseen realm. Maybe I can get him to believe. Before the good can happen for him, he's got to open himself up just a little, and believing in something like a conga line might be a good start.

I tell Houndy we'll call it a "Blix Out." He doesn't think much of this business of accepting death, but lord, he does love a party. I know him too well: he thinks that if I have a party, it will be such fun that maybe I'll start answering the letters from the cancer center in which they plead with me to go through with our "treatment plan."

"Who knows? Maybe they learned something after all those years in medical school and they can cure you," he says.

Ah, dear, delightful Houndy, with his red, rough face and his white beard and squinty blue eyes, cloudy now from all his years of being in the sun without protecting them. I always tell him he has a poet's soul. All that sea in him, generations of it. He's been a lobsterman forever, now transplanted to the city, where he stomps around and acts like the land is a compromise he's made. Who in their right mind would have thought I'd turn out to be a lobsterman's woman, going out with him on the boat between the Bronx and Long Island, hauling in nets? But here I am.

"No," I say. "They'll cut pieces off of me, and I need all my pieces."

"You don't need the pieces with cancer," he says. "I do not think you need this cancer."

I just smile because Houndy doesn't know what I know, that, as stupid as it sounds, sometimes you have to live alongside the things you don't want, like cancer, and doing that helps you go deeper into life than you've ever gone before. If we all lived forever, I tell him, then life really wouldn't have any meaning. So why not embrace it, prepare for it, love what is?

"Who needs meaning when we've got this life?" he says. He flings his hand out, taking in all of it—the apartment building, the chips of electric-blue sky between the rooftops, the park across the street where the children shriek with happiness in the swings, and miles away, the sea, that he claims he can hear.

But he doesn't know. I'm at the point where I'm *all* meaning. I'm not going to have a body much longer, but I am certainly going to have scads of meaning.

At night, curled up next to me, he whispers, "Blixie, I don't want you to die."

And there is nothing really to say to that. So I just reach across the vast expanse of blanket and touch him.

His hands are like big warm mitts, but somehow their shape is as delicate as stars. Houndy is made from stardust, that's for sure.

NINE
MARNIE

"How are you doing?" Sylvie asks me on the phone two days later.

I'm jobless and unloved and I'm currently lying under the covers, reading old issues of *People* magazine and eating granules of instant pudding out of the box, is how I'm doing.

I'm also having a little bit of a fascination with dust motes. I know, I know. They're fantastic. But they're really *more than fantastic*. They have a lot to tell us about ourselves, these dust motes. If you stay still for a long time, they stop falling, but when you move again, wave your arm in the air or shake your foot in the covers, then they come swirling around again, like little stars. Like whole universes. It makes you think—what if our world and the whole solar system are just contained on somebody's dust mote? What if we're that meaningless?

I throw tissues at the wall; I pace around the apartment and dance to wild music until the neighbors downstairs bang on my ceiling with their broom handles.

Maybe I could stay like this forever, suspended between worlds.

But what I say is, "Oh, well, actually I'm having all the feelings."

"Are you looking for another job yet?" she asks.

When I don't say anything, she says, "I'll make some calls for you, if you want. When you're ready. You really are a very good teacher, you know. This has nothing to do with that."

Later I call Natalie and tell her the whole story, and she puts me on speakerphone so she and Brian can both work on cheering me up.

They say all the right things—things I know I would say to a friend who'd called with this story: wow, what a tough year you're having; of course you're not crazy; you'll find something else; we love you; you could move back home. I chew on my knuckles while they talk to me so they won't hear me crying.

I have to figure everything out, but right now I have a headache, and I need a nap. Besides that, I need to watch the dust motes lit up by the setting sun before it gets too dark to see them any longer.

So one day, without any warning, my parents show up.

My parents live three thousand miles away; when they show up, it means that airplanes and rental cars have been involved. And this doesn't happen without about a million conversations ahead of time. But here they are, banging on the door, calling my name like they're expecting to wake me from a coma. For a long moment, I think maybe I'm hallucinating their voices. Has it come to this? But then I realize. Ah, of course. I should have known. Natalie and Brian have told them what's happened.

I open the door tentatively, aware suddenly that I'm covered with flour and chocolate and wearing a too-small Japanese kimono that my father brought back from Japan for me when I was thirteen years old. I have on one bunny slipper and one sock, and my hair is a tangled mess because I have let the braid from four days ago turn feral, like a bramble you'd step around in the woods.

I have been baking. Cupcakes with messages in them, if you want to know. Like fortune cookies, but cupcakes.

When against all odds Noah comes back to me, he will be so surprised to bite into a chocolate cupcake and see the message: YOU ARE NOW WITH THE LOVE OF YOUR LIFE.

Maybe this could be a business. Cupcakes with Messages. I'll have to come up with a better name, of course, but first I have to figure out how you can tuck pieces of paper into cupcake batter without getting them all wet. I've been puzzling over this for days, and so far nothing seems to be working.

My mother puts her hand over her mouth. Her eyes fill with tears as she and I both take in the full horror of my situation. My father pulls me into his arms and hugs me. I start to cry.

"We've been trying and trying to reach you," he says in a muffled voice. "Why don't you answer your phone? We've been calling you for days and days. We were out of our minds. Your mother finally said we should book a flight and rent a car and see for ourselves what's going on."

"I wanted to call the police," my mother says. "How could you do this to us?"

"I am so, so sorry," I say. But really—has it actually been that long? I might have lost some track of time.

They come into the apartment warily, like they might be entering a crime scene. Suddenly everything looks awful: the sun shining on the countertop where I spilled eggs and cream and flour. And the little slips of paper everywhere, with their simplistic sayings on them, look stupid and childish. Out of the corner of my eye I see that my mother has picked up one off the floor that reads: WHO CARES WHAT OTHER PEOPLE THINK? BE YOU!

She hands it to my father and stares at me with round, tragic eyes. "Marnie? Honey? What is going on?"

"It's . . . an idea . . . a business idea . . ."

"A business idea?" My father is all over business ideas. He looks at the slip of paper and then at me and then back at the slip of paper. It has chocolate smeared all over it.

"Throw that away, Millie," he says in a low voice.

The trash can is overflowing, and the window has streaks of dust. The sink is filled with soup cans and spoons and a cardboard coffee cup that has something green floating in it. I was studying it earlier, that green mold. Mold is life, after all. And now that I look around, seeing the place through their eyes, I also notice that there's a red high heel in the middle of the floor and the picture of Noah and me at Lake Tahoe smashed on the floor by the heater. (Yes, I smashed the picture with the high heel, so what? It was a satisfying symbolic moment.)

I go over and try to scoop up as much as possible of the detritus of my life, to hide it from them. But I can't hide it at all, and now that Natalie has told them that I've lost my job, they also can see that I haven't gone out and replaced it. Soon they'll point out to me that when MacGraws lose jobs, that's when they *double down*; they start making calls, sending out flurries of résumés and curricula vitae. That's when a MacGraw *gets into gear*.

"So what happened to your phone?" my mother wants to know.

I look around. Where *is* my phone, anyway? How could I have neglected it? Oh, yes. The phone. Well, the truth is I must have forgotten the charger at work the day I left, and I honestly have never thought of it again until this moment. No wonder nobody has called me. I talked to Sylvie and Natalie last week, and then never bothered to recharge it. I have been so—so lame. Maybe I am having what they used to call a nervous breakdown. I don't really know what one of those is, but that does not mean that I'm not having one.

"Oh, honey," my mother says. I expect her to say the things she wouldn't have been able to avoid saying back when I was in junior high: *stand up straight, comb your hair, and why didn't you do these dishes?* It's even scarier that she says none of that. Instead, she tightens the purse strings of her lips and sets herself to work making things conform to the standards set by civilization.

My father, clearly the designated hugger, comes over once again and holds on to me, and says, "You need some care." They must be really worried if he's not going to ask why I didn't get another job yet, or why I was so awful as to get myself fired, or what I think I'm going to do next.

Nobody says anything that would be upsetting.

I close my eyes in gratitude. My parents are here, and I can stop running from whatever has me, because they are going to take care of me now so I don't have to adult myself anymore.

They pack up my things, donate the furniture, clean the apartment, make the necessary phone calls, sell my old car to a guy down the street.

And just like that, it's over.

They are going to take me back home, back to the mother ship, for repairs.

TEN
MARNIE

When you fall apart and move back home, nursing a big heartbreak, everyone tiptoes around you, until one day they bombard you with all the opinions they've been keeping to themselves.

But here's the thing I didn't expect: I actually don't mind their opinions. I am back in suburban Jacksonville where I belong, back in the 1960s pastel-yellow ranch house on the cul-de-sac where I grew up, two blocks from a black-water creek in one direction and the low-slung pink brick elementary school in the other. Old oak trees, dripping with Spanish moss, stand guard among the palm trees, the same as they always did. Nothing truly bad could ever happen to you here—that is, if you have the good sense to come in during the daily thunderstorm that arrives around 5:00 p.m.

My father is sure that I need to find another job, but he is patient and willing to help me. He says I need something with security! Health benefits! A pension! He talks to Rand Carson, my old boss at the Crab & Clam House when I was a teenager (I was chief clam girl, I'll have you know)—and when I make a face and tell my dad, "Not the fried clams again!" he says I am in line for a much more senior position: dining room manager. I can boss the clam kids around while somebody else pays my health insurance premiums.

My mother has another life in mind for me altogether, as her sidekick. She declares happily that we are "joined at the hip" as we make the rounds of her social life and errands: to the pool, to the store, to the library, to the gym, to lunch with her friends, and then we do the whole circuit all over again the next day. I am the prodigal daughter, welcomed back into the neighborhood, complimented for how I've grown up, for my nice smile. And it's true; I smile brightly at all the people my mother knows, which is nearly everyone in town. The neighbors who are outside watering their lawns need to run over just to get a look at me, as does Rita, the cashier at the Winn-Dixie, and Drena, who has styled my mother's hair *since* forever at the Do or Dye Salon on Hyde Park Avenue. They all look at me with slightly pitying expressions on their faces. So they know the whole story. Of course they do, but they understand.

And then there's my sister, who lives only a half mile from my parents, in a new subdivision that features the kind of dream house that two full-time professional incomes can provide. She is just about to begin her maternity leave when I arrive, and she is the perfect example of how a perfect person can make a perfect life. I know, I know: I am using the word *perfect* too many times, and no life *is* perfect, but when I am with Brian and Natalie in their cozy house, with her cozy big belly, and the furniture all overstuffed and comfortable, and the walls painted muted shades of gray and beige with white trim, and the windows all clean and everything looking peaceful and restful, I think that this—*this!*—is what everybody had been hoping would magically fall into my lap, too. I, myself, did not see it, frankly; given a house like this, I'd be painting the walls real *colors*, colors from the red family or the turquoise family, and hanging modern art on the walls.

One morning I'm having breakfast with my father out on the patio, just us, when he asks me what I see myself doing in my life, so I tell him the truth.

"Well, I have a lot of plans actually. I'm really into that idea of baking cupcakes with little sayings in them—like fortune cookies, you know, but with cupcakes. *And* also I'd like to write love letters for people who can't think of the right words. Oh! And I also would *love* to make costumes. Maybe do a stop-action film with *figurines* in costumes. I could write the scripts. Or, say, I could be happy, um, working in a bookstore because I could help people find the novels they need to read for whatever is bothering them."

He folds his newspaper and smiles at me. "We should try to narrow this down and see how any of it could be monetized," he says. "When you're thinking of what to do with your life, whatever your occupation is, it would help to think *money*."

"Also, you're going to think this sounds crazy," I tell him, "but it's possible that I could turn out to be a matchmaker. I mean, I've had a few successes at it, so it's something maybe I could pursue."

He gets up and ruffles my hair on his way to leave for work. "Ducky, I'm gonna say it again. You're a fascinating human, but that's not what life's about. You gotta make some money."

It is not lost on me that this—Natalie and Brian's dream house—*this* is the reward for going to school and really applying yourself to a skill that people want and will pay for. You get to meet a nice person, and so what that he is maybe *not* the most zany, creative, handsome person you ever met, a guy who wants to play guitar all night long and write you love songs, and then cook omelets at three in the morning, like the guy I married by mistake—but he is instead that other kind of man: a provider, an ethical, strong, good man with an eye to the future. Your future.

Ah, you see how it is with me. You see how Noah creeps in. He has set up shop in my head with his goofy love songs and his Ray-Ban sunglasses and a storehouse of memories, like the way he'd claim he had a special delivery for me of one thousand smooches and then he'd kiss my whole body, up and down, every inch of me. Both of us laughing until—well, until we couldn't anymore.

There is no point in thinking about this, however. I'm in my real life now. Back where I started from, and where I will pick up the pieces.

My room, still painted pink, smells like being a kid again. The light still slants in through the pink cotton curtains just the same as it always did, a slant that is so familiar it may actually be installed in my DNA—along with the sound of the hinges of my bedroom door, chiming like a musical note, and the flat-yellow hall light shining up into the attic.

Late at night, after my parents have gone to bed, I find my way to the family room, the lived-in, comfortable space, where you don't have to pretend about anything. There's the same worn-out rag rug, the chipped bookshelves, and an old brown corduroy couch that hugs you when you sit down, like it's so very glad to see you.

Welcome home, Marnie, the couch says to me, and I sink farther into its soft cushions and let myself fall under its spell of safety and familiarity.

"It's so good that you finally came to your senses and came back home," says my friend Ellen one night when she and Sophronia and I meet for drinks and dinner. I've been home only three days, but my mom says I need to get out, and she's probably right.

Ellen and Sophronia are both working for an insurance company in downtown Jacksonville and are dating multiple men from the corporate world. They tell me they have a social life that keeps them on the go: Margarita Mondays and Wacky Wild Wednesdays and Thirsty

Thursdays. And then there are the weekends—parties at the beach, with plenty of beer and dancing. Dating intrigue, that sort of thing.

I can hardly remember that world. Maybe I wasn't ever really part of it, come to think of it.

"Oh, you should totally come with us," Ellen says. "It'll be good to get back out there, get that guy out of your system."

Sophronia gives her a meaningful look, and then they both look sad for me.

"So. Are you really over him, do you think?" Ellen asks.

"Yes. Oh, yes. Totally. Over him, over him, over him," I say. I'm glad they can't see the lump that has formed in my throat.

They both reach across the table and hug me at the same time, and I remember how I used to like them in middle school, before we went to separate high schools and I lost my way and they became the part of the popular crowd at their school. The Cool Kids.

They're still the cool kids, and maybe hanging out with them would be a good idea, now that I'm back here.

We drink a bunch of beers, flirt with some guys, and then I get tired and sad and tell them I've got someplace I need to be.

The corduroy couch is calling my name.

Natalie and Brian come over for dinner my first weekend at home.

I discover that they are now best friends with my parents. I am shocked—*shocked!*—to realize that the four of them have rituals together. There is Sunday dinner, and then most Saturday afternoons my father and Brian play golf while my mother and sister go shopping or go to a matinee. Also, my sister cooks extra for my parents on Mondays and Wednesdays, and my mother sends over some Thursday meatloaf each week.

Even more startling to me is the fact that they get together at least every other week and play quadruple solitaire. There's a complicated scoring system that no one can quite explain to me, not without laughing so hard they give up. I stand there, amazed, while my mother and sister try to tell me all about it, with my father and Brian tucking in little helpful remarks here and there.

"... and if you have more than a certain number of cards ..."

"Red cards!"

"No, not just red cards, any cards ... just more points for red cards."

"Well, yes, unless your opponents have an odd number of black cards."

"Solitaire?" I say. "But isn't that ... played ... alone?"

They fall over laughing at that quaint idea. I feel a flash of irritation mixed with envy knowing that I can never catch up to them, will never truly be a part of their cozy little group.

Natalie takes my arm and says, "Never mind. It's a silly game."

My sister looks like an advertisement for pregnancy and happy marriage, like it's the least tiring thing ever. Her formerly long blonde hair is now chin length and cut at a sharp angle that makes her blue eyes jump right out at you. And although she's definitely wearing a huge round thing on her front, the rest of her looks perfectly slim and regular, like somebody came along and randomly glued a basketball underneath her shirt.

And Brian—tall, handsome, dark-haired Brian, the personification of husbandhood and fatherhood, carrying the banner for good men everywhere—tells me about Natalie's brave march through pregnancy. "She's been such a trooper!" he says, smiling at her winningly. "All that morning sickness stuff that some women complain about? Not Nattie. She hiked and swam and worked full-time. I tell you, birth is going to be a breeze."

"Well," says my mother. "Let's not tempt fate, shall we?"

My eyes meet Natalie's, and we smile. If people had themes, this would be my mother's: don't anticipate anything good, or it won't happen.

"Marnie doesn't want to hear about all this," Natalie says quickly. "Let's talk about how awesome it is that she's moved back in time to be an on-site auntie."

"Of course I want to hear about all of it!" I say. "I've missed out on everything. And look at you—he's right; you look absolutely gorgeous! You make pregnancy look like fun."

"Well," she says. "Pregnancy is sociologically and scientifically the most interesting thing I've ever done. When you think about what's really going on in here! Like, did you know that a woman gets fifty percent more blood supply when she's pregnant? Fifty percent!"

"Astonishing," my mother says, rolling her eyes. "Maybe you should sit down and rest. Take a load off." She looks at me. "Please don't get her started on all this. She starts in with talking about mucous plugs and breast engorgement and I don't know what all else. Gametes—was that what you were talking about last week? *Gametes?*"

"That was at the beginning I told you about gametes," Natalie says cheerfully. "Now we're at mucous plugs and breast engorgement."

My mother throws up her hands. "Not in my kitchen! We will not talk like that before dinner!"

Natalie says, "It's life, Mom. Biology."

"Biology, shmiology. Not everybody wants to hear about this stuff. It's like you think you invented having children!"

"Wait, I thought you did invent having children," I say to Natalie. "Wasn't that one of your accomplishments? And I, for one, thank you for it."

"Now I have both of you ganging up on me," says my mother, but she's smiling. She starts cutting up iceberg lettuce and plunking it into a bowl with carrots and celery. (Noah's face rises up in front of me, and he says, "Not even *red leaf lettuce*? Not even *romaine*?")

The men, of course, have headed outside with a platter of hamburgers and their beers. I watch them out by the grill, my father listening to Brian, and then laughing as they clink their beer bottles together.

"Hey, I'd like to chop up some vegetables to roast," I say, and my mom says, "No need for that. We've got salad and that's enough."

"But I *like* roasted vegetables," I tell her.

Natalie winks at me. She goes to the refrigerator and gets out cauliflower and broccoli and peppers, and hands me a cutting board and knife, all the while telling me about the birth plan that she and Brian have figured out: no epidurals, no fetal monitors, no bright lights. Also, there will be soft alto flute music, and a doula and a midwife. Brian will cut the umbilical cord, which they will then bury. The staff is to speak only in whispers.

My mother puts her knife down. "Well, I think you just want to make sure to do what they tell you. Although that's all a good idea *in theory*, please don't overlook the possibility of a good epidural if someone comes around offering one."

"I'm not having an epidural," says Natalie.

"It's not good, being rigid about these things," Mom says. "If parenthood teaches you *anything*, it's how to be flexible. When you're a parent, you have no control. None. Might as well start getting used to that now, missy."

Natalie turns to me, smiling her high-wattage fake smile. "So! New subject time. How does it feel, being back here?"

"Fine," I say, too quickly.

"Just *fine*?" my mother says. "Haven't we been having fun? My God, we've done everything!"

"No! I mean, yes, we're having fun. It's been wonderful!"

Natalie gives me her dazzling this-is-just-meant-for-you smile. Like she *knows* all about my mixed feelings as I trot along after our mother like I'm a little kid again.

"Do you have olive oil?" I ask.

"No, we don't have olive oil. Use corn oil. It's fine," my mother says. "And we do not need those vegetables. I told you there's a salad."

"No, that's okay. I'll just run out and grab some at the store," I say.

"The *store*!" says my mother. "Oh for God's sake! Honestly! You kids with your olive oil! Corn oil is fine. You've been eating it your whole life."

"I know, it's just that it doesn't have the same *taste* for the marinade . . ."

Natalie, elbowing me in the side and hiding a smile, pretends to duck for cover, and sure enough my mother explodes: "For heaven's sake, what *is* it with this generation? All of you! There are only *certain foods* that can pass your delicate systems? Can't have American cheese—lord, no! Or canned vegetables! Or *bread*! Good ole ordinary Wonder Bread! A person could *die* from bread to hear you tell it! And now *corn oil*—innocent little corn oil—has to be replaced by the eighteen-dollars-a-bottle *olive oil*."

I look over at Natalie, who narrows her eyes at me and cocks one eyebrow.

See? her eyes say. *See what you've been missing?*

Brian comes in to get another beer, looks at my mom and grins at me, and goes back outside.

"Well," says my mother to me with a big sigh. "Give *me* the vegetables. I'm going to boil them and put some margarine and salt on them. They'll be just fine."

"Mom, let Marnie make the vegetables the way she wants them, why don't you?" says Natalie. "You know I'm not going to eat any margarine. It's bad for the baby."

"I am not going to listen to this!" my mother says. "Margarine is not bad for babies!"

"Mom, will you please just stop? I read a bunch of nutrition blogs, and I know what I'm talking about. So, Marnie, do you ever hear from Noah? Where is he, anyway?" Natalie asks.

My mother takes in a sharp breath and shakes her head. "Oh, so here we go. For heaven's sake, we are not going to talk about him! I just want tonight to be *pleasant*. Here we are, all together for the first time in such a long, long time, and I want us all to have a good time. Discuss *fun* things. Not Noah!"

"Fun things like margarine?" Natalie says, and then she walks over and takes my mother's drink out of her hand and starts massaging her neck. "Ah yes," she says. "Here's the place, isn't it? Oh yeah, I can feel the knot. *This* is the Noah Knot. I'm getting it."

My mother closes her eyes and tilts her head back and forth, and Natalie keeps working away at the spot. I take a sip of my wine so that I won't say anything—because, really? My mother has a *Noah Knot*?

My mom opens her eyes and says to me, "Honey, let's not drink *too much* now, before we have dinner. You and I didn't have much lunch today, remember."

"I'm not—"

My dad comes to the sliding glass door right then to say that the hamburgers are done, and my mother flaps her hands the way she does when events are happening too fast for her, and she starts gathering up the paper plates and the plastic utensils. I reach for the salad bowl, but she says I'm the guest of honor and shouldn't have to do any work, so I tell her that's ridiculous, carrying a salad bowl isn't work, and also I don't need to be the guest of honor.

"Oh, you!" she says. "We're just trying to take care of you, sweetie. I just want to make you feel at home here again. And oh my goodness, you two got me so distracted I forgot about boiling your vegetables."

"It's fine," I say. "I'll just put them on the grill."

"Can we just have the salad, please? Will you humor me on this for God's sake!" says my mom as she marches out the door. Natalie gives me her what-are-you-gonna-do face.

Outside, the heat hits me like a furnace. The late afternoon sun is still beaming right down on us, and the air is thick with humidity, like something you could roll around in. Brian adjusts the patio umbrella so that my mother will be in the shade while she eats, and my sister sets out the citronella candles while my dad lights the no-bug torches. It's like a dance they all perform, everyone knowing their roles.

"Sit here by me," says Natalie, and she pats my arm. And Brian hands me the hamburger platter saying I should get first dibs. My father grins at me across the table, holds up his glass like he's going to give a toast.

He stands up, looking formal and overcome by emotion. I feel a little pulse of alarm as he clears his throat. "To our sweet little Marnie, the survivor! I just want to say, Ducky, you've been hit with some hard blows, but I knew you were going to be all right the moment you opened that door to your apartment in Burlingame, and I saw you were baking. Baking! Isn't that what we said, Millie? This girl is going to take care of herself. She just needed to be back among family and old friends!"

There's the clink of glasses as they toast, and then we pass around all the food—the salad and the overcooked hamburgers (my father has a fear of medium rare that rivals what people feel about circus clowns and rattlesnakes)—and for a moment we're all busy with our plates, and I wonder what would happen if I were to suddenly burst into tears.

Maybe it's the fuzziness from the wine mingling with the excessive humidity and the argument about vegetables and olive oil (olive oil!) and also the tension from the sky, which I now see is gathering itself for its late afternoon performance event—a violent thunderstorm. But also there's something else, some huge hurting thing taking shape within me, what it means to be here with these two couples who know each other so well that even their squabbles—the ones that bring me up short and make my heart start palpitating—are simply routine for them. They fuss and argue and kiss and somehow just keep plowing along through life, racking up grievances and then forgiving themselves and each other again and again. No one is going to stand up and say, "You know what? I can't do this anymore."

And I am an outsider, and yet these people around me are my tribe, the people who have the right by birth and DNA and blood type to have opinions about my life.

"Are you okay?" Natalie whispers, and I wish I could stand up and tell them the truth, which is that my mother has no *right* to have a Noah Knot! A Noah Knot! That means that they have been discussing him and me so much that Natalie knows just where the knot is and how to cheer my mother up out of it. And just look, I'd say to her—just *look* at our father, who is so shrunken next to Brian, like he's already abdicating ever so slightly his own place as head of the family. Brian will soon be managing his portfolio and his lawn maintenance plan, will be scheduling the tuning of the furnace, and eventually suggesting nursing homes.

And I—I am just a damaged object they're all trying to patch up and haul back onto the sales floor. They love me and they will sit with me while I find the necessary prerequisites for their estimation of a happy life: a new job, a new man, a new car, and later on, furniture, a house, some babies. I need endless help, apparently.

In the meantime, they say, here's the story we're giving you: California was a mistake. Your life up to now has all been a big, blurry mistake, but luckily you're moving on. We caught you just in time.

My California life, my adulthood, quietly folds itself up like a map and tiptoes away. Nobody but me even sees it go.

ELEVEN
MARNIE

One night, I pass the door of my parents' room, and I can hear them arguing. It's nearly midnight, and she is saying, ". . . needs more time, she's recovering. Don't you *see* that?"

So of course I stop in my tracks and sit down on the floor outside their room.

He says, "She's got to get back out there. She needs to get back on the horse. Something bad happened to her, sure, but she can't let it get her down. Can't let it stop her in her tracks."

"Ted, that was not just 'something bad' that happened to her," my mother says. "Those were two big blows she suffered. Losing her husband and her job."

For a moment, it seems simply a fascinating discussion, as though they're talking about somebody else, or the Theory of Big Blows. I would love to join in. *Do* I need more emotional rehabilitation or to get back on the horse? What could be the point of either? What does the research say about such things? Fight or flight? Rest or work?

"You *know* what she needs," my mother says in that voice of certainty she uses. "She needs to find a man to go out with."

"Millie, for God's sake, that is the *last* thing she needs! Why do you always act like that's going to solve any problems whatsoever? She needs to find herself first! And why am I the only feminist in this conversation? The girl needs a career. Then, if she wants to, she can find a man."

"You don't know anything. She needs love."

"Well, fine. Maybe she'll meet a nice guy at work. But first she has to get a job."

"Listen," my mother says, and I'm surprised by the sudden intensity in her voice. "Don't you *dare* take this away from me! Ted, right now we have *two* daughters in town, and I want to keep it that way! Imagine how nice life would be if *both* of them could live in the neighborhood permanently and have nice husbands, and then their children could grow up as cousins, and they'll all be best friends, and they'd all come over on Sunday afternoons, and we could eventually put in a swimming pool—"

"A *swimming pool*?" he says.

"—and a swing set, and we could babysit for the kids, you and I. And I think we can get Marnie to stay here, unless you start pressuring her to get a job! She'll go off on her own once again, and we'll just have to worry about her like I did every single night while she was in California. Every single night, Ted, I worried! But—if she meets a *guy* here, then maybe they'll both stay."

"Oh my lord God in heaven. You are out of your mind."

"No! I'm right about this, Ted MacGraw. It's happened over and over and over again to my friends. If your kids fall in love with a local person, they stick around. It's love, not work that keeps a person nearby."

"And how do you plan to make this happen?"

"Well, that's just it. I can't."

"Well, there you go."

"Well, there *you* go."

"Turn off the light, will you? I've got to get up in the morning. *Somebody* in this house has to work."

I am getting to my feet, about to depart for the couch so I can think this over more comfortably, when she says quietly, "I did hear something interesting today."

I stop in my tracks.

"I cannot even imagine what that might have been."

"If you're going to be like that, then I won't tell you."

"It seems I am going to be like this. Please, I'm begging you, turn off the light. You've already got my blood pressure so high, I'm not going to be able to sleep."

"Fine."

"Fine."

"Good *night*. I hope you have *very* pleasant dreams."

"Thank you. I am certainly going to try."

"And when our daughter moves away because *you* push her to work—"

"Ah, Millie, you are driving me crazy; do you know that? Go ahead and tell me, so we can both get some sleep."

It's fortunate he says that, because I'm thinking I'm going to have to pound on the door and demand that she tell all of us.

"Jeremy's back in town," she says. She starts talking very, very fast before he can stop her: "He came back six months ago when his mom got sick, and now he's a physical therapist with a real practice, and he's living with his mother. And he's a nice guy, and she liked him a lot, and I think this could be just the answer we're looking for."

"Who's looking for?" says my father. "No, really, Millie, *who*?"

The couch is calling me. I stand up and tiptoe away before I have to hear my mother explain to my father her very misguided notion of my love life.

Okay, so Jeremy Sanders was my boyfriend during our senior year of high school, which is the very first year when boyfriends might start to mean something—like they could very well be a real part of your future. My parents certainly thought so, anyway. Even though Jeremy and I didn't have a whole, huge, madly passionate thing going, we were good together, that kind of good—companionly, sweet, adorable—that parents think is going to be enough for your whole life.

He was sarcastic and smart, and so was I, and because neither of us fit in with the desirables, we had a great time making fun of everything the popular kids cared about. We made it through high school on our snark alone.

And then one day, after we'd done nothing more than routine kissing for months and months, he said, "I think we should take our friendship to the next level."

I was only moderately cute back then. He was cute, too, in a kind of understated way: he had dark hair and nice eyes and a slight mustache that clearly needed years to grow into something better, and I didn't understand why he wasn't embarrassed enough at its scraggliness to shave it off until it could be magnificent. But that's the way Jeremy was. He shrugged off imperfections. He was kind of too normal, was the truth of it. Besides that inadequate mustache, he had a standard-issue nonathlete boy's body—a little too plump—and hands that sweated when I held them, oily hair, and pimples on his cheeks. Not that I was so dazzling in the looks department, you understand. I had blonde hair that had a definite greenish cast to it from the chlorine in the pool, and I wore both a dental retainer and glasses. I thought my knees were too sharp and bony, my feet too big.

All around us, our classmates were fucking like rabbits, and it struck me as crazy that here we were, sitting in his car one afternoon in the school parking lot, and we were talking about sex like you might talk about whether to go to Taco Bell or try something dramatic, like

Hardee's. Should we, or should we not? I was leaning against the window, facing him with my legs curled under me.

He presented the idea of sex calmly and scientifically, like it would be an experiment. Nothing more than that.

"Okaaaaay," I said. "I'll do it, but you have to go buy the condoms."

His face went pale.

"Or you could borrow some from somebody, I suppose," I said.

He stared out through the windshield. It was drizzling, the windows were fogging up, and soon we wouldn't be able to see to drive. "I don't know," he said. "I sort of wanted to do it right now."

"Sex? You wanted to have sex right this minute? In your car? Are you crazy?"

"People do have sex in cars."

"I know, but usually they do it in the dark. So all the other humans can't see. Like, the police get involved if they see you having sex in a car."

He twisted in his seat, drummed his fingers on the gearshift knob. "Anyway, I didn't say it *had* to be in the *car*. We could go someplace, maybe."

"Well, we're not going to my house. My mother is in and out of there all day long."

"We could go to my house. My mom is at work and my dad is back in the hospital."

"Do your parents have any condoms?"

"What?" He stared at me. "Ewww. I can't believe you said that."

"Well . . . if no one has any, then you're going to have to buy them. I am *not* going to have sex with you without a condom."

"I know, I know."

I looked at him and felt a stirring of interest. "Do you even know how to use a condom?"

"Yeah. In sex ed, they showed us with a banana." I'd been absent that day so he pantomimed pulling something over an imaginary banana, and that made me crack up.

"I don't know," I said to him. "What if we did it, and it didn't work out all right, and then we weren't even friends anymore?"

"I've been thinking about this, and that's one of my arguments for why we *should* do it. We're good friends, we'll always be good friends, and if it goes badly—like if we don't like it or something—we can both laugh about it. That's what we're so good at—laughing at things."

"Don't you think we should be like crazy in love so we can get through it?"

"Get through it!" he said. "Do you think it's going to be something *bad*? I think it's going to be awesome, and then we'll have it all out of the way so that when we end up with other people someday, we'll already know what to do. For once in our lives we'll be ahead of the curve."

So we drove to the CVS, and he went in—I refused to go with him—and then he came right back out and said it was too horrifying. He knew people in there. One of his mom's friends was buying shampoo right that minute, in fact.

So we didn't have sex that day, and I remember feeling a bit disappointed when he took me home. I mean, if it had really been important to him, couldn't he have worked up even an iota of courage?

So—and now we hit the tragic part for Jeremy and me—two weeks later he sauntered over to me at my locker and said out of the side of his mouth, "So, schweetheart, I got the goods. I ordered us some condoms by mail order, you see, and they came yesterday and somehow we've got ten boxes of the stuff. Enough for the rest of our lives." He pretended to smoke an imaginary cigar.

The thing was, it was *two whole weeks later*, which is forever when you're seventeen, and everything had changed. I had, against all odds, somehow been plucked from high school obscurity by a guy who was so out of my league that it was pathetic. Brad Whitaker, a guy that Jeremy and I had spent much of the semester making fun of, had asked me out! Never mind that I had had zero action before this point, now

I was on the verge of achieving something approaching coolness. And, as I carefully explained to Jeremy, I was in love.

Jeremy was devastated, which I felt terrible about. We had an awful scene, and he said I was making a humongous mistake, that I was a traitor to the cause of irony and sarcasm and normal human intelligence, and by the way, *good luck* dating a guy who didn't know his ass from a hole in the ground. Also—he couldn't resist pointing this out—he'd bought a lifetime's supply of condoms for *me*, and now what was he supposed to do with them? Sell them to Brad Whitaker?

Sure, I shot back. Why don't you do that?

I was in that dopey state of first love, first passion, and so I was immune to Jeremy's pain. I just wanted to get away from him. I was on the brink of one of life's great moments, and why did he have to make me feel so guilty?

Later that week, I lost my virginity in Brad Whitaker's bedroom while his parents were at work, to the soundtrack of the Backstreet Boys. I remember feeling slightly confused by the sweaty intensity of sex, all the writhing and the pushing, the way it felt more like an athletic event than what I'd been picturing from the passionate kisses in movies I'd seen. Jeremy and I could never have pulled off something that was this dead serious. We would have laughed ourselves sick.

Still, I was proud of myself for not complaining about the pain and the disappointment and also not minding the fact that, overall, Brad Whitaker didn't really care anything about me. I just did what you do in those times of your life when you're trying to make yourself be something you're not: I stepped up my game, tried harder, shortened my skirts, wore my hair in a side ponytail (you'll have to trust me that this was übercool), and took to lowering my eyes and holding my mouth in such a way that I looked charmingly bored.

It didn't really do any good. Brad turned out to be a heartbreaking narcissistic toothache of a guy, and he *forgot* that guys are supposed to take their girlfriends to the prom, and he took some other girl instead. I got to be the Wronged Woman and everybody felt sorry for me, and my mother said, "You should have stuck with that Jeremy Sanders. Now *there* was a nice guy!"

So, great. Just great. He's moved back home.

Cheers.

TWELVE
MARNIE

A week later, I'm at Natalie's house painting a mural on a wall in the nursery, having decided that a scene with a budding dogwood tree, a rolling green hill, and a garden of purple tulips would be just the thing to welcome little Amelia Jane to the world, once she makes up her mind to get here, that is.

Natalie has been in the kitchen reorganizing her spice cabinet, but when I look up, I see her leaning against the doorway of the baby's room, holding on to her belly and squinting at the wall. I do not think she really likes this mural. Her idea was to paint the baby's room *gray*. Gray! Can you even imagine what that might do to a newborn's psyche?

"Would you do me a huge, huge, huge favor?" she says.

"Drive you to the hospital because you're now in labor?"

"Stop it," she says. "Believe it or not, I have to go to the dentist to get my teeth cleaned, and I honestly don't fit behind the wheel anymore. So will you drive me?"

"How is it that you have an appointment for teeth cleaning *now*? What if you were in labor? What if you'd already had the baby?"

"I know," she says. "My appointment was actually for three weeks ago, but the dentist went on vacation, and they needed to reschedule."

Natalie does not look so good as she gets into the car, tipping herself way back so that she can maneuver her huge stomach without banging it into the dashboard.

"How's it going?" I say.

"Shut up."

I start the car and fasten my seat belt. "Oh, Ameeeeelia? Did you hear what your mother just said to me? Don't be scared to come out, baby. She's really a very nice lady. It's just that you're pressing on some of her vital organs, sweetheart."

Natalie bares her teeth.

I turn the car around to head out to Roosevelt Boulevard, and I'm surprised when she yells at me that I'm going too fast and that there are dips in the road I'm not feeling, but they're there and they are KILLING HER. I slow down obediently.

And then she says, "OW!"

"Nat. Are you about to have this baby?"

"No," she says. "These are Braxton Hicks contractions. Fake." She takes a deep, ragged breath.

"Because I'm just saying, since we're already in the car and all, maybe we should go to the hospital."

She doesn't even answer that, just lies back with her hands on her massive belly and looks like she's in the most amount of pain a human has ever endured, doing little puffing things with her mouth.

"Does it hurt . . . a lot?" I say. We pass a lumberyard and a row of shops. "I could pull in here, if you want."

"Please. I'm concentrating. This is not pain. We don't use the word *pain*. There is some . . ."

"Some what?"

"Marnie. Please. Be. Quiet."

We finally get to the medical building—a low-slung little stucco building with banana trees and azalea bushes planted out front—and I pull up to the door and get out and come around to help her. But she waves me off and then—just like that—she loses her footing and she falls down on the pavement with a loud smack.

"Oh, no, no, no! Oh my goodness!" I cry, and I bend down to help her. "Don't move. Let's see . . . oh crap . . . did you land on your stomach? Did you hit your head?"

"*No*, I didn't hit my head. Calm down, will you? That was my purse making that noise."

She's lying on her side in the flower bed, her head resting on a big old palm frond, looking up at me through her same old calm-as-anything Natalie eyes. She's not frothing at the mouth or bleeding or giving birth. She's just Natalie, lying there as if she meant to. Then she starts trying to pull herself up and can't.

"Here, maybe you shouldn't move. Really, Nat. It could be you broke something."

"Stop yelling," she hisses at me, which is weird because I'm almost positive I'm not yelling. "I'm fine," she says. "Just help . . . just help me up, would you? And don't attract attention."

"Okay, here, hold on to me. Can you hold on?" I go around to the other side of her and get down on my knees, but I can't figure out where to grab on to her, and she's so *big*, but just then a man's large hands show up in my field of vision, and somebody in a white coat is gently grasping my sister under the arms and gradually easing her upright until she's on her feet, and then supporting her gigantic body against his until she can steady herself. I'm still on the ground, scrambling around to get the contents of her purse, which have spilled everywhere, and I can't see his face, only that he has dark hair, and she seems to be leaning against him as he walks her inside.

"There," I hear him say. "Are you all right?"

"I'm fine," she says, which is so untrue it's not even funny. But leave it to my sister.

I finish picking up all her lipsticks and quarters and a wad of tissues, and then I run to catch up with them. A blast of cold air-conditioning hits my face when I open the door, and I can hear Natalie saying, "Oooh! It's freezing in here!"

"Ridiculously cold," he agrees, and that's when I look up at his face, and it's Jeremy Sanders holding on to my sister.

Jeremy Sanders! Of course it is! I almost laugh. At first I think this is all an elaborate ploy by my mother to get us together. She is a busybody with mysterious ways. The color seems to leave his face as he lowers my sister onto a bench next to the elevators. Once he gets her situated, he straightens up and looks at me with wide, round eyes.

I must look as shocked as he does.

I hear myself saying, "Hi, how are you?"

"Marnie." He looks stunned. But then he manages to recover and says, "And oh my goodness, this is Natalie? Hi! Wow. Are you okay? That was quite a spill you took. Here, take my coat. You're shivering."

He starts removing his white coat, which I notice says Jeremy Sanders, DPT embroidered over the pocket. Whatever that means. Something official, from the looks of him.

"No," Natalie says. She's back to being her brisk and competent self now, waving him away, thanking him for taking care of her, but saying she's got to get to the dentist's office, and she's fine, really she's just fine—it was just a little slip is all. Nothing to worry about. She's just going to rest here for a second, catch her breath, and then she'll be off.

I keep sneaking looks at him. He seems older, of course—but in a good, mature-guy way. My mind is filled immediately with the memory of his slouchiness, his nonconformitude, his sloppy snarkiness. None of that is left. He's obviously become a fully invested member of society. Who would have guessed?

"Hey, dude, it's great to see you!" I say. "So you're a DPT now! Yay, you!"

"Yes," he says and smiles at me with even, white teeth. I never noticed how really white and even his teeth were.

"And forgive me," I say, "but what *is* a DPT?"

"Physical therapist," he and Natalie both say at the same time, and then she grabs on to her huge stomach and lets out a yell.

"Um, I'd say your sister seems to be in labor. I think we should call an ambulance. That fall did not look good," he says in a low voice.

"NO!" roars Natalie, holding up one hand while she clutches her abdomen with the other. We watch her in fascination, and after a moment she straightens up and says, "I'm fine. I'm prepared for this."

"She's a warrior," I tell him. "So you're still living here? Or did you move back?"

He tears his eyes away from Natalie and looks at me. "Came back about six months ago. My mom's getting up there in years and needed some extra help . . . and so you're back here, too? Or just visiting for—?" He gestures toward Natalie.

"The baby? No! I've moved back. This is home. Now. Newly." I shrug and do a ridiculous little dance to show how carefree I am. I am beginning to regret that I'm wearing paint-splattered jeans and that my hair is shoved up into a big messy knot, although he's certainly seen me looking worse.

"No, totally," he says, which doesn't really make any sense, but who cares. He looks back over at Natalie, who is shivering on the bench and breathing hard, and his eyes are round with alarm. "Really. We should call an ambulance."

"No! This . . . is . . . false labor," Natalie manages. "If the contractions were real, then . . . my Lamaze teacher . . . said . . ." Suddenly she can't talk anymore and her face has turned pale and she slumps against the wall, panting.

Jeremy looks at me. "I don't know what the Lamaze teacher said, but whatever. She's not here, and we are. I think we've got to do something. So . . . I'm thinking hospital?"

"Definitely."

"Definitely *not*," says Natalie, resurfacing from her breathing debacle. "That's not the way this works. You have early labor for a long time before you have active labor . . . and I did *not* have early labor. So these can't be—"

Just then she looks horrified, and a huge gush of liquid goes all over the floor.

"My water broke!" she says. "Oh my God, this is not what I planned!"

"Ohhhkay. That's it. Ambulance time," Jeremy says, getting out his phone.

Natalie, who would still like to be running the world even while delivering a child, is not having it, however. "No. What we should do . . . is clean all this UP," she says somewhat slowly in her new-normal voice. "When the amniotic fluid breaks, you still have time." As though she's reading from some textbook.

"Natalie, honey, Jeremy's right. Let's go to the hospital, sweetie."

"But the birth plan!" she says. "I do not want an ambulance! Take me in your car. And call Brian. Tell him to bring my suitcase and the tennis balls and the lollipops."

Then another contraction hits, and she has to stop talking.

"Jesus," says Jeremy. "I'm definitely getting an ambulance." And he starts to punch in numbers.

My sister holds up her hand, and as soon as the contraction is over, she says, "Take his phone, Marnie! I've got this! I have trained and prepared, and I am the warrior-queen, and I am READY. Do not get in my way because I—"

And then she stops. Falls back on the bench. Starts breathing through her mouth. Eyes round with panic.

Right after that one, there's another.

And another.

Jeremy, looking more handsome and more in charge than I have ever known him to be, gives me a meaningful look and then quietly tells the emergency dispatcher the whole situation, and then when he hangs up, he suggests that I call my parents and Natalie's husband. So I do as I'm told. No one answers, but I leave messages all around.

While we wait, he tells me it's going to be okay, and somehow I believe him. Between contractions, Natalie is still screaming about her birth plan and yelling at me to get the car and then she gives us some information she learned in her childbirth class—information that no longer seems to apply, if you ask me.

"The warrior-queen is not going to be happy with you and me," he whispers.

I am freaking out, but I say the wisest thing I can think of, which is, "When she gets a healthy baby by the end of this, all will be forgiven."

And then I cross my fingers.

THIRTEEN
BLIX

On the morning of my Irish wake—aka the Blix Out party—I wake up to find the angel of death hanging out in my room.

So, okay.

"Hi," I say to the angel. "I know it's time. I can do this dying thing. I'll die at the party if that's what I'm supposed to do, although that is probably going to freak some of the guests out. But not me. I'm ready when death is."

Then I lie back and close my eyes and ask for some white light to surround me, Houndy, and the entire borough of Brooklyn, and then, for good measure, the whole country and the world. I bless the whole planet. Little stars going all over the place.

The angel of death swirls up around the high ceiling, settles into one of the plaster cracks up there, the one that looks like a dog's nose. That one may be my all-time favorite.

Houndy stirs next to me, moaning a little bit in his sleep. Then he sits up and does that epic throat-clearing thing he does every morning, making barking and snorting noises, so loud that they could stop traffic.

It always makes me laugh, like Houndy is composed only of phlegm and old tobacco products from his misspent youth, when I happen to know for a fact that he is made of seawater and strong coffee and lobster claws.

I reach over and rub his back when he's finished, and he turns and gives me a look I can't quite read, which is weird because I can read *all* of Houndy's looks. Always have been able to. He's the least mysterious man on the planet, which is why it's worked so well between us.

He is looking at me. "You're not going to get well, are you?"

"I don't know. I suppose there could still be a miracle. Anything can happen."

"It's getting bigger. You gave your tumor a name, and now it's bigger. Don't you think maybe you gave it too much love? You encouraged it." Then he shakes his head. "Listen to me, talking like this. Like any of this is really real. Blix! Why the hell couldn't you have used all your . . . whatever . . . your *power* to stop this from happening?"

"Oh, Houndy baby, everybody eventually has to make their transition, and I've done what I could, but maybe we have to face it that Cassandra is the way I'm meant to go. Come over here, you big old lug, and let me love on you for a minute."

He says no but then he scootches over and holds on to me. I'll bet he was a fine specimen when he was young, because he still has the strongest, broadest shoulders and the softest little earlobes and the reddest cheeks and a light in his eyes that you don't find on most humans today.

One time he said to me, "You know, I had a great six-pack when I was young," and I said to him, "Bragging about beer is so unbecoming for an old man."

The truth is that he is still a beautiful man.

"Why do you want to leave me?" he says, his voice all choked up, and I can't speak for a minute. I just rub his back in circles, closing my eyes tightly and drinking him in—the smell of him, the way his muscles ripple underneath my hands, the labored breathing that comes out of him in bursts.

This, I think, *is my life. I am living my life. Right now. This is the moment that we have.*

I stroke his head and look deeply in his eyes. There is no answer. I don't want to leave him, but I believe we all create our own reality, so I must have planned this. I can't figure it out, why it went down this way, and it hurts to try, to tell you the truth. I just know that some ailments aren't meant to be healed, and that Houndy and I—and Marnie, too, and everybody that I know—are engaged in some kind of dance of our souls and we are here to help each other. So I tell him this, and he kisses me, and then in his regular voice he says I'm his very favorite lunatic, and maybe I could do a spell to make the lobsters simply jump out of the sea so he doesn't have to haul them in today for the party, how would *that* be; and maybe while I'm at it, I could do a spell that his back would stop hurting, and that we would both live forever here in this perfect little brownstone that threatens every day to fall down around us but so far hasn't.

"Okay, I'll try to get the lobsters to come right to you," I say. "And I also have another new project, that I didn't tell you about yet. But I need to tell you."

"I hope it's you staying alive."

"Sssh. I think Marnie and Patrick are supposed to be together. I'm working on that."

He pulls away just slightly. "Marnie and *Patrick*? Are you out of your mind?"

"No, she's right for Patrick. I'm convinced of it. They're supposed to be together. That's what all this has been about, Houndy. All of it. My meeting Marnie at the party. Patrick coming to live here in the first place. Who knows how far back this goes?"

"Oh, no," he says. "What are you doing this for? Blix! You can't possibly want to torment poor Patrick any more than he's already been tormented."

"*Torment?* Love is not torment," I tell him firmly. "Trust me. These two are a match. I knew it the moment I saw her, but I just didn't know I knew it."

"Blix."

"Houndy."

"He doesn't want love. He's hurt." He gets up out of bed, pretending to be all grouchy. "Patrick just wants to be left alone."

"That is the most ridiculous thing you've ever said to me. Everybody wants love, and the ones who appear to want it the least actually *need* it the most. Remember when you first came to me? Huh? Remember that? You didn't know you wanted love."

"Yeah, but, with all due respect to your matchmaking ways, let's not overlook that Marnie married Noah. What about that? He's the one she wants."

"Well, she did marry him. But he's left her. The universe works in mysterious ways, Houndy, and I know what I'm doing. You just have to trust me." I hug myself and laugh.

He starts waving his hands in the air around his head, like there are gnats bothering him. He can only go so far with this kind of talk. And sure enough, he's pulled his clothes on by now, and he goes to the bedroom door to leave, grousing again about how he has to go get the lobsters, and I remind him that Harry said *he'd* get the lobsters, and then I say, "Okay, you. I think you need to come back to bed for some special attention."

"Blix. I don't wanna."

"Oh, Houuuuuuuundy . . ."

"No."

"Ohhhhhhh, Houuuuuuuundy . . ."

"No, no, no." But he is standing at the bedroom door again, trying to hide his smile.

I waggle my fingers, like I'm sending over some fairy dust. I crook my finger at him. "Houndy, Houndy, Houndy!"

"Damn it, Blix. What are you doing to me?"

"Youuuu knooooow."

He comes over to the bedside, and I reach over and lift up his shirt, and unbutton the cargo pants he's just buttoned up.

"Blix, it—it's not going to . . . ohhhhh!" And then he comes down onto the bed, tumbling really, and he's laughing in surprise, so I roll him over and put my nose right up to his, and then—and this is an effort, let me tell you—I hoist myself up on top of him, and sit there, straddling him. And slowly, slowly the light comes back into Houndy, and he gives himself over to me. It's almost like that moment when you're sautéing mushrooms, and they give up, yield themselves to you, and the alchemy is complete.

That's Houndy and me, making love. Mushrooms in a pan.

Like we've done for so long, thick and thin, sickness and health, all that. You never know which time is going to be the last time.

He wasn't my first love, or second, third, fourth, or maybe even thirty-fourth. But Houndy, as I've come to see—simple, uncomplicated, straightforward Houndy—is the love of my life.

And when I tell him so, he squeezes his eyes shut tight, and when he opens them again, the light of his love nearly blinds me.

Lola comes over to help me get ready for the wake. I'm washing bowls and trays while she unpacks the streamers and tiaras and confetti left over from our last bash early in the summer.

"I don't know," she says. "Somehow I don't think streamers are quite appropriate for a wake, now are they?"

"Everything should be appropriate. I'm changing the rules of wakes, remember? I'm going out with a bang. Streamers and whatever else. I personally will be wearing a tiara and I hope you will, too. I'd like to die in a tiara, as a matter of fact."

She turns and smiles at me sadly. "Ah, Blix, you're not dying. I've seen people who are about to die, and they're nothing like you. They're not washing bowls for a dinner party, for one thing. And they're not thinking about sex."

"Oh dear, did you hear us?"

"Did I *hear* you? Are you kidding me? Damn straight, I heard you. I was walking outside on the sidewalk, and I thought, that Houndy sounds like—wait, is *that* why he's called Houndy? It is, isn't it? He baaaaays like . . . Oh!" She bursts out laughing.

"That's it. He's an old hound dog."

"God, I miss that."

"Sex? Do you, really?"

"Yeah."

"No. Really really?"

"I said yes. But it's been so long, it would probably kill me. It'd be like sandpaper down there."

"Oh, that's no excuse. They have stuff for that now. At the drugstore. And you could be having sex, you know. You know you could." I can't resist saying it. "And speaking of which, how come you're not telling me about that guy who comes and picks you up? He would sleep with you in an instant."

"Oh, him." Her face goes cloudy. "You sent him, didn't you?"

"Of course I did. Not *him*, per se. I don't even know who he is. I just put out in the universe that you needed somebody to love again. So tell me why you're so secretive about him."

"You want to know the truth?"

"Yes, damn it. You tell me everything, except now suddenly you're keeping this man all to yourself. Don't think I haven't noticed how mean you're being."

"Well, I haven't told you this because I don't want you making a big deal out of it. Putting all your magic dust all over it. He's a friend, okay? From the past. Nothing more than that."

"Uh-huh," I say. The truth is, I did concentrate real hard on having her find someone who could win her trust, someone she'd perhaps known from before, because Lola is a little bit cowardly when it comes to meeting new men. I wrote journal entries; I did chanting; I threw the *I Ching* coins. I did a couple of spells just for good measure. And I sent prayers out into the universe. It's all a mix.

"See? There you go, doing it again. Matchmaking when there's nothing there. Sorry. Just wishful thinking this time, Blix."

I simply smile.

Just before the wake starts, Patrick sends word that he can't come. He's feeling pugly, he says.

Pugly. This is code for Patrick thinking he's too ugly to be in polite company. It's the word we use between ourselves. Patrick isn't just shy, it's that he has a disfigurement, you see—a scarred face and a jaw displacement. He was once in a fire when his kitchen exploded due to a gas leak, and in one instant he went from being relatively handsome and well-adjusted, he said, to being a hideous beast. His word for himself, not mine, because the light that shines out from Patrick's eyes transforms his face. You see that light, and you don't even know about his jaw and his skin, which is stretched so tight in places that it's almost translucent. His light makes you forget all that.

But that's how he describes himself, as a hideous beast because *he* is the only one who can't see that light, and periodically I have to go down to Patrick's apartment, which he keeps dark and musty smelling, and also it's filled with old computers and one grouchy cat, and I sit down there with him and try to tell him about the light that other people see in him and also that he has a soul that anyone would love.

He breaks my heart, Patrick does. He promised he would come to the Blix Out.

"I'm going down to see him," I tell Houndy and Lola, and they exchange a look, but nobody tries to stop me. I put on my long spangled skirt, and Lola helps me zip it up over Cassandra, and then I put on the purple tunic and the shawl that has the lace and the mirrors sewn everywhere, even on the fringe. Lola fluffs up my hair, which is sticking up everywhere—and off I go, trundling down the stairs, down to Patrick's lair.

"I can't do it today, Blix," he calls from the other side of the door when I knock.

"Sweetie, I need you to come to my wake," I say. "Just open the door a little crack. I have something I need to tell you."

After a while, I hear about five locks being unlatched, and then he lets me into the apartment, and I go tromping around, and I open all the shades and turn on lights. He's standing there in the darkness, wearing what he always tells me is his work uniform: baggy sweatpants and sweatshirt, way too big. He's a thin, waifish guy now, somebody who would barely leave a shadow, and that's what he intends, I think, to waste away until he's just a smear in the world, as small as a piece of gum you'd see on the sidewalk. He can't be loved anymore, he told me once, so now he doesn't want to bother anybody. He has some horrible job, writing about diseases and symptoms, and so he's steeped in troubles and doesn't want to bother the people of the world with his yawning, gaping need. I get this, I do.

"Patrick," I say. "Honey."

"I can't do it. Listen, I love you and I think it's fantastic that you're doing this amazing party—"

"It's not just an amazing party, as you call it. It's a *wake*. An Irish wake."

"Whatever it is, but you don't want me there having a panic attack. I'd ruin the whole mood."

"We'll stick together. We can do our dance, and then you won't need to panic." One time, when it was just the two of us, we made up a dance in which we wore hats that we pulled down until they nearly covered our faces, and then we threw them up in the air. We might have been drunk when we invented that dance, but we could be drunk again, I tell him. I pick his Hawaiian shirt out of his closet, which contains exactly three shirts, all meticulously hung up and evenly spaced.

"You look devastating in this shirt, and you know you do. So you can put on that and your straw hat, and we'll dance and drink. People *need* you there. If you're not there, I'll have to answer the question all night long: Where is Patrick? Where's Patrick? Think of how that's going to be for me. It's going to ruin my whole evening having to explain your absence."

He just keeps looking at me sadly and shaking his head.

"Patrick," I say. "Honey. We can't undo the scars and the burns. We can't go back to that day, so we just have to figure out how to move forward from it."

I go over and gently touch his face, touch the place on his cheek that is nearly sunken in, and the smooth, bright part near his eye where the skin was stretched taut. I take his hand and hold on to it.

He is silent, unmoving, while I do this. A praying mantis of a man.

"Can't we find a way together to be in the world in spite of the fire?"

He tilts his head back and closes his eyes. And I take his hand, and very carefully, slowly, drag it over to Cassandra, where she is resting beneath my shirt, and I lift my shirt ever so gently, and place his hand on this ball of tumor that even Houndy doesn't want to look at or touch. I wrap his hand around Cassandra, and I tell him her name. I am terrified that he will pull away, that he'll recoil, that I'll see the horror in his eyes before he turns away.

Instead, what flickers across his face is compassion. He doesn't move his hand. He says, "Oh, Blix," like a slow exhale.

"We are all broken," I say to him. "And we all still have to dance."

He sucks his breath in. "I scare *children*, for God's sake."

"And yet we still have to dance."

"I-I don't know."

"Also. I didn't want to have to bring out the big guns here, but I think this really is a wake. I think tonight is the night I'm going to die."

"Damn it, Blix. What are you talking about?"

"I have some evidence I'm not going to go into. But I'm just saying you might want to come and hang out. Otherwise, I'll have to haunt you for the rest of time."

And then I kiss him and kiss him, kiss all the scarred-over parts of his face, kiss his eyelids and his forehead, and then I go back upstairs, and I am not surprised—not a bit surprised—when an hour later he shows up to the party, and we slow dance together, him in his Hawaiian shirt and sweatpants and me in my spangles and sequins, with Cassandra bouncing around like a baby in a pouch.

The tiki torches by then are bright flames against the dark night sky, and people are gathered around the fire pit, where Houndy is cooking the lobsters he and Harry somehow got from the sea today. Jessica comes out with pots of melted butter, and Sammy, recently returned from his visit to his father, is playing his guitar in the corner. There are clusters of people everywhere, people playing music and people just talking, and oh, so many people, and Lola is bobbing here and there, putting out platters of things, pouring more wine. There's a keg in the corner, and Harry is pumping it like it's a musical instrument.

I am twirling around in the middle of everything—very slowly, very gently—and I am smiling when it happens. Smiling, as if life is just going to continue in this iridescent way, and I will always be a body, and Houndy will always have a body, and we have time for so many more wakes before the very end comes.

But no. There's a sudden commotion next to the fire pit, and at first I think too many people are trying to put too much wood on it. But no—somebody is down on the ground, and others are gathered around, and somebody says, "Quick! Call nine one one!"

Lola turns to find me, and when our eyes meet, I know the very worst has happened. "Houndy," she mouths to me.

And it's true. I push through the crowds, and there he is. My Houndy.

Lying on the ground on his back and he is not breathing, and by the time I get there he is already dead, but no one knows that yet, only I know it because I see his spirit leaving, and I can see his face growing more gray, the pink of him vanishing like a magician's trick, and somebody pushes me aside and does CPR on him—for the second time, I'm told—and Houndy is gone from his body, but part of him is still there with me. I feel him leaving, feel him slipping away, but first he's drifting around telling me he loves me, and then soon he's small enough that he can fit in the folds of my shawl, where I will hold on to him forever.

People are all murmuring, the crowd is like a tide, bending and waving, and gathering and subsiding. There are hands on me, people trying to lead me away from him, and good luck to them, because I can't be led anywhere. And then there is the sound of a siren, and the pounding of boots on the roof, as EMTs come and do their work, bending over him, coaxing him into coming back, trying to use their machines to persuade him. But he's in my shawl, I want to tell them. He's not where they can reach him, not really.

Lola leads me away, but I insist on going in the ambulance. It's too hard, she says, but I am firm about this. I need to go. And she says she'll come, too, in that case. We have to be there with Houndy, even though it's not Houndy. Not anymore.

Houndy/not Houndy.

I pass everyone on the way down, take hold of their hands, look deep in their eyes, and see all the love reflected back. All the amazing, smashing love. The universe of stars. The dance of summer.

The angel of death, you messed everything up. You came for the wrong person.

Somewhere, I know, a baby must be being born—a life arriving and a life leaving. And I feel both things, the joy of both. Houndy is gazing at me through the mists, Houndy so close he can still reach out and touch me. He's sorry. He's happy but he's sorry.

And me saying, don't worry I'm coming soon please wait for me Houndy love wait because I'll be there I promise.

FOURTEEN
MARNIE

I text Brian as the ambulance pulls up.

"It's okay, it's going to be okay," I hear myself saying. Two EMTs jump out and come inside the building to Natalie, who is now panting with each contraction and swaying on the bench just slightly. Her lips look a little white to me, and sweat is pouring off her forehead even though she's shivering.

It's hard for me to let go of her, but these guys know what they're doing. They squat down next to her and take her pulse and blood pressure, and ask a lot of questions. "When is the baby due? When did you last eat? What hospital are you using? How far apart are the contractions? When did your water break?" And then they put her on a stretcher and take her inside the back of the ambulance, and one EMT slaps an oxygen monitor on her finger, and the other starts an IV. The radio crackles news of other people, but they are intent on Natalie. One of them talks into the handset for a minute, but I can't pay attention to what he's saying.

I sit beside her, trying not to freak out in front of her. Also, I'm trying to help her breathe through contractions, which she is not doing such a hot job of. She keeps looking like she's going to pass out.

"Okay, Natalie, my name is Joel, and I'm going to help you get your breathing under control," says one of them, leaning down close to Natalie's face. He is young and ruggedly handsome with kind eyes and large, capable hands. "I think you're hyperventilating, sweetheart, so let's try to slooow down your breathing, okay? Take . . . it . . . easy . . . like . . . this." He demonstrates how to breathe slowly and deeply, and then gives her a paper bag to put over her mouth. "My wife just had a baby," he tells me. "Trust me, she's going to be fine."

"I'm *not*—" says Natalie, and then she lets out a yell that I haven't heard from her since she got a B minus on a research paper in seventh grade, on sea lions, after she had read four books about them. I grab her hand, and Joel says to me, pleasantly as if we're discussing soccer goals, "Yeah. That was a big one. Okay, Natalie, let's get ready to ride the next one. They're coming about forty seconds apart now, so just rest for a minute . . . and okay now, be ready!"

"Are we going to the hospital?" I say to him, and he nods.

"Just want to get her stabilized first," he says, holding on to her wrist.

Natalie suddenly makes the most unearthly sound I've ever heard—and I'm stunned when the other EMT guy, Marcus, slams the back door of the ambulance and comes over to us. Joel leaps into action and starts ripping off her pants, which are wet from that water-breaking incident, and hard to get off, and Joel motions for me to help him, because we seem to be suddenly in a huge hurry.

He exchanges a word I can't hear with the other EMT, who takes out a tray of something from a drawer. There are towels and cloths and some silver equipment-looking things. I don't know, but I *think* we're about to deliver a baby. My sister's eyes are closed, and her face is all scrunched up.

"Breathe. Ride the contraction," says Joel. "It's fine . . . you're doing great, Natalie."

Suddenly it hits me that Brian is possibly going to miss his own child's birth unless he gets here fast. I turn to say that to Joel, as though there's something he might be able to do: delay things or something—who knows? But before I can say it, Natalie starts screaming her head off, and Joel motions something to me, and I suddenly understand that this is it. *This is it.* There isn't going to *be* a ride to the hospital—we're going to deliver this baby right now, in the parking lot, just these two guys and me.

Well, mostly the two EMTs.

But I am here, too. No one is going to turn to me and say, "Um, miss? Could you please get out of here? I don't believe you're authorized for this kind of activity, are you? Did you take the baby delivery test? No? Then I'm sorry, you'll have to leave."

And I know nothing about this! In fact, I don't even know what you're supposed to read to get ready for something like this. It's like that dream where you signed up for a course and then forgot about it so you didn't do any of the required reading, and now you've realized your mistake but it's too late to withdraw . . .

"AARRRUUUUUUUUUUGHGHGHGHGH," my sister says.

I take her hand, and when I look down, I see that there is the top of the baby's head. Like, coming out of her.

"Crowning. She's crowning," Joel says. "Amazing, isn't it?"

My sister's face is all red and contorted and her eyes are squinched closed. I am thinking a ridiculous thought—that she is not going to like the fact that she didn't get to have the birth plan she wanted. She was so emphatic about the whole thing. Natalie is swamped by another contraction, and she yells and grabs my hand and grips it so hard that I'm halfway certain that my fingers are going to turn black and fall off by Wednesday.

Joel instructs her on one final push—"Give me a good one, a nice steady push!"—and then, my God, somehow a tiny human, gray and mottled and covered in what looks like cottage cheese, comes sliding out, guided by Joel's gloved, capable hands. A baby! Oh my God, there's a baby girl! With eyes open! Looking around! And little fists, curled up tight, legs folded in so compactly, now stretching out, kicking, yelling, breathing like a champ. Joel is holding her in the crook of his arm.

I look up at Natalie, and her eyes are bright with tears, and my face is streaming wetness. My heart is galloping all around, and my hands look like they might soon start bleeding from the little half-moons of Natalie's nails pressing into them.

"Good job," says Joel softly. And Marcus smiles and rips off his gloves. Both of them are so calm and methodical, it's like they're injecting calm into the air. Like pure love. I hear that voice again—*you are love; you are going to be all right.* And my niece—Amelia Jane—is now looking around with wide, navy-blue eyes, making little peeps of protest, her tiny body turning pinker by the second, as though she's under some kind of cosmic light. She has a fringe of dark hair, and little arms and legs, and fingers and thumbs—all of your most important equipment—and she's alert and aware. Her filmy eyes lock on to mine, and I am smitten, stunned, thinking: *How can this be? How does such a thing happen around us every day—and we just go about our lives like it's nothing out of the ordinary?*

The two guys are busy doing official medical stuff, cleaning Natalie, covering her up. Joel hands the baby to me, which makes me startle. *Me?* Are you *serious*? I look around, venture out of my trance. Wow. We're in an ambulance, sitting in the parking area of the dentist's office. Outside, there are cars honking, voices of people walking past the ambulance, unaware. Somewhere out there is Jeremy; did he go back upstairs to help somebody with a backache?

But here, in this cocoon, plopped into my arms in a little blanket, is my niece, round and rosy and just as startled as I am.

"Here, let me give her to her mom," I say. Natalie is propped up now, the stunned look gone from her features. She takes the baby from me, and our eyes meet.

Joel says, "Beautiful baby. You did a great job. Boy, these are my favorite kinds of days, when I get to help a baby come into the world."

After a bit, I'm aware that the ambulance is moving. Marcus is taking us to the hospital. But slowly. No sirens. Our own little traveling safe place is moving, taking with us all the equipment we could ever need.

"Look what we did!" Natalie says, and her eyes are locked on to mine. "You are the best, the best sister in the world! How did you know—to be here—that I needed you?"

We both gaze down at this little life we just brought into the world. My heart is so full it feels like it will spill out of me somehow.

"You know, of all our antics, I have to say that this is the best sister act we've ever pulled off," I tell her. "Even though it wasn't the birth plan you had in mind."

"Yeah," she says, "but only because I didn't think I could get this one to work."

I think I might just die of this.

That evening, the whole family comes to my sister's hospital room, where she presides beautifully, wearing a lovely peach-colored nightgown I fetched for her from the gift shop, and her hair is clean and shining. She is even more radiant than ever, with her skin looking dewy and lit from within—and little Amelia—rosy little Amelia lies contented in her mother's arms, pooching out her sweet pink little lips.

Joel, the delicious EMT, shows up at one point with a bouquet of flowers, and my whole family goes gaga over him. He explains that he hardly ever gets to deliver babies, and that he was, in fact, a mess when his own wife went into labor. And that makes everybody laugh, and my mother wants to invite him and his entire family over for dinner, except that my father quietly puts his hand on her arm before she can quite squeak out the invitation.

Brian, sitting by my sister's side, is clearly smitten with the whole scene. I was a little worried that he was going to feel he'd been cut out of the deal somehow, but he doesn't seem to mind in the least. Here he got a perfect baby girl without having to even endure one of my sister's high-pitched screams, screams that will never, ever be mentioned by anyone, though they are going to live on in some pocket of my memory until the end of time.

"She looks like your brother," says my mother to my father.

"Joe? I think you're just saying that because he's bald."

"No. Look at the chin. It's Joe's chin."

"But that's just because he had his teeth knocked out playing street hockey. People with no teeth—like Amelia, for now—have those kinds of chins."

To my surprise, my mother laughs. And my father tucks his head over her shoulder, and for a moment they're both smiling down at the baby. It seems impossible to believe that this is a couple who communicates mainly through bickering. Maybe, it occurs to me, this is what marriage ultimately turns into: you have to tough it out through the bad times so that you can get to these pinnacle moments when life has just handed you a shiny star.

I'm not even surprised when Jeremy shows up, carrying balloons. Or when my parents greet him like the long-lost son they never had. Nor is it shocking that he and I leave the hospital together, going out for dinner, and that after that, we go to his mother's house and sit on the screened porch where we spent thousands of hours doing homework and gossiping about other kids.

He's grown up to be a good-natured, good-looking man who takes care of his mom, and I'm suddenly so sorry I broke his heart, except that I think that we all do need to have our hearts broken at some point, and so maybe I actually did him a good service. It's something we need to know about ourselves, how that heart breaks and grows back.

My own heart, given away to Noah, now stirs somewhere deep down, stretches, yawns, looks at its watch and rolls over, tries to go back to sleep. But it has one eye open, I notice.

In no time, over a glass of wine, we've covered our college years and our employment decisions (his good, mine questionable). And then, because this is what you do under these circumstances, we rehash our own breakup, casting it in a new, more philosophical, forgiving light.

After he razzes me for falling for Brad Whitaker, I say to him, "Did you ever think that maybe you could have tried harder to fight for me? Like, you at least could have said you cared about me. Maybe asked me not to date him."

"Um, I was not equipped at seventeen to have that kind of conversation," he says.

"Yeah, well, you treated me like I was just one of your buddies and I honestly had no idea you cared one way or the other."

He smiles and his eyes hold mine a lot longer than necessary. "Didn't you, really?" he says. "Yeah, I know I wasn't any Prince Charming, more's the pity. But on the other hand, I'm the one who gets to sit here with you tonight, while he's some loser out in the world *not* spending time with you. So maybe the good guy triumphs in the end, you know?"

He is gazing at me so directly that I have to look away.

Then he says, "I've, um, heard through the grapevine that you've had something of a rough go. We don't have to talk about it if you don't want to, but . . ."

"Oh," I say. "Well. Yeah. Pretty much your average stood-up-at-the-altar situation. Not really ideal."

"Well, that certainly sucks." He looks at me like he wants to hear what happened, and not just so he can gloat a little bit over my poor judgment.

So I go through the story—the long version, including the two years Noah and I were together, the engagement excitement, and then him showing up late to the wedding and our horrible talk in the meadow, blah blah blah, and then I tell him about the honeymoon and the screaming monkeys, because by now it's becoming The Story I Tell about My Marriage, and it always gets a laugh as well as a sympathetic clucking, depending on how I tell it.

With him, I confess the part I hadn't told anyone but Natalie—how I dismantled my wedding dress—because he is the only person who would understand something that bizarre and find it funny. Sure enough, he laughs in all the right places—and he does this thing that I now remember he used to do as a kid: he sort of wrinkles his nose and closes his eyes before he laughs. It's just a little quirk, but seeing him still do it makes my heart glad.

And then things shift slightly. Jeremy is looking at me without having to look away. He says that this is a momentous day, because not only have we been present at the miracle of birth, but he's also gotten to hear about a jerk who is perhaps even worse than the jerk I ditched him for senior year.

When he comes over to the couch where I'm sitting and puts his hand idly on my arm, I slide over closer, and it turns out that, thank God, he's learned something about kissing in the intervening years because I realize that I haven't been kissed in quite a while, and I need it badly.

It's still a slightly cautious kiss around the edges, of course, because it's Jeremy—and also because I have hurt him before, and so maybe he's wisely holding something back, but I throw myself into it, kissing him as passionately as I can, holding *nothing* back, just to show him how it can be done, and then—my God, in no time at all, we're breathless and shocked at the heat we've generated.

He looks at me in surprise, and I see his Adam's apple bob up and down. He smells like aftershave, and my mind briefly wobbles, goes to the backseats of cars in high school, to the hot breath of boys and their heavy aroma of sex—was it Old Spice? Something else?

"So, listen," he says roughly. "Will you . . . I mean I know it's weird, with my mother upstairs sleeping, but we used to be good at sneaking around, and—"

"Yes," I say. "I will."

He pulls away, wide-eyed. "Yeah? Really?" He blinks, and I think maybe he'll lose his nerve. But then he says, "Okay then! Okay. Let's do it!" And he takes me upstairs to his boyhood room, and I swear, it's like time has stood still up there, with his single bed still in there and his old posters of Harry Potter.

"Dude, your room!" I say. "My God, everything's still the same except the *Star Wars* sheets. How in the world have you not changed anything?"

He looks around like he's seeing it all for the first time, too, and runs his fingers through his hair. "I'm hopeless, I know. I guess I was thinking I'd move out sometime, so why get new stuff?" He looks very concerned. "It is weird in here, isn't it? The question is, is it *too* weird for you? Deal-breakingly weird? Are we going to have to go to Kmart before we can make anything happen between us, do you think?"

"No," I say. "No! But seriously? *Harry Potter?*"

"Everybody knows that Harry Potter is cool, and besides"—he wraps his arms around me and puts his face up against mine, whispering—"full disclosure: the *Star Wars* sheets are in the wash. They'll be back on the bed next time you're here."

I'm laughing as I wrap my arms around his neck. "Well, I can certainly see that you don't bring a lot of women home."

He gets all serious. "No. Well . . . I guess I don't. My mom being here and all." He starts planting little kisses all along my jawline, down to my neck. With his right hand he unbuttons my blouse. "And can you please . . . could we both stop laughing so we can have sex? Am I going to have to go get a paper bag for you to breathe into, because hysterical laughter really ruins a seduction scene."

"Oh, brother. *Is* this a seduction scene?"

"Well, I'm *trying*," he says, and he reaches around to unfasten my bra, and I attempt to be serious, which makes me start laughing all over again. "Could you?" he says. "Stop?"

He walks me, backward, over to his bed, and we fall down on the mattress, with him on top of me, and he says, "I can't believe how long I've waited for this," and I say, "Me, too," as you do. It's just the slightest bit awkward, but I'm wondering if life would have been altogether different if we had done this long, long ago—that day way back when he *didn't* buy condoms. If I could go back in time, I'd insist we try another drugstore.

This is what I'm thinking, lying there underneath him and looking into his eyes—and then, all of a sudden, I'm not thinking anymore at all. Sex has a way of taking over, all the body parts waking right up and taking their stations.

Afterward, I think how nice it is, lying there in his arms, as though no time at all has gone by. Press a button, and—bingo, you're back to safety.

When I go home that evening, I realize that I, too, am sleeping in my girlhood room with the same posters and sheets. We're not so different after all, he and I. The walking wounded, coming home to heal.

FIFTEEN
BLIX

So I don't die.

I don't die that night, and I don't die the next week or the next after that. In fact, I have never had a larger appetite, or more of a piercing sense of what it means to be alive. All this feels like bonus time, like the days that get tacked on to a vacation trip because the airline cancels your flight.

There's a kind of holiness to these days, this time, painful as it is.

Maybe I am meant to simply cruise along. Maybe there's still something I am supposed to accomplish.

Or maybe when death came for me, Houndy jumped out in front and took his turn first. He's a scoundrel, that one.

Ah, well, but if you believe, as I do, that there are no mistakes, then clearly I am supposed to be here.

Summer ends, and Brooklyn ushers in September. I am tired. The mad current of life goes on around me. A bright ribbon of humanity exists outside, coming back to life now that the summer's heat has dissipated some; there is laughter and there are doors slamming, and sirens and cars backfiring, and conversations and arguments in the street and out the windows. Houndy's chrysanthemums bloom in his rooftop pots, as though he's saying hi. The nights grow chilly, and Sammy goes back to school and doesn't come home now until after six o'clock every day because he's in an after-school program. Patrick is still writing about diseases, but he comes up to see me sometimes when he knows no one else will be here.

In this bonus time I've been given, I trundle down the steps, bringing him cakes and pickles and delicate mushrooms, and once a Prosecco that I need him to taste—but no matter how often I throw open his curtains and rub his head, no matter how many times I hug him and bask in his presence, I'm not sure anything I've said has yet convinced Patrick that he deserves love.

Sometimes the universe has its own ideas, and I have to accept the fact that I may run out of time here on the planet, and I have to hope I can watch people from the unseen realm. I wonder if that's true, if I'll see them and hear them. If I'll be able to communicate from beyond.

I take a deep, deep breath—breathing in the city around me, all its sounds and voices, and the car horns and the laughter and uncertainty of life on planet Earth. And then a voice says to me, *There is nothing more important than this.*

One morning I make my way out to the stoop. I have sciatica, I have a pain in my chest area, an arm that feels on fire, and my eyes are burning. I haven't been able to sleep since four o'clock, that blackest of hours, so at first light I go outside where I can watch street life happening in front of me, and perhaps be healed by the jangle of personalities and car horns. I want to stop thinking of pain as a problem I have to solve.

I'm sitting there on my blue flowered pillow thinking about endings when I notice a man loping down the sidewalk. He is swinging a backpack behind him, and I watch him come toward me because it is more effort to turn away, frankly, and because I have a little tingly sense that something is about to happen. He looks elegant and disheveled at the same time, animal-like in the way he moves, his arms swinging and his long legs in their khaki shorts striding down the street, looking around him the way a tourist would. He comes closer and closer, until I finally have to put my hand over my mouth, seeing who it is.

"Noah?" I say, and I cannot even stand up, cannot hold on even another hour, because I am suddenly so tired, and here is Noah to catch me when I fall. Maybe he is the miracle I've been waiting for, the savior coming to console me, to pay his respects, to say good-bye. Wouldn't it be amazing if, after all our family history, the universe has sent *him*, and he turns out to be the one who helps me?

He comes closer, peering at me from under a fringe of long hair, and I don't see very well, but I feel his shock at the look of me. All that terror. "Aunt Blix, what happened to you?" he says. "Look at you! What—? Oh, are you ill?"

"Yes," I say. "I'm actually about to drop dead. That's why you're here."

"That's why I'm here?" he says. He doesn't hug me. He runs his hands through his mop of hair and looks around. "You're dying?" he says. He licks his lips nervously. "Shouldn't you be in the hospital? Who's taking care of you?" He looks up and down the street, like he's hoping a team of doctors and medical professionals with their stethoscopes will step out from behind the shrubbery and tell him everything is under control. I almost want to laugh.

"No, honey. There's no need for hospitals. I'm dying," I say. "Perfectly normal thing to do at the end of life. Come and sit with me. I'm so glad to see you."

"Aunt Blix, I think we need to get you to a doctor."

"The hell. No doctors, darling."

"But doctors could help you!"

"I've been dying for some time now, and I have no intention of seeing doctors now. Sit here, please. Hold my hand."

He looks so sad, so frightened. Like if he could, he'd rewind the tape, spool himself walking backward down the street, back down the subway steps, back into the subway car, perhaps all the way back to the airport and maybe even back to Africa, the plane flying in reverse. But he sits, perched on the steps, and I take his hand in mine, and he lets me hold it there. I flow an abundance of love and energy to him.

Ah, my grandnephew. How we loved each other when he was a little kid, but as can so easily happen with distance and time, things went bad between us later. I remember that he came to visit Houndy and me when he was about nineteen and full of himself. I was shocked at the change in him. He was so much his mother's son at that point—arrogant and judgmental, challenging me about all my beliefs, laughing at us for being old hippies, as he called us.

Even worse, I felt the first inklings of a brittle vanity in him, as though appearances were all that mattered, in the same way Wendy was renovating our old mansion without curiosity for the past or any attention to the details that made the old house beautiful. Just pave over what you don't appreciate. That's what my family seems to say.

And mock in others whatever you yourself don't understand.

But now maybe we have another chance. Clearly that's what his presence here means.

"Well, then—what?" he says. "What can I do?"

"You can ease me over to the other side," I say. "That's what I'm hoping you'll do."

"Wait. Does my mom know how sick you are?"

"No. Nobody in the family knows. That's the way I wanted it. But now you're going to be here, and I hope you're going to stay with me while it happens. And it's going to be the kindest thing you could ever do for me."

"I can't. I don't—"

"Shush. Yes, you can. Everything is going to be fine," I tell him. "Whether you know it or not, you were sent here, and now that you're here, you can stay with me while I go. It might take a few days, but it's coming soon. And, sweetheart, this is going to be good for you. Something elemental about life that you need to know."

His beautiful face looks so uncertain. I almost want to reach over and pinch his cheeks between my fingers like I did when he was small. "But—when?" he says. "I mean, what's going to happen?"

"Well, that's what we don't know. I thought it would be by now. But it hasn't. I think I must have been waiting for you. The universe has sent you."

His shoulders slump. I close my eyes and surround him in white light so that I can forgive him for being his mother's son. He's a child, a novice, what J.K. Rowling would label a muggle. Unsuitable for the task at hand, but maybe he'll get there.

"Here. Let's begin with this. Walk me inside the house," I say.

"Okay," he says and manages to support my arm as we slowly walk up the stairs. It's funny how I'd come down these steps all alone—slowly, but still—but now I have to lean on him to get back up. I stop when I need to, which is about a million times, because this may be my last look at this beautiful scene, at my life here that I have loved with all my heart.

"Do you—do you think you're going to suffer?" he says.

"Oh, my darling, I have decided not to suffer," I tell him. "Suffering is optional."

We get to the top of the steps, and he opens the big wooden door. I see our reflection briefly in the pane of glass as it catches us in the sunlight when it swings open. The smells of breakfast, of the parquet floors, the curtains blowing. The wind chimes tinkle above us, a comfort.

"It's really going to be all right," I tell him. "I'm not scared, and I don't want you to be scared either."

SIXTEEN
MARNIE

Summer has turned to September, which in Jacksonville means it's Summer 2.0. The days are still bright and hot, the nights are filled with the electric sounds of buzzing insects and flashes of heat lightning, the air is still as humid as the inside of a dog's mouth, and—yes, I'm still living with my parents and hanging out with Natalie and Brian and the baby.

And now there's Jeremy.

We go running on the beach; we play cards with my parents; we cruise around in his car like we did in high school. It's like when we were teenagers, except for the stunning fact that we're adults so we also have sex now.

There is something so sweet and uncomplicated about these days—being with a guy who speaks your same language, who knows all the old jokes, who loved you even when you had braces and hair tinted green from chlorine.

We know the smell of each other's houses. Which cabinet holds the drinking glasses and which drawer has the flatware. He already likes my family. I already like his mom.

Sometimes these days it's already noon before I think of Noah.

Another good thing is that Jeremy has asked me to work with him in his office, which has happily put aside forever the talk of me having to be a dining room manager at the Crab & Clam House. So now three days a week—the days I'm not helping Natalie with the baby—I put on a skirt and blouse and little heels and go play receptionist, sitting there in his tastefully appointed office talking on the telephone and ushering in his patients.

His patients tell me they all love him because apparently he's simply magic with his hands, as one woman put it. He makes back pain and knee pain vanish.

I felt a little pang of jealousy when she said that, which for me is a sure sign that I'm falling for him. After all, he's in that exam room looking at women's *bodies*, and not only that, thinking about how their muscles and tendons could be made to feel better. And I get to be the one he sleeps with!

I feel a little bit of a thrill when I see him do all the things he used to do—the way he flips his hair out of his eyes, that nose-wrinkling thing, and how sometimes he rubs his hands together when he's anticipating something wonderful. He has never really appreciated deep, long kisses—but he's the master of divine mini-kisses, all along my jawline, a whole trail of kisses.

What can I say? I know it's way too soon to make any huge pronouncements—I'm not crazy or anything—but, as Natalie keeps pointing out to me, he and I seem more and more like a couple every single day.

And she ought to know. We visit her and Brian in the evenings after work, and we've become a lovely foursome: two ordinary, happy couples in the family room, with the guys making sports conversation and Natalie and I sitting with them, cuddling the baby. The four of us pass the baby around like she's a big platter of happiness we all share.

I tell you, it's as though I've walked through a door called Normalcy, the door I was always trying to find.

Most nights when we leave Natalie and Brian's, we go back to his house, and we talk to his mom for a little while, and then, because he's the best son in the world, he helps her get settled upstairs in bed with her cigarettes, her heating pad and her paperback book and her glass of club soda with lime and her sleeping pill. I wait for him downstairs because Mrs. Sanders is kind of shy, and since her husband died, she likes things done a certain way.

Once we are sure she's asleep, we tiptoe up to his room and get into bed. (Yes, there are *Star Wars* sheets.) It's a little bit like being a kid again, because we have to whisper since his mom's room is right next to his. Jeremy says she is probably quite aware that we're having sex in his room, but he says there's no need to "rub her nose in it" as he put it, since she doesn't approve of sex before marriage. He's always having to remind me not to make any sex noises at all, clamping his hand against my mouth, and many nights, to tell you the truth, it seems more trouble than it's worth so we simply lie there chastely holding hands while we read our books before we turn in. In the mornings, I have to make sure to leave before she gets up.

But it's worth it. He and I haven't hit our sexual stride yet, but we will. He gives wonderful back rubs, and between those and all the soft little kisses, I'm quite turned on by him. And every couple has *something* to work on.

"It'll be so much better when I get my own place," he says. "I just have to approach my mother with that idea very delicately, but I'll do it. And maybe sometime we could get a hotel room if you want."

Late at night, sometimes I lie awake and watch his calm, unlined face as he sleeps. He might have been my snarky best friend back when we were teenagers, but now we've both been a bit humbled by life ("HBL" he calls it) and so here we are, milder and gentler versions of our old selves, waiting to see what life will serve up to us.

I'm aware that he's the counterpoint to Noah, that he'll never wake me up in the middle of the night to go stand in line for a Lady Gaga concert.

That he doesn't even know his car is hopelessly uncool, or that his hairstyle wouldn't meet California standards. He'll never get drunk at a restaurant and start doing the samba around the tables until we get kicked out, as Noah did when we first met. He'll never throw out a case of seltzer water because the one I bought wasn't a brand name, which is also a Noah move.

But he wants kids. He loves his mother. He loves me. *And* he appreciates my mother's meatloaf.

And I am watching myself fall in love with him.

One day I'm at work at his office—and I've straightened the magazines and cleaned the little glass window between my cubicle and the waiting room—when he comes sauntering in from the back. It's lunchtime, so there aren't any patients.

"So," he says, leaning against the doorjamb with his arms folded. He has on his nice, crisp, professional white coat with his name embroidered in maroon script, and he's smiling at me. "So," he says again, in this pseudocasual tone he uses when things are more important than he wants them to be, "when do you think you're going to be over this other guy?"

I give a little uncomfortable laugh. "Noah?"

He wrinkles his nose. "Please. Don't say his name in the office. This is sacred space." He looks around, and I see that his eyes are more serious than I've seen them since the day of the condom incident in twelfth grade. "Just level with me here. Before I invest any more of myself in this relationship, you've gotta tell me if you're ever going to be really done with him."

"I think—well, I think that in all the ways that count, that I'm already done with him," I say carefully.

I am pretty sure I am telling the truth.

"No," he says, "it doesn't work that way. You were married to the guy! He did a horrible thing to you. It's only been a few months, and people don't bounce back that fast."

"But I have bounced back. I work extra fast." And then I tell him about Blix, who said some words that steered me toward happiness—a spell that suddenly seems to have come true in a way that none of us were expecting. And here I am. I have arrived at the door of happiness, I say, thanks to some words to the universe that someone chanted for me. For a moment, it occurs to me that I should call her and let her know how it all worked out. But then that thought dissipates; Blix might not see this as the big life she'd promised I'd get. Why disappoint her?

I look back at Jeremy, who is shaking his head comically, like he has water in his ears or something. "Oh God! Please don't tell me I'm basing my whole future happiness on some fortune-teller's notion of the universe!"

So I laugh and kiss him right there in his office, right on his smooth, clean-shaven cheek, but then the phone rings, and I have to go back to my desk to answer it. He stands there watching me while I switch around some appointments. I watch him out of the corner of my eye, and I suddenly feel all the doubt dragging on him, and I know that to him I'm the Louisville Slugger and he's the ball. And, well, it pierces my heart, is all, that he doubts me.

I take it up with Natalie, my personal enabler and therapist, the next day. What I want to know is this, I tell her: Can a person (say, me) actually be ready to move on from a devastating heartbreak so soon? Or am I just kidding myself?

"Well," she says. She is busy changing Amelia's diaper, so she's facing away from me. "Well, of course you *can*. Anything can happen where love is concerned. How do you *feel*?"

"I feel . . . I feel like I'm in the right place. Where I'm supposed to be."

She turns and gives me a big smile. "Oh, I'm so glad to hear you say that, because that's what I think, too. You and Jeremy have such great chemistry! Brian and I were talking about it last night, as a matter of fact."

"Really?"

"Yeah, you're so easy together. And he's funny and he's cute, and you seem really, really healthy and happy. Best I've seen you in years."

"I am. I mean, I think he's great. The only thing is, I just—well, I'm not nervous and scared around him. You know what I mean? I don't feel . . . all fluttery. It's just comfortable. So is that what love is?"

She looks at me like she knows something very wise that I haven't figured out yet. "Of course it is. It's such a relief to be with a guy who loves you more than you love him, isn't it?"

And oh my God, I think, she's exactly spot-on. That's what this is: he *does* love me more than I love him. In fact, he's kind of like a little puppy dog around me, always wanting to please me. So *that's* what my teeny tiny little sense of hesitation is: he adores me, and although I can make a list of all his wonderful qualities and I know that he's perfect for me, I am not suffering the way I usually do when I'm in love.

She's talking away. "That's the way it is with mature love, you goose. And it's wonderful! You'll see. It's one less thing you have to worry about. He's not thinking about somebody else or about to realize he doesn't really love you after all." She picks up Amelia, who kicks her fat little legs and flaps her arms. She's so adorable that it's all I can do to keep myself from going over and whisking her right out of Natalie's arms.

"Wow," I say. "You're right."

"Just one thing: How's the sex? That tells you what you need to know, I always say."

"Wellllll, his mother—"

"Oh, right. You've got that prim mom of his in the next room, don't you? Okay, so he's got to get his own place. And then everything will be perfect. And to tell you the truth, sex falls off as the most important thing in the whole world. You'll see."

I look over at my sister, who is possibly the luckiest person in the whole world, managing to celebrate the daily mundanity of marriage without having one iota of regret. She's shown me the texts she and Brian send back and forth, and they're all about who'll pick up the milk and should they have tacos for dinner, and did she take the car in. Not even one pronouncement about undying love.

When we go into the living room, she puts Amelia in her windup swing and we sit on the couch and drink Diet Cokes while the baby falls asleep to the soft whirring of the swing. The air conditioner is a soft hum in the distance, and the refrigerator motor comes on. Adult life seems to be full of the sounds of motors. Even lawn mowers. Outside there is the glistening blue jewel that is their swimming pool; inside, I watch as a shaft of sunlight flickers across Natalie's thick beige carpet.

"Look at her," Natalie whispers, and I turn to the baby, slumped over in the swing, looking like a sack of rice. We both laugh softly, and then I say, "I want one of those. I want to do this, too."

"You know what would be like the greatest thing in the whole world? If you had a baby, too, and we could raise them together and it would be just like when we were little girls playing house, only now there are real guys here, too. Husbands."

"That *would* be the coolest thing," I say.

We both start talking about how Jeremy and I could buy a house in this neighborhood once we're married—it's totally not too soon, Natalie says—and then when it feels right, we could start having kids, and blah blah blah, something about the guys playing tennis and Natalie and I being together all the time, having barbecue nights, and growing old, and I can barely hear her because my blood is pounding in my ears and maybe I am so excited at belonging somewhere. And soon I get up and go take a dip in her pool, and I lie on my back in the crisp, cool water gazing up at the blue, blue sky with little white clouds that look just like a child painted them.

And this, I think—no, I *know*—is exactly what happiness feels like.

SEVENTEEN

BLIX

I am still me. I am still me. I am dying, but I am still who I am.

I think I see my mother, feel her hand on my forehead. But then it's not my mother at all; it's Lola here with me.

And so is Patrick. I feel his hand holding mine.

"You have to keep breaking your heart until it opens," I say to him. "Rumi said that."

Houndy, from somewhere, tells me that Patrick's heart has already broken more than any heart can stand.

"Sssh," I say. "So much light is left for you, Patrick."

I hear him say, "Blix, I have no idea what you're talking about. Do you want some more ice chips?" and I do not.

"Love," I say to him. "That is what I'm talking about."

Ah! The moon is here again. And the sea. Our blood and the sea have the same pH.

Does Noah know that? I'll bet Patrick knows.

Lola has gone away again. She says it won't be long.

He knows so little, poor beautiful Noah. Wants me to have professional people here instead of my friends. Doesn't want to know from death. How it can be part of a well-lived life. He sits on my bed next to Patrick and plays the guitar, his hair falling over his gorgeous face, but I don't really hear the music as much as feel it. It's as though my bones are making the noise. *Plink, plink, plink.*

I feel myself say, "Houndy."

And Noah laughs and says, "Houndy?" so I know I must have said it aloud. Funny how some sounds exist but don't come into your ears.

I love to hear him say that name.

Lobsters, I think.

"Yes, I remember. Houndy brought us all lobsters that time I was here." He sings that to the tune of something I almost remember.

Patrick says that Houndy was a good man. He wants to know if I can see Houndy right now, and Noah says death doesn't work that way.

The light circles around me, and I am outside the old elementary school in my own hometown, and a girl named Barbara Anne is offering me a chocolate, and I smile at her and reach over to take it, and my arm hits something. A person. Houndy? No, Patrick.

"I'm here," he says.

Solid, warm. And I'm walking on the cliff looking at the stars. I might be a star. I used to think we became stars when we died. From stardust to stardust, someone told me.

When I told Houndy that, he said, "Nope. Not stars. I want to become a potato chip."

His eyes fill up my whole head. His laughing eyes. *Are you coming, my love? Do I have to keep waiting for you?*

All is love. Just love.

Don't be scared. Don't clutch. It's like yoga, those hard poses, where if you resist, it hurts.

It doesn't hurt just to let go. That's Houndy talking now in my head.

I can't think of how. What do you drop, what makes letting go happen? The blackness comes over me, but still I don't let go. There's something else I have to do.

"What do I do . . . after?" Noah says.

You call the coroner, bunion head. This guy really knows nothing, does he? Houndy again. *What does he think you're supposed to do?*

Patrick says he knows what to do.

"I called my mother," Noah says close to my ear. How much later is it? His voice is too close; it tickles me. "She says I have to call the doctor for you. She insists on it. You need medical care fast."

No. No. NO.

Patrick, tell him.

Patrick says no.

Oh God. Is this going to be my last thought? My last thought on earth is going to be NO? I want to think of something peaceful, not how Wendy is directing me from Virginia, how my family thinks my death should go. Why can't they let me die the way I want to die? I need to go NOW. How do I make myself die?

Patrick and Noah are arguing. Noah says maybe there's something else they can do. To buy more time. I can't hear what Patrick is saying, but I hear his tone of voice—low, loving, gentle.

Patrick knows I don't want more time. Not unless I can have eons of it.

Marnie. That's it, that's what I will think about. I wrap her in love and light. I send her a message: *Love is the only thing that matters.* I want to stop the men from talking; I want to tell Patrick about her, but something says not to, that Noah would hear. What a funny business love is, and these two men sitting here, one the past and one the possible future.

There was so much I still wanted to do.

And then I'm up on the ceiling, looking down at myself, a perfect little wrecked body there in the bed, beautiful and strange. That body of mine, so useful and brave, wrapped now in a white gown. The gown I'd picked out and made Noah help me get into. Patrick is there on the bed, too, looking down at me. I feel it when he notices that I'm not there anymore. He reaches over and touches my hand, curls my fingers in his own large hand, the hand that was burned.

Thank you, I say. *And now it's time. So much left undone. So much I still want to feel and know.*

But I've already let go.

EIGHTEEN
MARNIE

I wake up in the middle of the night, startled into sitting upright in bed, noticing my heart hurts.

The air feels sharp in the room, as though it has an unfamiliar smell. Like a candle has burned down somewhere. I want to awaken Jeremy, just for company. It's so nice turning over at night to find somebody next to me in the bed again.

Yet I don't wake him up. I lie there, longing for something I can't quite name.

What woke me up?

Happiness. Happiness woke me up, but there's something else. Something about life feeling so fragile. Something about love being the only thing that matters.

I go to the window and look out at the blackness of the night. There's a shooting star and I watch it, unsure whether it's really the trail of an airplane. But no, it's a star. Blazing out, probably from millions of years ago. Isn't that what they say? That when we look at the stars, we are seeing the past.

NINETEEN
MARNIE

The envelope is from the law firm of Brockman, Wyatt, and Sanford, and by the time it arrives at my parents' house, it looks like it has been through the worst that the postal system has to offer.

I pick it up by its halfway torn and blackened corner and take it inside with the rest of the mail. It's about a million degrees outside, and I'm excited because tonight Jeremy and I are going to talk about taking a vacation together, just the two of us. He says we should rent a *red* convertible and drive up the coast through Georgia, go to Savannah and up to Charleston.

And—well, there is some indication that Jeremy might propose. That's what Natalie thinks, and just talking about it makes her so happy that I go along with it, even though I told her that it seems crazy somehow, even trashy, to have *two* marriage proposals in one year from two different men.

She said, "It's not trashy if it means you're getting your life on the right track. And anyway, it's a great story you can tell the grandchildren when you and Jeremy are celebrating your golden wedding anniversary. The year you married two men. I think that'll be a wonderful story."

I walk into the kitchen, ripping open the envelope as I go, and then I hold the letter in one hand while I open the refrigerator to get the pitcher of iced tea and then get a glass out of the cupboard. The birds are chirping madly at the feeder—probably complaining about the heat—and I stop to watch them while I'm sipping my tea.

When I look down, Blix's name jumps out at me.

"Dear Ms. MacGraw . . . I am writing to you because our law firm is representing the estate of Blix Marlene Holliday . . ."

Estate?

Blix is dead?

Oh my God. Blix is dead.

I sink down onto one of my mother's kitchen chairs. I put the letter on the table and close my eyes for a moment, remembering the night of the wedding when she said that she was at the end of life, and I didn't make her tell me what she meant. So long ago.

I have meant to keep in touch with her—honestly I have meant to—to tell her about Jeremy and that I'm living in Jacksonville now and that I'm going to be okay and to thank her for all the good wishes about the big life and all that . . . but, well, I've been terrible. So much has happened to me in such a short time, and I didn't keep her filled in about any of it. But, really, why would I? She was Noah's great-aunt, and yes, she was kind to me, but she belonged to *him*. And even as I'm saying this to myself, I know it's just an excuse I'm making up because I feel so guilty. All this new life in Florida: Had she somehow known this would be where I would end up? And damn it, I never even knew that she was sick.

And now she is dead.

Shit.

I pick up the letter again and scan it quickly.

"Our client, Blix Holliday, recently deceased, has named you in her last will and testament as the owner of a property belonging to her, a house on Berkeley Place in Brooklyn, New York . . ."

I drop the letter.

Of course this is a mistake. It has to be. Surely Blix left it to Noah, and the post office forwarded it on to me because he's in some forsaken place in Africa with no forwarding address . . . or maybe she left it to the two of us during the twenty minutes or so that we were husband and wife, and she never got around to changing her will and taking my name off.

But nope. I pick up the letter and read further. I am the sole owner of the house, according to Mr. Sanford.

Me, Ms. Marnie MacGraw.

Mr. Sanford urges me to come to Brooklyn as soon as I can. Right away would be nice since there are decisions I need to make.

Decisions.

He ends the letter with, "I know this may come as a surprise to you, Ms. MacGraw, which was exactly what my client wished. She spoke to me many times of her great hope that you would live in Brooklyn and take care of the house. Most recently, right before she died, she urged me to impress upon you the urgency of coming to Brooklyn immediately to review the terms of the will and to participate in the pending decisions that must be made. And she asked that I assure you that your expenses would be paid in full. She wishes for you to stay in the house while you are here making arrangements. Also, I am to tell you that there are tenants living in the house who are anxious to meet you. And if you knew Blix, who was a dear personal friend, you also know that she liked to do things a certain way, and have her wishes respected. Sincerely yours, Charles F. Sanford, Esq."

Holy cow. I put the letter down and rub my head. Blix is summoning me. That time she invited me and I turned her down—now she's *insisting* that I come, now that it's too late. Too late to see her, that is.

But why? What does she want with me?

I can almost hear her voice: *This is your adventure. Take it.*

Is that it? An adventure right when I'm in no need of one? I look out the window. A dragonfly is dancing past the glass.

That evening, I hand the letter to Jeremy, who reads it once and then starts over and reads it again. He's about to embark on a third reading when I take it out of his hands. He has such a disapproving expression on his face that I feel I should tuck Blix back into the safety of my purse, nestled up between my sunglasses and the little bag that holds my art supplies.

"So I take it you're planning to go to Brooklyn for this," he says in the flattest voice anybody ever used. Of course. He's a practical person, and this makes no sense to anybody who didn't know Blix.

"Well, yes. I've made a reservation for Friday."

"Friday!"

He sighs. I know what he's thinking: here we are, in our favorite diner, on an evening when we're supposed to be talking convertibles and beaches and islands—and now we have to deal with *this*. Decisions that have nothing to do with us. A house that we also never thought about. And a trip. Tenants. Brooklyn. Freaking New York. Who cares about any of it? And . . . worst of all for him, I imagine, is the fact that the great-aunt of my ex-husband, a man whose name I am apparently not even allowed to say in front of Jeremy, has somehow stepped back into my life, even indirectly. It must feel to him as if Noah himself has just tossed a hand grenade into our relationship.

"But how do we know this isn't a scam?" he says. "Maybe there are going to be legal problems. Complications. I mean, what are you really walking into? You didn't *know* her."

I stir my glass of iced tea. "It's not a scam. And I did know her."

"She didn't even have your new address," he points out. "How close could you have been?"

"That's more my fault than hers. I haven't kept in touch. I didn't know she was actively dying or I would've. She left me this building as a good thing. A nice gesture. It's not a punishment."

He's smiling. "Okay. Maybe I'm missing something, but I still don't see why she wouldn't leave her property to her family. Isn't that what people do? No offense, but why give it to her grandnephew's ex-wife?"

"Well, I think—well, I think she liked me." I shrug.

He eats more of his hamburger and then pushes his plate away. "Also, we were planning such a fun trip. I thought you *wanted* to drive up the coast with me."

"I do," I say. "And we will when I get back. But first I have to go to Brooklyn and see about the building." I finish off two of his French fries.

At the booth across from us, a man and woman are on a first date, and without even paying attention to what they're saying, I almost feel the need to go over and tell them that they are perfect together. The air around their booth shimmers a little. I'm startled to realize that this is the first time in so long that I've noticed anybody falling in love, that I've seen sparkles.

"You're not going to want to *live* in Brooklyn, are you? Because I do not see myself as a city guy, and I didn't think you wanted that either." He laughs a short little laugh.

"Jeremy. Don't be ridiculous. Nobody's talking about *moving* to Brooklyn. I'm going to look at the building, most likely put it on the market, and come right back. You know . . ." I lean forward and lower my voice. "This could be really good for me. I could sell it and get some money and that could give me a fresh start here. Some money for a house here. You know?"

"Okay," he says. His face softens a little, goes back to its non-paranoid state. "Well. So listen." He swallows. "Along those same lines.

I've been thinking about this, and I really didn't prepare any speech or anything. But . . ." He reaches for my hand across the table, nearly knocking over the ketchup bottle. "But, well, when you come back and everything, what would you think about us getting engaged? I know it's soon and all—" His face is so full of fear and trepidation that it stops my heart.

"Oh, Jeremy! Really? Are you *serious*?"

He blanches, as if I've just turned him down. "Well, I don't know, it just seemed like everything is going in the right direction, and I just thought maybe . . ."

But then he has to stop talking because I am coming over to his side of the booth, and when I get there, I put my mouth on his, hard. He tastes like salt and fries and hamburger. When I finally let go of him, my heart is hammering away, and his face is shining and he's smiling so big, and I see my life figured out just as I'd hoped, gloriously unfolding like a movie in front of me. We'll work together every day in his office, and we'll come home together weeknights to our own place, kick off our shoes, put music on, smile while we cook dinner together, and on weekends we'll go biking and eat brunch with my family, and I'll tend to his mother, and he'll drink beers with my father and Brian, and wow, it's a whole built-in, secure life and all I have to say is yes.

So I say it. "Yes." He's laughing as I keep my arms around his neck, kissing him on both cheeks.

"Holy shit," he says. He kisses my nose and my eyelashes. And finally I settle down and go back over to my side of the booth, and he mops his forehead, grinning at me, and he says, "I did not expect that kind of reaction. Whew!" Then after we sit and smile at each other for a while, basking in this new decision, he says, "So you'll go to Brooklyn and then when you come back, what do you say we tell our families we're getting married and then we'll find a place? Move in together? Give it the old trial run?"

"Okay! Yes! The old trial run!" I can't seem to stop myself.

"So . . . are we engaged? We're engaged. Is that what this means?"

"I think it means we're engaged," I say. "This is how it happens."

"Wow," he says. "Who knew it was that easy?"

It is so very, very easy when it's right. I sit there smiling and holding his hand, and the one thing I know for sure is that everything is going to be all right.

TWENTY
MARNIE

My family is not at all pleased to hear about my newfound building in Brooklyn, or my trip there. They're so upset that I don't even tell them the part that would make them happy—that Jeremy and I are now engaged.

Instead, I just listen as they point out that I don't know anything about real estate, that I haven't ever even seen Brooklyn, that this bequeathment is from a woman who at best had shown herself to be a possible crackpot (this was from Natalie, who saw Blix's mind meld while we were waiting for Noah to arrive for the wedding) and at worst, was a psychopathic meddler who is trying to involve innocent people in her shadowy real estate deals (this from my father, who said he knows the ways of the world).

But I stand my ground with them, and here I am three days later, landing at JFK International Airport, waiting for a shuttle to take me to the subway, then trying to use an app on my phone to figure out which subway would get me to Park Slope, Brooklyn. Apparently I am supposed to find Grand Army Plaza. Which I totally will do. I can do this city thing when I have to. I have been to San Francisco many times, thank you very much, so I can *certainly* find my way around a city that has a grid. And no crazy hills.

My mother keeps texting me:

Did u land yet?

R u keeping safe?

Do NOT ride the subway!!!!!!!! My friend Helen Brown says it's VERY dangerous.

Alas, the shuttle never comes, and a woman in a brown coat, juggling a toddler and a baby, tells me that I don't want to take the subway from the airport anyway—"You'll be on there *forever*, trust me; you should go stand on the taxi line instead!"—so that's where I go, and sure enough, all the New Yorkers there seem to be also heading to Brooklyn. Led by a man in a black knit cap who seems to be part of a comedy team and who makes jokes out of the side of his mouth in a gravelly voice, they're all having fun complaining about the slow service, the fact that it's starting to rain, and also arguing about whether or not the Mets are going to win the World Series. A woman with a blue streak in her hair lines up behind me, bumping into my arm as she juggles her suitcase, then shoots me a brief apologetic smile.

Just then my mom sends a screaming text, all in capital letters: *OH GOD! WATCHING THE NEWS. SOMEBODY GOT STABBED IN A CLUB LAST NITE IN NYC. DO NOT GO TO ANY CLUBS!!!!!!!!!*

I turn off my phone quickly and put it back in my coat pocket. And then I do the little concentrating thing I do—the thing that makes stoplights turn green and taxis show up, and suddenly it's my turn for a cab.

It works everywhere.

Brooklyn, just like San Francisco, is so overcrowded that the cab is forced to meander its way in traffic inch by inch. The driver is practically comatose with indifference, and finally, after he has had to slam on his brakes for three bicycles as well as swerve around another car that suddenly just parks in the middle of the too-narrow street, he drops me off at the address I gave him and tells me that I owe him eighty-seven dollars. He seems quite serious about it. Which is so ridiculous that I can't think of anything to do except pay it. He says thank you, helps me with my suitcase, and then drives off. For a moment, I stand, dazed, on the sidewalk, looking around me.

Supposedly I'm at the law office of Brockman, Wyatt, and Sanford, but the only signs visible are for City Nails (mani-pedis are twenty-five dollars, a good price) and Brooklyn Burger (now with gluten-free buns). The whole street smells like hamburgers cooking, along with a load of garbage festering near the curb, and the strong perfume of an angry-faced woman who race-walks herself right into me without even bothering to say *excuse me*.

I square my shoulders and go inside a dingy little hallway. The directory sign is missing all the *A*s, but apparently I'm to go to the fourth floor to see BROCKMN, WYTT, AND SNFORD. When the elevator door creaks open, there's a magenta-haired receptionist in a black dress who buzzes me in, looking annoyed as hell. A little sign in front of her says her name is LaRue Bennett.

I give her my best Florida smile. "Hello. I'm Marnie MacGraw, and I'm . . ."

"What?" She peers at me. I see that she has a tattoo of a rose on her wrist.

I begin again. "I'm Marnie MacGraw, and I'm here to pick up the keys to Blix Holliday's apartment, or house, or whatever."

"Blix Holliday? Do you have any ID?"

"Oh. Sure." I put down my suitcase and open my purse, which is filled with my boarding pass and my package of gum and my hairbrush and—well, everything except my wallet, which seems to have disappeared. I channel my mother and go immediately into panic mode—the wicked New Yorkers have already stolen my wallet!—but then after

I've emptied everything onto the counter, with LaRue Bennett watching me, I remember that I put my wallet back in my pocket when I got out of the cab. Sweat is starting to trickle down between my breasts by the time I get out my ID and hand it to her, and she lets out a sigh. Possibly she was on the side of the wallet being gone forever.

She looks it over and then pushes it back to me.

"Okay, well. Charles isn't here. He's gone for the weekend. Back Monday."

"Oh," I say. "Oh." I shift my weight to my other foot. "Well, um, I just flew in from Florida. He said I should get here as soon as possible. I've apparently inherited Blix Holliday's house, and I'm supposed to make arrangements, I guess."

"But he's gone."

"Can you reach him? I mean, I was hoping maybe I could at least get the key to the house. I'm to stay there, I think."

Her face is impassive. "There are stipulations to the will he needs to talk to you about first."

"Stipulations?"

Oh, yes. Apparently Blix didn't just do a straight blah blah blah . . . She did things her own way . . . blah blah blah . . . not until Monday . . .

I can see LaRue Bennett's mouth moving, but my brain has suddenly gotten all staticky. Ha! Did I really and truly think that I had somehow managed to outrun my usual luck, and that I had seriously *inherited* a building in Brooklyn, New York? *Of course* there are stipulations! I am the biggest idiot there ever was, falling for this kind of thing again and again throughout my whole life. Thinking Noah was really going to marry me! Thinking it was my turn to be Mary in the Christmas pageant! Even thinking that Brad Whitaker was going to take me to the prom!

And of course the *stipulations* are going to turn out to be that Blix didn't leave me the house after all, which, now that I think of it, is totally fine with me. I just wish I had known before I paid airfare and then taxi fare of nearly ninety dollars plus tip to get to a place that smells like garbage and hamburgers. She probably meant to leave the house to Noah anyway, but he was married to me when she wrote the will, so my name got put on it by accident. Probably happens all the time.

"What am I supposed to do next?" I say, looking around the room and starting to panic just the slightest, tiniest amount. Maybe I should forget this whole thing and simply go back to the airport and get a flight back to Florida. Go back to that diner, have another shake and fries, and pretend this never happened. Later this year, I'll marry Jeremy and have a baby.

LaRue sighs. "I'll try to reach Charles and see what he can do for you. Go sit."

The chairs actually do look good. Beige upholstered armchairs with a Queen Anne table between them. Magazines about architecture. Botanical paintings on the wall. I make my way over to the nearest chair and collapse into it as LaRue disappears into the inner sanctum.

My phone dings.

Hope you're not on your way to becoming a Brooklyn hipster. LOL!

Jeremy.

Yeah. My clothing turned all black the minute I crossed into Brooklyn.

After what feels like forever, LaRue returns with the news that she reached Charles and he'd authorized her to give me the key.

"There's a letter, too, but he says he wants to be with you for that. He'll meet with you Monday morning and go over all the details then. Can you be here at ten a.m.?"

"Okay." I get to my feet and take the manila envelope she offers with a ring of keys jingling inside. Outside, I hear sirens coming closer and closer and the bleating of horns, the squealing of brakes. Hot, spoiled city noises.

I wish I were back at home, floating in my sister's pool, listening to the hum of lawn mowers.

TWENTY-ONE
MARNIE

"This is it," says the cab driver who is taking me to Blix's building. We've been in stop-and-go traffic on a huge, busy avenue for quite a while, passing everything from ridiculously pricey boutiques to a giant natural-foods store, little restaurants and cafés with handwritten signs in the windows advertising matcha tea and kale smoothies. But after a while, he turns onto a leafy side street, and scoots over to the curb to let me out. I'm in front of a series of towering brownstones all jammed together and hovering near the street, with wide staircases leading up to the landings.

So this is where Blix lived. I take a deep breath and look down at the address, written on a piece of paper that LaRue Bennett gave me. Blix's building appears a little worn out, frankly, with rusty-looking wind chimes hanging off the peaked roof over her door and some ragged Tibetan prayer flags clinging to the railing.

Next door, which is closer than you might think, an older woman is sitting on the stoop, drinking a can of Coke and watching me.

"Are you lost?" she calls out to me.

"Not really. I mean, I don't think so! I think this is the place I'm looking for."

She stands up. She must be in her sixties or seventies, but she's wearing yoga pants and a sweatshirt that says FREE TIBET and red tennis shoes, and her gray hair is all nestled in curls around her face like anybody's sweet old grandmother. "Are you Marnie, by any chance?"

"I am!"

"Oh, for goodness sakes. Marnie MacGraw! I've been expecting you. I'm Lola! Lola Dunleavy!" She comes sprinting down the cement steps and over to me and holds out her arms to hug me.

"Lola. Yes," I say, dimly remembering Blix talking about her friend who lived next door.

"You are exactly who I pictured!" she says. Her eyes, in their nest of lines, are shiny. She grasps my hand and looks as if she might burst into tears. "You're probably tired and just off the plane, so I should stop talking to you and let you get inside, but oh, honey! It was so sad, her passing, I still can't get over it. Although I have to say she did it her own way. If you've got to pass, and evidently it was time, nobody does it with more flair than Blix Holliday." She pauses for a moment and closes her eyes briefly and then lowers her voice, leans in. "So do you know everything that's going on? I mean, did you get the *lay of the land*?" When she says *lay of the land*, her eyebrows go up into a little peak.

"I think so. I mean, I got the keys." I drag my eyes away from her and reach inside my coat pocket.

"From the attorney's office? Oh, good. I mean, I would have given them to you myself, but I guess we're doing things all official now. Although"—she glances up toward the house, gestures at it like it might be overhearing us—"I don't really know what exactly is going on. I mean, at the moment."

"No," I agree. No one seems to.

"So maybe I should leave you alone, and you can go in and figure things out? Or do you want company?"

"Well. I guess I'll . . . just unlock the door . . . maybe . . . and go in?"

"Okay!" she says brightly. "And then, if you need anything later—well, you can always call me. I might be able to cast a little light if . . ."

"Sure."

She follows me up the steps.

"Blix never did like to use the newer lock," she says. "She didn't like locks at all, actually. I was always coming over and finding the place wide open. One time the UPS guy came by—I think it was UPS—and he opened the door and called out her name, and she sings out, 'It's okay! Come in! I'm in the bathtub!' That was our Blix."

The door does not open when I turn the key. I look through the ring of keys I have, and start trying different ones. Some don't go in at all, others go in but stay stuck in place. There's a noise from inside, footsteps walking toward the door.

"Oh dear," says Lola in a low voice. "So he *is* here. Now we've probably disturbed him."

"Him?"

"You don't know, do you?" She leans closer to me and cups her hand. "*Noah* is here."

"Noah?"

Just then the door flies open, and damned if Noah isn't standing right in front of me, looking from me to Lola with shock on his face, although it would be hard to guess who's more shocked, me or him. I feel my knees wobbling just the slightest bit.

"Marnie? What the *hell* are you doing here, girl?" He's smiling, his eyes crinkled up into little slits.

I cannot seem to find words, so I simply stare at him like he's a mirage. He's wearing jeans and a black sweatshirt and holding a bottle of beer and a guitar, of course.

This is going to ruin everything, everything. All of my recovery, all of it.

"I could ask you the same thing," I manage to say. "What are *you* doing here? Aren't you supposed to be in Africa?"

Just then Lola, who turns out not to be the bravest human on the planet, touches my arm and says softly that she might have something boiling over on the stove and she'll be available later, in case I need her. I hear her saying, "Oh dear, oh dear, oh dear" as she heads to her own house.

And then I look back at Noah, who is smiling at me like the proverbial cat who is about to swallow the canary.

"It's so good to see you!" he says. "I'm afraid, though, that if you've come to see my Aunt Blix, you're too late. But maybe you know that already."

"I do," I say softly, putting down my suitcase. "I was so sorry to hear."

He is rambling on and on. Blah blah blah. He wants to know why I'm there and not in Burlingame, and I tell him that I've actually been living back in Jacksonville for a while now. (Which he could have known if he'd so much as even looked at my Facebook feed. I mean, who doesn't do that with an ex? I would know everything about him if he ever bothered to post anything. The last time he posted it was to say that the African sun is hot. And that was right after he left.)

So he goes on and on, and I'm frankly having an out-of-body experience. How is it that just the day before, I was safe and in love and getting engaged *again*, and now I am standing on some steps in Brooklyn, looking into the face of Noah? Noah, whom I now realize I have missed—and still miss—with a desperation beyond all reason. Which is a horrifying thing to realize.

Meanwhile, he's kept talking and now, from the way he's staring at me, it's apparent that he's asked me a question that he's waiting for the answer to. I review the last few seconds of the tape in my head and realize he wants to know why I am living in Jacksonville.

"Complicated reasons involving certain financial obligations of an overpriced apartment, I believe," I say.

"But you had three months! I paid my portion of the rent for three months."

"Yes, but as you may be aware, those months ran out." I am smiling.

"Yes, and then you were supposed to find a roommate."

"Well, I didn't. Do you really want to stand here in the doorway and discuss the problematic roommate situation in Northern California, or may I come in?"

"Of course, of course!" he says, stepping aside and flattening himself against the wall so I can get past him. When I brush against him, several of my more alert cells notice that he's something we all once liked. They have conveniently and traitorously forgotten that we are not Team Noah anymore. We are Team Jeremy.

"You brought a suitcase, so I guess that means what—that you're planning to *stay*? I get to enjoy your company for more than just an afternoon?"

"For a few days, I thought."

"That's wonderful," he says. "If I'd known you were coming . . ."

"Well, I couldn't very well let you know when I didn't even know you were here!"

"No, no. I'm not saying you should have. It's just a surprise, is all. A very nice, wonderful, amazing surprise. Here, go through that door," he says, motioning with his head. "Blix has the first and second floors."

I feel like I have jet lag, even though technically I'm still in the same time zone. Maybe I've somehow gone into a kind of weird time warp. As we go into Blix's living room, I'm struck by the parquet oak floors, the exposed brick walls, the light from the bay windows, the art everywhere. It's beautiful, in a rundown, funky, Blixish way. I exclaim over it, and he says, "You want the tour? You've never been in a Brooklyn brownstone before, have you?"

"I'd love a tour."

He keeps stealing little looks at me as he shows me around her apartment—the living room and two bedrooms are on the first floor, and the large eat-in kitchen is upstairs along with a study and a hallway and staircase leading to the roof. Also off that hallway, he tells me, is another two-bedroom apartment. A woman lives there with her son, he says. She's quite attractive. Amazing curly hair, nice body. (He always has to comment on women's bodies, because, he says, that's what life is about: noticing the beauty around you.)

"There's also a guy in the basement," he says. "Sort of a recluse. Something wrong with his hands and face. Blix collected characters, you know." He tilts his head charmingly. "Perhaps, now that I think of it, you were even one of them."

Was I? "There's so much light in here," I say. The kitchen is astonishing, with two huge windows looking out onto all of Brooklyn—buildings, rooftop gardens, condominiums under construction blocks away. Outside I hear sirens, crashing sounds, voices, car horns.

"So, wanna go up on the roof?" he says. "We could grab a beer or something, and then maybe you can finally manage to explain why you're here to see my old auntie who happens to be dead."

"And you can tell me why you're not still on your year-long stint in Africa."

"Oh, well, *Africa*—that's a very long, weird story of great bizarreness," he says, opening the refrigerator, an old model, oval-shaped at the top and painted turquoise. Everything in this kitchen looks old and worn out and possibly hand-painted—a scarred wooden table in the center, and a countertop that runs along the wall—something that looks like it came from a French country kitchen around the turn of the century. The last century. There's a soapstone sink in the corner and a gas range, little vases with dried weeds and flowers and half-burned candles sitting in saucers on every surface—and the walls are painted a wonderful off-red color, with white trim around the windows and cabinets. The floor is worn and scuffed in spots. There are dishes piled in the sink, and half-emptied cups of coffee on the table.

"I have plenty of time to hear it, and the more bizarre the better," I tell him. He hands me a beer with some unfamiliar Brooklyn label, and points the way to the hallway and a steep stairway going up. He pushes the door open at the top, and suddenly we're on an unlikely terrace, with planters filled with grasses at one end, surrounding a fire pit and a low table. There's a gas grill pushed over toward the corner, and several padded wicker couches, a couple of chaise lounges, and a portable basketball hoop. I have to catch my breath. The view of Brooklyn's skyline is kind of amazing. I can see rooftops all around me with gardens and water tanks. Big windows blankly looking back at me, catching the sun.

"How long have you been here?" I say.

"I've been here, ah . . . three weeks maybe?"

"Were you here when she . . . when she died?"

"Yeah. Although she would prefer we said when she *made her transition*."

"I didn't even know she was sick. I'm so sorry."

"Thank you. Yeah. Me neither. Not until I flew in. And then I found out she was dying. She'd been sick for months, maybe even years without telling. But then once I was here, she wanted me to stay, to see her across, you know." He opens my beer and then his own and puts the opener down on the table. "She was a funny one. Kept things like that a secret, I guess. Didn't want sympathy. Of course she and I weren't all that close as you know." He looks around the rooftop and shakes his head. "She was always just my crazy Aunt Blix, saying such weird woo-woo stuff it was hard to pay attention to. But you never know, do you? What's going to happen to the people you somehow belong to."

"Odd that *you*, of all people, would be telling that to me."

He laughs a little bit through his nose. "Okay. Fair enough." He looks at me for a long moment, and I'm surprised to see how sad his eyes are. "You have every right to be pissed off at me," he says. "That was a horrible thing I did to you, and I want you to know that I've kicked myself many times."

I sit down on one of the wicker couches, feeling woozy. "Really? Have you now?"

"Well, let me clarify. I've kicked myself for the *way* I handled it."

So there we have it. He's not sorry he left. Just sorry for the way it went down. Nice.

He laughs again. "Please. Let's don't talk about this. It cannot lead to anything good."

"So what happened with Africa? Why aren't you still there? You had to dump Africa, too, did you?"

He grimaces a little at my joke. "Yes. Africa. Well." He sits down on the couch across from me and starts peeling the label off his beer, the way he always used to do, and launches into a story that involves Whipple signing both of them up to teach music to schoolchildren as part of a fellowship he'd gotten, but then, as he puts it, *bureaucracy* happened. Whipple, in typical fashion, hadn't filed all the papers they needed and after a long, drawn-out time of bobbing and weaving and trying to go through other channels, finally they got kicked out of the country.

"Same old Whipple bullshit," he says with a sigh. "Fun but sketchy. For a month or so, we hid by traveling around, trying to keep from getting deported. But it was touch and go, and then . . . well, I decided I'd had enough, and—well, I figured I'd come back to the US, and I arrived here in Brooklyn just before Blix died. I think he's still backpacking around trying not to get jailed."

He's silent, picking something off his shoe. Then he looks right at me, and my heart does a little unauthorized flip-flop.

"She liked you, didn't she?" he says. "That's why you're here."

I look down, suddenly shy. "Yeah, I think she did. She was nice to me."

"I know. That horrible party at my mom's. The way she stayed there talking with you the whole time. God, my mom was so pissed that you weren't circulating! Neither of us circulated much, I guess. Did you know that's a guest's job according to my mom? Apparently you can't just go and have a good time, you have *responsibilities.*"

"I think I've heard something along those lines."

"Yeah, well—fuck that! I went off and played pool with Whipple because I couldn't take listening to my mom and all her fakey-fake friends. And—didn't something else bad happen?"

"Yeah. The Welsh rarebit situation."

He throws back his head and laughs. "Ah, yes. My mom said you wouldn't eat it due to some snobbish thing?"

"No, I wouldn't eat it due to who knew what the hell it even was! We didn't have such things at chez MacGraw in Jacksonville, Florida. You might have warned me, you know, that there'd be an exam on British culinary practices. But *you* weren't anywhere around. I had only Blix to defend me."

"So that's when it all started," he says absently. "That's when the whole thing unraveled. Whipple and I were playing pool, and he started telling me about his amazing fellowship and talking me into getting in on the act with him, and I was thinking about the need for one more big adventure. You were talking to my Aunt Blix outside in the snow, as I recall. And everything got set into motion."

"*That* was it?"

"That was the moment."

"So you're saying that if we hadn't gone our separate ways at that party, then we would have just had our regular wedding and you would have stayed with me? Because, I have to say, that is absurd, and you know it."

"Well, who knows for sure?" he says. He looks right into my eyes. "All I want to say is that I did love you, you know. I really thought I wanted to get married."

"Until you didn't," I say, and he laughs.

"Yeah, until I didn't. My bad."

"So are we to conclude that in the great scheme of things, I lost you but got your great-aunt?"

He puts his hands behind his head and looks up at the sky. "Maybe. Oh, hell. There's a lot I regret, you know, when I think of her. Our family wasn't very good to her. I tried to make it up to her at the end, but we never did really connect in a huge way, no matter how much I tried. She was always—well, you know . . . crazy." He pauses. "Listen," he says suddenly. "Want to grab some dinner? I haven't eaten anything today but a peanut butter sandwich. I know this sweet little place on Ninth that's got amazing burgers and stuff. Some local beers. Good people. Because as long as we're both here, we might as well have fun, right? No hard feelings for all that bullshit that happened?"

I realize I haven't eaten in a long time either. "Okay."

"Are you really not so angry with me, then?"

"Not so much," I say. "I think I'm having an Insufficient Anger Response, actually."

"Yeah. You probably should be mad as hell. But I'm glad you're not." He stands up and stretches, giving me a view of his nice flat belly and low-slung jeans. It hurts, the deep long familiarity of him, the *badassness* of him, and finally I have to look away, so I take the last drink of my beer and look out at the lights of Brooklyn instead.

I am supposed to be here. I am supposed to be here. I take a deep, full breath of the new unknown. I should call Jeremy. I have so many feelings that I'll have to sort out later.

"And hey, while we're eating," he says, "you can tell me everything that's going on with you—and why you serendipitously showed up on Blix's doorstep today."

I guess that's when it really hits me that he probably has no idea that Blix has left me the house. That thought arrives at the back of my neck first and works its way around to the front of my brain, rather like a bug making its way around a nerve-wracking circuitous path.

Just then, the door to the roof bangs open, and a kid who looks to be about ten years old, with a mop of pale hair and a huge pair of round black plastic glasses, comes charging onto the roof, dribbling a basketball and dancing all around. He leaps up onto the edge of a planter, but he doesn't notice us until he's making his last mental calculation, and when he does, he's so startled that he doesn't quite make the height he needs. The ceramic planter falls over and smashes on the ground, and dirt goes everywhere.

"Sammy, my man! What the heck you doing?" Noah says.

"Oh! Sorry!" The boy stops and looks instantly horrified.

"Nah, it's okay. It's just a planter. You scared me, that's all."

"I'll clean it up."

"No, go get a broom and dustpan, and I'll take care of it. I don't want you to get cut." Noah turns to me. "This is Sammy, our resident lovable juvenile delinquent and breaker of pottery. His mom is Jessica, the one I was telling you about. And Sammy, this is Marnie."

Sammy says hi to me, and pushes his hair out of his eyes, and then he runs off and comes back with the dustpan and the broom, and Noah and I get to work sweeping up all the shards while Sammy bounces his basketball over in the other corner of the roof. I keep stealing little glances over at him because he's so adorable—like a serious little owl with good dance moves.

"Hey, Noah, guess what!" he calls after a few minutes. "My dad's coming to get me tomorrow morning, and we're going to Cooperstown for the weekend."

Noah gives a fake growl. "What's so great about Cooperstown? You don't care about *baseball* or anything, do you?"

"Yes, I do! You know I do! And we're gonna stay in a B and B and have pancakes for breakfast, and he said maybe there's gonna be a pool."

His mom appears just then. She's thin and gorgeous and wearing jeans and a gray cardigan and she sighs a lot. She looks over at Sammy like any minute he might turn into something that's going to disappear on her.

Noah introduces us—"Jessica, Marnie; Marnie, Jessica"—and she holds out her hand for me to shake.

"Oh, Marnie!" she says. "I've heard Blix talk about you! Oh my goodness, it's so awful what happened—I miss her every single day." She glances over at Sammy and lowers her voice. "He does, too. He adored her. There was nobody like her."

Sammy is listening to us talk and dancing over by the fire pit, like a goofy bird ready to take flight.

"Sammy, it's bath time, and you need to come in and get your stuff packed up," she says. Her eyebrows are all knitted up in a frown. "Wait. Did you break this planter?"

"I didn't mean to."

"It was an accident," says Noah. "No biggie."

But she is clearly worried about Sammy being careless, and now he's destroyed this planter that was Blix's, and those were Houndy's red geraniums planted inside, and everything, she says sadly, seems to be crashing to an end all around them—and right then, my phone starts buzzing in my pocket, and I would be so deliriously happy to be able to escape from this conversation except that when I look down at my phone, I see the faces of all my family members grinning and waving—all of them, plus Jeremy—wanting to FaceTime with me. It's as though they're suddenly right there on the rooftop with me.

I go tearing inside, down the stairs and into the hall and skidding into Blix's kitchen before they can see where I am and—oh God—who I'm with.

"Hi!" I say, and there they all are, jockeying for position in front of their little screen: Natalie holding up Amelia, who is blowing bubbles—"Look, Auntie Marnie, I talks with spit!" Natalie crows in a baby voice—and my mother and father peeking in from the side, trying to ask me a million questions. All of them at once.

"Where *are* you right now?"

"Is that really Blix's house? Show me the kitchen!"

"Is it old? It looks really old!"

"Don't even tell me those walls are red!"

"You look tired, sweetie cakes. Bet you wish you could just come home!"

And Jeremy, last of all, smiling so winningly. "Are you having a good time? Do you like the house?"

I hear Noah coming down from the roof, and so I dash with the phone downstairs toward the living room and sit down on the floor, as far away from the window as I can get.

"Oh, yes, it's lovely!" I say to Jeremy, and if my face is turning ashen or bright red, either one, I can only hope he doesn't see in the dim light of the living room. From the kitchen, I hear Noah throwing our beer bottles into the recycling bin and whistling.

"We just wanted to make sure you're all right, that you made it in and everything," says my father. "Also, honey, just so you know: we've had a family meeting and we've decided to teach Jeremy the quadruple solitaire game tonight."

"Yep, I'm in way over my head," yells Jeremy from off camera.

"So how are you, sweetie?" says my dad.

"I'm fine. Nothing much to report as yet."

My mother's face now looms in the phone. "CAN YOU SEE ME, HONEY?"

"Yes, Mom! Yes, I see you just fine. I hear you, too."

"So just tell us this much: ARE YOU GOING TO BE ABLE TO SELL THAT HOUSE, DO YOU THINK?"

I look up then to see Noah standing in the doorway of the living room, his arms folded. And if I had thought he looked shocked when I was standing at the front door earlier, that's nothing compared to how he's looking at me right now.

TWENTY-TWO
MARNIE

So. Here we go.

When I hang up, Noah comes all the way into the living room, walking so deliberately it's as though the floor might be made of pointy little rocks. His eyes are round and bright with shock. He sits down on the floor across from me and shakes his head.

"Okay, Marnie," he says slowly, "why don't you tell me what's going on? What are you doing here?"

I swallow. "Oh God. It's so confusing and complicated. I thought you knew what was going on, but—well, apparently your Aunt Blix left me this house when she died. You didn't know that?"

"No, I didn't know that! How was I supposed to know that?" He falls back against the couch and rubs his face briskly with both hands. "She left her house. To you. My ex. Oh my God. I can't *believe* this." Then he puts his hands down and stares at me for a long moment. "Why would she *do* this? To my mom?"

"I don't know. I'm as shocked as you are."

He gets out his phone and looks at it. "Oh, fuck. I've had the ringer off, and there are, let's see, um, nine, ten . . . no, *thirteen* calls from my mom in the last day and a half. And three texts saying I've got to call her immediately." He sighs and puts the phone back in his pocket. "And my mom doesn't believe in texting. So this means she's *really* desperate. Fuck, fuck, fuckity fuck. What am I supposed to do?"

"Wait. Seriously? You don't check your phone?"

"Correction: I check my phone, but I keep the ringer off because if I didn't, I'd go crazy from my mother wanting to be in touch with me all the time. Trust me, this is only slightly more calls than I usually get from her. My policy is that I return about every fifth call."

"Noah! What if something's ever really wrong?"

"I'll find out eventually. She's *insane*, my mom. You know that." After a moment he says, "Before I call her, could you please walk me through this? How did this all happen? Did you *talk* to Blix?"

"No. I got a letter from a law firm."

"A letter. I'm going to need to know more than that now, aren't I? What did the letter *say*, Marnie?"

"Just that I had been left this piece of property in Brooklyn, and that I should come as soon as possible because there were some things that needed doing. Some decisions."

"Some *decisions*."

"Yes."

"And what *kind* of decisions?"

"Noah. I don't *know* what kind of decisions. Stipulations, I guess. Things I need to know about or do or . . . something. That's why I'm here. It said I should come as soon as possible."

He doesn't say anything for a long time after that, simply stares off into space. He's flicking his thumb against his index finger, a nervous habit he used to display in meetings, back when we were teachers together. Back before everything. When we were still falling in love.

But I remind myself that we are so not anywhere near falling in love anymore. He left me. He's not sorry about that. And *I* inherited this house. And why? Because maybe this is all part of the big life Blix thought I should have. I can't very well tell him that, though.

He gets up and starts pacing in circles around the middle of the room, rubbing his hair. "But were you *in touch* with her since the wedding? Did you *know* she was doing this? Have you ever talked to her?"

I sigh very heavily, to show him that I am nearing the end of my patience with this line of questioning. "Look. I talked to her once. One time. But she didn't say anything about this. I swear. And I didn't even know she was sick, much less dying."

"Tell me the truth. Just so I know. Did you somehow get her to do this to get back at me?"

"Noah! You know me better than that."

"But now you're going to sell it? That's what your mother said. 'Are you going to be able to sell that house?' Those were her exact words. She was practically screaming it. So that's what you're planning, right?"

I don't say anything.

"Yeah. That's what you're planning. Oh my God. And here's what's so ironic. If you sell it, then what? You'll take the money and move to some three-bedroom house in the suburbs, won't you? You don't even *care* about it." He keeps shaking his head in disbelief. "Too, too unbelievable. Just incredible. But that was my Aunt Blix in a nutshell. Totally zigging when you thought she was going to zag. Always keep 'em guessing." Then he stops walking and sighs. "And you know what? What I'm most sorry about here? The conversation I'm about to have with my mother. She's going to have a million things to blame me for in this little scenario. Trust me."

"Well. I do feel bad for you."

He laughs. "No, you don't. This is all fucking unbelievable, you know that? I was the one here when my great-aunt dies, and yet somehow she manages to say *nothing* to me at all about the house or what's going to happen, so I of course just *assume* I can stay here because it'll belong to my family—and then *you* show up."

There's a loud noise from downstairs. "What's that?" I say.

He runs his hands through his hair. "I told you. There's a guy living down there. He has a life. Sometimes he drops things."

"What's his name?"

"Patrick Delaney. He's disabled in some big way. Burn victim. Doesn't come out much."

"I think I'm going to take a walk. I'll see if he's okay." I can't stand looking at Noah for one more minute.

Now he's pacing again. "Wait. I just thought of something. Do you think it's possible that she left the house to both of us before we got divorced, and that my letter didn't come to me yet because I was in Africa, and that what my mom wants is to tell me there's this letter for me from the law firm? Is there any way that could be what's happening?"

"Maybe," I say. "Actually, I have an appointment to meet with the attorney on Monday at ten. Why don't you come with me, and maybe we can get some answers?"

"Okay," he says after a moment. "At least I can tell my mom that."

I get up off the floor and go outside, closing the big heavy door behind me. Even though it's night, it's still bright from the streetlights, and there are plenty of people outside, walking their dogs, talking into their phones. There's a coffee place four doors up the street, filled with people wearing scarves and jackets. I go down the little stairs to the basement apartment. It's narrow and dark, and probably infested with New York cockroaches and rats, but I bravely knock on the door anyway. I keep my eyes on my feet, just in case something should try to run across them.

No answer, so I knock again. And then again. And again. There are bars on the windows. I shudder.

Finally there's a muffled voice from inside: "Yes?"

I put my mouth near the door. "Um, Patrick? Listen, my name is Marnie. I'm Blix's . . . friend, I guess you'd say. Or maybe grandniece-in-law. *Friend* sounds better, though. Anyway, I was upstairs and I heard a crash. Just wanted to check you're okay."

There's a pause and then the voice says, more muffled than before: "I'm fine."

"Okay," I say. "Well . . . good night then."

Another pause. Then, when I've given up on him having anything else to say, I hear, closer to the door this time: "Welcome to Brooklyn, Marnie. Is Noah with you?"

I lean against the door, close my eyes, almost brought to my knees by the question. And the kindness of his voice.

"He is," I say finally. "Well, not now, but he's upstairs. I think I'm going to go over to the coffee place and get something to eat. You want to come?"

"I'm sorry, but I can't."

"Well, that's okay. Can I bring you back something then?"

"No. Thanks. Listen, Blix has my number upstairs. Call anytime you need something."

"Thanks. Can I give you my number? If you need anything?"

"Sure. Slide it in the mail slot, will you?"

When I get back upstairs, Noah has gone into the back bedroom and closed the door. I can hear him talking, though, no doubt on the phone with his mom. His voice is rising and falling, and when I pass by, I hear, "*I'm trying to explain to you*—she's here now!"

The larger bedroom at the front of the house, with its sienna-colored walls, is open, so I go in there and close the door. The room is kind of surreal, with posters everywhere, and a big lumpy double bed, a kantha quilt, and all kinds of crazy little knickknacks on every surface, and crystals and banners hanging on the walls, little pieces of art, pieces that Blix no doubt loved and that still seem to hold on to some part of her.

I lie there looking up at the ceiling, which is illuminated by the streetlights. You could shoot a movie in this room it's so bright.

The ceiling has a crack that looks like a sweet little chipmunk eating a burrito. *Don't give up. Everything is going to be fine,* the chipmunk says. *It's all unfolding just the way it's supposed to.*

It's a long time before I can close my eyes and go to sleep.

And that's the end of the first day.

TWENTY-THREE

MARNIE

Noah already seems to be gone when I wake up in the morning, which is nothing short of a divine blessing.

I take a shower in Blix's fabulous claw-footed tub and then go up to the kitchen, where I have to search for a coffeemaker (she has some press device that seems to be missing some key parts). There's hardly any food in the refrigerator, just bags of dark chocolate and green mushy things, possibly lentils, and some bottles that look like dietary supplements. And of course beer. Lots and lots of beer.

Luckily, as I'm about to plan a journey into the outside world in search of food, there's a knock at the back door.

"Helloooo!" calls Jessica. I open it to find her standing there wearing a pink flowered kimono and blue jeans, her wet hair tied up in one of those divinely messy knots.

"Oh, hi," she says. "I just wondered if you might want to get some breakfast with me." She makes a sad face. "The truth is that my ex, Sammy's dad, came and picked him up this morning, and that's always tough for me, so I could use a little distraction. And I'm guessing you might possibly want to get out of here, too."

"I'd love to."

"Well, great. I can show you the neighborhood! Park Slope rocks, you know."

I go grab my thin, little, good-enough-for-Florida sweater, and she dashes into her apartment to get her real sweater, then she tells me about all the great places around here. As we're leaving, Lola waves to us from the stairs next door and calls out, "You doing okay, Marnie? Settling in?"

"I'm doing fine, Lola!" I holler, and she says, "Come over sometime! I have stories to tell you!"

Jessica murmurs, "She and Blix—such a pair! Always out on the stoop talking to everybody who came by. Playing with the babies, inviting the old people to come sit with them. Blix knew everybody."

It's a beautiful day outside—warm for October first, Jessica says, and the sidewalk is filled with people: kids in soccer uniforms heading off to games, families with strollers, groups of young guys all wearing black clothing decorated in zippers, a man on the corner who seems to be lecturing a brick building, a guy setting out buckets of flowers in front of a little grocery store. Cars lurch along the streets, then come to screeching halts as people double-park and jump out to run into various shops, setting off spates of annoyed honking and swearing—and although everything that happens makes me jump, Jessica pays no attention to what's going on.

I keep wanting to slow down and soak it all in, pause somewhere and just watch for a while, but Jessica is walking along, at a brisk thirty-miles-per-hour pace, cheerfully ranting about Sammy's father, who cheated on her while they were married, and who is now living with that woman. And now the judge has said that Jessica is supposed to be sharing custody with him! Can I even imagine? She has to share weekend time every other week? The precious time she has to be alone with her own *son*, the time when they're free from work and school responsibilities—and now she has to share *that* with her *ex* the scumbag, the guy she calls Creepasaurus?

"I know what you're probably thinking, and you're absolutely right: I should get over it already. He's Sammy's father, and Sammy needs to see him, *but*—and this is a big but—he lost some of his privileges when he betrayed me, and how can I get over that? Anyway!" She looks over at me, and I see that she is puffed up with anger, puffed up and beautiful in her outrage. "You've had some complicated stuff, too, I gather. All of Blix's people have. I mean, you were with *Noah*, for starters."

"Complicated, yes," I say, and she says, "Hey, what's your policy about waiting on line for a table? There's this excellent place I love, but it takes monumental patience because it's so awesome, and also it's got hundreds of reviews on Yelp."

"I'm fine with waiting," I say, even though my stomach is growling. I'm surprised she can't hear it.

"Great. Because it is *the* place for eggs in Park Slope! You like eggs, I hope? And it's Southern food, which I know you'll like. Goes with your accent. Oh, here we are! See how cute? It's called Yolk!"

Sure enough, we've arrived at a tiny little place that has about thirty people milling around outside, sipping mugs of coffee and chatting. Inside, I can see that there are approximately five tables we'll be competing for. But we put our name on the list and then she suggests we walk around, look in the shops. I try to resign myself to the fact that I won't get breakfast until sometime in the middle of next week.

"I know it must be so much worse for you, but I still can't believe Blix isn't here any longer," she says. "I miss her so much, it's like my own grandmother died or something. I saw her every single day! Sammy couldn't leave the house without stopping by her place. She was *everything*."

"Did you know her for a long time?" I say.

"Since Andrew left. I met her that same week. So, yeah, three years? But it seems so much longer because she was always the person I could talk to about anything. She was like my guru and my grandmother and my therapist and my Reiki master and my best friend, all rolled into one. Even while she was sick, she kept up with everybody."

"I-I didn't even know she was sick. I met her last Christmas and then she came to my wedding . . . but that's it."

"Oh my goodness, she loved you a lot. She told everybody about you! The whole borough of Brooklyn probably knew that you were coming. And then Noah showed up right before she died, so I thought that might mean you weren't coming after all. But I couldn't ever get her alone to ask her, you know? I hope you don't mind that I know all this. That's the way it is when you're one of Blix's people. We all seem connected somehow."

"I have to admit that I didn't know I *was* one of Blix's people."

"No? There are a bunch of us. I met most of them at the wake slash good-bye party she gave for herself. Did you know about that?"

"Sadly I am way out of the loop on everything."

"I'll fill you in, then," she says. "There's Patrick downstairs. He's an amazing person, an artist and sculptor, but he doesn't come upstairs anymore since she died. Have you seen his sculpture in Blix's living room—the woman holding her hands up near her face? Incredibly beautiful. Too bad he doesn't do that anymore."

"Did he stop because she died?"

"Oh, no. Even before she died he had stopped." She looks at me and laughs. "I am talking way too much. Sorry. So! But Blix left you the house—am I right? She left you the building?"

"Surprisingly, yes."

She stops walking so abruptly that two people nearly run into her. "How's Noah doing with that?"

"It's kind of a mess," I say. "Noah and his mom believe that *she* should have been the one who got the house, and I kind of agree, if you want to know the truth. And no offense, but I don't really want to live here, so I guess I'll just sell it."

"Oh, no!" Her face changes. "You're just going to sell it and go?"

"Well . . . yeah, I mean this isn't really *home*, you know. I have a life elsewhere. In Florida."

She is searching my face. "I hadn't even thought about that. Of course you have a life! Oh, man! This would be like somebody in—oh, I don't know—*Oklahoma* or somewhere leaving me a house and expecting me to pick up and go there."

"It does feel kind of random."

She shifts her bag over to her other shoulder and purses her lips. "I have got to tell you that this is so Blix-like. Doing something like this. No warning, no explanation. We all call this 'getting Blixed.' Although mostly it works out for the best once the dust settles."

"Ha! So I've been . . . Blixed?" I say.

"You, my dear, have been *sooo* Blixed. And you probably haven't even finished processing your breakup with Noah. That takes forever to get through, and you're going to have to start the whole thing all over again, now that he's all up in your face again and reminding you of the past. Is he being—weird? He is, isn't he? He's being weird. I can tell. Just from the way he was last night."

"He is being a little weird," I say. "But I get it. He's in shock."

She frowns. "Can I tell you something, even though I probably should just keep my big mouth closed and keep out of it?"

"Okay."

"She didn't want him or his family to have the building. She left it to you on purpose."

"Really."

"Yeah, she wasn't all that happy when he showed up." She comes to a full stop in front of a shop like she's slammed on the brakes. "Hey, this is one of my favorite stores," she says in the same chirpy tone of voice she's been using all along. "Want to go in and look at the coats? You might need one."

"Okay," I say, "although Florida doesn't really call for a lot of coats."

"Well," she says in a singsong, "but you *never* know what's going to happen when Blix is involved! You just might find she wants you to stay here."

"Since she's dead, though, she doesn't have much of a way of getting that to happen," I say.

"So you'd think," she says.

We go inside and she goes over to the coats, starts flipping through all the shades of gray, black, and brown. And then suddenly, without warning, she stops moving and looks straight ahead, stiffening.

I follow her gaze and see that a man is staring at her and making his way over to us, and behind him is Sammy. If Jessica were a cat, her back would be arched, and she'd be hissing.

"Andrew!" she says, and her face has turned angry. "What in the world are you doing here? Aren't you supposed to be on the way to Cooperstown?" She looks around. "And where's your girlfriend, huh?" She reaches over and puts her hand on Sammy's arm, protectively. Sammy has a stricken expression on his face; I see him mouthing to her, "It's fine, Mom, it's fine."

The man looks abashed, as though he's been caught at something, which is exactly how she sounds. Sammy, pushing his mop of too-long hair out of his eyes, scoots out of her range and says, "Easy, Mom. It's *okay*. We just wanted to get some food first, and now we're looking at gloves."

She turns to her ex. "If I had known, Andrew, that your girlfriend wasn't going to cook for you, *I* could have fed him breakfast."

"It's fine. We had a nice breakfast down the street. I always like eating in this neighborhood." Andrew puts his hand on Sammy's head, which I see Jessica register as some possible violation, and Sammy looks down miserably and kicks at something on the floor.

"So where *is* she?"

Andrew mumbles something, and then the two of them glare at each other, and then he dips his head, smiles, and steers Sammy over to where they were before, the glove section.

"Good-*bye*!" she says. "And don't come home later than you said, okay? We've got to stick to the schedule we agreed on, Andrew." She turns to me. "Let's get out of here. Do you mind?"

Sammy is giving me an imploring look. Me! Like I could help.

"Of course I don't mind," I say. And I smile at her son.

"Sorry that was awkward," she says. "That man is constitutionally unable to stick to a plan, even if he's the one who made it."

"So I'm not the only one *processing* about an ex," I say lightly, and am glad when she laughs.

"Gah! No, I'll be processing this guy for the rest of my life if I'm not careful," she says.

By the time we get back to Yolk—after threading our way down the street as she points out the best places for beers, for East Asian clothing, for jewelry, for hamburgers, for muffins, for coffee, for everything—it's somehow become our turn to eat, and we snuggle into a tiny table near the back.

The waiter comes by, a hot-looking guy with a black knit cap and red plastic glasses, and I order a cheese omelet with bacon, coffee, and whole grain toast and grits, and she says she'll have the same. As soon as he's moved on, she says: "Okay. So we've established that we're both dealing with exes who are in our faces right now, but I don't really know the story of you and Noah. Before we get to be best friends, do you want to tell me what happened between you?"

So I haul out the usual story—the wedding, the honeymoon, the walkout, all of it minus the wedding gown dismantlement—and then a waitress comes by and puts two coffees down on the table, and I suddenly know that she has recently broken up with the waiter, and they've not been able to put things back together between them, but there's a guy walking down the street who would be perfect for her. Maybe she should take off her apron and take a few minutes off to go run into him. She could make it look all casual-like. Or maybe the guy will come this way. He needs breakfast. He needs a hug. He needs her.

At the next table, a couple is falling in love. Outside, a golden retriever has run down the sidewalk and is licking the face of a toddler. A toddler who laughs and says, "Mommy, I want doggie!"

My head feels funny. It's like there's a golden light spreading over everything, like maple syrup poured on pancakes.

I look up and Jessica is smiling at me quizzically.

"Jessica," I say. "You need to get back together with Andrew. You do know that, right?"

TWENTY-FOUR
MARNIE

The maple syrup haze stays with me. It's like I'm moving in some sort of glow-filled fog. All the moments stand out somehow. Everything is brilliant and bright and etched in my brain like it will always stay in my memory. Even when Jessica laughs and assures me that she will *not* be getting back together with Andrew. No thank you, not now, not ever.

"He. Is. Sleeping. With. Someone. Else," she informs me icily.

"But you match," I tell her. "You both match. You don't see that?"

She laughs. And then she pays the breakfast tab, and we walk back to the house—and along the way she says, "You and Blix with your get-back-together-with-Andrew talk! I'm beginning to see why she wanted you to have this house, so *you* could take up her song and dance about me and Andrew. Come on, tell me the truth. Did she put you up to this?"

"No," I say and feel that dazed, shaky sensation again, like the air is wobbling.

"Well," Jessica says. "I *cannot* forgive a man who's been unfaithful! Sorry, but that is a deal breaker, pure and simple. Period. No excuses. No backsies."

I try to remember exactly what Blix had said about all the people in her crazy little community. Certainly she mentioned Lola and Jessica. But she just said that all of them needed love, and all of them were fearful of embracing it.

But the thing is, I can almost feel her around me just now, feel her thinking that Jessica and Andrew are meant to be together. Maybe that's what this hazy feeling is about.

"Listen," I say, "one day I called her up when I was so miserable, when Noah left. And I asked her to do a spell to get us back together. I could tell she didn't think it was a great idea. She said she'd send some words for me to have a good life, for energy, for love . . ."

"That's because she probably didn't think Noah was right for you. Also I can't imagine her agreeing to manipulate somebody's path that way."

"And then—right after that, I lost my job, which sucked, but then I moved back home, and then I fell in love again with Jeremy, my old high school boyfriend. So! That was obviously the spell she sent, right?"

"Well . . . sounds like it."

"Only now! Well, now I get the news that she passed away and that she left me her house, and I come here, and here's Noah! He's back in my life. So . . . well, what I want to know is: Is *this* the spell? Is this what she intended to happen?"

She stares at me. "Wow. That's the way this stuff goes. It might be the spell is working. Or not. We don't know."

"I like to think I believe in free will."

"I think Blix would say that you have to trust what makes you happy," she says. "She was always telling me that: trust joy. That's free will, isn't it?"

My phone pings just then with a text message. I'm expecting it to be from Jeremy, but instead it's from a number I don't recognize.

Marnie, this is Patrick. Downstairs. Sorry for the crashes last night. Cat knocked vase over, which fell into computer printer, drowning motor.

Flashes of light ensued. Sparks. New printer being delivered next Monday. Cat very sorry. Told him he can't keep getting by on his looks. He's looking for new apt.

Jessica is watching my face. "Patrick," I tell her. I smile and type back to him:

Yikes! Just make sure your wallet is safe when he decides to move out.

And he types:

Too late. Wallet already missing, and coincidentally, tuna fish cans are arriving by the boxload.

A few minutes later he writes: *By the way, welcome to this house! Blix told me about you. Glad you're here at last. Hope you like it. It's crazy but in a good way. I think.*

The golden haze is still around me when I get back to Blix's house, where I find Noah practicing his guitar in the living room, and the haze is still there even when he sees me and wants to tell me again how he helped Blix over to the other side, and how he knew she should have called on the medical professionals, but instead she turned to him—HIM—and how bad it feels that even doing *that* for her apparently wasn't enough. He's clearly been brooding about this all night long, but I am in this *haze* like nothing I've ever been in before, you see, and everything seems so fraught with meaning.

The haze stays with me through the thirty-seven text messages (yes, THIRTY-SEVEN) sent to me by my family members and Jeremy, asking what I'm planning to do, if I've listed the house for sale yet, when am I coming home, and by the way, don't even tell them I like it in Brooklyn because *we are not New York people*. (That, from my sister, who says she is holding the baby while she types, and she just wishes I could somehow hear the gurgling sounds the baby makes when my sister tells her my name.) Jeremy types over and over again: *COME. HOME.*

The golden haze peaks when I happen to go outside and see a car pull up next door, and an elderly man gets out and goes up on the porch where Lola is waiting for him. He puts his arm around her, and

Lola eases herself away from him, shifts her hip just so, and they walk down the steps together. She ducks into the car without even glancing in my direction.

Noah goes out alone that night, and I get takeout and eat in my room, chatting with Jeremy on the phone. I tell him Brooklyn is big and dirty and complicated. He tells me that he went running on the beach, that it's still so warm he almost was tempted to go swimming, and also that he had dinner with Natalie and Brian.

"And guess what. I was the one who finally got Amelia to sleep," he says. "She put her little head on my shoulder and I walked her around and around the dining room table until she fell sound asleep."

"That's so nice," I tell him. I want to tell him about the golden haze, but there are no words.

It might be part of the magic, and Jeremy doesn't believe in magic.

The haze has disappeared, though, when Noah and I get to Charles Sanford's office on Monday morning. Charles Sanford, a very nice-looking man with hair so slicked back it seems like it may have been buttered, studies us sitting across the desk from him and rattles his papers and lowers his spectacles and then says a bunch of words in a very lawyerly voice that confirm the fact that Blix Holliday has indeed left me her house.

Left it to me. Just me.

"However, there's a stipulation," says Mr. Sanford in a quiet, careful voice, looking at me. "And that is that you, Marnie, will have to agree to live in the house for three months before it is officially considered yours. Meaning that you can't put it on the market until that period of time is up. Blix did not want you to simply sell the house and leave."

Noah exhales loudly.

"So it's not mine unless I live there?" I say.

"For three months," says Mr. Sanford.

Three months. Three months.

"It's an unusual stipulation," he says, "but then Blix was not a usual type of person, now was she?" He shrugs. "What can I say? That's the way she wrote it up. It doesn't have to start right this minute, of course. You can go get your affairs in order and come back . . ."

"But whenever I come back, it's for three months," I say.

"Yes. That is correct. Perhaps you need some time to think it over."

I become seriously interested in the little hammered gold nails decorating the upholstered armchair I'm sitting in. I run my fingers across them again and again, tracing the indentations. The light in the room is purplish. The carpet is soft underneath my shoes. There's a tiny spiderweb in the upper left corner of the ceiling, near the window. My brain is ticking off the fact that three months will mean I'm there until the end of the year, pretty much.

Three months, three months.

My whole family is going to be so upset! And I'll miss Jeremy. Taking a three-month break from him is not what I would have chosen. Oh, and Amelia, too. I was just getting situated back in Florida, beginning to feel connected and secure. Damn it, I've been *happy* there . . . and after such a big, huge unhappiness, this has felt like a gigantic gift.

Blix, what have you done to me? I'll need a coat. And sweaters. And what will I live on?

And, oh my God, then there's Noah.

I look over at him. He's holding a piece of paper in front of him, which I happen to know is a checklist of questions that he's been directed to ask by his mother.

He starts in, his voice heavy and serious. Might there be another will that's more current somewhere? How do we know Blix was of sound mind? Can this will be contested? Blah blah blah.

When he asks Charles Sanford point-blank if I had any input into the terms of this will, and when exactly was I informed about it, I bristle and make a little squawking noise of protest. But Charles Sanford is patient, explaining that I had nothing to do with the terms of the will, but I can tell he's getting fed up with Noah and his family, and anyway there's a loud buzzing sound in my ears that means I can barely pay attention anymore to what's being said. I work on rubbing the little nails in the chair and wonder what in the world Jeremy is going to say when he hears this news.

Do I even *want* this?

Yes. Yes, darling. You want this.

Somehow while I've been consumed with my own anxieties, Charles Sanford seems to have found the combination of words to make Noah shut the hell up, and then we all say more words and apparently I've agreed to everything because I'm signing papers, and it is growing darker outside, like the sun has disappeared, which I don't *think* has anything to do with the fact that I've just signed a scary legal document, but you never know.

A thunderstorm is coming, LaRue says. Would anyone like some coffee? Or some bottled water? But no, we say we're fine.

"Wait. One more question. So what if she *doesn't* live here for the three months?" Noah is saying in a voice that feels like it's coming from the bottom of a well, distorted and strange. "What happens to the property then?"

Charles Sanford clears his throat and starts looking through the papers. "She was actually quite certain that Marnie would meet the stipulations. You know how your great-aunt was. There's hardly anything that she had doubts about. But in a separate document sent in right before she died, she said that if Marnie didn't accept the terms, the house would go to several charities she named."

"To charities," says Noah flatly. He glances over at me in shock. I shrug.

"Yes, Mr. Spinnaker. I know." Charles Sanford clears his throat again. "She did leave you a bit of money. Not what you're hoping, I'm certain, but still . . . your great-aunt did mention once that you're the heir to a rather large family fortune, so perhaps she didn't think it necessary to provide for you in her own will."

"Well. That remains to be seen," says Noah in such a small, defeated voice that I feel sorry for him. I see him as a boy with his hand tucked into his great-aunt's hand, and maybe she is telling him something, and he is gazing into her face. Aunt Blix. *Kiss your Aunt Blix, Noah.*

Charles Sanford is looking at him kindly. "Please know that this kind of thing happens all the time. There's no accounting for what people want done with their property when they're gone." He turns to me. "And here, Marnie, is a private letter she requested that I give to you, to be opened when you wish. There's another letter in the vault for when the three months are up."

I reach over and take the letter. I still feel dazed. Perhaps it's not too late to speak up and change my mind. In one second, I could reverse course and my life would go right back to normal.

Still, I can't help but notice that I am keeping silent.

Charles Sanford stacks all the papers, and then he stands up to signal that the meeting is over. "So if you don't have any more questions, I'll file the necessary paperwork and get things moving. Marnie, feel free to contact me with any questions you might have, or if you have any problems going forward. Because you've chosen to accept the terms of the will, Blix has provided a stipend for you for your living expenses. I would suggest you open a bank account here and I'll see that checks are deposited to the account as needed. Blix also wanted you to know that she's paid the taxes on the property for the next five years, and she's also provided some gifts for the tenants, which I'll be disbursing."

The blood is beating in my ears so hard that I can only barely hear what he's saying.

It's time to go, apparently. Noah, walking along beside me, is reading his phone. "Just so you know, I'm pretty sure my folks will want to contest the will," he says.

We're in the waiting room by then. Charles Sanford frowns. "They are welcome to try, of course, but I assure you it's a waste of money and time. Your great-aunt was knowledgeable in how to make her wishes known."

Just then there's a huge clap of thunder, and Charles Sanford says, "Hi, Blix," and everyone laughs.

"You both have my deepest condolences on her loss," Charles says, and he shakes our hands, and says we'll be in touch.

There is not a taxicab in the world that could contain both me and Noah right after that meeting, so I make sure to turn down the taxi he hails as soon as we get outside. He is a big brown bruise of a man just now, furiously texting with his mom, and I feel like I'm in a dream I can't wake up from.

I decide to take my chances with the thunder and lightning and the rain that is splattering all around us. I wave him away and start down the street, pulling my sweater up over my head.

As soon as I get to a Starbucks—a familiar landmark!—I duck inside and find myself surrounded by a zillion rain-soaked people, all tapping on their phones and ordering skinny chai lattes.

I'm shivering and reading the sign, trying to decide what to get when a woman next to me says sharply, "Are you on line?"

"Pardon?"

"I *said*: Are you *on* this line or not?"

"Oh, you mean am I *in* this line? Yes, oh yes, I am," I say. "I thought you were asking me if I was *online*, like on the Internet."

She stares at me, shakes her head, and then turns away, muttering about *some people*.

Huh. So people in New York stand *on* lines instead of *in* them. Good to know.

After I get my chai latte, I find an armchair in the corner that a guy with a laptop is just vacating and sink down into it. I'm going to be living in this city for three months.

At the table next to me, two women are talking, leaning forward in intensity like no one else in the world is there. One of them has deep-purple hair, and both of them have on coats that look like they're made of quilted black parachutes. And by the way, they're in love, and later today they'll probably go out and get a dog.

I need a coat, probably. And a job. A pair of warm gloves. More black clothing so I can fit in.

I take a sip of my chai. And all of a sudden, just like that, I know that I don't want to be in Brooklyn. I want to go home.

This is not a good place to live. It's dirty; it's loud; it's impersonal—and for heaven's sake, it doesn't even know how to have a proper thunderstorm! I like my thunderstorms to arrive in the late afternoon after a buildup of humidity and heat so that by the time the storm comes, you're grateful for it. It does its job, chasing out the sticky air, and moves on, and the sky clears right up. But this—this is a constant gray drizzle with intermittent booms that seems like it could go on all day. Who needs this?

I tap my fingernails on the table, push all the crumbs into a little pile. Maybe I should go back to Charles Sanford's office and tell him that I've made a horrible mistake. I'll tell him that I'm simply not up to it.

This was an amazing gift, TOTALLY amazing, and I am very appreciative of Blix's kindness, but, sadly, I myself am not up to it. But . . . thank you.

Let the place go to a charity, and I'll take the next flight home tomorrow, and later this week, I'll tell my family the good news that I'm marrying Jeremy.

We'll go to Cancun for our honeymoon like Natalie and Brian did. In a few years, we'll have a kid, and then another, hopefully of the opposite sex, and I'll decorate the house and garden and join the PTA and drive in carpools and keep a color-coded calendar hanging on the kitchen wall and get to say things like, "Honey, did you do your homework?"

I kind of love this idea. And in thirty or so years, I'll be there to help my parents when they need to move to a nursing home. Jeremy will close his physical therapy practice, and maybe we'll go back to Cancun for our fiftieth wedding anniversary when we're eighty. And we'll say, "Where did the time go?" like everybody else in the history of the planet. And then we'll die fulfilled and people will say, "They were the luckiest ones."

That's a life, isn't it? A person could do that. There will be so many, many good moments to that kind of life.

So why does it feel like right this minute I'm at a crossroads, trying to decide between the unknown and the known? Between the city and the suburbs? Between risk and safety? Didn't I already make that choice? I told the guy I'd marry him! I kissed him right there in the diner, and I saw the happy look on his face, and how surprised he was—and now all I have to do is tell him that there's a little piece of real estate that's holding things up.

Blix, I am so sorry, but I already decided all this about my life. And now you've come to give me a gift that is going to muck up my whole life, and I'm sorry, but it's just such a huge, huge mistake! I am not the person you thought. I don't want a big, big life.

I know that if I called Natalie right this minute and told her everything that's happening, she wouldn't even have to think about it. She'd say I should run, not walk, back to Charles Sanford's office this minute and insist that he rip up all the pages with my signature. Refuse to leave until every last shred of my signature is gone.

I'm about to punch in her number when I remember that I am carrying a letter from Blix right in my handbag. With my heart pounding, I take it out and open it, somehow knowing it will change everything.

TWENTY-FIVE
BLIX

Dear Marnie,

Sweetheart, an hour ago I got off the phone with you. You were asking me for a spell to bring Noah back to you, a request that pierced me to the core of myself. You love him. YOU LOVE HIM. At first I thought I'd go over to my book of spells—yes, I really do have one, but it's more a joke than anything else because the best spells just sort of happen without any need of external stuff—but then I thought, what the hell, I'd try to find just the thing you could drink or eat that would make you a magnet for Noah once again. Maybe it would be only a placebo spell, but it would work because that's how it all works. They work on BELIEF. And some directed energy. Here's the truth, sweet pea: we are all vibrational beings in physical bodies, and thoughts actually become reality so you have to make sure you're thinking about what you want and not about what you don't want.

But then it hit me: there's something else I can do instead, an immediate remedy—I could give you my house.

My funny, weird, crazy Brooklyn house. I should tell you: It has a plumbing issue. The floors slope in some of the rooms. It's filled with tenants who don't have perfect lives. The light switch on the first floor flickers sometimes, and once it shot a spark at me. I shot one right back. There's a loose shingle on the roof. A tree branch batters the upstairs windows when storms come. What else? Oh, yes, one of the planters on the roof wobbles even though it's supposedly cemented in place. The sun coming up in the morning can shine directly in your eyes, even with the bamboo shades pulled all the way down. The full moon will wake you up if you sleep in the front bedroom. Still, that's the room I recommend. It's the best because you will hear the sounds of the outside world, and that will keep you grounded and sane.

It's a messy, forgiving, rambunctious house, filled with love and mischief. There have been so many good times here, and perhaps you already know the truth that good times beget other good times. And so there are plenty more to come. This house wants to be yours.

And I want it to be yours. You and I are messy, forgiving, rambunctious people, just like the house. That is what we share, Marnie dear. I hope you will stay.

Because you see, I am dying. I have this cancerous, tumorous thing growing inside me—it's been here with me for months, and I know the end is coming soon. I haven't told so many people, because sometimes people think I should go get treatment, like treatment is something I want to waste my time with. I do not want to have parts of me cut off, and I don't want to be burned and slashed and poisoned in the interest of "getting better." I want the kind of treatment where the universe looks down and says, "Hey, Cassandra!" (Cassandra is the name I gave my tumor. I thought she deserved a name.) I think the universe should have said, "Cassandra, you know you don't belong there. Get out of Blix's belly, will you, and go evaporate back into the atmosphere. Go turn into part of a glacier, or a little nest for a squirrel, or go back to wherever you were before you came here. Sweet Cassandra, if you kill off our Blix, then you will die, too, because Blix has all the nutrients for you. So think about that."

But the universe didn't come through with any such thing, and Cassandra apparently did not think about the consequences, and she has grown bigger and stronger, and she nestles down next to my heart when we lie down together, and I know soon she will be the bigger part of me.

So I'm excited for what I know can happen. I am calling my attorney, and I'm drawing up a will that leaves you the whole mess of a house. My heart beats faster when I think of how that is going to be for you! I know that the house will set your life off on a new course, just the way it did that for me. I know that you and I are in many ways connected, and maybe you'll feel that when you get here.

Think of me here, welcoming you. Will you do that? See me on the rooftop, or sitting at the beat-up kitchen table drinking tea, or out on the street talking to the people who come by. I'm the car horns, the bus that rounds the corner, the subs over at Paco's across the street. I am all of it. And you are, too, although you may not know it yet.

I know, I know, this will come as a shock to you, getting a house from someone you think you don't know. But I know you. I have always known you. And I see myself in you, believe it or not.

And here's the main thing of what I know about you. I told you when we met that you are in line for a big, big life, and this, Marnie, is where you will find it. There will be love and surprises here in abundance, I promise you that. Be open to what doesn't seem possible, and you will be amazed what can happen. Darling, this is your time.

Love over lifetimes,

Blix

P.S. Will you stay for at least the three months it's going to take you to get over the shock of this? Please? Tallyho, my love!

TWENTY-SIX
MARNIE

I read the letter three or four or ten times, then I fold it up carefully, and put it back in my bag.

For fun, I do the little exercise Blix showed me at the engagement party—the one where you beam some energy over to somebody you don't even know, and watch what happens.

I choose a baby in a high chair, banging his cup on the table in front of him. I picture him all bathed in white light and happiness—and then I wait to see the effect. And yep, he stops banging and looks around, and then his eyes meet mine and he laughs out loud.

I made a baby laugh! This is so cool.

After the rain stops, I go to H&M to buy a sweater to replace the wet one I'm wearing. My eye gets caught by a long, bulky white cardigan, a black knit tunic, three pairs of leggings, a short black dress with red slashes on it, four pashminas, some heavy socks, two weeks' worth of underwear (most of it sexy just because), and a blue knit cap. The clerk is ringing it all up while I'm looking at the jewelry display next to the counter, when a woman behind me in line—an older woman who has kind, crinkly eyes—says, "You need to buy that turquoise medallion there. Look at the shape of it. I think it's your good luck charm."

So of course I buy it, but I have that weird feeling again—the maple syrup sensation. A good luck charm. Just what I need. When I turn around to show her that I've bought it, she's moved over to another cashier and doesn't look back.

Outside, the weather has cleared up dramatically, and above the tall buildings, I can see wisps of white clouds scudding across the sky. The air feels clean and crisp. I put on the cardigan and go into the closest bank branch and start filling out the paperwork for an account.

Apparently I'm staying.

It's not that Brooklyn suddenly looks so beautiful, or that I miss my family any less, or that I've come to a momentous decision. It's as though I can feel Blix's presence all around me, that her words have landed in my soul somehow . . . and I want to bask in that for as long as possible.

Three months suddenly seems like nothing.

A little break from my life perhaps, before it goes rumbling off on its normal track—toward marriage and children and, yes, lawn mowers.

I have a chance to pause. I feel like that woman we sent energy to that time at the engagement party—and just the way she did, looking up to see who's called her—that's what I'm doing right now.

I text Patrick, for no reason at all: *Just bought the heaviest sweater I've ever owned in my life. Question: Is life really possible for a kind of weird person from the South to make it here?*

After a long time, he writes back: *Sweater is a good start although December can be frosty. Hell, November can be frosty! Also Bklyn is welcoming to weirdos. It's normal folks who have the most trouble. BUT: Do you say "y'all"? Might be harder to assimilate if you say "y'all."*

I don't say "y'all." My time in Northern California whipped that out of me. (BTW, nice punctuation! Colon AND quotation marks! ☺)

Then I'd say you have a good chance. (I've been told I'm a punctuator extraordinaire.)

If I can make it here, I can make it anywhere, or so I've heard.

That's Manhattan. Making it in Brooklyn guarantees nothing.

So I need a coat?

Most def. (That's Brooklynese for "most definitely.")

I figured.

I go over to Uniqlo and get one of those adorable little parachute-type coats. In dark purple. Because why not?

Then I walk home, trying out my part as a regular Brooklyn girl strolling through the hood.

I'm staying! I'm actually going to live here for three months. I feel like when you're at the top of a roller coaster and are just about to start the whooshing ride you paid for, and you just hope you don't freak out.

It's a long walk back to Blix's house, but I'm not up to figuring out the subway system just yet, and it's too nice a day for a cab. And anyway, what else do I have to do but walk? I just want to look at everything, all the nail salons and brownstones and nondescript apartment buildings and restaurants, everything big and noisy and filled with ordinary life. For a while I try keeping track of how many people smile at me, which is not all that many, but who cares. It occurs to me that when it's this crowded, you can't afford to be smiling and chatting with everybody. You'd be exhausted within two blocks.

I see a woman sweeping her steps, and her brown arms in her floral-print housedress look majestic. A bird's nest is perched in a gingko tree. A leaf on the sidewalk is shaped like a heart.

And all three of those things feel like Blix saying, "Welcome. You're here now."

My entire family, of course, loses their respective minds when I tell them the news that I'm staying for a bit. But I'm ready for them.

My mother calls it abhorrent and manipulative, and says Blix was probably certifiably crazy. My father says that I should come home and we can let our family attorney look over the papers.

"No one can keep you against your wishes," he says. "Believe me, I'll figure out how you can sell the property and still be at home."

"It's not like that!" I say, but they are not having any of that kind of talk.

When I get Natalie on the phone, I try a different tack. I start with the good news that I just walked through Brooklyn, and people smiled at me, and that even though it's loud and dirty here, it's also kind of amazing and full of stories—and that Blix was perhaps onto something when she said I needed to be here.

"What?" says my sister. "No, to all of this! What happened to our plan to have babies and hang out by the pool? You said you were happy here! Why are you letting this woman, who's *dead*, by the way, change your whole life around!"

"It's not changing my whole life," I say. But the truth is, I'm not so sure. I finger the good luck charm I'm still wearing around my neck and listen to my sister's diatribe, which is getting more shrill by the minute. The thing about sisters is they have your whole rotten history right at their fingertips.

She runs through the greatest hits of my misfit life: my admittedly checkered history of dropping the ball, changing the plan, not following through. How, sadly, it's no wonder that things go badly in my life—I assume she means my marriage, my job—when I let myself be swept along by somebody else's vision for me. Where is my backbone? What do I stand for?

Think of Amelia! Think of Jeremy! Don't I care that people here *need* me? Our parents!

I sit and listen, looking around the bright kitchen, at my shopping bags on the floor, my new coat, my beautiful white sweater that she won't see. The sun is coming through the kitchen window. Blix's plants on the windowsills are still in glorious bloom.

Finally I rouse myself enough to tell her I have a pot boiling over on the stove and have to hang up.

I try a new tactic with Jeremy, simply stating the facts. Not coming right home. Three-month residency required for the inheritance. Staying here. All is well. We'll be fine.

"Whoa, whoa, whoa," he says. "Back up. I've never heard of anything like this."

"Yep," I say. "Me neither. But there we have it. It is what it is. It doesn't have to be a problem. It just delays things a bit for us, is all."

"But wait. It does seem like an odd situation, doesn't it? Having something unusual like that written into a will? Why do you think she did it?"

"Well, she *was* unusual."

"It just doesn't sound like a very nice thing to do to somebody. You know? No offense because I know you liked her, but a gift with such strings seems really . . . well, suspect."

"I can see that way of looking at things," I tell him slowly, but what I am thinking is that it's extraordinary how the late afternoon light slants in the kitchen window and hits the scarred top of the brown table. I love this table. The heft and solidity of it. And the turquoise refrigerator. I love that this whole place seems to hold Blix's personality—and how does something like that happen?

"Can you come home for a visit, do you think? Or should I maybe come up there and see you?"

"Okay," I say. I shake myself back into the conversation.

"Okay to you coming home for a visit, or okay for me to come and see you?"

"Either one," I say, and yawn.

He's quiet for a moment. Then he says, "Look. I'm sorry I'm not such a good phone guy, but I just want you to know that this makes me a little bit sad. And in case you didn't know, I really loved having you working with me right in the next room, just knowing you were there, and my mom will miss having you to talk to because you know just how to make people feel good, you know? We all need you here. My patients, my mom, *me*."

"Well," I say. "Thank you."

"And this *is* really temporary," he says. "Right?"

"Oh my God! So temporary! Very temporary!"

"Because I love you, you know. I'm going to be so lonely without you!"

"I love you, too," I say. "We'll talk every day. I miss you." And then I add, "It'll be lonely here without you, too."

And then, wouldn't you know that when I hang up and turn around, Noah is standing there next to the refrigerator. Shit, I didn't even hear him come back in the room. He gets out two beers and holds one out to me, cocking his head and looking way too amused.

"Wow. That was so sweet," he says sarcastically. "Really. You'll have to tell me who the lucky guy is."

"Actually, it was my fiancé," I say.

"Excuse me? Your *fiancé*? Soooo . . . *how* long have we been divorced—and you've already got somebody else lined up?" He's smiling. "What? Did you have a guy waiting in the wings or something?"

"Oh, Noah, stop it. It's not like that at all. He's my old boyfriend, and we've gotten back together and we have a lot in common, so . . . we recently decided to get married."

"Your old boyfriend. Who might that be? Let me see if I remember the pantheon of guys." He puts his finger on his chin, a pantomime of someone thinking. His eyes are bright with laughter. "Wait. I hope to God it's not the one that ditched you before the senior prom!"

"No. Please. Stop. You're embarrassing yourself."

"Oh my God! Is it the guy *you* ditched to go out with the hot guy? It is, isn't it? You got back together with *him*?"

"Why are you doing this?"

"Because I'm curious. Because I care about you. I did this terrible thing to you, and I've felt horribly guilty over it, so I'm glad to see you're fine. That's all. Also . . . I'm a little jealous, maybe. You got over things kind of . . . *rápidamente*, if you ask me."

"I suppose you think I should still be pining for you."

"It would have been nice to have at least a six-month pining period. I think for a two-year relationship a person should get six months of pining."

"Ha!"

He's gazing at me like he's seeing me for the first time. I sip the beer he's handed me, and then I say I'm going to see if Jessica's around, and then *he* says that we never actually made it to that burger bar the other night, and why don't we grab a bite to eat *now*, and the truth is, I'm a little bit hungry, and I can't think of a good reason why not, and so we walk there. I keep meaning to ask him when exactly he might move out of the house now that he knows it's not going to be his. Because surely that's his plan. But the conversation is instead going all over the place—Whipple and Africa and playing music and what living in Brooklyn is really like—and I never quite get around to it.

Okay, I know this is shallow of me, but all my nerve endings and I had kind of forgotten what it's like to be with a man who is so handsome that everyone stops and looks at him. It's so unfair. Did separating from me and going to Africa have to actually *improve* his looks? And while we're at it, at what age will looks cease to matter to me?

But, well, here we are—me and my nerves and him—and we're laughing and talking, and he's holding court, telling his magnificent stories and being the life of the party. And every now and then his eyes meet mine and he smiles, and I dig down into whatever sanity and strength I possess, and I say to myself, *Not this time*.

And when we walk home, with him smiling and taking my arm and laughing about the people in the bar and being as charming and engaging as Noah can ever be, I hold myself very tightly together. I let my footfalls tap out the rhythm as I walk: Not. This. Time. Not. This. Time.

And later, lying there alone in the dark, I resolve that tomorrow I will tell him he has to leave.

The next morning I wake up to a knock at my bedroom door.

"Please. Go away," I say from the mound of pillows and covers.

"That is not a nice way to talk to a man who is bringing you breakfast."

"Um, thank you anyway, but I don't eat breakfast."

"What? It's the most important meal of the day," he says. "And also I made my specialty—German pancakes."

He pushes the door open. "Come on, I know you, and I am not buying the fact that you don't want at least two bites of a perfect German pancake! Look at it!"

Making German pancakes was his specialty back when we were together. They're thick wondrous concoctions with powdered sugar. Irresistible. Now he's bringing them on a tray with coffee on the side. Bacon. A folded napkin. He's a rich guy, the son of a woman who makes Welsh rarebit, so he has always been all about the presentation.

His face is flushed from all the effort he's gone to.

"I thought you might like a reminder of happier times. That's all. It's just breakfast. If you really want me to, I'll go away."

"It's okay," I say grouchily.

"Scoot over. I'm joining you." He stands there while I contemplate whether to move or not. Then he says, "*If* you don't mind."

So I haul myself over to the other side of the bed, and he sits down and puts the tray down between us. I tuck my feet under and arrange the covers around me. This is not good.

"Um, why are you doing this?" I ask him. The pancakes really are perfect—round and golden brown, with melted butter oozing across the top. And the bacon is how I like it—snappable. My stomach does a traitorously appreciative growl.

"Because this is my way of saying I'm sorry. I'm asking for pancake absolution. Aaaaand . . . well, I also want to ask a favor."

"What?"

He grins at me. "Such a tone of voice! It's just that I kind of *need* to stay here, so just hear me out, if you please. I promise I will be a good roommate, and I'll behave myself and not throw wild parties. I'll make pancakes and I'll clean up. And fix faucet leaks. You know. That sort of thing. I'll even put the toilet seat down ninety-five percent of the time, which is something I have never been successful at before."

"No, Noah. That's an absurd idea. We can't live in the same house. It won't work. You need to go."

"But I don't have anywhere *to* go," he says. His eyes are twinkling, like he knows how to make himself adorable. "Come on, Marnie. We're cool."

"Call your family. Go back to Virginia and live with them, like I had to do with my family. Do whatever your people do when they run out of money, if that's ever happened to any of them. But staying here is not an option. You know it won't work."

"I can't call them. I really screwed up in Africa, and they're pissed." He starts stroking my arm.

I pull it away. "So teach. You have a teaching certificate."

"I'm not licensed here. And I'm burned out. I don't want to teach. *Please*, Marnie. I started some classes in September, and I intend to stay here while I finish them."

I don't say anything.

"Okay, hear me out. Look at it this way. This is a massive social experiment, okay? No, no. Don't roll your eyes. Listen! We were good friends before we were lovers, and we were lovers for a while before we moved in together and decided to get married. And then I screwed up royally, bigger than I've ever screwed up in my whole life. And clearly, because of that screwup, we're never going to be *together* together again. You've got somebody else now, and I respect that. So what if we just have *this* time in Brooklyn, in my great-aunt's house? Just this little slice of time while you wait to inherit this place for real. We'll be nice to each other. We'll be friends again, repair all the holes in our relationship. And then—well, when we're old and gray and decrepit and married a hundred years to other people, maybe we'll look back and say, 'Wow, that was such a cool thing we did, living together *nicely* even though we were divorced and had all that baggage.' It can be like a spiritual practice—both of us here, in Blix's house. I think she'd think this was really cool of us to do. Closure."

"I don't know, I don't know." I can't look him in the eye. I go to the bathroom and pee, and then I stare at my reflection in the cracked, mottled, wavy bathroom mirror.

He calls through the door: "Did I mention that I'll make pancakes? And I'm also throwing in the fact that I'll kill all the spiders."

"There are no spiders!" I call to him, but I have lost. I know I will say yes. I just wish I knew for sure *why* I'm saying yes. Is it to please him? Or to keep from being alone? Or is he right, that we really could bring some closure to our relationship?

And then I know for sure what it is.

I am not really done with him.

The place where he lives in my heart—well, he's still in there. Still rattling around. And it was okay as long as I wasn't seeing him. I had paved over so many emotions. And now I really, really do need to get over him.

So maybe this will do it.

After too much time has passed, I go back into the bedroom. "All right. You can stay. But, Noah, I hate this. Really. Whether you think it's a good thing or not, I am seeing someone else. Somebody nice who's waiting for me—"

"I know, I know," he says. "Believe me, I respect that. I do."

"Noah. Don't."

"No funny business, no regrets. Just us."

"Okay," I say, and he does a fist pump in the air and then he comes over and kisses me, a chaste kiss on the cheek. But there's a history behind that kiss, and we both know we could tumble right into our old story. He gives me a knowing glance and then picks up the tray with the dishes, and he takes his arrogance and his kisses and his magnetism and leaves, trailing a little whiff of possibility. I hear him walk up the stairs to the kitchen, hear him put the dishes in the sink, and only then do I exhale, and then collapse on the bed and find myself in tears.

I'm not sure what I'm crying for, to tell you the truth. Maybe I'm crying because there's something in me that can't seem to quit him, or maybe at last I'm crying for Blix who, despite how everybody talks about her in the present tense, really is dead. And I'm crying because the legacy she left me—this house, all these characters, this life—is something I would never have chosen and don't intend to keep.

That's it. I'm crying for Blix's mistake. She was so wrong about me.

TWENTY-SEVEN
MARNIE

Later that day, when Noah has gone out, Lola brings over brownies, cookies, two pumpkins, and a pair of hand-knit socks with hearts on them. "The socks are because it's going to get cold here, and the pumpkins are because I thought we should decorate them," she says. "The brownies and cookies are self-explanatory." She smiles at me, and I see that she has smiling gray eyes that crinkle up nicely, like they are nested in a crisscross of lines. Grandmotherly, sweet pink skin topped by a haze of gray cottony hair. "Blix and I always did pumpkins together," she is saying. "Kids will come for Halloween, you know. And by kids, I mean hipsters and *their* kids. Very entertaining."

I blink. Halloween is still weeks away! Why are we doing these now?

Lola smiles and heads past me, upstairs toward the kitchen. "So how are you settling in?" she calls over her shoulder. "It's a fine place to live, isn't it? So Blix!" She looks around, smiling brightly, like this house is an old friend she's needed to see.

"I'm so glad you're here," I say when we're both in the kitchen, and Lola is taking off her gray cape that matches her eyes, and draping it over one of the kitchen chairs. The way she looks around the kitchen makes it obvious that it belongs much more to her than to me.

"Ah!" she says and holds her arms straight out, as if she could hug the whole room. "Wow, so she's still here, isn't she? I feel her everywhere around!"

"I'll put some tea on," I say.

"And then let's get to work on these pumpkins. Want to?"

She's the one who goes and gets the kettle out of the cabinet and fills it with water and sets it down on the back burner. "So tell me about Monday. I guess you got the news?"

"The news? Oh, you mean the three-months thing."

She looks at me closely. "Yes, of course that. Were you surprised? Believe me, this three-months thing was not my idea. I told Blix that was crazy. I told her that you already have your own life somewhere else. And I said that when you give somebody a house, you either just give it to them or you don't. You don't try to give them a whole *life* in the bargain. But there wasn't any reasoning with her. I guess you know that by now." She opens a drawer and gets out what look to be some alarmingly sharp carving knives and brings them over to the table.

"Lola," I say quietly. "You get that I didn't really *know* Blix, right? I've had maybe three conversations with her in my whole life. And then she goes and does this. I don't know what to think. Noah was positive the place should go to him and his family, and I can't say I disagree with him."

Her face darkens, and she picks up a knife and waves it around in the air. "No! Blix would *not* want to hear anything about that! She calls Noah an unevolved scoundrel—and trust me on this, she did not want him to end up with this place—and I've gotta tell you, somewhere, in whatever realm she's in, she knows you're letting him stay here now, and she'll probably be all up in things trying to get you to change your mind. If there's any way she can reach you from the afterlife, that is, and I wouldn't put it past her."

"Wait," I say. "Is it because he wanted a divorce? Because—"

"No. It was all long-ago stuff—her entire family has always been so condescending, ever since her father died. He was her champion," she says. "Blix was pure love, and they couldn't see that. They treated her with such disrespect, and finally she got fed up with it. No way was she going to leave them her house!"

She hands me a knife. "Are you good at this? I've never done it without Blix, so I'm just faking it. But the main thing is, Blix says she knows *you*. She's unexplainable, always doing the thing you'd least expect. I say to her, 'Blix, nobody's going to benefit when you go around trying to remake somebody's whole life for them without their permission,' and then *she* says, 'I have my reasons for what I do.' I feel like my whole thirty-something years with her has been and still is one big argument. In between the fun, of course."

"Do you know you always talk about Blix in the present tense?"

"That's because she's right here with us. I know you feel it, too."

I slice into one of the pumpkins, take off the stem, and lay it on the table. I haven't done this since I was a kid, but I used to love cutting designs into the pumpkins. My mother was always telling me to cut out triangle eyes and mouths, but I liked doing spirals and curlicues.

"Know what I'm going to miss?" Lola says after a while. "It sounds crazy, but it's the dinner parties. Blix and Houndy gave the best—"

"Houndy, the lobsterman? What happened to him?"

"He was her true love. They were together for over twenty years, but then in the summer, she was giving a party to say good-bye to everybody because she knew she was going to die soon, and Houndy died right at the party. Dropped dead just like that." She takes off her glasses and wipes at her eyes with a napkin.

"Oh!"

"Yeah, it was quite a shock to her. To all of us. I think he just couldn't face the idea of life without her, so he went first. They were something together. Only people I ever knew whose priority was just to be happy, no matter what. Most people don't have the knack for that day in and day out, you know. But they did. They danced. They gave dinner parties. Oh my goodness, those parties! Blix was a marvelous cook, but she was even better at knowing who needed to be there to share it with her. She'd just meet people on the street and become fast friends. They had musicians and poets and homeless people and shopkeepers. People would come again and again." Her eyes are shining with tears. She gets up to pour the tea into the cups and brings them over to the table.

"And they'd do just about anything," she says. "That was the thing that struck me the most. Never thought of how old they were, or if they were sick. They had all the usual aches and pains, and Blix, as it turned out, had that tumor. And yet she's out there in the ocean, skinny-dipping, even in her eighties! Traveling all over. Then there was the year she taught herself the harmonica and she'd go to bars and play it. To bars! Right there with the young people, the hipsters, like she was one of them. And it wasn't like she was just pulling some cute old-lady routine. She fixed them up with their partners and gave them advice and dragged them home with her. Bought them presents. And Houndy—oh, that Houndy—he gave out lobsters like they were nothing more than old rocks he'd happened to find on the beach."

"I'd love to be like that."

She puts her hands in her lap and looks wistfully at me. "You know, when you watch people like that live, you start to realize that the rest of us are just counting off the days until we die. *They* were the experts at life."

I slice a paisley shape into the center of my pumpkin. "She rescued me at Noah's parents' house at Christmas. I made kind of an idiot of myself, and she just swooped in and made everything all right for me. Got me laughing. Telling me outrageous stories, making me laugh."

Lola's face scrunches up while she works on the eyes for her pumpkin. She does standard-issue jack-o'-lantern triangle eyes. "Oh, yes! I heard all about that. She was so excited when she came back. She was just stunned to find you. She told me how you reminded her so much of herself at your age." She tilts her head at me like she's trying to see if I'm anything like Blix, which I know I'm not. "I think she came home full of ideas about you."

"But look at me, Lola! You can see that I am nothing like her! Nothing! She got it all wrong about me. I'm the least . . . *able* person that I know. I'm not even brave. Not the tiniest bit brave." I fling my arm out and knock over my cup of tea, and have to run to the sink for a sponge to wipe it all up.

Lola moves the newspapers aside and says, "None of that matters to Blix. I'm her best friend, but she's miles ahead of me. For God's sake, I was a secretary for the board of education for forty-two years, a place Blix wouldn't have put up with for one red-hot minute. *And*"—she lowers her voice and leans toward me—"you know how many men I've slept with in my life? Exactly one! The man I was married to for forty-seven years—a trustee for the railroad. I didn't dance in the streets. I didn't go skinny-dipping, and if I had, believe me, the cops would have showed up and hauled me away. We just have to trust what Blix sees in us, maybe." Then her expression changes. "Also, aren't you a matchmaker? She told me you're a matchmaker."

"I don't know. Am I? I mean, sometimes I do sort of see when people should be together. But it's not—I don't really know how to make it happen, you know. I just know that it *should* happen."

Lola is smiling. "I think one of the things you might want to be prepared for is that you're not going to get to stay ordinary. She said you have a big life ahead of you."

I grimace. "Yeah, she told me that, too. But I'm afraid there are things she didn't know about me. I mean, I'm appreciative and all about getting the house, but I can't stay here," I say to her. "I've gotten involved with my old high school boyfriend. I'm actually scheduled to get married when I go back home. He's a physical therapist with a practice in Florida, and we've got this whole life that we're planning on. Blix didn't know that was happening, you see . . ."

Lola is still smiling her unwavering smile and nodding up and down like nothing I'm saying makes one bit of difference.

"By the way," she says, as if she's just been told to say this. "Have you met Patrick? You kind of need to go see Patrick."

I would like to meet Patrick, but Patrick famously does not come outside. So the next day I bake some cookies and go downstairs and knock on his door.

Forever passes and there is only silence from inside. Finally I type to him:

Hey, Patrick! You around? I'm on your steps. With cookies.

Enticing. But I'm not my best self today, as Oprah would say.

Did I mention that they are CHOCOLATE CHIP cookies? And that I made them with my bare hands?

Marnie . . .

And they're HOT and JUST OUT OF THE OVEN.

Marnie, has anyone explained to you that I am hideously ugly? Disfigured and curmudgeonly and introvertish and possibly malodorous. Hard to know since it's just me and the cat down here, but one of us is definitely NOT FRESH.

Patrick, has anyone explained to YOU that chocolate chip cookies transcend all that and more?

All right. I am opening the door. But you have been warned. Also, spoiler alert: I am much better in texts than I am in person. So adjust your expectations accordingly.

And then there he is. He's slightly built, with a black Mets hoodie on—with the hood up, even in the house—and sweatpants. His face is partially obscured by the hood, but I can see blue eyes. Some scars. Dark hair.

"Hi," I say. "Cookies." I hold out the platter.

"Hi, cookies," he says. "Patrick."

Then we stand there. Finally he says, "Oh, I'm guessing you want to come in, even though I am doing everything I can to make you feel unwelcome."

"Well . . ." I laugh a little bit. "Um, I thought I would. I mean, if it's okay. I don't have to stay long."

"Sure. Enter the palace. You do now own this place, I believe." Before I can protest that I'm not there as the *building owner*, he steps aside with a flourish, and I go into a little tiled hallway that leads into his living room, which smells amazing—like cinnamon and sugar and apples.

The place looks more like a computer library than a home. Along one wall is a plywood desk that has three computer monitors blinking away, with various keyboards and a desk chair on wheels. The monitors all have lines and lines of writing on them. Across the room, over an expanse of tan carpeting, is a black leather couch with some books and magazines piled at right angles. And a coffee table. There are pole lamps and intriguing sculptures everywhere.

"You have such amazing artwork!" I say idiotically. "And so many computers!"

"Yep. I work at home so I don't have to inflict myself on the American citizenry. It's a public service I perform, and it seems to require electronics. The sculptures are from a previous life."

I turn and look at him. Even with his hood up, I can see that he's smiling—and yes, it's a crooked, damaged smile in a face with a ruined nose. He looks craggy and roughed up. I feel myself take in a deep breath, which might have sounded to him like a gasp, but which wasn't that at all.

"Oh! What kind of work do you do?" I say. My voice sounds fake even to myself, probably because I am worried that he thinks I was shocked by his appearance, when I was *not*. I was just taking a breath, but how do I explain that to him without sounding like it's a lie? I look at him helplessly, hoping he'll rescue me.

He looks right at me, and he lets the awkwardness be there in the room with us before he answers. "Actually, I scare people by telling them what disease they probably have, based on their symptoms. Like, if you go to the website and type in that your back hurts, I'm the guy who asks you to click on further symptoms until eventually I tell you that you might have back cancer or that your kidneys are exploding."

"Actually, this is amazing because I may be one of your best customers," I say. "I'm often up in the middle of the night reading about brain tumors and stuff."

"Thanks," he says. "It's good that I'm here to help you with your light reading." He lets out a sigh, and I worry that I am boring him. Really, this is so difficult, and I so want him to like me. "And you?" he says politely. "Blix told me that you're something of a matchmaker."

"Oh my God. Has she told *everyone* that I'm a matchmaker? I am so not a matchmaker."

"Well. That's what she said. 'I'm leaving my house to Marnie, and she's a matchmaker, so I think she'll be very happy here.' Exact quote."

"Wow. Did she tell you the part about how she actually only laid eyes on me two times? Did she tell you that she didn't even really *know* me?"

He gives me a mild look. "It's okay. I know better than anyone that Blix had her ways. I'm not going to ask you for your matchmaking union card or anything."

"It's just so crazy. I have no idea why I'm even here. I keep explaining to people that I didn't really even know her, that I feel like I'm some kind of imposter getting this house from her. My parents are aghast. Like, who is this old lady and why couldn't she have left this house to her own family? Why did she pick me? They seem to think it's some kind of punishment and that I need to be very, very careful!"

He is looking at me with a little half smile, or what seems like it might be a half smile. Hard to tell with the hoodie he's wearing and the fact that his face isn't quite like other people's faces. "And are you?" he says. "Being very, very careful?"

"Not by their standards, I'm sure. Also, what if she left me the place so I could do matchmaking, and it turns out I'm no good at it? She should have left it to Noah."

"I think—well, do you want to know my true, uncensored thoughts?"

"Do I? Yes, I do. Tell me. Uncensored thoughts."

"Well, my first thought is that Blix didn't ever do *anything* she didn't want to do, and when she met you, I can tell you this: you made a huge impression on her. I don't know if you were demonstrating your abundant *matchmakery* skills in front of her, or if she was just discerning them—but she was taken with you, and that was that. End of story. When she decided you needed the house, you were getting it, and nobody else could have it."

"But it's so . . . surprising. Who does that?"

"Blix Holliday does that. Also, she did not think that Noah should end up with her house, nor should any of her relatives from Virginia. She told me that over and over. And now I'm really not going to say any more."

"I've been here less than a week, and yet every single person I've talked to has made sure to tell me how little she thought of Noah. Even he tells me that. It must have been epic. Maybe you're the one who could tell me why?"

"No more. I've taken a vow."

"A vow?"

"A vow of silence when it comes to criticizing other people, particularly ones who were married to the person I'm talking to. And who are currently also living with that individual. It's my policy."

"Well, we're not doing *that* kind of *living with*," I say. And when he keeps looking at me, I say, "It's *not* that way at all. Believe me. He's only staying here because he's enrolled in classes and also we're doing some experiment to show that we can live together for the three months without killing each other. It's so that when we're old, we can look back and see that we were kind to each other. A different sort of breakup."

He smiles at me. "I am so not going to comment on any of that." He leads the way into the kitchen, which is really nothing more than a tiny stove, sink, and refrigerator all jammed into a little closet-sized room off the living room. An apple pie is sitting on the counter, with one piece missing.

"Let's eat cookies, shall we? Or would you like some pie? Or maybe both?"

"The cookies are for you," I say, and he laughs. "So that's a vote for both, then!"

He cuts us each a slice of pie and piles some cookies onto some paper plates, and we stand in the kitchen, eating them. The pie is exquisitely buttery and sweet, with tart apples and a flaky crust. Kind of amazing actually. I can't stop exclaiming over it.

"Yes, I've been experimenting with crusts lately. The old lard or butter question, you know? This time I went with butter. Flakier with lard, I think, but . . ."

"Oh my God. I vote for this pie. Butter all the way."

"I'll make a note of it," he says.

We're quiet, devouring our pie, when I say, "Have you lived here a long time?"

He frowns. In the greenish cast of the fluorescent light from the ceiling, I can now see more of his face. It's a shock, a little, to see that the skin on his face is pulled taut around his left eye, leaving it extra pink and smooth like the inside of a shell. The other eye is fine, looking back at me with some attitude to it.

"Well, three and a half years, I guess it is now. Are you thirsty? Are you the kind of person who wants milk with your pie?"

"No that's okay," I say. "So . . . did you know Blix before that?"

"Nope. Met her outside the art museum one day. I was having, shall we say, a rather unfortunate moment, and suddenly, there she was, bossing me around even though I was a stranger. Talked to me for a while and then said I had to come live in her building."

"Really? And so you did? You just moved in here because she told you to?"

"And didn't *you* come here because she told you to?"

"Well. I mean, I guess I did, when you put it that way."

"Yeah. She knows things about where people are supposed to be. So, am I allowed to ask the big question? Now that you've purchased a coat, may I assume this means you're intending to become a Brooklynista for good? Are you staying?"

This is when it hits me, really, that my decision to sell the place actually affects his life. What if he has to move?

I put down my plate on the counter. "I feel weird about saying this, but I don't think I'm staying, really. I've kind of got a life to get back to. And I'm not really a city person, you know? Blix wrote into the deal that I need to stay for three months, so of course I'll do that—"

"Yeah. I knew about the three months."

"Really? Did she tell everyone everything?"

"Everyone? I'm not sure *everyone* in Brooklyn knows about it, but we, her closest friends, certainly do."

"So people are going to be upset if I don't stay here. I'll be abandoning her plan. Is that right?"

"It's not like we all expected everything to stay the same forever. If this isn't the life you want, then you shouldn't feel you have to have it. I don't think Blix ever intended that you should be a prisoner here."

"But, oh man, I feel guilty. She obviously believed I'd keep it."

"Oh, Marnie, for heaven's sake, don't put that on yourself. Maybe she gave you first dibs on the house, but if you don't want it, then we just have to know that she's operating in the unseen realm and will bring around the next person who should get it. How's that?"

I stare at him until he asks me to stop looking at him. He says he can't bear it when people stare at him. Then he says, "Anyway, the very last thing Blix would have ever wanted from you is guilt. Either keep the house or pass it along to someone else. Suit yourself. That's what she would have wanted. Do what makes you happy."

"But what will you do if I sell it?"

He stiffens. "What will *I* do? I'll either stay here or I'll go someplace else. And so will Jessica and Sammy. We're all very portable humans, you know. I realize I look like a guy who doesn't have any options, but even I can find another place to live."

I feel my face reddening. "I'm sorry. I didn't mean—"

"No more sorry or guilt for this conversation. It's met its quota."

Just then a tabby cat comes running into the room, meowing like he's in midconversation and needs to tell Patrick something immediately.

"And who is *this*? Are you the guy who steals Patrick's wallet and orders cans of tuna on the Internet?" I lean down to pet him, and he runs right over and brushes against my hands.

"This is Roy. He's the real tenant here, and he's after your cookies. I'm the one who misses Blix, and he's the one who thinks we should have cookies and possibly fry up some fish and clean the litter box more often."

I straighten myself up. "You miss her. I'm sorry. It must feel like a huge loss."

He turns away a bit, looks toward the living room. "I do. Very much. And although it's been great to meet you, I'm afraid I really do have to get back to alarming the population about rheumatoid arthritis."

"Oh! Of course," I say. "And, Patrick, thank you. It—it really is so nice to meet you." I want to say to him that he is far from hideous, that the light that shines out from his eyes knocks me right out—but how do you say those things? So I stick out my hand, and after only a flicker of hesitation, he takes it. His hand is leathery and I can feel the rough ridge where new tissues were probably grafted on. I feel an involuntary shiver go through me, and Patrick looks right into my eyes.

"You see?" he says. "I warn people, but it gets them every time just the same."

And then the very worst thing happens, which is that as I'm backing out of the room, I turn too quickly toward the front door and trip on a piece of carpet and bonk myself into a sculpture that's sitting on the bookshelf, and it goes toppling over into the bank of computers, bouncing once and then smashing on the floor.

"Oh, no! Oh my God! Oh, I'm so sorry!" I say, but even as he's shrugging his shoulders and telling me I shouldn't worry about it, I notice he's heading for the kitchen, probably looking for paper towels or a broom. I say that I'll sweep things up, but he keeps saying, "I shouldn't have left that piece there, it could have happened to anyone."

"No, it's me, I'm far too clumsy!" I tell him. "I'm so, so very sorry!"

I feel like I'm about to cry. I am over-the-top sad and crazy, and finally there is nothing to do but leave. The quota of sorries has been said for the whole day, and I have to leave this sad, funny man sweeping up shards of a sculpture that he probably made with his whole heart and soul and that I have now broken forever.

TWENTY-EIGHT
MARNIE

The next week, Jessica takes me out for Brooklyn Lessons. Apparently I have not been doing well at Brooklynizing myself.

It's all because I referred to the subway as the metro. I mean, I knew it was the subway, but I figured the words *metro* and *subway* were interchangeable. Same thing, right? Wrong! Then I said that Lola was sweeping the steps, not the stoop. Then later I called Paco's store down the street "a convenience store."

That brought Jessica charging right down the stairs, banging on the door, and holding up her phone and laughing. "Has no one ever said the word *bodega* to you?" she said.

"I thought a bodega was kind of a bar and possible whorehouse," I said, and that made her come over and hug me, she was laughing so hard.

"Okay. What's the cheese they put on pies? And by pie, I mean pizza."

"Pies are pizza?"

"No. Pizzas are pies. Come on. What's the cheese?"

"Mozzarella."

"No! Oh my God. It's *muzzarell*. You can call it *moots* if you want. Do *not* say moz-za-rella in a restaurant around here. Promise me. And do not ever let anyone see you eating pizza with a fork, no matter how hot it is or how hungry you are. The ridicule and shame will be everlasting."

So today, her day off, we ride on the subway—where you use a Metro*Card* but God forbid you call the whole enterprise the *metro*.

"I still like driving a car the best," I tell her. "Except here, where I'd probably go insane and start driving on the sidewalk."

"You're such a Californian and Floridian. Subways are much better for people- watching, although it's very important that you do not make direct eye contact. The best part is that you get to learn gymnastics routines on the subway when the school kids get on."

The gold shimmers so much I am nearly blinded.

I know what that means. It means that Jessica is going to start talking about Andrew again. She thinks she's complaining about him, but as I watch her speak, all I can see is the pink aura around her, and the way her face lights up when she talks about him. Oh, but there is such a wounded heart underneath that light.

It's okay. She'll be okay.

Later I give money to a homeless man, who tells me he has a secret for me. He was once president of the United States, he whispers, but they made him sleep outside the White House in the park, so he resigned. He says that there are some things people should not have to put up with, especially when they're too hungry, and so I go into Brooklyn Muffin and buy him a sandwich, and when I come out and give it to him, Jessica shakes her head and says I am just like Blix.

Walking home, we're on Bedford Avenue when I see an adorable little flower shop, with pots of chrysanthemums and other greenery outside on the sidewalk. The name, scrawled on the door, in white script, is Best Buds. And I know I have to go in there.

"You know what? You can head home if you want, but I need to get Patrick some flowers."

Jessica's eyebrows go up in little peaks. "You have to get *Patrick* some *flowers*?"

"Yes. I took him some cookies the other day, and—"

"Wait. You took him some *cookies*?"

"Will you stop it? Yes, I took him some chocolate chip cookies because I wanted to meet him, and we were having a conversation, and things got a little animated, and I knocked one of his sculptures off the table and smashed it."

"Oh, no."

"Oh, yes. It was kind of horrible actually. So I've been trying to think of how to make it up to him. And maybe flowers would be nice. It's kind of drab in his apartment."

"Is it? He's never invited me in."

"Besides the smashing of his artwork, I think I made at least five hundred other mistakes with him."

"He's tough. Only Blix had the magic touch with him. I've never been able to get so much as a conversation going." She shifts her bag to her other shoulder. "Listen," she says. "If you don't mind, I'm going to head straight home. Sammy's going to be getting off the school bus soon, and I should meet him. Good luck with your Patrick project, though." She wrinkles her nose. "You're kind of sweet, you know that?" She starts down the street and then turns and points at me. "The cheese on the pizza! Go!"

"Moots!"

"And how do we eat pizza?"

"With our hands!"

It's glorious inside Best Buds—all tropically fragrant and moist, with greenery in every corner, along with spikes of flowers: roses, tulips, gerbera daisies, mums. The perfect place for a Floridian. Orchids tower in one corner of the softly illuminated cooler, looking like birds preparing for takeoff. I take deep breaths and try to think what would be the best flower for Patrick: the gerbera daisy or the mum plant? An orchid he'd have to take care of, or a bouquet of roses?

I finally take a bouquet of red and yellow roses up to the front counter and wait in line to be rung up by the slightly harried cashier. Two women are standing at the counter, looking unhappy, and the dark-haired one says to the other, "Come on! We're getting a baby because of him, and I want to thank him. I'll write him the letter if you won't."

The other woman, who is wearing a ponytail and an emerald-green pashmina that I am coveting, folds her arms over her chest and says, "No! The flowers are enough. More than enough. If you write to him, believe me, he'll be over all the time. I know this guy. He'll be all up in our business."

"Some daisies and a nice short letter then. He doesn't even know yet that the pregnancy test was positive. I think he deserves to know *that*."

The ponytailed woman scowls and looks away. Our eyes meet and she suddenly laughs. "Can you *believe* this conversation?" she says to me. "How to thank your sperm donor and make sure he knows he's *only* a sperm donor."

"Well," I say. "What about this? What if you sent him the flowers and a card that says, 'Thanks for the strong swimmers! We got a hit!'"

They look at each other and grin. And then the first woman grabs the pen and writes my message on the card, and they both give me a high five.

After they leave, the next man in line orders a gigantic bouquet. The cashier, who by now has chattily told me that her name is Dorothy and that she's actually the owner of the shop, is trying to get his bouquet just right. He's kind of grim faced and unhappy looking, with such a muddy aura. Then the woman in line behind him laughs and says to him, "Wow, *dude*! Tell me this: Are you in trouble at home, or are you just a fantastic person?"

I see Dorothy flinch a little, and the man looks down at his shoes and mumbles in a low, dreadful voice: "Not in trouble. My wife died of breast cancer two months ago, and every Friday I put a bouquet on her grave."

There's a horrible silence as he reaches over and takes the bouquet. Dorothy thanks him and squeezes his hand. Nobody knows where to look, and I don't know who I feel sorrier for—the woman customer or him. She's turned the color of wax paper, and she tries to say something to him, tries to apologize, but he roughly turns away, and walks out, head down, ignoring all of us.

"Whew," somebody says. Dorothy mops her forehead.

"You didn't know," I say to the woman.

She puts her head in her hands. "Why am I always, always *doing* this kind of thing? I shouldn't be allowed out of the house! What is *wrong with me*?"

"You didn't mean any harm," I say. "He knows that. He would have been nicer about the whole thing except that he's a wreck just now."

"That's it. I am taking a vow of silence," she tells me. Dorothy says, "Aw, you don't have to do that. It's all going to be okay. People gotta get through as best they can, you know?"

"Come over here and smell these gardenias," I say. "They'll change your brain chemistry."

"They will?" the woman says, and I shrug. I really have no idea. I tell her they *might*. She laughs. As soon as she's gone, along with all the other customers and their problems, Dorothy turns to me and says, "So when can you start?"

"Start what?"

"Working here. Can I get you to take a job here?"

"Well . . ." I look around. Really? Should I go to work? And then I know that I definitely should. I'll get to come here every day and smell flowers and talk to people. "I'm afraid I really don't know much about arranging flowers," I say.

Dorothy shrugs. "Flowers, schmowers. I can teach you that. What I'm needing is a listen-to-the-story person. When can you start?"

"Well. Okay," I tell her. "I could start tomorrow, I guess."

She comes around the counter and hugs me. She has a slight limp, and straight gray hair pushed back off her face, and a sweet, sweet smile that transforms her tired eyes. "Come tomorrow at ten, okay? We can go over some things. I can't pay a lot, but we'll figure out something. Part-time okay?"

"Yes. Yes, part-time is great!"

I'm halfway down the block before I remember I need to tell her something critical—so I hurry back to the shop and call out to her.

"Dorothy! One thing: I'm moving away at the end of the year! So this is temporary. Is that okay?"

She comes out, holding on to a rose stem. "What? Oh! No, that doesn't matter a bit," she says. "Whatever."

And that appears to be that. I'm employed.

I write to Patrick:

Studying Brooklyn today with Jessica as my teacher. Pizzas are pies! Metro is subway. Convenience store is a bodega. #whoknew

Youse are doing awesome. Watch out, or soon you'll be saying fuggedaboutit.

Also I accidentally may have gotten a job in a flower shop.

I didn't know people could accidentally turn into florists. Are you happy about this?

I think so. I also think I need to go do a bunch of New York things. Carnegie Hall, jazz clubs, Brooklyn Bridge, Empire State Building, Broadway show, Times Square.

(Patrick shuddering involuntarily, can barely type) Report back. I'll be cheering you on from the curmudgeon seats inside my dungeon.

You wouldn't come?

Marnie? Hello? I thought I explained to you that I'm an introvert. #ugly #recluse #irredeemablymisanthropic

And what is there to say to *that*, except what I do say, which is:

Open your door when you get a chance. I've left you a present. A pitiful attempt to make up for your beautiful sculpture that I smashed. Though nothing ever can, I know.

Marnie, Marnie, Marnie. You didn't have to do this. That sculpture was from another time. Another Patrick who doesn't exist anymore. Not worth thinking about. You did me a favor. #outwithold

TWENTY-NINE
MARNIE

One evening, as I'm putting away the supper dishes and Noah is sitting at the table scrolling through his phone, he says, "I just want you to know that losing you was the worst thing that ever happened to me."

I look out the window at the lights of Brooklyn. I can see right into other people's apartments—see them gesturing; a man and woman are talking in one window; in another, a man is lifting a barbell high into the air. My stomach has dropped to my knees.

With difficulty, I manage to say, "Noah. Come off it. You don't believe that even while you're saying it."

"I do believe it," he says. "It's true. And now some other guy has you. I lost out, and it was my own fault." He shakes his head and smiles at me. "I'm just not husband material. Waaaay too fucked up."

"Way," I agree.

He says a whole bunch of things after that.

He says, forgive me for saying this, but I don't think you are even remotely in love with the guy you're seeing now.

He says, remember the time we woke up in the middle of the night and we were already having sex, but both of us had been sound asleep and we don't know how it happened?

He says, this is kind of like a secret time in our lives. Time out of time. Together but apart.

"Not together," I say with difficulty.

"Have you told your family I'm here?"

"Of course not."

He smiles and comes over and takes the platter out of my hands and places it up on the shelf I was straining to reach. He's Noah, so he doesn't simply *come over* and take the platter—he kind of *saunters* over. And when he reaches for it, his hand brushes against me very, very slightly. And then after he puts the platter up where it belongs, he stays there, standing so close I can see the little dots of stubble of his beard, can feel his breathing as though it's my own breath he's taking. His eyes are on mine and I know from the expression on his face what's going to happen next. He's going to lean down and kiss me.

I brace myself against it. I think as hard as I can: *no no no no.*

Then to my surprise, he turns away and goes back to the table, where he picks up his phone, and giving me a short wave, he leaves the house. The front door bangs behind him.

I am shaking. I get a glass of water from the sink. A man in a window across the way is dancing. A man is dancing, and I am standing here drinking water, and somehow now I know that it is only a matter of time until Noah and I get to the kissing part.

I have never wanted anybody more in my life.

Jeremy calls me the next day on his way to work. I can tell I'm on speakerphone in his car, because I get to hear all the Jacksonville traffic—the whooshes of trucks going by and the snippets of other people's radios as he passes them. I'm on my way to work, too, walking along Bedford Avenue to Best Buds, studying the people who are rushing past.

"Hey! How are you?" I say when I pick up.

As he always does, he plunges right into the list of things he's done since the last time we talked. Went for a swim last night. Played checkers with his mom. Had pork chops for dinner. Went to bed early.

"How are the patients? Any good stories?"

"Well, Mrs. Brandon came in yesterday, and you know how it is. Poor thing, her sciatica is still bothering her, and she's blaming the treatment, so I asked her if she's taking the anti-inflammatory drugs, and she said she's not because they hurt her stomach, and I said she should take probiotics at the same time, and she said she'd heard of those but never knew if they were safe."

"Huh," I say.

"Oh, but there's this. You'll be happy to know I got the carpets cleaned in the waiting room. Looks nice. A guy came in and said he could clean the whole office for fifty dollars, and I didn't know if that was a good deal or not, but I don't think the building management has cleaned the carpets in the entire time I've been there. Did you notice how soiled they were?"

"I'm afraid I didn't," I tell him.

"Well, they're awful. I thought you would have noticed."

"But sounds like they're clean now," I say.

"Yes. Oh, yes."

I let a beat of silence go by and then say, "Hey, guess what! I got a job."

"You got a job? In Brooklyn? Why would you do that?"

"Because—because I think it'd be good for me to be out around people more, and this woman in a florist shop asked me if I wanted to work there because I was sort of talking to some customers there, and she—"

I stop talking because I realize he's been trying to interrupt me the entire time.

"No, I realize what a job will be like," he says. "But what I'm wondering is—why are you embedding yourself in this community if you're going to leave soon?"

"Well, it's three months. I can work for three months, can't I?"

"I don't know. I thought you'd be busy getting the house ready to sell or something. Not going out and working in—what? A shop of some kind?"

"For a florist."

"Yeah. A florist. You do realize I'm counting on you coming back, don't you?" He laughs, a stiff little chuckle that rings completely false.

"I told the woman that I'm only here until the end of the year," I tell him. "Don't worry. I'm coming back."

"Well," he says and pretends to growl. "See that you do. Because there's *somebody* on this call who's getting very, very lonely without his girlfriend around."

I toy with the idea of dropping my phone in the storm drain.

After that, it takes a little bit to put this conversation back on solid ground again. He tells me the weather is still hot, that he hopes to go see Natalie and Brian tonight, that he thinks Amelia looks like me. And then he says brightly, "Oh! I told my mom about our engagement. I know, I know. We agreed not to tell everybody until later on, but she was so down the other night that I wanted to cheer her up. And it did! She was thrilled. Over the moon."

"Oh, you know what? I've just gotten to work!" I say. "Gotta go! Have a good one!"

I click the button, and jam the phone back in my bag. I'm nowhere near Best Buds, but I can't take any more.

What I want to know is what happened to the old snarky boy from high school, my old misfit friend, the one who could make me crack up with his constant sarcastic little asides? More and more I'm aware that

that guy went through some kind of unfortunate cleansing or deprogramming situation.

I'm going to have to figure a way to bring him back.

In the flower shop that day, I help a woman pick out a bouquet for a man she loved who left her when they couldn't have children, and then he married someone else and now that other woman has just had a baby, and—well, she wants them to know that she is happy for them, that she is genuinely, tragically, fully, and confusedly happy for them. After I make up the bouquet she requests, I make up one for her, too, and pay for it myself. I think she needs it more than the couple, frankly.

There's a guy who comes in and tells me proudly that he just proposed marriage to his girlfriend of nine years, and also today happens to be the day she gave birth to their triplets, and now he wants to send her three bouquets of pink roses. He disappears while I'm making the bouquets, and I find him sitting on the floor, his head in his hands, sobbing. "How do I deserve this?" he says to me over and over again.

And an old woman in a baggy dress and sweater who comes in for one red carnation and pays for it with coins. She buys one every week, which is all she can afford, she tells me. It's to remember her son who got shot. She tells me about his life, and how when he was five he told her that he was going to take care of her always, when he grew up.

A man with laughing eyes orders daisies for his girlfriend and writes: "I'm going to be with you forever—or at least until I get deported."

I feel leveled by every story I hear.

One afternoon I'm at home, talking on the phone with my mom, who is telling me about the progress in her lifelong argument with my father over which way to hang the toilet paper—she goes with under—when the doorbell rings.

When I go to answer it, there's an older, smiling man with deep-blue eyes standing on the stoop. He's holding a brown paper bag that seems to be thrashing around in his hand. He takes his other hand to steady it, and I *think* I hear him talking to the bag.

"Hello?" I say.

"Oh! Hi. I was just trying to calm the boys down a little bit here."

"The boys?" This may be why a person shouldn't open the door without getting a background check on whoever is standing there.

"Sorry," he says. "I'm Harry. I'd shake your hand but I better hold on to this bag instead. Anyway, I was friends with Houndy, and I don't know why, but I went to his traps today, and found these beauties, and I just thought—well, I knew you were living here now, and I thought maybe . . . you know . . . you like lobster, and since these were Houndy's really, I'd, uh, bring them over and see if you might want them."

"Oh!" I say. This is a relief. "Lobsters! How wonderful!"

"Yeah. Well, they're for you. I feel like Blix . . . and Houndy . . . they woulda wanted you to have them." He has that expression that everyone else here has when mentioning Blix and Houndy: sad yet smiling. Remembering something.

I ask him in for a cup of tea, but he says he can't. He points to a pickup running at the curb. A woman waves to me from the passenger seat. So I thank him and take the bag of wiggling lobsters upstairs and wrestle the bag into the refrigerator and slam it shut.

I think I can hear them in there disrupting the eggs and the milk.

I text Patrick.

Refrigerator is possessed by an alarmingly active bag of sea creatures with claws and tails. A gift from Houndy's friend. Please help!

What nature of help do you wish? Pro tip: I hear that some people like them with drawn butter and lemon.

May I . . . could we . . . I need help with all aspects of this project. Chasing, cooking, eating.

Ah, well. In the interest of being a good neighbor, I invite you to bring your sea creatures down. Also I believe Blix has some rather formidable lobster pots. We can take care of this problem.

It turns out that there are four actual living beasts in the bag when I finally get it down to Patrick's kitchen, and they are not interested in hanging out quietly while we prepare to boil them on the stove.

Neither one of us has ever cooked a lobster before, so we call up a YouTube video on how you do it, and we drink a glass of wine to fortify ourselves while we watch it. Apparently someone has to boil water and then pick up this *thing*, this animal, and plunk it in the boiling water. It might make a noise when that happens.

I take a deep sip of wine. "Okay, I'll go back upstairs and make a salad while you plunge the lobsters, and then I'll come down when they're done."

He says, "*I* don't want to plunge the lobsters."

"Well, somebody has to."

We sit there, staring at the computer monitor. There's a crash from the kitchen, and we turn to each other.

"They're taking over," he whispers. "They're going to try to put *us* in the boiling water."

"We've got to go see."

"Don't let them lure you into the pot. That's the important thing."

We go to the kitchen in time to see all four lobsters scuttling along the floor, waving their claws at us.

"What the hell?" he says. "They're making a run for it! The video did *not* talk about this part!"

"I think we're going to have to pick them up," I say. One's gone behind the stove. "We have to chase them down. And by *we*, I hope you know I mean you."

"Wait. Why me?"

"First of all, because it's your apartment, and secondly, because I am a known coward, and you're not. Also, they now look like giant cockroaches to me."

"Okay," he says grimly. He puts on an oven mitt and starts running around after them, while they clatter along, going in circles. He finally gets one and holds it in midair and does a mock bow. "Now what am I supposed to *do* with this monster?"

"Put him in the sink. Or no. He'll get out of the sink—in the bathtub."

It takes twenty more minutes to catch two more, and then we have to move the stove in order to capture the fourth, and by then we're laughing so hard we can't even stand up.

And we have a tub full of lobsters that we cannot ever imagine eating.

The night's dinner turns out to be pizza, and the lobsters spend a luxurious day and night in Patrick's bathtub, until Paco finally comes over and takes them away.

I don't work at Best Buds on Friday, which is good because that means that Sammy can wait here every other Friday afternoon for his dad to pick him up for their weekend together. Jessica has to work, and besides, she's never gotten all that good at being nice when Andrew comes to get their son.

"Do you think my dad and my mom will ever get back together again?" Sammy asks me one day. I glance at him. He has a nonchalant look on his face behind those huge round glasses, but I can hear the anxiety in his voice. He keeps tapping on the kitchen table with his pencil.

"Well, what do you think?" I ask, stalling for time.

"I think they still love each other. They're both always asking me about the other one. My dad goes, 'How's your mom? Does she mention me?' And my mom goes, 'What did he say to you about the breakup with what's-her-name?'"

"Hmm."

"Blix said they still love each other. They *match*, is what she said." He draws a circle on the table where a drop of milk has spilled.

"Really? She said that?" I look at him with interest. They *do* match, I want to tell him. They absolutely belong together. I'm gratified to hear Blix thought so, too.

"Yeah. I think she was going to do a spell or something on them, but . . . well, then she died." He shrugs and looks away.

"Did she do a lot of spells?"

"Yeah," he says. "Like, one time when I couldn't find my backpack, she snapped her fingers and she said we could *imagine* the backpack, and then I knew where it was, but a few minutes earlier I couldn't have ever remembered that. So that makes me think she put spells on things."

"Really!"

"Yes, and one time the subway wouldn't come and wouldn't come, and Blix said she had to put a spell on it, and then it came right then. But she said it like it was kind of a joke. And the subway would have come anyway, you know."

"True."

"That's why I like coming here and hanging out. Because sometimes if I close my eyes, I think Blix is still right here, too."

He puts down his glass of milk just so on the table and turns his face to me. His eyes are wide and wise; like a lot of only children, he's older than his years. "So do you believe in all that stuff Blix believed in?"

"Like what are you talking about? Specifically."

He looks me over. "Oh, you know." He waves his hand around. "How she could make stuff happen. Do spells and stuff like that."

"I'm not so sure."

He gives me an appraising look. "She told my mom that you were a matchmaker. So I think you could get them back together again. How are you going to know if you won't even *try*?"

"I don't know, Sammy. I mean, your mom is pretty sure she doesn't want to have anything to do with your dad right now, so maybe we have to wait and see. Not try to change things. You know? If it's meant to be, they'll find their way. Right?"

He gives me a look that holds so much disgust that I almost laugh out loud.

"My childhood is practically over!" he says. "I'm in double digits already. What if they don't get together until I'm all grown up? That would be the stupidest thing in the whole world."

"But isn't your dad . . . living with somebody else?"

"No! That's the thing! My mom always liked to say that, but he wasn't really. He had a girlfriend who would stay over sometimes, but I think she's gone because I never see her anymore, and when I ask him about her, he gets very quiet. Says it's nothing for me to worry about."

He slumps down in his chair and then looks up at me from underneath his fringe of bangs. "Blix had a book of spells. You could use that and maybe you'd learn how to do a bunch of stuff. It could help you."

"I heard she had a book, but I've never seen it."

"It's right over there," he says. He gets up and points to a bookcase in the corner, filled with cookbooks. "This is the book she showed me when she looked up a way to make my sore throat go away."

Sure enough, there's a book called *The Encyclopedia of Spells* sitting right out there for anybody to see, a book I'd somehow never noticed. The binding of the book has a picture of a vine with red flowers. Frankly, it doesn't look all that legitimate. I think a real book of witches' spells would look secretive, with hieroglyphics. You wouldn't be able to read the title from across the room.

Just then the doorbell rings, and he jumps up and grabs his backpack. "Don't tell my dad," he says. "And think about it. Read the book! Pleasepleasepleaseplease!"

After he leaves, I finish drinking my tea. Periodically I glance over at the book and think about getting it off the shelf and looking at it, just to see . . . you know . . .

But something holds me back. I go outside, sweep the stoop, then go get some chicken salad at Paco's bodega for dinner, and find myself watching a lively neighborhood conversation there between the regulars about which kind of people read the *New York Daily News* and which ones read the *New York Post*, and whether you can tell the difference merely by looking at people. Paco, in the minority, maintains that you can't, and looks to me to back up his position.

I shrug and he laughs at his mistake. "How you going to know? *You're* an incomer!" he says. "Now, Blix—she would have talked all day about this."

Everybody gets quiet. It's as though they're observing a moment of silence for Blix.

"She was *la maga*. Our magician," Paco says softly. And he wipes his eyes.

THIRTY
MARNIE

I am not a *maga*, so I don't pretend to know how these things happen. But two nights later I'm walking home from Best Buds and I look up and see Noah approaching the house from the opposite direction—sauntering, really, that sexy walk I remember—and the air fills with little crackles of something, and when we reach the front door, my heart is pounding like it's going to shake apart. He takes my hand, and we practically fall inside, mashed against the wall with our bodies pressed against each other and his mouth hard on mine.

All I can think is: *Oh my God.*

The door slams; he's closed it with his foot, and the noise of that makes us open our eyes.

His hands are in my hair, removing a clip I'd used to pin it up. He says into my neck, "You've got me crazy! Being near you but having you no longer in love with me is killing me."

My phone rings right then, and I work it out of my jeans pocket and look at it. Natalie.

"Listen, I've got to take this," I say, and he releases me with a groan and we go inside the apartment, and he heads upstairs to the kitchen.

"How are you?" I sit down on the floor and listen as she launches into a litany of complaints. Brian is working too hard; she's lonely at home with the baby. She needs me there. Nobody keeps her company in the daytime. And she's sorry but she feels betrayed by my decision to stay in Brooklyn, even for three months. It's as though we'd reunited and worked out a wonderful plan for our lives, and then I went and changed everything. Backed out. And now she's just heard from Jeremy that I even have a *job* here—and what is *that* about?

Listen, I want to say to her. *I am . . . I am . . . falling again.*

Noah comes back downstairs, with a plate of grapes and some cheese. He sits down next to me and starts peeling grapes and dangling them in front of my mouth very suggestively, which makes me laugh.

"This isn't funny," says Natalie. "You didn't even tell me about the job! How come I have to hear it from *him*?"

Noah starts unbuckling my sandals and easing one off my foot. I'm having a little trouble breathing.

"I have to go," I say to her. "I'll call you back."

And then—well, it's as though we've gone mad, ripping off each other's clothes and then making love right there on the rug in Blix's living room, and it's like no time has passed at all; he's what I've been missing, his mouth and hands and his breath against my cheek, and I have about a million feelings because he's so familiar and exciting, sexy and infuriating—but then, it's over. And the second we're finished, as he's rolling off me, it slams into me that I'm the worst person ever. Jeremy's face rises up before me, his eyes wide and hurt, and I hate that I have betrayed him.

But you know something? Even as I'm sitting up, grabbing my clothes in the cold air, feeling both guilty about Jeremy and disappointed in myself, there's a big part of me that wants to block out all thoughts and live in this blinding light of a moment.

And so I do. I just do. Maybe making love with Noah is something that is bad but necessary. Maybe I'll understand later what I'm doing. Maybe I can't think about it now.

Noah stays in my room that night and the night after that and the night after that, and the moon outside the window shines on us, and cold air seeps through the cracks where the window sash doesn't quite meet the frame, and branches scritch against the building like in a horror movie. These are the first really cold nights, and he puts his arms around me and we lie there each night after making love before sleep overtakes us, and I listen to him breathing and look at the little chip of the moon from my pillow.

There's something that felt so inevitable about all of this, like he's an old habit that won't go away. I don't ask myself if it's love, or if I can trust him, or if this is the right thing to do, whole-life-wise. Because it's not. God knows it's not even close to being the right thing.

I feel awful. Here's Jeremy in my head: *You're doing this to me again?*

I close my eyes. During the day, I tell myself to stop. I tell myself that this is simply my need to resolve the past before I truly can accept my grown-up life with Jeremy. And maybe this is a little moment in time—*closure*, that's it—and I'll get Noah completely out of my system and I can move on.

The fact is, this is just a thing I'm doing right now.

I'm sleeping with my ex.

And like the job at Best Buds, like the house in Brooklyn, like the way the sun slants through the trees that are rapidly losing their leaves—it's all only temporary.

A time out of time.

I may have forgotten to wonder what *Noah's* motivation is.

And then one night when I'm nearly asleep, he asks me if he can see the letter Blix wrote to me—you know, just out of curiosity. I am suddenly wide-awake, on alert. Little prickles go off behind my eyes, like the beginning of a headache, and I say no. So that's what he's after—Blix's letter? The thought that he may try to use it against me flits across the landscape of my mind.

"But why not?" he says. He's propped up on one elbow, trailing his fingers down my arm, tickling me slightly. "I just want to *read* it. See what my great-aunt and my wife had in common."

"No. It's private. It was only to me. And please don't forget that I'm your ex-wife."

"But she was *my* great-aunt, and she didn't leave me a letter. I feel like—well, I wish I'd gotten to know her better. I'm having a moment, that's all."

I sit up in the bed. Sleep has vanished.

He laughs, seeing my face. "Okay, forget it! Forget I even said anything. Go back to sleep."

But of course I can't. He closes his eyes, but I stare at him for so long that he finally opens his eyes and lets out a loud, exasperated sigh. "Marnie, for God's sake. What's with you? I merely asked if I could—"

"I know what you asked. But it's intrusive. And disturbing. You want this house, don't you? That's what this is really about. You think if you read the letter, you can find out something that might mean I shouldn't get the house. That's what's going on." I put my face right down next to his, eyeball to eyeball.

He moves back, batting my hands away from him. "Stop it! I don't know what you're even talking about."

"Yes, you do."

He flops over on his back and puts his hands behind his head. "Okay, stop being a lunatic and I'll tell you." He takes a deep breath. "My parents are really *perturbed* about the way the will worked out. As you know. So my mom—it was my *mom's* idea—*she* thought that as long as I'm here, one *avenue* we should check out is what Blix said to you in the letter. That's all. She asked me to ask you if I could read it, you know, just to see."

"One *avenue*? *One* avenue? See? I knew this wasn't all aboveboard."

He gets up on one elbow. "Well, what's it to you, really? I mean, you're going to sell this place. You don't really care anything about it. And I'm not defending my mom because you *know* I am not one hundred percent in agreement with Wendy Spinnaker about *anything*, but she said to me that there's at least a chance you're not going to want to stay here the whole three months since you're a *Flah-ridian*, so they should be on the watch for ways to keep the house from going to a charity. And she wondered if I might just ask you if I could see the letter. Okay?"

"Uh-huh," I say. "Right. Sure. I'm surprised she's not rigging the place with booby traps to get me to move out."

"Don't give her any ideas. Now could we go back to sleep, please?"

I flop back down on my pillow and spend the next ten minutes tossing and turning.

Finally I say, "Noah, I think I need to sleep alone tonight."

"Fine," he says. He gets up and goes back to his own room, and I close the door behind him and lock it. Then I get the letter out of my purse and sit on the floor reading it again.

The letter, Blix's voice, pulls at my heart.

I told you when we met that you are in line for a big, big life . . . Darling, this is your time.

I sit there for a moment trying to figure out why I feel so violated. Then I roll up the letter and hide it in the sleeve of my sweatshirt way at the back of my underwear drawer.

THIRTY-ONE
MARNIE

One morning later that week the doorbell rings at just past eight. Surely not more lobsters! I have the day off from the flower shop, so I'm still in my bathrobe, losing my daily fight with the coffee press thing, and Noah is choking down a piece of toast and reading the messages on his phone, getting ready to go to class. Of course we argue about who has to answer the front door. I say he should since he's dressed; he says I should since he has to leave in a couple of minutes.

So I go, and Lola is standing there, wearing her marvelous red sneakers and a gray sweatshirt, carrying coffees in a cardboard holder and a bag of something that I'm thinking could possibly be scones. Or doughnuts. She looks up at me with a huge grin.

"Wow, are you the coffee fairy?" I say. "And does this mean that today I don't have to vanquish the evil spirit that lives in that coffee press? Please, please, come in!"

"Are you sure, dear, because I don't want to interrupt your privacy," she says. "But today I just couldn't help myself. I used to come over and eat breakfast every morning with Blix and Houndy, and I—well,

I just feel like this is where I'm supposed to be." She shrugs. "I know that's not right, this isn't my house, and Blix isn't here anymore, but—"

"Stop! Come in! I've been wanting to see you."

"Well, if you're sure . . ." She steps in and looks around, and once again it's like she's drinking in the surroundings, gaining strength simply from being in Blix's house. Then she turns her eyes to me and says quietly, "Also, I need to talk to you about love if you have some time."

"Love? Sure, I have time. Who doesn't have time to talk about love?"

Then, wouldn't you know, Noah comes charging out of the kitchen as though the word *love* summoned him, juggling his coffee cup while he shrugs his way into his backpack, and I see her eyes widen just slightly at the sight of him. Of us. Even though we're not an us, I know we look like it.

"Hi, Lola," he says. "Off to school. Marnie, see you later."

"Fine," I say, embarrassed.

He looks for a moment like he's going to come over and kiss me good-bye, but then he just says, "Keep it real, ladies." And he's gone, slamming the door behind him so hard that the glass rattles. I look over at Lola and her knowing little smile.

"Yep, he's still here," I say. "It's weird."

"Well," she says. "It's certainly on topic."

"Noah is not about love. Noah is about the convenience of living here because he's taking classes."

"Oh," she says. "You forget that I've learned a few things from Blix."

We go upstairs to the kitchen, and just as she's gotten settled in the rocking chair by the window, there's the sound of footsteps on the stairs. Sammy bangs his scooter into the kitchen door, like he does every morning, and I hear Jessica saying, "You've got to stop doing that. Marnie isn't Blix, and she might be sleeping," and *he* says, "She isn't sleeping. And I just want to say good morning to her!"

Lola claps her hands. "Oh, I've missed this so much! Sammy heading for school! Ah! It's been way too long!"

I open the door, and Sammy runs into my arms. Jessica told me that I've inherited him along with the house. Then he goes over and hugs Lola, too, and Jessica dabs at her eyes and blows kisses, and once we're all hugged and they're on their way, Lola looks at me and says, "So do you think you love him?"

At first I think she means Sammy, but then I know what she really means.

"Who? *Noah*? No. You can't be serious! *No!*"

"It's okay if you do," she says. "Love is so complicated, isn't it? You probably had him figured out and filed away, and then look what happened: Blix gave you this house, and railroaded you right back with your ex! Damnedest thing in the world. Unintended consequences, I call it."

"But I don't love him."

"No, but you're sleeping with him," she says. "So there's that."

"Oh God. You can tell?"

She nods. "So, if I may ask, what happened to the guy back home?"

I groan. "He's still hanging in there. Listen, I'm just bad, I tell you. I was always the good girl who did everything she was supposed to. And now every day I tell myself that I'm not going to have anything to do with Noah again, and then at night . . . I don't know . . ."

She smiles at me. "I get it. You're just having that year of life when you're like a magnet. Sweetie, you're *attracting* everything to you. Situations and lovers and life—you're pulling stuff in all over the place! It's my theory that everybody gets one of those years. It passes, don't worry."

"It's not dangerous? Because it feels kind of awful."

"Well. If you stop at one year, then it's not dangerous. How old are you anyway?"

"Twenty-nine."

"Perfect! See? You're going to be fine. It'll run its course, trust me," she says. "And just so you know, I think Blix approves of this."

I look at her closely while I'm stirring cream and sugar into my coffee. "So . . . am I allowed to ask about the man who comes and picks you up? The man with the New Jersey plates? Is that the love you wanted to talk to me about?"

She scowls at me. "Well, yes. But first you need to know that he's not anywhere close to being somebody I could ever love."

"No?"

"Marnie, he was my husband's *best friend*."

"So . . . ?"

She purses her lips. "Can't you see what's wrong with that? I can't believe you matchmaking people! Do you have any scruples?"

"Clearly *I* don't. But I don't see why this—"

"Okay, I'll explain it all to you. Blix sent him to me. She told me as much. With all her little tricks and sending out vibes into the universe. Whatever. She *said* she was going to work on finding me a man to love, even though I said I didn't need one, and time passes, and one day, out of the blue, I get a call from William Sullivan. William Sullivan, my husband's best friend! Wants to see me. Catch up. Old times. You know. Has no idea that he's the subject of any kind of vibe being sent out! He just shows up."

I look at her blankly. "And . . . ?"

"And, Marnie, this is never going to work because I can't be romantically involved with William! He was like a brother to my husband! Walter and I used to go on family picnics with him and his kids and his wife!"

"He has a wife?"

"Had. He's a widower. Patricia, her name was. Perfectly lovely woman. And I am not going to kiss her husband."

"Does he want kissing? Maybe he wants a nice friendship, too."

"Oh, I don't know. Sometimes we'll be sitting in his car, and at a certain point I can feel his hand start to crawl along the back of the seat—in a very suggestive way."

"Wait. It *crawls*?" I am fascinated with everything about this story, and also intrigued with Lola's animated face, turning pinker and pinker, and then the spirals of sparkles distracting me by going off behind her head.

"*You* know how they do," she says. "How a man will just *snake* his hand along the back of the seat, thinking he's being so innocent, but clearly he's intending to put his arm around you. To pull you in! And he gets this shy, sort of sly look on his face. It's awful. Just awful. I'm embarrassed for him really."

I burst out laughing. "Lola, really? *Snakes*? And his *crawling hand*? Do you hear yourself? It sounds to me like it might be lovely, talking to somebody who knew you from before. He's safe. He knows you. He likes you." She is glaring at me, so I say, "But if you don't want him, then why are we spending so much time talking about him?"

"Because I saw you looking the other day when he came to pick me up, and I know you're like Blix, and I want you to stop thinking everything you're thinking about William and me. Just stop it. Blix thinks everybody should be like her and Houndy. If you've lost your partner, get another one. As if everybody's replaceable."

"Huh," I say.

She looks at me. "I was happily married for forty-two years and that chapter of my life is over. Who *needs* it? Who needs the bother of it? I've got my television programs and my bridge club ladies and the neighbors who come by, and the people at church—and do I really need to take a chance on some other *man*? Right now I've got everything just the way I like it. I told Blix I don't need another man. Somebody with opinions I'd have to pay attention to."

"Soooo . . . I take it this didn't sit too well with her?"

She shakes her finger at me, and there's an explosion of sparks all around her. "Let me tell you something about Blix. Blix the adventurer! I'm quite sure she still thinks that someday she and Houndy and this man, William Sullivan, and I are going to be frolicking around together in the afterlife—and we are so not, because when *I'm* in the afterlife, I'm going to be over in Walter's corner, sipping tea with him and not having to explain to him that I have a second husband who happens to be his old friend."

For a moment my mind is boggled with this view of the afterlife, in which we're all traipsing around between little bistro tables where our old friends and lovers are drinking their tea and noticing who we're talking to more than them. It sounds so much like eighth grade.

"That can't be what it's like!" I say. "And don't you really think that if it is, both Walter and William Sullivan will be evolved enough to want to know that you can sit with *both* of them at the same table in the afterlife—you and everybody else they ever loved? I think that's what the afterlife is going to be all about—that's when we're finally going to understand all the love stuff that confuses us now. It's going to be magnificent, all the Walters and Williams and Lolas and Blixes and Houndys all together!"

I look over at her: all the color has left her face, and in a low, panicky voice, she says, "Marnie. Oh, no! I can't breathe so well, and my heart is . . ."

And then, almost in slow motion, she falls right over.

Patrick takes one look at her and says she has to go to the hospital.

By the time he gets upstairs, of course, she's come to, and is even arguing about things. She wants to go home and get in bed.

But he's not having it.

She needs to go to the hospital, he says. Find out what's going on.

"What could it be?" she says in a wavery voice. She looks so nervous, it's like she's a little child dressed in a grandma costume, perhaps to be in a play.

"Well," he says, "it could be nothing, or it could be you drank too much coffee, or it could be . . . something they'll want to help you with." He's already calling 911.

Our eyes meet, and he smiles at me. She makes little murmuring sounds of distress.

"Marnie, are you going with her to the hospital, do you think?"

"Of course," I say. I know that Patrick can't go. He'd have a meltdown in a medical place, among strangers. He mouths the words "Thank you" and then he's talking to the dispatcher.

While he's on the phone, she gives me specific directions for what items she needs, and I go next door and get her pocketbook and her warm jacket, both of which just happen to be in her bedroom. No clothing because she won't be staying—she's positive of that.

I love how her house is dark and cool and filled with large pieces of old-people upholstered furniture, grandparent furniture. It's like a cave in here, with the shades all pulled down. There are tons of pictures of her and Walter and their two boys set out on every surface and hanging on the walls—Lola with red, fluffy hair cut in layers like petals, and Walter a slim, handsome man with laughing eyes. The boys look just like boys of any era: crew-cutted and freckled, wearing striped T-shirts, grinning at the camera, and then turning into handsome teenagers and finally bridegrooms—and then there are snapshots of them with their families. Far away.

There's a framed portrait of Walter next to her bed, and I pick it up and look at his aquiline nose, his blue eyes. "Walter," I tell him. "You old rascal, you know as well as I do that you've got to give her a sign you release her, don't you? You and I both know she needs the love and care of your old friend now."

When I turn, I notice the little gold sparkles are back, showing up tentatively around the curtains, like little fireflies at dusk.

I'm no *maga*, but it does seem to be kind of a coincidence that all those sparkles showed up right when we were getting to the heart of love in the afterlife.

I come home from the hospital that evening to find a dog on the stairs—or rather, the stoop. He's lying there at the top, and when I reach him, he stands up and wags his tail and licks my hand, like I'm his owner and he's been told to stay there until I return, and now his whole body is vibrating and saying, AT LAST YOU ARE HERE! HOW DID I GET SO LUCKY TO FIND YOU AT LAST, YOU WONDERFUL, BEAUTIFUL, KIND, ELEGANT CREATURE OF LOVE AND BY THE WAY DO YOU KNOW HOW TO OPERATE A CAN OPENER?

"No," I tell him. "I am not looking for a dog. I am moving back to Florida in another two months, and I can't take you with me."

He looks away and then looks back at me. I search through my purse for my keys, glancing over at Lola's dark house. The hospital is keeping her for a few days, so tomorrow morning I'm to take her a change of clothes, a decent nightgown, and some toiletries. She'll be fine for tonight, she told me in a quavery voice that had a distinct "not fine" undertone. Still, she is being brave. She has a room overlooking the river, and a roommate who likes the same television programs as she does. I sat in a chair next to her and didn't leave until they made me.

The dog makes a little sound and licks my hand with his soft, pink tongue.

I stare at him helplessly. I know exactly nothing about dogs except that they are dirty and they like to eat things, particularly human shoes. This one is a medium-sized brown-and-white one with floppy ears and big brown eyes, and when I open the front door, he bounds inside like he knows where the bones are hidden.

He hasn't been here for five minutes when some switch in his doggie brain gets activated, and suddenly he's dashing through the rooms, racing around in circles, leaping up on the couch and off again, zooming up the stairs, then down again, zigzagging through the bedrooms, and back into the living room. I can do nothing but stand by in amazement, leaping out of his way when necessary, and then finally laughing so hard I have to run to the bathroom.

Later, because he seems hungry, I go over to Paco's and buy some dog food and ask if anybody might know who he belongs to.

"A brown-and-white dog with floppy ears? I think he's *your* dog," says Paco with a laugh. "At least now he is. No, seriously. He's a stray. He hang around here sometimes and then go somewhere else for a while, but he always show up again."

Great. So he's a freelance dog. Available on the open market. Everybody in the store has advice for how much to feed him and how to check him for fleas and ticks, and then in the back, it turns out, Paco has shelves with dog collars and one leash, so I buy those, too. As well as a water dish and a food dish. A brush to brush him with. Just because.

"And I'd give that boy a bath before you let him up on the furniture," says a woman who's carrying a fat, smiling, drooling baby.

So when I get home, even though I'm exhausted, I fill up the bathtub with warm water and put towels down all across the bathroom floor. I get out my bottle of shampoo and go out in the hallway and say, "Here boy, here boy!" and Mr. Floppy Ears comes crashing around the corner and into the bathroom, where I scoop him up and try to lower him into the tub. He is having none of it. You would think I'd decided to drown him by the way he thrashes around and tries to use my body to help himself climb back out.

"It's okay . . . it's okay . . . ," I keep saying, but he is all wild-eyed, panting, and scrambling now to get out of the tub, churning up the water until I'm hit with a tidal wave so huge that even as it's soaking me, I'm laughing. This doggie, this bath—both are such antidotes to the earnest, businesslike, life-saving hospital with all its protocols and forms, all the danger lurking right around the next doorway.

"Okay! Okay! You gotta stop with this!" I say to him, and then clamber into the tub with him, still wearing my jeans and sweater, and he settles right down, as if even he is amazed at such craziness. He stands still then while I lather him up and scratch his ears, and he's panting and I'm trying not to get soap in his eyes and scare him even further. Then he gives me his paw, almost like an offering. A handshake of thanks.

That's how Noah finds us when he opens the bathroom door—both of us in the tub, covered in soapsuds, the dog with his head propped on the side of the tub, looking contented.

"What the hell?" Noah says. "What is *this*?"

"This is my new dog. I think I'm going to name him Bedford. It's my favorite avenue, I've decided."

"Wait. You bought a *dog*?"

"No and yes. I didn't buy him. He picked me, as it turns out. He was on the stoop when I got home. Waiting for me. And I do have a favorite avenue. Bedford is everything Driggs Avenue wishes it could be."

"Oh my God. Who *are* you, really? I don't even know you anymore."

"I'm me. And I'm giving him a bath so he can sleep on the bed. A lady at Paco's said I had to."

"I'm sorry, but that mutt is not sleeping with *me* in any bed."

I smile at him. Because that's just fine with me. I had already decided today that I am going to try not to sleep with Noah Spinnaker anymore. After he closes the bathroom door, I write my vow in soap on the tile. Not that it shows, but I know it's there.

"Bedford," I say, scratching him under the wet chin. "Already you are solving so many problems, boy!"

The next day is Halloween, and when I go to the hospital to visit Lola, I take her some candy corn as well as some clothes to wear. She looks dried out from the hospital air and exhausted from all the tests, but she says she's feeling better. They keep poking her with needles, she says. She misses her houseplants and her pictures of Walter. I tell her that I've somehow acquired a dog, and she says, "See? Your attraction quotient is at work! You've now manifested a dog for yourself."

"I need to figure out how to manifest you some good health so we can spring you from this joint," I say, and she sinks back among the pillows and says, "Oh, would you, darling? Let's forget about love for me and just get me some good health."

"Maybe both," I say.

"Just health, sweetie."

Also there is this: I think the nurse's aide who comes into the room is in love with the guy who brings the wheelchair to take Lola for a scan. I also think the woman in the next bed is in love with her doctor. I wouldn't be surprised if I wandered around the hospital for hours and found so many matches we could hold a dance party on the roof and have everybody paired up.

Later that day I take Bedford to Prospect Park, where we find ourselves partaking in a Halloween street fair/farmers' market clearly attended by every child, parent, and dog in Brooklyn. There are games set up and face-painting booths, an artisanal ice cream truck, a guy selling both organic vegetables and hand lotion. I spend a lot of time looking at a table filled with vintage clothing, candles, soaps, and stained glass lamps. And here I am, just another human who has a dog on a leash, a human carrying a take-out cup of coffee and a phone.

And then he is out of sight. The leash slips from my hands when I stop to pick up a bar of olive oil soap, and away he goes.

I walk for a bit, then sigh and lie down on the grass. Okay, I think, watching the sky. I *had* a dog. Maybe this is what life is teaching me now, how to let go. I had a life in California and a marriage. Then I had a life in Florida with a man who wants to marry me. Now I have a moment in Brooklyn with a house and my ex and a guy downstairs who is maimed and claims to be irredeemably misanthropic, and I have a new friend who has a child and a wound where her heart is supposed to be, and an old lady who thinks she can't possibly love again.

The gold sparkles are all around me still. If I squint, I can see them. The same ones Blix saw. It makes me feel so close to her, as if maybe she's somewhere nearby, floating about in the ether.

After a while, I feel something touching my leg, and then I hear panting and feel hot breath on my face. I sit up quickly and put my hands over my mouth. But Bedford doesn't care that I don't want dog slobber all over my face. He stretches out next to me, wagging his tail, smiling, and his eyes look right into mine.

I'm back, he says. *When shall we head back home? Oh, and by the way, I brought you a baby shoe.*

Please know that I am totally on your side, no matter what is going on upstairs, but IS there a cattle drive situation you are living with? Should I be concerned?

Oh, sorry. I seem to have acquired a canine.

You see? I thought it must be a greyhound, but Roy was sure it was a whole pack of wolves.

LOL. A mutt. Named Bedford. His middle name is Avenue, but that's only used on formal occasions or when he has ripped up all the garbage in the kitchen. Which, by the way, he just did.

I suspect you are turning into a Brooklynista. There is no other excuse for that name. Fun fact: Roy's original name was Seventh, and Avenue was HIS middle name, too. #justkidding

Perhaps Bedford and Roy need to meet each other, as the two animals of the house.

You are so adorable. Cats and dogs don't so much enjoy meeting each other.

Patrick, would you ever go for a walk with me, do you think?

Hey, how is Lola doing?

She's fine. They're doing tests. Lots and lots of tests. Patrick, would you ever go for a walk with me?

When is she coming home?

Not sure. Patrick, so you never go out? Never? At all? How do you get groceries?

Marnie, where you're from, do they not have delivery services? It's a wonderful system! But now, sociologically interesting as this is, I really must get back to work. Toenail fungus is a serious disease, and people are waiting to hear my thoughts.

Fine. Gotta go because a stormtrooper is at the door anyway, wanting candy. #mightbesammy

Oh, these quaint customs of people and their children! Pro tip: Sammy is one thing, but if other children come to the door, you don't have to open it for them.

You are a curmudgeon of the highest order.

The very highest. A higher curmudgeon you will not find in today's world.

I stare at my phone for a few minutes, wondering if I dare take a chance, say what I want to say. And then I type:

Were you always such a high curmudgeon? Or is this because of what happened?

Whoa. Good talk. Off to describe toenail fungus! The fun doesn't stop. Ask Roy.

"Look at this magnificent stormtrooper!" says Jessica. "At least I get him for Halloween!" She's standing in my kitchen doorway, pointing to

Sammy, who is all dressed in white with a white helmet. He's carrying a pillowcase full of candy. He says, "Oh, *Mom.*"

"Well? If Halloween had fallen on one of those *alternate weekends*, then you would have been in Manhattan with your father and with *her*. And *she*, being all of about twenty-four, probably wouldn't know that children even go trick-or-treating. And that they need costumes. Or who knows? Maybe she's so young she still goes herself." She shrugs, both hurting and pleased with herself.

"You're my costume person," he says. He looks at me and rolls his eyes, the universal signal of the exasperated child. "Also, Mom, Dad told me he isn't even seeing her anymore."

"Dream on!" says Jessica. "This is the relationship for the ages, to hear the way he described it to me."

I interrupt her before she can continue with her tirade. "Come on in. I've made hot chocolate for you. And show me all your loot! Oh my goodness, you've filled that whole pillowcase to the brim!"

Jessica and I make him spill out his whole sack of goodies on the table—luckily it's a huge surface—and for a while the three of us are laughing and picking through the candy bars and lollipops and bags of M&M's and toys, exclaiming over everything. We drink our hot chocolate and eat candy bars and Skittles, and Bedford organizes one of his cattle drives—a "puppy blowout," Sammy calls it—and the two of them race through the apartment, barking and laughing, until Jessica says enough is enough and they have to go back home.

Before he leaves, though, Sammy sidles up to me and whispers, "Have you looked at the book yet?"

I shake my head, and he says, "*Please.* You've got to at least look at it."

I glance over at it, still on the bookshelf. But I don't go open it up.

Although I can't say for sure why not.

THIRTY-TWO
MARNIE

Once it's the first week in November, the weather turns sharply colder, becoming at last what I've been expecting from New York all along. The wind whips around corners and up and down the streets. It plays with the litter, sending papers and plastic bags dancing along the sidewalks. Taking Bedford out for one of his daily walks and squirrel-chasing sessions, I watch a white plastic shopping bag do a tantalizing waltz until a bare treetop reaches out and holds it close.

I tell Jeremy in one of our daily phone calls that it's as if a referee suddenly blew a whistle, and said, "CHANGE!" and the old summer team limped off the court, and the wild, windy fall team came dashing out, young and energetic and whirling around. It is so un-Florida-like. So un-California-like.

Winter will come after that, and it will be Christmas, and then I will leave. Less than two months from now. My family is already talking about how fun it will be when we're all together again, Amelia's first Christmas, the stockings, the Christmas turkey, the millions of little shiny ornaments my mother thinks it's fun to hang everywhere.

Jeremy says it's going to be amazing, having a big family Christmas for once, and not the tiny little twosome Christmas he and his mom usually endure. Already my mother has invited him to bring his mother over to be with my family. He's actually been taking our two moms out for breakfast some weekend mornings, and he says it's lovely, seeing them chatting so amiably about us. I cannot imagine.

"*Us*," he says, and my nerve endings curdle with guilt when he utters that word. Then he says, "You know, maybe you should contact a real estate agent so that when the time comes to sell, everything will be in place." He says, "I miss you so much that I'm going to have to be physically restrained from carting you off somewhere when you get off the plane."

"Huh," I say.

One morning I awaken because the entire building is banging and clanging, and then shuddering like the Huns have arrived and are pelting its bricks with iron bars. Noah is up, already taking a shower. The whole commotion seems to be originating from downstairs, so I grab my phone and start typing.

Patrick, are you okay?

Yes. Welcome to the heating system poltergeist. Harbinger of winter.

What does it want? Money? An animal sacrifice?

No, it's friendly. It just has air in its pipes. Wants you to know about it. (By the way, curious that your thoughts go right to animal sacrifice. Things going okay, dog-wise?)

Why do you ask? I happen to LOVE wearing chewed-up shoes.

This is what gives dogs a bad name. And I'm not referring to the rather brilliant name of Bedford.

You think that's a brilliant name? THANK YOU!

Oh, shucks. I think anything beyond Rover or Spot is brilliant. By the way, what does the Gentleman of the House think of your canine friend?

Um, he's not the Gentleman of the House.

Could've fooled me. Could've fooled HIM, for that matter.

It takes me a little while to compose myself again. And then I type:

It's complicated.

Is he planning on leaving anytime soon?

Good talk. Gotta go feed the dog.

A few days later I'm at Best Buds when an elderly man comes in. He has the pained appearance of a man who needs to ask somebody a huge question, and so I ask him if there's anything I can do for him. He says no, looking around furtively like he's sure I'm hiding something in the palm tree.

So I leave him to ramble with his thoughts. He drifts over to the orchids in the cooler and stands with his hands in his pockets, looking at the tight little roses, and then he moves along to gaze for a while at the feathered greenery, and then his eyes suddenly swerve over to me. I look down at the counter quickly.

He clears his throat, and I smile at him. Our eyes meet.

"I guess I'm not ready," he says abruptly.

And, just like that, he leaves the store.

If I were a different sort of person—if I were, say, Blix—perhaps I would run to the door and call after him. Perhaps I would say, "Oh, but, sir, no one ever thinks of themselves as ready. From the look of you, you are ripe right this minute."

But I am me, Marnie MacGraw. And so he slips away, down the street.

Two months ago today I was with her when she died.

I'm walking home from Best Buds, and it's dark now that we're back on Eastern Standard Time. I have to walk fast because it's freaking cold. But this text stops me in my tracks. I lean against a mailbox and type:

I need to talk about her. Can I come down?

No. Well, maybe. Yes. OK.

That seems to cover all the possibilities. I tell you what: I'll bring a chicken because I'm starving.

I wait to see what he'll say, and when he doesn't say anything, I stop at Paco's and pick up a rotisserie chicken, some mashed potatoes, and broccoli rabe. Paco, standing behind the high counter near the front of the store, is almost giddy with happiness tonight, but he says he can't tell me why. Not yet but soon. Still, he comes around the counter and hugs me when he gives me the bag of food.

"How many people you feeding tonight? Just you—or you and that . . . bandito?" He makes a face. "Sorry, I shouldn't say that."

"Who's the bandito? Oh, you mean *Noah*? Noah is Blix's grand-nephew, Paco."

"I don't like him." He turns to his assistant, George, who's squatting down stocking the shelves, and George laughs.

"Nobody like him," George says. "Even Blix didn't like him."

"Are you kidding me?" Paco says. "Blix *for sure* didn't like him." Then he says, "We gotta stop this kind of talk. Marnie—she like him fine. Sorry."

"Well, it's not him I'm eating with anyway," I say. "It's Patrick."

"Ohhh, *Patrick*!" they say in unison and then they exchange glances.

"What? What about Patrick?"

"Nothing, nothing at all. You go see Patrick. Here, extra potatoes. Patrick need potatoes. And here's a bone for your doggie. Tell Patrick I got the special almond flour he wants. And the Irish butter."

"I'll pay for them and take them over to him. It'll save him a trip."

George laughs a little. "You mean, it saves *me* a trip."

"Patrick no comes here," says Paco. "We take to him."

"Oh," I say. "Of course."

Patrick lets me in when I ring the bell. I notice he's not wearing his hoodie tonight, which gives him a welcoming look, much less ominous than usual. Also, Roy runs right over to say hi—a function of the chicken I'm carrying, no doubt. Still, I feel as though they're both happy to see me for once. The lobster incident must have been forgiven.

The place smells like something amazing is about to come out of the oven.

"Vanilla cheesecake," he tells me. "My old standard."

I give him the almond flour and the butter, and he looks like a kid at Christmas. "This butter is the best! Let me pay you for these," he says, but I wave him off and take everything into the kitchen.

Then, as happens sometimes, I suddenly remember that I am a dog owner. And that you have to let dogs out. Often. I've learned this the hard way. Also, he needs company. He gets lonely.

I look at Patrick apologetically. "I need to go take Bedford for a little walk, and then I'll come right back. You can start eating if you want. I know it's late."

"No, no. I'll wait for you."

"Well, thanks. I'll hurry!"

Bedford is frantically happy to see me, way happier than anything I can imagine Roy doing, even at his best. I take him out of the crate and he races to the front door, his ears flying. So I clip the leash onto his collar, and we go sailing down the front steps—the stoop—and he tears over to the little patch of dirt near the gingko tree and lets loose a long stream of pee. Then he has about fifty things that require sniffing and some items he has to stop and chew, like a candy wrapper and a piece of somebody's shoe. I take these things away from him and he briefly considers whether we know each other well enough for me to take those kinds of liberties. But I win because I know the secret phrase, and I'm not afraid to use it: "Do you want to EAT? Do you want to go inside and EAT? Eat??"

And boy, does he ever! We go racing up the stairs and back into the house, and I feed him in the kitchen. Some dry kibble mixed with a little meaty wet food that smells awful. I clock his eating time at thirty-six seconds, and then I tell him the bad news.

"You have to go back in the crate, my dear friend."

He lies down with his head on his paws and makes his eyes look round and innocent.

"I know. But it's only for a little while. It's because Patrick is worried you would eat his cat."

He wags his tail. Which is probably a yes.

When I get back downstairs, Patrick has put food on our plates, and we sit down at his table, which I notice he has cleared of papers and books. He's using a nice yellow tablecloth, and there is even music coming from one of the computer monitors. Bach fugues. Very tinkly pianos. He's poured us glasses of wine, and made an incredible salad with walnuts and seeds and butter lettuce.

I unfold my napkin in my lap and look across at him.

"You've gone to some trouble," I say. "Thank you."

"Well, it's the least I can do for a fellow trooper." He smiles and lifts his glass in a toast. "To Blix, away from us for two long months now."

I look closely at him, but he's holding his emotions in check. Probably for my sake.

"To Blix! Who is still watching over us," I say.

"And also I have some news for you. I'm moving. I wanted to tell you in person."

"You're *moving*!" I put my fork down.

"You sound shocked."

"Well, I guess I am shocked. I never meant to disrupt your life! And also—I haven't even talked to a real estate agent yet, so who knows if this place is even going to sell? And when I go back, I was thinking I could rent out Blix's place, and you and Jessica could stay on. Also, even if it did sell, you could probably negotiate staying—"

"No," he says. "Thank you but no."

"May I ask—without you getting mad at me—what you're going to do?"

"Yes. I'm going to my sister's in Wyoming."

"Wyoming?!"

"Wyoming. The wilderness. My sister lives in a town with a population of twenty-eight. That's what it says on the sign year after year. So obviously when somebody dies, somebody else in town has to step up and reproduce. It's the law of the land."

"Can you really be happy there? I mean, with no people around?"

He laughs. "Have you noticed that I don't have a lot of people around already? Frankly, I'm worried that twenty-eight people are going to be too much for me. I'm counting on my sister to fend off the hordes."

"Patrick."

"Marnie."

"Can you tell me . . . what happened to you? How . . . ?"

He looks surprised. He refills our glasses, which is really just to give him an excuse not to look at me, I think, because we both have plenty left. And then he says, slowly, "Ah, actually, no. I can't."

"Patrick, I—"

"No. I don't want to talk about it. Let's talk about you. We covered my life at your last visit." He looks up and smiles. His eyes are hard to read, maybe because of the scars that pull that right eye so taut, but I can see that he's making an effort to look happy. God knows he probably wishes he could shift this back to a nice, light, polite conversation. "So here's what I know about you. Let's see. You were married to Noah for about two weeks, you met Blix at his family's party, she went bonkers over you and decided to leave you her house. You, however, don't really *want* her house. And so you're moving back to Florida, but you feel guilty. Unnecessarily guilty, I should add."

"Yes. Those are my facts."

"And, if I may ask, what are you doing in Florida that is so much more compelling than Brooklyn, New York? Which you seem to have taken to, I might add."

"Well." I feel my mouth getting dry. "It's kind of hard to explain. But at the time I inherited this house, I had actually only just settled in Florida, and I had—well, if you want to know the real truth, I have this sort of fiancé there."

"What?" He raises his eyebrows, as best he can. He's trying not to laugh. "What, may I ask, is a *sort of* fiancé? Excuse me, but given the evidence around here, I've been under the, um, impression that you and Noah were back together and rekindling your . . ."

"No. We're not. I mean, not really."

"You are certainly an interesting one, aren't you?" he says. He raises his glass and clinks it against mine. "To an interesting life!" I know then, by the look on his face, that he knows we sleep together. My bedroom is just above his main room. The sound travels downward, I'm sure. I feel my face grow warm.

"It's not—" I say, and at the same time, he says, "No, really. You don't have to explain anything to me. I know that life is complicated, believe me. These things—really, don't be embarrassed."

We go back to eating. I pick up my fork and spear a piece of chicken. My silverware clinks together. The Bach fugue has stopped for a moment, and in the huge silence that yawns before us, there is only the sound of me trying to rip some meat apart. I feel him looking at me.

At last I put down both the knife and the fork and square my shoulders.

"Okay, yes. God, this is awful to have to say out loud, but you're right. Everything you're thinking is right! I am cheating on someone, and he's probably the nicest guy in the whole world, and I never thought I would do anything like that! I'm actually horrible and insensitive and incompetent at life, and oh my God, I'm having sex with my ex, who I don't even love. And I don't even mean to be doing it! It's all a big mistake. And I don't even know if that makes it worse or better, having sex with somebody by default."

I am slightly aware that he says under his breath, "Really, I wasn't . . . you don't have to . . ."

But I am in this now, so I plow on, MacGraw-style.

"And my fiancé—he's so *trusting* and *nice*, and yet—and yet, Patrick, can I tell you something I've never told anyone? He is so god-awful boring that sometimes it takes all of my willpower *not* to throw my phone into the nearest gutter just so I don't have to hear him talking to me anymore. There."

I stop, because Patrick is looking at me, and it looks, shockingly, like he's suppressing a smile.

"Do you even *know* what I'm talking about? That level of boringness? He can go on and on about the way the cleaning service *shampooed* his office rug and how long it took them and how many guys they sent to do it and what the first guy said and then what the second guy said. And he can also talk until the sun comes up about highway routes! *Highway routes*, Patrick! And I'm supposed to love him, and I probably do, but he loves me so much more than I love him, and what's so really terrible is that I broke his heart back in high school so I can't do it again, even if it turns out that I can't love him. Do you see? There's a special kind of hell for people who break nice people's hearts *twice*, don't you think? And I know I don't deserve him, and that just makes it worse somehow! Oh God, please stop looking at me! I don't even know why I'm telling you this! I am not a good person, Patrick. I came here to Brooklyn scared out of my mind, but now I see that way deep down I was just hiding from my real life and hoping Brooklyn would show me an answer, and instead I'm stupider than ever—sleeping with my ex, who doesn't love me and *never* loved me! Like that's going to lead to anything good! Some experiment, he called it, in behavior for exes. We're going to have *closure*."

My voice breaks, and I make myself stop talking. I carefully set my napkin down on the table in the heavy silence that follows and put my head in my hands. What will he do when I start to sob? I can feel the tears, all right there—a big cry is organizing itself and is going to break all over both of us soon.

"Well," he says at last. "Well. My goodness. I'm wondering if this night doesn't call for whiskey instead of wine. This may be a Chivas Regal situation." He gets up and goes over to the cabinet and brings down a bottle and two glasses. On his way back to the table, he grabs a box of tissues and puts it in front of me.

He hands me a glass of whiskey, and I stare at it because I don't drink whiskey. But I take a sip anyway, and God, it's the most terrible taste in the world, burning all the way down, but also warming me up, inch by inch. Who can drink this stuff? I take another sip and set my glass down. He's downed all of his.

"You know what? I thought—when I came here—I thought Blix left me the house because maybe she wanted me to be with Noah. That she set this all up. That's how crazy I am. Right after he left me, when I was desperately unhappy, I asked her once for a spell to get him back, and I thought maybe that was why she gave me the house, and why he was here. The spell."

He clears his throat. "I have to say that I don't think she wanted you to be with Noah."

"I'm getting that idea. But why not? Why did she not really like him? You know the whole story, don't you?"

He hesitates, pours himself another glass. "Really? Are we going to do this?" Then he sees my face. "We are. Okay, she saw him as something of an opportunist, I think. Somebody who would take advantage. He wasn't . . . so wonderful when she was at the end of her life and needed him to step up."

"Please tell me what happened. I need to know everything. He told me he was the one who took care of her."

"Are you sure you want to hear this?"

"I think I need to know, don't you?"

"All right." He stretches out his legs and cracks his knuckles. "Well, he showed up one day when it was right near the end for her. We were *all* taking care of her—all her people, you know. Coming and keeping her company, fixing meals, straightening, that sort of thing. Mostly sitting and talking to her. And he comes along one day with no idea what's going on, doesn't even know that she's sick, much less dying. And he was shocked, of course. We all tried to help him with that, because it can be upsetting to see a loved one dying, but we started getting uncomfortable because of the way he just kept badgering her to go to the hospital. He thought she should have had surgery for the tumor. Get some chemotherapy, whatever. We kept trying to talk to him, to explain to him that the time for all that had passed, and that we were there helping her make her transition, but he wasn't having it. He kept insisting that professionals needed to be called, that only they know how to take care of people who are dying."

"Oh, Patrick! How did she stand it? What did she do?"

"See, that's just it. The essence of Blix is to try to solve things. To love what's there. She was sad, but I think at the end she thought that she could use love to help him. She wanted to fill him up with love. The way she did. You know how she was."

There's a silence. Roy climbs up on my lap and I pet him. Patrick is looking at us with a serious look on his face.

"On the last day, he was panicking at the idea of having her die in front of him, and I get that. It's scary, watching somebody die. But she had planned it all out, and she wanted to die at home in a peaceful state, and he was determined to have medical authorities. So Lola took him next door and fed him something, just to keep him away. And . . . well, I sat with Blix while her breaths just kept getting farther and farther apart, and I held her hand. I told her I'd stay with her for as long as she needed, and for her to take her time, to go only when she was ready. And—well, that's it."

"Oh, Patrick."

I want so badly to get up and go over to him and hug him—the air is practically demanding that we hug—but I know better. The air may want us to hug, but he's not inviting that kind of attention. Instead, he gets up and walks to the sink with our plates.

I lean down and give Roy my last little piece of chicken, and he takes it and jumps down from my lap and eats it next to my foot.

"Hey, congratulations. You're now Roy's best friend," Patrick says. He picks up the cat, and Roy rubs his head along Patrick's chin, along the place where the skin is pulled tight.

Maybe it's because I'm possibly drunk, or maybe it's because Blix is right now in the room with us, but I suddenly get an amazing idea. It feels like the very best idea anybody in the history of the world ever had, and I stand up to deliver the news of it, so it will have the fullest possible impact.

"What if—what if I threw a big dinner party? Or—I know—Thanksgiving! I'll put on a Thanksgiving dinner upstairs and invite everybody who loved her, and we'll all celebrate her life. It can be my good-bye to her. And my thank-you. Both at the same time."

Patrick is smiling. "Look at you," he says. "Glowing like this. This is a big plan."

"Will you come?"

"Well—no. But I think it's a good idea for you."

"Patrick!"

He leans across the table and speaks in a husky voice. "Look at me, Marnie. Look at my face. You and Blix . . . you are the only people I've let into my life. Don't you know that by now? The only people who see me on purpose. I'll send up some cookies, some pumpkin pies, and I'll cheer for you from down here. But I can't go up there. The hideous factor kicks in."

"But you are the furthest thing there is from hideous," I say. "You're *luminous*."

"My tolerance for absorbing sympathetic remarks has reached the breaking point," he says. "So I think it's time to call this evening quits."

I say, "Patrick," and then I look at him and set my mouth a certain way, and then I give him my most exasperated expression and roll my eyes, and then I say, "Patrick, you and I both know—"

And then I just leave because there's no point. Patrick's heart is closed for business. He's told me every way he knows how.

THIRTY-THREE
MARNIE

"I'm afraid you're not going to like late November up here," Sammy tells me. He's waiting in my kitchen for his dad to come pick him up for their weekend together. "I don't know if you realize it, but November is when everybody's teeth start to hurt."

"Really!" I say. "I'd heard about all the leaves falling off the trees and possible early snowfalls. But I didn't know that about the teeth."

"Well, my mom works for a dentist, and she says it's because of the cold weather. That when you're outside and you breathe in the cold air, your teeth get sensitive. And then *everybody* goes to the dentist. That's what she said." He starts beating on the table like it's a drum, and then gets up and does an effortless cartwheel across the kitchen floor. Then he stops and looks at me. "Also, can I tell you something else? Did you know everybody has a superpower? You know what my superpower is? I have the magic power to notice when the clock says 11:11 or 1:11. I always, always look up then. It's kind of amazing."

"Wow. Well, that's a good one to have."

"Sometimes I see 2:22 or 4:44, also. Not so many of the other ones, though."

I concentrate very hard on trying not to laugh. "You are clearly on your way to superhero status."

He nods seriously, then sits cross-legged on the floor for a moment, looking at me so directly that my heart stops. He swallows hard before he speaks. "So, I have a plan for getting my mom and dad together."

"You do?"

"Yeah, so there's a concert at school, and I'm performing at it—and I think they should both come, and then I'll get up and play my flute or sing or read a poem or something, and after we'll all go out for ice cream and you can do a little spell or something on them, and I think they'll decide to get back together."

"Really."

"But *you* have to do the spell. All we need is a little bit of magic to get them to both come to the concert and be nice to each other. So far all they do is fight about it."

"They do?"

He sits down at the table next to me and rests his head on his elbow. "My mom yells at my dad that he won't remember to come on time. And that he won't be wearing the right clothes. And then she said that *I* had to tell him no girlfriends allowed because she will walk out if she sees him there with some woman."

"But you said he doesn't even have a girlfriend."

"He doesn't. But my mom is worried anyway. Maybe she thinks he'll get one." He starts drawing on the table again with his finger, outlining the same star that I love to outline with my finger. Then he gives me a little smile. "So we need to look at the book of spells and find a good spell you could use on them."

I think about it. "I think we should let the concert do the magic. Play your flute and that will be magic enough. All that beautiful music curling out over the audience . . ."

"No," he says very firmly. "We need more than that."

"And if it doesn't work," I continue, "then it's just not the right time. Because if it's meant to happen, it will. But things have to develop. We can't force it to happen."

"Would you please even *look* at the book of spells? I know you could find *something* in there to help us. This girl at my school said she knows this psychic lady and she rubs people's heads and tells them what's going to happen. So I know you could just *read* some words. I'd do it myself except you and Blix are the ones with the magic."

"How do you know that?" I say.

He shrugs. "I dunno. I just know it."

I glance over at the bookshelf, where the book of spells sits, bulging with papers. Its cover looks torn. Funny how some days I don't even see it there, and some days it's the focal point of the whole kitchen.

Like now.

Andrew, with his usual hangdog countenance (what I assume is the result of a perpetual, lifelong guilty conscience) arrives then, and Sammy leaves with his dad, trailing his overnight bag and holding on to his soccer ball, giving me backward looks and wagging his eyebrows at me. He mouths, "DO IT" as they leave. I sit there drinking my tea for a long while, listening to the way the house settles and creaks. The windows need washing. *Everything* needs washing around here.

I should call a real estate agent, find out what I have to do to put the place on the market. Why don't I ever seem able to set all this in motion?

Bedford, lying at my feet, turns over in his sleep and thumps his tail. *Tap tap tap.*

I wash the dishes and sweep the kitchen floor, then go outside to get some fresh air. The wind is whipping up the trees. Patrick has put the recycling out by the curb and it's full of cardboard boxes and containers. I look longingly at his apartment; the windows with the wrought-iron bars are a perfect metaphor for everything about Patrick.

Lola's shades are up, I'm pleased to see. She got a pacemaker last week, and it's made her feel worlds better, she says, filled with energy she hasn't felt in years.

I pull the dead leaves off the rosebush and then traipse up the stairs and straighten the Tibetan prayer flags on my way inside. Maybe I should call my sister—but then I find myself standing in front of the book of spells.

It would not hurt to look at this book.

I could open it up and see how ridiculous it is—probably just a book of parlor games. Somebody probably gave it to Blix as a joke, a nod to her interest in unconventional things.

I open the front cover. There are a whole bunch of papers shoved between the pages, so I take them out very carefully and set them aside. They are grocery lists, little doodles, a note Blix evidently wrote to Houndy reminding him to bring home four extra lobsters because Lola and Patrick were both coming over for dinner. (Patrick came up for dinner? Really?) All the stuff of life that you shove away somewhere when company is coming over and you aren't ready to sort through the papers cluttering the table.

But the book itself. The book is trying very hard—too hard—to be serious. It has a whole section about the history of spells, blah blah blah, an explanation of how humans have always thought they needed to claim some influence over the vagaries of life. And then, getting down to business, there are some five thousand actual spells for *everything*: cleansing energy, winning court cases, ensuring protection, finding lost objects, healing disease, getting money—and, of course, a huge section on love and sex.

In the love section, there are mentions of ingredients for a proper spell: rosemary, roses, chamomile. Some vanilla beans wouldn't hurt.

A piece of paper falls out onto the floor.

On it, I see that someone has written in a scratchy light scrawl: "Lola open heart love brave dream. You know the man now. The man who will love you."

At the very back of the book, there's a thin green leather journal wedged between a couple of pages, wrapped up with a brown cord with a star charm attached.

I shouldn't open this. Blix's secrets are there, I'm sure of it.

But maybe—maybe she wanted me to see it. This isn't exactly hidden away, after all. She *could* have destroyed all the things she didn't want found. It wasn't like her death surprised her; she knew for ages she was going to die. No, I am certain she put everything exactly where she wanted it, and for a purpose.

My hand touches the leather cord, and I take a deep breath, and then I'm pulling on it slightly and opening the journal. I'll read a little bit, I tell myself. See if she mentioned me. I have a right to know if I was mentioned in her journal, don't I? After all, she left me her house—maybe there are instructions here on what else I should be doing.

And there it is, the thing that breaks my heart.

She has listed the spells she was using for healing, and the date she employed each one, and the results. The Acorn Good Health Spell, for instance, that she used the previous fall. "I threw the acorns in the air. They scattered over the ground."

On another page of her journal: "I'm frightened sometimes in the morning. I look at Houndy and I feel the fear. But it's not like I'm desperate," she wrote in a beautiful, looping scrawl with curlicues and little stars. "Everyone thinks medical science can cure this cancer. Why don't they see what I see? That death is not the enemy." Here she drew a starburst. "I know that my tumor is a living entity and that the tumor and I together can heal ourselves if it is meant to be that way."

I turn the page and see, "I am not afraid of death, and I am not afraid of life. These days are full of passion and love and richness, now that I know the end is coming. I carry the ocean in my blood. I float out into the night, knowing that when the time comes, I will leave on the luminous huge milky moon. I am disappearing by degrees, yet I want to stay longer, look back at my whole glorious life. Where did you go?"

Later, she invoked Obatala, whoever that is, and said she'd gone out at night, offering him milk and coconut, for healing. She summoned the Dark Moon Spirit and the Ancient Egyptian Fumigation for Expelling Disease Demons.

My heart is beating hard.

Oh my goodness, she did use spells.

"I am wearing the special blessing crystals and the amber beads," she wrote. "But Cassandra is strong. I am making myself ready, but sometimes I am filled with a longing to stay. Is that so bad, to want to stay a bit longer, to see my projects through?"

There's a buzzing in my ears. I run my fingers over her printing. Where she wrote Cassandra's name the handwriting is jazzy, almost childlike, with lowercase letters all in different colors. She dug into the paper so hard that when I run my fingers over the name, the writing feels almost three-dimensional.

A few more pages in: "Houndy calling to me from the other side. Last night I saw my mother and my grandmother and sat with them in an orchard. My mother told me that I know what I need to do. I had a conversation with Houndy, and he reached over and touched my arm and it left a little mark. He says Patrick will see me through. Patrick knows the way."

I am fingering the pages, letting my eyes drift over them—when I hear the front door slam.

I jump up, startled and guilty. Bedford lifts his head and wags his tail.

"Marnie! You home?" calls Noah up the stairs, and I close the book quickly, shoving the journal deep inside—except that as I do, I see my name on a tiny piece of paper lodged into the binding of the book, and I pull it out, fast.

At the top she's written the date, September 10, which I remember was the day before she died. The handwriting looks like it was scratched with a pencil that had hardly any lead left to it. I have to strain to see what it says.

Then my heart twists. She has written in capital letters, each one etched deep into the paper:

> MARNIE NOAH HAS TO LEAVE DO NOT LET HIM STAY!!

THIRTY-FOUR
MARNIE

I've only barely managed to stash the book of spells away when Noah clumps up the stairs, bringing his jangly, disruptive vibes into the room.

Blix didn't want Noah here. Blix didn't want Noah here. Blix didn't want Noah here. That sentence runs through my head on a continuous loop—and now here he is, standing in front of me, eyes crinkled in a smile—and I'm in the middle of the kitchen, feeling like a trapped animal. Who stands in the very middle of the kitchen, for heaven's sake? And who stands there looking like she just completed the hundred-yard dash to *arrive* there, cheeks flushed, hair standing on end, looking like she's just seen a ghost?

I feel I am seeing the truth of things. Everybody tried to tell me that she didn't mean to leave the place to Noah, that she didn't want him here. And somehow I dismissed everything they said.

But now here it is, in her own words. The day before she died.

He stops and stares at me, and a grin spreads across his face. "Hey! What are you doing?" he says. "What's going on?" And for some reason, his eyes drift over to the bookshelf. Maybe I've run from there so fast that a trail is still visible.

MARNIE NOAH HAS TO LEAVE DO NOT LET HIM STAY!!

"Nothing. Just fixing up a few things. Cleaning a little bit. This place gets so dirty!"

He laughs, then comes over and puts his arms around me. I feel myself bristle, but he pulls me to him, presses my face against his chest.

"No, really. What's with you? Did I scare you when I came in?"

"No," I say into his shirt.

"God, you look sexy today." He kisses the top of my head. "Soooo . . . whattya say we go downstairs and have sex? I just got done with my paper, it's the weekend, and I feel like celebrating. Especially when you look so hot! Did you do something to your hair?"

"Nothing. It's just uncombed. And actually I was about to go out."

"Yeah? Where to?"

"Um, I was going to see Lola, see how she's doing."

"She just left. I saw her when I was coming in. Leaving with that man again."

"Really?" I pull away from him. "The New Jersey guy?"

"I didn't exactly talk to him to find out where he's from."

"His car has out-of-state plates. If you looked at them, you'd know."

He laughs. "What do I care what the license plates say?"

"I bet it was him. Which is great. But never mind."

"Anyway," he says. He points to himself and to me, tries to take me in his arms again. "So . . ."

I don't want to have sex with him. *I do not want to have sex with him.* I manage to extricate myself and go over to the sink and turn on the tap. I'll water the plants; that's right.

"Actually, I can't just now. After I finish up in here, I'm going out."

"Mmm. So you said. But Lola's gone."

"Yeah?"

"I told you. She left with the guy, and you said that was great news. What's up with you anyway? Are you all right?"

"Tell me something. What was Blix like when you got here?"

I walk carefully to the window with the water glass. I can feel him looking at me as I drizzle some water over the roses and then the chamomile.

"She was dying," he says after a moment. "I got here a week before she died."

"And, tell me the truth . . . did she want you here?"

"Are you kidding? She said I was the one who could help her make the transition to the other side." He comes over and takes the glass out of my hand, puts it on the table, and holds on to both my arms. "What. Is. Going. On?" He leans closer, starts running his lips down across my jaw.

I pull back and look at his face. "Nothing. I was just thinking how it must have been very hard for you. To see her that way. Dying."

He flushes. "You know what was hard? It was hard that she wouldn't do anything to help herself get well. God forbid anybody call a doctor. I wanted to help her, but she just wanted me to sit there and watch her die."

I pull away from him. "But she had the right to do it her way."

"Well, sure. But my point is, why was *I* the guy who had to watch it happen? That's what hospitals are for! But whatever. I did it anyway. For her. And then . . . she goes and leaves her place to you." He gives a short, bitter little laugh.

"I don't think her death was about you."

"Well, whatever. It's done. I did what she wanted. Case closed. It's all good." He runs his eyes over me and holds out his arms, smiling. "Why are we talking about this anyway? Let's go make ourselves happy. You and me? Downstairs?" He motions with his head toward the door.

But I can't. In fact, looking at him right now, I can't believe I ever let myself get involved with such a self-absorbed, egotistical *child*. Who can only see things from his own perspective. I actually feel a little sick.

"No," I say. I swallow, trying to locate some moisture in my mouth because it has suddenly gone dry. "Actually, I have to tell you that this isn't really working for me anymore."

"What?"

"I feel weird about what I'm doing. I shouldn't be with you like this when I'm getting married to someone else. I feel guilty. This is a terrible thing I'm doing."

He looks shocked for a moment and then he smiles and revs up the charm machine.

"Ah, guilt! It's a terrible thing when guilt gets in the way of fun, isn't it? But here's what I think. We shouldn't feel guilty because in the grand scheme of things, you and me having sex is not taking anything away from your boyfriend. I'm no threat to your relationship because, one, I'm a known quantity and, two, I'm screwed up and can't maintain a decent relationship. You're his, as far as I'm concerned. This is all recreational. Look at it this way: I am strictly for fun."

"I don't work that way, unfortunately," I say.

"Yes, you do. That's exactly what we've been doing, having fun. And there's nothing wrong with it."

"I can't do it anymore. I'm sorry I ever started. So please respect my wishes on this."

He gives me a sideways look. I know I'm sounding weird—so stiff and formal, but I can't help it. I'm still shaking. He goes over and opens the refrigerator, stares into it, and finally gets out a beer. I know he's playing for time, waiting to see if I come to my senses. When I don't say anything else, he finally lets out a big breath, takes a swig of the beer, and says, "Okay. Have it your way. I'll respect your wishes, and we'll chill on the sex, but I have to stay here until the semester's over."

"No. I want you to leave."

"Marnie! Fuck! What *is* this?"

I stand in the middle of the kitchen, shaking my head, standing my ground. It feels like Blix and everybody who loved her is standing right there alongside me.

"No. I can't have you here. You have to leave."

He stares at me, and for a moment I think he'll challenge me, or refuse, or even throw a fit. But then he laughs, takes another big drink of beer, and shakes his head as though this is the most insane request he's ever heard. He picks up his backpack and goes downstairs. I hear the shower running. Soon after, there's the sound of drawers banging shut, and his footsteps in the hallway, and then the front door slams. I watch from the window as he heads down the street, talking on his phone.

That night I take the book of spells down to my room and lie in bed, anxious to get back to Blix's journal. I love how she filled pages with stars and filigrees and comets. I love the stories of little glimmers she felt as she watched people falling in love around her. She wrote that she sometimes sent out messages and energy through the atmosphere and saw people turn in surprise when they got zapped with love.

She was a person like no one I ever met.

Then I smile, remembering the engagement party and how we surrounded a red-haired woman with white light. And for a moment, I feel her there with me in the room.

I read lists of things she was grateful for: the random heart-shaped leaves on the sidewalk; the pigeons who talked to her from the windowsill; her kantha quilt; Patrick's sculptures with their grace and power; the way she and Houndy would sit by the fire pit on snowy nights, curled up together under fleece blankets; Sammy's smile.

How important it was to add to every spell, "For the good of all and free will of all."

And then, in the very back of the book, on the very last page, she'd made a list, called "My Projects."

JESSICA AND ANDREW.

LOLA AND WILLIAM.

PATRICK AND MARNIE.

PATRICK AND MARNIE.

PATRICK AND MARNIE.

PATRICK AND MARNIE.

I close the book very carefully and place it on the floor.

Patrick?

Patrick is the one she thought was for me?

It's so impossible as to almost be laughable. Patrick is so locked up in himself, he's so unreachable and . . . and . . . what did she think I was supposed to do? Spend the rest of my life writing to him on my phone? We could gradually work up to love notes in our texts! Maybe after twenty years of me texting *I love you,* he might let me actually touch him.

Oh, Blix. Maybe you got some things right, but this was so very, very wrong.

THIRTY-FIVE
MARNIE

The next day, I'm at Best Buds texting the news to Patrick that I've asked Noah to leave, when I look up to see the elderly man coming in the door. The one who wasn't ready. This time, however, he masterfully strides over and picks out calla lilies, roses, some baby's breath, some gerbera daisies, and some greens.

"Gerbera daisies are my very favorite flower," I tell him when he brings them over to the counter.

This seems to please him. He has a sweet face, lined and gentle.

"I am about to do a very brave thing," he says. His eyes are shining. "Braver than anything I did in the war, that's for sure. I am going to ask a woman to marry me."

"Really!" I say. "That's wonderful. Is she going to be surprised or does she already know?"

"It's a surprise. Actually, do you have paper so I can write a note? It occurs to me that it might be a very good idea to include a little note, convincing her."

"Oh, boy. You're going to propose marriage on paper?"

He stiffens a little. "I am."

"No, that's cool. I get it. Do you want some help?"

"I have to do this myself," he tells me sternly. "This has to be all me. Though it's been years, you know, since I had to . . . well . . . convince a lady that I'm worth investing in."

"Of course. Here, you can sit over here and take your time." I lead him over to a little white table in the back. "Can I get you some water? Or maybe a thesaurus? Or a romance novel?"

He laughs at that.

He sits for a long time, chewing on the end of his pen.

Patrick texts back:

Great! Did he go peacefully into that good night? (Did you see what I did there?)

Ha! He did go peacefully. So far, at least.

The man turns, clears his throat, and says, "Maybe I *could* use a little help, if you have some time."

I put down my phone. "I love doing this," I say. "Tell me something about her. And you. I'll see what comes up."

He sighs. "All right, maybe that would work." He closes his eyes and begins: "So I've been seeing . . . this lady. I drive from New Jersey to visit her. Been doing it for about six months now. Every chance I can. Every chance she'll let me."

Little sparkles are dancing around in front of my eyes. Oh my God. This is him!

"And . . . well, she's the widow of my best friend. She doesn't know I want to be more than a friend to her because I haven't wanted to scare her off. But we only talk about our dead spouses. And current events. Weather. Plays. She doesn't know I have . . . feelings. She's very proper with me."

I clear my throat. What are the ethics of this situation? Should I say, *Hey, you're William Sullivan, and I know your whole story. Let me tell you what the lady in question has said to me about you!*

Instead I go with, "But is it the kind of proper like 'keep your distance' or is it the kind of proper like 'I don't want to assume this man loves me'?" I really do want to know which one it is.

"Now how would I know that?" he says. "That's why I'm going to propose marriage—to see what she says." He gets a mock serious look on his face. "I am, as they say, *taking the plunge*."

Ohhhh. Lola is going to break his heart. This is not going to go well.

"Yes," I say. "But . . . if . . . I mean, won't it be too sudden? It might put her on the spot, you know. Why plunge when you could wade? Tiptoe in, test the waters."

"No. Absolutely not. When I asked my wife to marry me, that's what I did, and it worked out just fine. I asked her while we were getting some ice cream—popped the question, and she dropped her ice cream cone on the ground she was so surprised. And then she said yes. I had to buy her another cone. Best money I ever spent."

There is something so lovely about his face, the expression in his eyes, all that cluelessness. And even larger, there's something so sad about men of that generation crashing through life, taking plunges, with no idea of how women are going to receive them. Or maybe it's adorable, and these are darling men, heroes on the mysterious frontlines of love, and women need to pamper them and save them from their craziest impulses.

I can't think of what to do.

"I think we may need us some proposing music to help us along," I tell him, to stall for time.

I go put on some Frank Sinatra love songs, and then we sit side by side in the shower of gold sprinkles and let the fragrance of the flowers wash over us. I close my eyes and say Blix's mantra, "Whatever happens, love that," to myself.

"So I need her to see me as a bold romantic partner," he is saying.

"But could she perhaps be . . . shy around you? Have you considered that maybe you want to take it slow?"

He laughs. "I now realize what's wrong with your generation. You don't take chances. You're always on your smartphones and with your texting and your swiping and your online dating, and you don't show up in person when it's needed! I am going to woo her and wow her—"

"Dude!" I say, and he laughs. "You haven't even tried to kiss her yet, and yet you think it's going to work to write her a *note* asking her to *marry you*? See? I do not understand males!"

Oops. I hope he's not going to wonder how I know he hasn't kissed her yet. But it doesn't even cross his mind to wonder.

"Trust me, it's going to work out," he says. "She'll think it over, and she'll remember all the good times we used to have years ago, and she'll think of the future . . . and then by the time I show up there ready to kiss her, she'll say yes."

After that, I can see there's hardly any argument I have that's going to hold any appeal for William Sullivan, so I sit down at the table, and he tells me to write that she is beautiful and kind and that when he is out with her in the world, he can't stop smiling. He wants me to tell her that he lives for the times he drives to see her, and for that moment when she opens the door. And that when she was sick, he was also sick—sick with worry—which is why when he showed up at the hospital, he maybe told too many jokes when he should have listened.

Then he leans across the table with his eyes dancing. "Say that I'm peanut butter and she's jelly," he says. "And that she'll never have to go to the hospital alone again."

"Really?"

"Okay, now say she's the bees in my knees and the cats in my pajamas."

I write it down, smiling. "This is starting to sound a little sketchy, but okay."

On the speaker by the cash register, Frank Sinatra starts singing "All of Me," and William Sullivan makes me write, "So I am asking now for your hand in marriage. Please make me the happiest man in the world and marry me. With love and sincerity, William Sullivan."

"Both names, really?" I say.

"Both names. When your name is William, you have to be specific." He is smiling, ear to ear. "Write *William Sullivan* if you please."

"Okay, dude. Done!" I write it down and hand it to him to look over. He reads it very solemnly, and clears his throat a few times, says it's fine.

"I kind of like it when you call me dude," he says. And then fear seizes him again and he says, "I hope this works. And now if you'd kindly address it to Lola Dunleavy. Here, let me get the exact address out of my pocket."

And that's when I have to tell him the truth—that I know Lola and love her already. "She's my neighbor," I say, and his face breaks open in a smile when I tell him I see his car when he comes to pick her up.

"Do you think I have a shot?" he says.

"You always have a shot," I tell him. "Of course! Of course!"

I tell him that, in fact, Lola is going to be at my house on Thanksgiving for dinner, and we come up with a plan. We decide that the flowers should be delivered on Thanksgiving morning, and if she accepts him, then he'll come over to my house, too. If it's no, he'll go back home, eat his turkey dinner in a diner somewhere.

We smile at each other, and then I come out from behind the counter and hug him. He's a bit reserved at first, and I say, "Dude, you can hug me. We wrote a love letter together, and that means I'm on your team," and then he gets into the hug.

It's raining outside, and he leaves Best Buds looking like he's one umbrella away from performing "Singing in the Rain" right out there on Bedford Avenue.

THIRTY-SIX
MARNIE

So I do a spell for Sammy.

It's not a big one. But it feels big to me. I clip off some rosemary and basil from the plants on Blix's windowsill, and grind the leaves with a mortar and pestle I find under the sink. Then, when I'm in Best Buds the next time, I collect some petals of wild pansies (for love) and some hibiscus blossoms (for fidelity), and I mix everything up together.

The spell book didn't tell me any words to say, but Sammy says we have to say something. So, at his insistence, we close our eyes and hold hands and say some magic-sounding words, calling on the forces of love and forgiveness and happiness for everyone. He makes me laugh when he shouts, "Hocus-pocus!"

Best of all, he and I sit together while he practices his flute and I sew a little pocket out of red silk. (Red for passion.) He'll put that in his mother's purse and have her carry it to the concert, I tell him.

"But what about my dad? We need him to be in the spell, too," he points out.

So then I grind up more flowers and leaves and sew them in another red pocket, and Sammy says he'll put that in his dad's car.

We do a high five.

"But the most important thing is what *you're* doing," I say. "Right? The flute, and the love you beam right over to them."

The school auditorium is packed with parents and grandparents, all buzzing around and smiling and waving. There's an excited hum about the place. Jessica saved me a seat right next to hers, and I get there to find her waving and smiling and motioning me over.

Her cheeks are bright pink, and she looks beautiful, with her long hair in loose, shiny curls. Andrew will melt when he sees her. "Look at this program! It turns out that he's not only playing the flute," she says, "but he's also reading a poem. A poem he *wrote*! He didn't tell me that, the little scamp. Oh my God, I may have to be carried out of here." She starts fanning herself with the program.

"That's actually wonderfully cool," I say. "You look beautiful, by the way. I think you should relax if you possibly can, because all this is going to be fine."

Jessica is smiling. "It would be more cool if I'd gotten to see the poem first."

"Hmm. Maybe not."

I turn the program over and over in my hands. And even though the spell book told me that you have to do a spell and then release it and not worry, I can't help it. I keep craning my head around to watch people entering. And finally, *finally* there's Andrew arriving, dipping his head just so, humbly standing at the back while he scans the auditorium, and you can just see he's marinating in his own little sauce of nerves. I see the moment when he spots Jessica—his eyebrows go up—and he starts to head our way.

She says to me, "Don't let him sit next to me. Is there a woman with him? No, don't *look* at him! Is he with someone?"

"It's hard to look and not look at the same time, but no, I do not believe he has a woman with him."

"Okay, then. Still, let's hope he sits somewhere else."

"He's not going to sit somewhere else. In fact, he's almost over here. Smile and be calm."

When he gets to us—smiling and wearing his usual guilty-but-hopeful expression—I slide over so that he can have the seat next to Jessica. She gives me a look that might be gratitude or it might be hatred: right now those looks are the same.

May you be blessed and bold, I think to him as hard as I can and surround him with white light. *May you stop looking so guilty.*

He glances down at his program. He fidgets, tells me how he played the flute as a kid, and says he never could have played it in public. He says his kid is braver than almost anyone he knows.

I'm about to ask him if he will come to Thanksgiving dinner, but then the curtain opens, and a teacher gets up and says this is a sacred space when children are performing things they've practiced so hard, and he personally will come out into the audience and confiscate any cell phone that happens to ring, and the audience laughs nervously, and then he adds that he will also smash it to pieces, and we all laugh even harder when a man yells out from the audience, "Please! I'm begging you! Take mine!"

Then the music begins and kids tumble out onto the stage, jumping all around, singing songs. Some perform cartwheels and some leapfrog over big beanbag pillows. And they sing about freedom and happiness, and I can't concentrate on the words because I'm suddenly smiling so hard that my ears aren't working anymore. The whole stage is a blur of colors and radiance.

When Sammy comes out and does a series of cartwheels across the stage, I sneak a peek at Jessica and see that she is no longer in this hot, hard auditorium; she's gone someplace else, and Andrew is right there with her. They are smiling at each other! I say this to Blix, who might not hear me, being dead and all.

There are choruses and dances and the bright, shining faces of kids. A group of boys reenacts "Who's on First." A girl does an improbable series of handsprings all across the stage to thunderous applause.

And near the end of the show, when the moment comes that Sammy edges over to the front of the stage, I think we are all going to die there. The spotlight beams on him, and oh, he's such a *little* boy standing there in the yellow pool of light, so sturdy and yet so vulnerable. He starts out in a wavery voice: "The day my dad moved out I ate a plate of eggs . . ."

The room falls silent, and Jessica puts her head in her hands. Andrew, next to me, stops breathing. He reaches for Jessica's hand and holds it.

The poem isn't long. It's about a boy looking at a plate of over-easy eggs and thinking how his father is the yellow part and his mother is the white part, the surrounding stuff that holds the family all together, but then later when he's eating a hard-boiled egg, the boy sees the yellow part hop out and fall away. Then there's something in there about the boy noticing that he's the piece of toast; he's not the thing that holds the yolk and the white part together, but the thing they can both join with, like he's an egg sandwich maybe?—and then it's done, and the air comes back in the room, and everybody claps for him. People stand up, clapping and cheering. And several of the other parents smile at Jessica and Andrew, and one woman pantomimes wiping away tears while she's smiling. Andrew is now holding fast to Jessica's shoulder and she's leaning against him and they're both shaking their heads and smiling.

When it's all over, we walk outside together, but I find a reason to separate from this fragile, private love between Jessica and Andrew and Sammy because it's at that stage, you know, when the night is holding it so delicately and I could blink and it might all disappear, all the magic might be gone, and Jessica would be complaining again about Andrew's supposed maybe girlfriend, and Sammy would look miserable instead of triumphant.

And anyway I want more than anything to be back in Blix's bedroom, sitting on her kantha, looking at her book of spells. And of course getting ready for Thanksgiving. That.

I walk to the subway, and my phone dings with a new text message.

But I am already underground, having stepped out of the cold, blowy night into the harsh yellow of the underground world, which always feels like stepping inside a huge world of light and noise, and the train is coming now. It's here, having screeched to a halt, all the metal clanging as if it would fall apart. And people are getting off and then getting on, and I have to hurry to make it.

I look down at my phone, but the train is crowded—at this hour of the night!—and all I see, before the cellular service disappears completely, are two words, from Patrick:

Can you

And suddenly I am so happy. It's ridiculous how those two words can have such an effect. They're not even words you'd expect could make somebody happy; they're not, for instance *love you*—but there they are, lighting me up just the same. I'm beaming as I hold on to the pole, bobbing back and forth, smiling into the faces of strangers, thinking how lucky I am to be here.

I send some white light to the rumpled-up guy who is panhandling, and the older woman who has rolled down her stockings and has her eyes closed, and the girl in the cloche hat, the one who keeps running her fingers along her boyfriend's neck and then leaning over to kiss him. There is so much love for all of us, and Patrick needs me to do something.

Can you, can you, can you.

Whatever it is, I can!

When my stop comes, I press the button, and the phone lights up again, and I can see his message for real. And my heart drops into my stomach.

Can you come here as soon as possible? Don't go upstairs first!!

THIRTY-SEVEN
MARNIE

Patrick has made cream puffs filled with vanilla pudding, and he hands me one as he lets me in.

"What do you think? Should I have made them with ricotta instead? That's more authentic Italian, I think."

"I like pudding best," I say. "So, why couldn't I go upstairs? What's happened? After that text of yours, I expected to see police tape outside the building!"

"Oh. Was I overdramatic? So hard to get texting just right." He looks at his phone, scrolls back. "Oh, yes. I see. It was the two exclamation points. Sorry. It's just that there have been new developments this evening, and I wanted you to come here in case Noah is upstairs."

"You think he's there?"

"Well, I don't know for sure—I haven't heard noises up there for a while, but earlier he had a long, loud conversation on speakerphone with his *mother*, right on the sidewalk here. I had taken the recycling out, so I was where he couldn't see me, and so of course I stayed there and listened. Not nice of me to eavesdrop, I know, but I think you ought to know that she's furious with him. About the will."

My heart sinks.

"Yeah. Apparently she and his father want to contest Blix's will, and she was yelling at him that he's not been doing his part."

"His part?"

"Yes. His job has been to figure out how *you* might have manipulated Blix into leaving you the property. I guess because you're such a known vixen who probably goes around getting old ladies to leave you stuff all the time."

"Only if their grandnephews dump me. Otherwise, I let them give their stuff to anyone they want."

"Well, sure. You're chill that way."

"So how are they going to decide if I'm guilty? Did they say?"

"I don't know."

"Blix wrote me a letter that the attorney gave me . . . and in it . . . oh God, in it she talks about how I asked her for a spell to get Noah back. And he—well, one night he asked me if he could read it. Oh my God." I put my hands over my mouth.

"Wait. There's more," Patrick says. "His mom said that if they can't prove you tried to influence Blix, they most surely can prove that Blix wasn't of sound mind when she wrote the will. On account of her doing magic and all. She was a practicing witch, is what his mom said. And she thinks maybe that would stand up in court."

"Witches aren't of sound mind?"

"She kept saying she knew they could prove whatever they needed to, and that their family attorney was only too happy to get involved in this case, but—and I think this is *really* creepy—in the meantime she wanted Noah to look for any supporting stuff he might find—you know, stuff that showed she was crazy—and mail it to her. She said they'll have someone do a psychological evaluation so he should mail *everything*. Artwork, good luck charms, talismans—whatever he could find."

"And did he go back upstairs after that? Could you hear him?"

"No. He didn't even seem all that interested. But she kept pestering him, asking him questions about Blix's state of mind when he first got here, and then he started telling the story about how Blix wouldn't go to the hospital. He told his mom that she did spells and stuff instead. Honestly, you would have thought, to hear how his mother was reacting, that Blix was out drinking bats' blood in the full moon."

"Oh my." I swallow hard. "This actually might be a good time to tell you that I found Blix's journal. It was in a book of spells she had in her kitchen, and I read it, and she did have all kinds of spells and remedies—not bats' blood that I remember, but she talked to her ancestors, and she contacted some spirit god and went out in the dark of the moon."

"Well, I'm going to go out on a limb here and think we need to put that in a safe place. Do you know where it is now?"

I try to think. I'd been reading it in bed, but then I'd taken it downstairs, hadn't I, when I made up the little pockets for the spell for Sammy? I *think* I'd put it back in the bookshelf. That's right. I did. I tucked the whole thing back where it had been, there among the cookbooks.

Right out in the open.

Where it's always been and where anyone could find it.

I stand up. "I think I have to go."

"Call me if you need backup."

All the lights are off in the apartment when I go upstairs, and Noah is nowhere to be found.

Feeling ridiculous, I call his name, walking through, turning on lights, looking into corners. I've watched enough thrillers to know that people always hide behind doors and curtains, so I make sure these do not go unchecked. I even go into the bathroom and rip aside the shower curtain while I yell.

I've got myself all worked up just the way Natalie and I used to do after watching horror movies. Still, it's true that there is a strange vibration in the house tonight. Bedford is cowering in his crate and he whimpers when I let him out. There's something . . . it's as though the air has gotten all messed up somehow, like the molecules got scrambled and weren't able to reassemble themselves before I came in.

"Noah!" I call. "Are you here?"

There's no answer. His bedroom door is open and the light is off. "Noah?" I flick on the light. The bed has been stripped, and his closet has about eight empty hangers and nothing else. Bedford licks my hand.

There's an empty cardboard box in the hallway, and one of Noah's gym socks is stuck under the bathroom rug. So he'd finally come back for his stuff.

But did he come back in after talking to his mom? That's the question. I run into my room, and head for the underwear drawer. The sweatshirt is still there, and I shake it out, searching in the sleeve for Blix's letter.

Nothing. It's gone.

I turn it inside out to make sure, but no. I can feel hot tears just behind my eyes. Why hadn't I known he'd look for this at some point? Why, when he'd even *asked* me for it, did I think it was safe in the underwear drawer? Of course he was going to look!

Patrick texts me:

I hear you running around. Is he there?

Not here. His closet is empty.

Is the "eagle" safe?

Patrick, the letter is gone! The one that Blix wrote me. I just want to cry.

What about the OTHER eagle?

Checking now. Walking, walking . . . in the kitchen . . . YES! The spell book and journal are on the shelf! Safe and sound.

For God's sake, speak in code! What kind of evidence hider ARE you?

Sorry. Forgot my #spyeducation. Going undercover now. Call me Natasha from now on.

SHUT UP I NEVER HEARD OF YOU

I remove the book from the shelf and take it downstairs with me. I'll sleep with it tonight in my bed. And tomorrow I'll call Charles Sanford and tell him what's happened.

Bedford's professional opinion is that we should go outside so he can pee, and then we should lock the bedroom door tonight, just in case. He actually lies on the floor with his nose by the door and growls every few minutes to make the point.

I'm pretty sure that Noah isn't going to come back tonight, but then what do I know? I never thought Noah cared all that much about getting this building in the first place. And clearly he does.

I go over and scratch Bedford behind the ears. "No one's here but you and me, boy. Come on up on the bed. Everything's fine."

He finally, worriedly comes up on the foot of the bed, but every car that goes by sends a cascade of light darting around the walls, ending in a point in the corner. And each time he lifts his head and growls a bit. There are noises, the settling of the house and the banging of the radiator, voices of people going past in the street, laughing even though it's the middle of the night. A car backfires and Bedford and I both leap into the air.

At last he puts his head on the pillow. But he keeps his eyes open long after I think we should both be sleeping. It's like he knows we're not done with the bad vibes just yet.

And I feel so sad about the missing letter. My connection to Blix.

THIRTY-EIGHT
MARNIE

It's after noon on Wednesday when I finally get back to the house from the store, lugging the eighteen-pound turkey and the bags of groceries—so many that I had to take an Uber instead of the subway.

Bedford is even more hyper than usual, so after I put all the food away, I leash him up and take him outside. But then he's not interested in anything in particular. Pees on the curb with a lackluster air. He sits on the stoop and looks at me expectantly, like *I'm* the one who needed to come out here, not him.

When we go back inside, he charges into the bedroom.

My head is full of cooking plans, but he's barking and running around . . . and that's when the little prickles of dread start.

I follow him into Blix's bedroom, which looks different, even since two hours ago when I left it. My dresser drawer is open a crack, and my flannel pajamas are on the floor. And the walls—they're bare! Not entirely bare, but things have been taken down—Blix's artwork, her talismans, her weavings.

And the bed—the bed is all in disarray, with the covers tossed everywhere.

My breath is high up in my chest as I run and lift up my pillow, which is where I had hidden *The Encyclopedia of Spells*.

It's gone. I feel around under all the sheets and blankets, look under the kantha, look on the floor on the other side of the bed.

Bedford looks at me.

Blix's secrets are gone. I slide down onto the floor.

Patrick comes right up when I call him. I let him in, and we walk through the rooms, and I show him all the places where there was once artwork. The living room, the kitchen, the hallway—everywhere you can see little pale patches on the wall with nails sticking out.

I think my heart is breaking.

Patrick says I should immediately call Charles Sanford, and I do, but he's not picking up. Right. It's the day before Thanksgiving. A lot of people are going over the river and through the woods today. They are not in their offices.

"Should we call the cops, do you think?" Patrick says.

"I feel too sad," I tell him. "I don't want the police going after Noah. For God's sake, his great-aunt has died. And maybe this stuff had some sentimental value to him. Also, who's to say Blix wouldn't want him to have some stuff from here?"

"Yeah," says Patrick, but he doesn't look convinced.

"Do you want some coffee?" I ask him. "I fight every day with this damned coffee press, and I'm willing to go another round with it."

"Oh, I know how to work that thing," he says. And then he very competently makes coffee. He's wearing jeans and a blue sweater. His dark hair brushes his collar, and I love that, for a moment, at least, I have an excuse simply to watch him, since I'm pretending to care how to work this abominable coffee thing that hates me.

Normally, Patrick doesn't like it when I look at him. But now, as I see his miraculous, stitched-back-together hands and fingers, see the nimble way he has of moving about, I can't help but think how stunning it is that he is here at all, that we're together in this room, in Blix's kitchen. Standing close together. I think of the spell book, Blix's journal, and my breath goes up high in my chest. This feels so momentous.

He straightens up, hands me a cup of coffee.

"Would you like a little help with piecrust?" he says. "Because I am, as you well know, the Prince of Pastry."

"Prince of Pastry, Chief of Cheesecake . . . you could have many titles."

"At Thanksgiving, though, I try to stay with pies. It's only fitting."

He rolls out some piecrust on the table, and I get busy chopping carrots and celery for the salad, and then, maybe because I'm feeling bold because there's nothing left to lose here, or maybe because I know I'm going home in a month and he's leaving for the depths of the Wyoming wilderness, I say very carefully, "I want to know what happened to you. I've now told you every embarrassing thing about me, and now I need to know about you. What happened. Please tell me."

"A lot of people don't know that the true secret ingredient to piecrusts is that the baker cannot talk to others while making it."

"Don't joke with me about this. I have to know. Is there somebody you love? Is that why you're going to Wyoming, because one of the twenty-eight people there loves you and wants you back?"

He lifts his chin up, looks for a moment like he's not going to say anything, and then he sighs. Maybe my persistence has worn him down, but somehow I prefer to think that Blix is making him tell me—Blix operating from the other side.

"She died," he says finally. "The person I loved died."

The sentence hangs in the air. I swallow and say, "Please tell me."

There's such a long silence that I think he has decided to completely ignore me. But then he sighs again, and when he starts, he speaks haltingly, lightly, like maybe it won't land so hard that way.

"Four years ago. A gas leak." He stares out the window. "We were in the studio together. I was making a sculpture. She was finishing a painting. She went to make coffee, lit a match near the gas stove, and there was an explosion. Blue light, the whole room engulfed in that light. I looked up and she was on fire. She was *in the flames*, and there was no getting her out."

He stops, looks right at me. "I was across the room, but I remember running toward her, pulling her away . . . grabbing a blanket and rolling it over her." He holds out his hands, spreads his fingers apart. I see the scars and the patches, the scaled-away parts, the ridges. "These, believe it or not, are medical miracles. For some reason Anneliese didn't get the miracles. I did. Even though I didn't want them." He flattens the dough with the palm of his hand. "What *I* wanted was to have died right along with her."

I hold myself very steady. It's like he's a wild animal and I don't want to frighten him away with too much sentiment, too much sympathy. I feel almost as though I am outside of myself. Maybe this is how Blix would have handled things.

"For the longest time death was all I wished for. Instead, I got surgeries. Thirteen surgeries. And a settlement. I lost my love, my art, my ability to even look at my old sculptures without wanting to throw up, but apparently society gives you money for that kind of loss. I went from being your typical poor, starving, happy artist to being a rich guy with literally nothing in the world that I wanted."

Bedford comes over and puts his rubber ball on the floor next to Patrick, and Patrick strokes his head, scratches him behind the ears. He actually smiles down at him.

"Where did Blix fit in? Did you know her at the time of the accident?"

"Really, Marnie? Really, do we *have* to talk about this?" He looks back down at the dough. "Blix found me one day in Manhattan. It was after. Long after. I was rich, living in a luxury hotel, eating room service every night, drinking myself to death, or trying to. And my therapist said it was time I went and looked at art again, tried to make friends with it. 'Art,' she said, 'wasn't the thing that hurt you. And maybe it has the power to heal you. You should give it a chance.' So I got to the Museum of Modern Art and I tried to make myself go inside. Walked five steps in, and then turned around and went back out. Then I talked to myself and went in again, and turned around and came back out. Five times, in and out again, in and out. And then a voice said to me, 'Are you imitating a person who's attached to an invisible rubber band? Is this an art installation you're doing outside the museum? Because I'm sold, if that's what this is.' My immediate response was that I wanted to kill whoever had said that, but then I saw this old lady standing there wearing crazy clothes, with her hair sticking up and her eyes so kind and compassionate. 'Hi, I'm Blix,' she said. And you know how she is—how those eyes would reach over and look right into you! Oh my God! The first person who ever looked at me like that. 'Or maybe,' she said, 'there's something inside that you can't bear to see.' She's there, just looking at me, human to human. It was like she didn't even see all my scars. 'Maybe there's something inside that you can't bear to see.'" He shakes his head, remembering.

"Wow," I say.

"Yeah. So she takes me by the arm—my arm, which was still hurting, I'll have you know, but Blix didn't know from pain—and we go have a cup of coffee together. I'm too exhausted to resist her. I feel like I'm under hypnosis or something. She takes me to this dark restaurant, like she knew instinctively that's what I needed, some shadows, and we sit in the back. And she says, 'Tell me.' So . . . I told her a bit of the story. And she wanted to hear all of it. I said no at first, but then the story starts pouring out of me. And it was the first time I'd told it. The fire, the operations, the therapist. She listened and then she said we should go into the museum together. And so we did."

"What happened?"

"Before we even got to the art, a child started screaming at the sight of me, and old Blix—well, she was *not* having any of that. She held on to me, walked me through the museum. Steeled herself for whatever was going to happen. Gave me her strength. I could feel it flowing to me. After that, I started meeting her every week. We didn't go to the art museum anymore, where people stared at me. She would come to my fancy hotel room with the maid service and the room service, and we'd just sit there and talk. About life, about art, about politics. And then one day she said to me, 'Listen, I like the look of you, and this is no fucking way to live your life. This is false and harmful and dangerous to your health. You're coming to live in my building with me. In Brooklyn. You'll have people.' And so I did.

"I didn't *want* any people, mind you, so I saw that as a big drawback, but I got Houndy and Jessica and Sammy in the bargain. And Lola. Five people, counting Blix. All I could handle. I took the job writing up symptoms. Because I wanted something to do. I thought this was the way to do it, stay so busy thinking about other things—people's symptoms—that I wouldn't think. And it works. I get to stay away from the outside world, from the children who cry when they see me. I don't go out. I don't have to. Why should I let in the awfulness out there, the people who stare at me and make me feel like a freak?"

"Did . . . Blix think that was okay? You not going out?"

"Well, yes and no. She gave me the space to live my life, and I loved her for it, and when she was sick, I didn't say 'Go to the hospital, get your tumor looked at, let them cut you up,' because I knew that wasn't what she wanted to do, and why should she? And she didn't say to me, 'Why aren't you trying to find art again? Why aren't you out there working on being a social guy?' We didn't do that to each other. I knew why she didn't want to turn herself over to surgeons, and she knew why I needed to mend in the quiet."

I am having a traitorous thought. I am thinking that maybe it would have worked out better for him if, say, she had pushed him just a little, nudged him back into life. Not right away, of course—I'm sure it took everything to dislodge him from his grief and get him to move to Brooklyn. But at some point.

As if he's reading my thoughts, he says, "Things changed after a while, though. She would come down and put on music and say it was time that we danced together. Or she'd insist that I come upstairs to her dinner parties and mingle with nice people who weren't going to stare. People she'd probably prepared in advance. She said once—she said it was time I realized that most people are way too self-absorbed to be looking at somebody like me and thinking pitying thoughts. She said—ha! I still can't get over this—she said that it would be such a more wonderful world if people *did* care enough to stare. But they don't, she said. They're thinking of their own lives."

"That sounds about right."

"Then she started in with this campaign to make me believe in love again. She claimed to have magic, and she kept saying there was love coming for me." He wiggles his floury fingers in the air and rolls his eyes. "She and Lola were these old ladies, always trying to drag the topic over to love. Like we were in a sitcom or a happily-ever-after Disney movie. Like *Beauty and the Beast*! One day we had an actual *serious* conversation about whether or not Belle—was that her name?—yeah, whether *Belle* really loved the beast from the beginning or if it was just pity." He eases the piecrust into the pie pan, turning it just so, tilting his head while he works it perfectly. "Read the text, people! It's fear and pity. Fear and pity—how's that as a cocktail for a doomed relationship?"

I can't speak. I've put down the knife I'm scraping the carrots with, because my hands seem to be shaking.

"Anyway," he says. "Here are the facts I've accepted: Anneliese will always be dead. I always will have tried to get to her in time and failed. When it really counted, I was powerless to change the outcome." He swallows and goes silent for a moment. Then he says, "You know, I used to dream that she made the coffee and the explosion didn't happen. Then I'd dream that the explosion happened, but that she and I weren't there; we came back to a studio that was gone but we were safe. Then other times, I'd dream that she lived through the burns and the pain and didn't love me anymore. So that's my life now. I endure. I'm not waiting to die anymore, but I'll never be the way I was before."

My voice feels clotted over when I speak. "Do you ever go anywhere? At all?"

He swings his eyes over to me, like he's just remembered I'm there. "Ah, goodie, another caseworker! Yes. For your information, I do. I walk sometimes at night, or I go to the twenty-four-hour gym and work out with weights in the back room in the middle of the night where no one has to see me."

"What is this feeling about people *having* to see you? You're you! You're a person in the world, and okay, so you have scars. Does that mean people can't look at you? Why can't we just go somewhere you and me? In the daytime? We could take the dog for a walk maybe. We don't have to care what people think."

"Haven't you heard anything I've said? I don't *need* anything that's out there in the world. I don't want to go fucking *out*. And you will find in your life that a man who lives alone with a cat doesn't usually want to be walking a dog. What's next is that I'm going to *Wyoming*, where my sister has a house in the middle of nowhere with a spare wing for me. She's good at Scrabble and she reads books. And I get along with her fine."

"God, Patrick, I have to say that sounds like giving up."

"Yeah, well, I get to do that if I want to. I have the right to give up after what I went through." He leans down and scratches Bedford's ears.

"Don't I, boy? You want to give up, too? Is this the good boy who'd like to give up? Oh, yes you would! Oh, yes you would!"

"But isn't there some kind of art you want to do? Maybe, okay, not sculpture, but something else? Painting? Drawing? Photography? You're a creative guy, and you've convinced yourself to just shut off that whole part of your personality."

"Wow, look at the time!" he says sarcastically.

"I know. I shouldn't be offering any advice to anybody. Look at what a mess I've made of things. Also, may I just say that I think you have potential as a dog person. Just saying."

"No. It's cats for me. They need so little. I'm only trying to humor this mutt, with his neediness. Dogs are shameless self-promoters."

He stretches. His shirt rides up, exposing his belly—which I can't resist looking at. It's all smooth, regular, unburned skin. His burns are all located on the parts of him that show.

"What I feel worst about just now is that Noah's parents are going to have Blix's journal," he says, "and then they're going to try to take her house, and that's just what she didn't want to happen. Just another example of powerlessness in the face of fate."

"You know something? I don't care if they take her house. You're leaving, and I'm leaving."

"You don't mean that," he tells me quietly. "They can't have Blix's house, because even if we're not here, it has to house her spirit. It's not meant for them."

"No. I think her spirit is somewhere else altogether. I think it's in the relationships she had with the people. If I have to give up on this house, then I will. I'm not going to do a whole court battle for a building I can't even take care of."

He looks stunned. And then I make things so much worse, because I can't help myself—I go over to him and stand on tiptoe and kiss him on the cheek, right below his eye, where there's the smoothest, pinkest skin. I just want to touch him.

It feels like silk. But he jerks away from my touch. He says, "No! Do not do that!"

"Does it hurt?"

"I can't stand being pitied."

"But I don't pity you. Why do you have to read affection as pity? Maybe that's what Blix was trying to tell you." I feel myself start to cry, which is even worse than trying to touch him.

Everything's weird after that. I've made the worst mess of things. He's rattled and angry. And I'm apologetic, but nothing helps. Nothing feels right.

After he's gone, I go in the living room, and stop beside the sculpture on the mantel. At least this is something Noah didn't take, maybe because it's so big. I touch its strong, deep lines, feel the taut seams underneath the welding, underneath the smoothness. Patrick made this back when he was healthy and whole. But he says he will never be that way again.

I close my eyes. *Do* I pity him? Am I drawn to him because of how fragile he seems?

Is it that I feel sorry for him because he's burned and damaged?

You are okay, says a voice.

You are so meant to be where you are.

And you can love him. He is meant to be loved.

THIRTY-NINE
MARNIE

Thanksgiving dawns rainy, windy, and cold. The first really cold day of the season. The wooden floors chill my feet when I get out of bed. It's five fifteen, time to start the turkey.

It hits me that I seem to have accidentally invited thirteen people for dinner (fourteen if you count Patrick, but he won't come), and I have no idea what any of them are bringing to share. They all said they'd bring *something*, and until this moment that seemed good enough for me. Back when I planned this whole thing, I figured whatever arrives is going to be just the thing we need.

But now—what if we end up only with the turkey, my green bean casserole that probably no one is going to like, my pile of mashed potatoes, and a pie that Patrick made? This will be the first Thanksgiving that people will have to call out for pizza.

I'm pretty sure I could qualify for my adulting license on the basis of this day alone, especially if it turns out there's enough food. I turn on some kick-ass rock music and crank it up loud while I work in the kitchen. I put on an old apron that I find in the cupboard and twirl around before I confront the massive, eighteen-pound turkey looming in the fridge. The happy homemaker, that's me.

"Tom," I say to him. "You're my first. Just so you know. So I'd appreciate it if you could do the right thing here, feastwise. I mean, I'm sorry and all about what you must have gone through. But I want you to know I'm deeply appreciative. Giving thanks for your life."

I have to borrow chairs, forks, knives, spoons, tablecloths, plates, and platters. Jessica says she has some, and so does Lola, and if those aren't enough—well, then some people might have to sit on the floor to eat, or else we'll eat in shifts, Jessica says.

Eat in shifts! I think of my mother with her white damask tablecloth and her candlesticks and the sterling silver turkey platter and dessert forks. She would *die* at the idea of people sitting on the floor or eating in shifts.

Jessica shows up first, at nine o'clock, bringing two pumpkin pies, coleslaw, four pounds of clams, and an apple crisp.

How stunningly random and un-Thanksgiving-like. "What are we going to do with these clams?" I ask, a little nervous.

"Clam chowder, of course! I know, I know; clams and coleslaw aren't the first things you think of when you're imagining Thanksgiving," she says, "but I thought it would be fun. And I feel that Thanksgiving should be about giving thanks for everything you like, not just the turkey. Which, by the way, smells fantastic!"

Lola, somewhat more of a traditionalist, comes in at ten with a squash casserole, some homemade dinner rolls, and two pumpkin pies.

After an hour, I baste the turkey like any expert would. Paco runs over with slabs of roast beef, a beet salad, a vat of onion soup, and some Grey Poupon mustard. And three more pumpkin pies. The waitress from Yolk shows up with her boyfriend, and they get busy playing with the dog, and also with another dog, who has come along with one of Blix's dog walker friends apparently.

Andrew and Sammy come downstairs and start making a pot of clam chowder that could feed the entire borough. This reminds Lola to mention that she's invited Harry, just as he arrives with enough lobsters to feed the Eastern Seaboard.

"You are Blix's favorite niece," he tells me, and when I correct him, he says, "Okay, okay. Great-niece-in-law, have it your way!" and I feel silly for bringing it up.

I also have no idea how we're going to cook these things—it seems every burner is being taken up, and there are dishes still waiting for their turn at the stove. Two of my Best Buds customers—the lesbian moms, Leila and Amanda, who were writing to the sperm donor—come and bring rolls and a pumpkin pie.

We are now full up on pumpkin pies, I notice.

Leila starts asking questions about when I'm selling the place and leaving, and I tell her all the problems, blah blah blah, and it turns out that she knows a real estate agent who would be happy to come and look at it and give me some advice. She whips out her phone and makes a call and then she yells over to me, "Tomorrow morning okay? Elevenish?"

"Sure," I call back to her.

Jessica comes over right then and taps me on the arm and whispers. "Um, just so you know, *Noah* seems to be here. He's in the living room, chatting with people and acting like he's the host."

"Noah?"

She smiles. "And also—I should tell you, there seems to be something going on with Lola. She's on the stoop with the New Jersey man, and things do not seem to be going well."

"Oh my God. I think he's proposing to her."

"Proposing? To Lola?"

"Are there flowers involved?" I yell to Jessica over a sudden din involving pots and pans, and she says there seem to be.

"I'll report back," she tells me.

The kitchen is starting to resemble a restaurant warehouse—except, you know, way more random. In the corner, Harry and the waitress's boyfriend are talking politics. Leila and Amanda are trying to set up tray tables in the living room, but the legs of one are broken so Andrew says he'll get a screwdriver and asks me where one might be kept, then it turns out that Bedford is happily chewing on it behind the couch.

The Yolk waitress says she'll set all the tables, but then she needs help locating the serving spoons and then the tablecloths and the water glasses.

And then she stops and says, "Andrew? *Andrew?* Oh my God, *you're* here! Are you with your wife? And *son*?"

I can't. I just can't.

Andrew, his face having gone white, is looking around the room, searching for Jessica, probably, and I hear him say, "Please—if you could just *not*—"

"Not mention that you dumped me? Of course I won't," I hear her say, and he takes her by the elbow and steers her into another corner of the kitchen. He's saying, "I mean, I've told her about you," as they go past. "It's just that we're so newly back together . . ."

Harry stops yelling about Republicans long enough to ask me sweetly if I think the lobsters are ever going to get their chance with the burners. And do I know where Houndy's lobster pots are?

"Where are the serving spoons, again?" someone wants to know.

"Who made the squash casserole? Does it need oven space?"

There are a million conversations going on around me, and I'm basting the turkey one more time, and juggling the piece of aluminum foil I'm holding and the turkey baster, when suddenly I'm aware that Noah is talking to me.

"Ta-*dah*!" he's saying. "Marnie, look who's here! What a surprise!"

At first I think he means himself, and I am ready to glare at him and tell him he shouldn't be here, not after what he's done—I never invited him anyway—but when I turn my head, oh my God, it is Jeremy's face that fills the room.

Jeremy. It takes such a long time for his face to make sense to me—why in God's name is Jeremy's face here in Brooklyn, standing here at *Thanksgiving*, with Noah, of all people, standing beside him, smiling at me with a shit-eating grin that could light up the whole freaking world?

And as I turn my head, my hand in the oven mitt goes with it somehow, and then the turkey—Tom, the pan, the juices, the stuffing, all of it—slides in slow motion to the floor, and I go down with it, hard onto the floor, banging my head on the table in the process, and in the screaming that follows, all I can think is that this is when it would be so good to be the sort of person who faints.

But no such luck. I am conscious for everything that comes next.

FORTY
MARNIE

This can't be happening. Of course it can't. In a minute I'll wake up and this will have been a dream, and I'll get out of bed and life will be normal.

But no.

Noah's arm is still slung over Jeremy's shoulders, and Jeremy looks blank eyed with shock while Noah is smiling this horrible grin, and oh my God, if so many things didn't hurt me at once, and if I wasn't stuck in this puddle of turkey fat, I'd get to my feet and I'd figure out something to say or do that would smooth things over, except that even in all the confusion and chaos and din of voices, it's dawning on me that there isn't going to be anything I can say or do. That this will never be smooth.

"Why?" I manage to say to Jeremy, which is, of course, the question *he* should be asking me. But I mean *why are you standing here in this kitchen*, and *why didn't I know you were coming*. He doesn't answer me, and somebody is trying to help me up, then she slips, too, and goes smack down in the turkey fat with me. And I want to laugh because it's possible that this one turkey is going to take out the entire party. We'll all be slipping and sliding here trying to save ourselves and each other in the very worst Thanksgiving party ever.

Jeremy's face is saying: *You are the worst person in the whole world.*

And then he is gone.

"Wait!" I say, or maybe I didn't actually get that word out in the din and pain and craziness. Two more people are sliding in the grease, and someone is tracking it across the kitchen, and Bedford is drinking the turkey drippings. I can hear Jessica and Andrew arguing by the kitchen table.

I get myself up, and head for the hallway. It hurts like hell to walk, and then Bedford dashes by me, holding the turkey carcass, with people chasing him, but I don't care. I limp into the entryway and there is Jeremy heading for the front door, and I say to him, "Please. Could we go somewhere and talk?"

"Is there anything to say?" he asks. "I think I've got the whole picture."

"Let's go outside," I tell him, and we go out on the stoop, where the rain is still listlessly falling, winding down to a gray, depressing, end-of-the-world drizzle. I don't care. I'm covered in grease and turkey bits, even in my hair, and my hip is killing me, and I think my head might be growing some kind of huge lump where I banged it.

But all that is nothing compared to Jeremy, whose eyes look like black holes in the middle of his face, and I can see that his wide, capable, physical-therapy hands are actually shaking.

I have broken this man.

Again.

"Talk to me," I say. "Go ahead. Say it. Say it all."

He shakes his head. I can't bear to look at him. "There's nothing . . . I'm in shock," he says.

"No. Please. Say it."

He exhales and looks around. I can see him taking in the whole rainy, desolate street scene. And then his eyes come back to me and he says in a low voice, "I've talked to you fifty times since you've been here, and you didn't even once think it might be good to mention that your ex-husband was here? Not even once?"

"Well? I didn't think you'd understand."

"What part of it wouldn't I understand?"

"How two people who were married to each other can stay in the same house."

"I can understand that. I trust you."

"No, you wouldn't."

"Try me. Please," he says. "Just tell me you weren't having sex with him, and I'll believe you. I'm not a suspicious person."

That's when it hits me that he really doesn't know. I look down at my shoes.

"Oh my God," he says. "Oh my fucking God. Marnie! I can't believe this! You've done this to me *again*! How could you *do* this?"

"I didn't plan this."

"What does that even mean? You didn't set out to crush me, is that it? But *why* did you do it?"

"Oh, God, I am really and truly very sorry. Jeremy, listen. I didn't know when I came here that he was here. And then when he was, I was thinking it was still okay and that I'd come back home next month and you and I would get married, and—"

"That's bullshit. You've been lying to me! Talking to me almost every day and never telling me anything near the truth. I-I'm speechless."

He stares out again at the dismal, dreary street, littered with leaves, and then he turns back to me. "This place sucks. You know that? This is what you're picking, instead of the life we had talked about? *This?*"

"It doesn't look so good right now," I admit. "But it's really kind of beautiful in its way. You're not seeing it at its best. And under the circumstances . . ."

He looks at me a long time, and then he shakes his head. "I've got to get out of here. I don't think I can take any more."

"Before you go, can I ask you one thing? Did Noah set you up for this? Did he get you to come?"

"Wow. You really are delusional, aren't you? I came here because I missed you, you idiot, because I thought it would be *fun* to surprise you since I felt bad that you were away for the holidays. Your whole family and I thought this up. That's why nobody's talked to you on the phone for the past week, because we were all so excited and worried that we'd spoil the surprise."

"Oh," I say. "Well. This may sound beside the point, but I've always said that I hate surprises. Now I know why."

He gives me an incredulous look. "You suck, you know that?" And then he shakes his head and walks down the steps and turns down the sidewalk.

"Want me to call you a cab?" I call down to him. But he doesn't even grace that offer with a backward glance, which is fine. I don't deserve anything from him. Nothing at all.

"I'm sorry!" I yell. "I'm really, really so very sorry!"

He doesn't turn around for that either.

FORTY-ONE
MARNIE

"I have never heard so much yelling associated with Thanksgiving," Patrick tells me. He's walking from the kitchen to the living room with a cup of tea, which he hands me, and a teapot. "Well, maybe the very *first* Thanksgiving had that level of tension. Possibly Myles Standish caused this much trouble with the Native Americans—he was a bit of a brute, from what I've heard. But I'm not even sure about *that*."

He looks over at me, sitting on his couch with my foot propped up and ice that's supposedly going to help with the bump on my head. He may have forgotten that he's mad at me for the crime of trying to kiss him. At least he let me come here. Even came upstairs and got me. Fixed the ice pack. Gave me drinks of water. And now herbal tea. Put aside his deadline about colon cancer, he said.

"Doesn't matter in the least," he told me. "People are digesting their turkey dinner, and they should be giving thanks and not rushing to read about colon cancer. Any symptoms they're having tonight are just that they ate too much."

"Yet another thing I'm responsible for today."

"Oh, you, stop with the self-pity. It's all going to be fine. For the rest of your life, you're going to have the most exciting Thanksgiving dinner story anyone's ever heard."

Yes. After the madness died down—after I'd gone back inside and screamed at Noah, and pulled Bedford away from the turkey drippings, then cleaned up the puke when he *didn't* stop licking up the drippings; after I'd cried with Lola, who told me I was a traitor, and after I'd tried to persuade Jessica not to break up with Andrew once again; after I'd packed Harry off with his bag of wiggling lobsters that never *did* get cooked, and sent the waitress limping off with her new boyfriend—well, Patrick came upstairs and retrieved me and gave me a place to hide. He checked out the bump on my head, peered in my eyes, asked me some arithmetic questions, and declared that I don't have a concussion.

Things may not be *fine* fine—there was way too much crying for that—but maybe it's livable. That's the best I can do right now. Patrick walked Lola home. I think he comforted Sammy. I think he may even have cleaned up most of the mess while I was dealing with all the fall-out. He tied a piece of gauzy cotton around my head where it might have been bleeding a bit.

I feel bad about so many things. Maybe one of the worst things is Lola, who told me in no uncertain terms that she was furious that I'd been conspiring, as she put it, behind her back to get her married off to William Sullivan. Aiding and abetting the enemy behind the front lines! How dare I! Helping him write that letter! Encouraging him! Giving him hope, even though I knew—I *knew*—her position!

Which I did know. She's absolutely right.

"How could you *not* have told me you were talking to him!" she said. "Is there *nothing* that you matchmakers won't do?"

But the magic, I wanted to tell her. The *sparkles*.

And then there was Jessica—well, she was just devastated, plain and simple. Not so mad at me, thank goodness, because how could *I* have known that the Yolk waitress happened to be the woman who Andrew had cheated with? Jessica says it's simply humiliating (her word) that all this time, she and I had been friendly with that waitress, and in fact we'd exchanged little tidbits of our lives with her—not even knowing who she was! (And excuse me, not for nothing, but who knew that Brooklyn was such a small town after all? That's what amazed me—that with all the millions of people milling around this place, how our waitress at Yolk could *possibly* be the woman who had enticed Andrew away from his marriage vows!)

This might as well be Smalltown, America, I tell Patrick.

He smiles.

"Don't," I say and hold up one finger. "Too soon for smiling."

"You look sort of jaunty with that bandage on your head," he says. "Rather like a drunken sailor."

"Did I tell you that after Bedford had dragged the turkey carcass into the living room, and I went by there on my way to talk to Jeremy, Noah was taking the opportunity to remove things from the walls and put them in a box—presumably to send to his parents?"

"Classy Noah move."

"Probably just to make me mad."

He is sitting at the other end of his couch, as far away from me as he can get, I notice. And he's grinning happily.

"What's so funny?"

"I'll tell you. But first, in exchange for all the excellent care and rescue, I need you to tell me every single detail. One by one. And start with what happened with Jeremy," he says. "That poor guy."

"Yes. God, I'm the worst. And of all the things that happened today, the fact that Jeremy came here without telling me, and got my whole family to keep it a secret as well—I still can't believe it."

"You had no clue?" Patrick says. "None?"

"Well, he'd vaguely said a time or two that it was too bad we couldn't be together, and he'd offered to come and help me sell the place . . ."

"But nothing like, 'See you at Thanksgiving, my plane gets in at eleven'?"

"Nothing. In fact, I hadn't even talked to him for a week or so, because I was so busy worrying about Noah and the Blix stuff." I put my head in my hands. "I can't believe I've done this to him. That look on his face."

"So . . . did he yell and scream? How did you guys leave it?"

"He was monumentally disappointed and sad. And yes, he yelled. Quite out of character for him. I believe we left it that I suck. Which I do."

Patrick now actually laughs. "Stop it. Who do you think you're talking to? You weren't ever going to end up with him. The first thing you told me about him is that he is the most god-awful boring man you'd ever met. I believe those were your exact words."

"But boring is not a crime. And anyway I led him on. And betrayed him."

"First of all, you weren't leading him on. You were *deciding* about him. And I happen to believe that your *betrayal*, as you call it, was part of the deciding. Also, for the record, I think Blix considered being boring a crime," he says. "Which it is. I agree."

"You're right. She did. She was married to that boring legal aid person, or was it the boring bug guy? And I told her she couldn't just leave somebody because he was boring, and she said of course she could! She had to, she said. So she did."

He reaches over and pours me some more tea from the teapot. "So anyway, we're all agreed that you weren't going to end up with him. And even though this was a shock for him, we have to acknowledge that he bears some responsibility for finding out the way he did. When you set up a surprise, you have to figure that you're the one that might get surprised. Right?"

I stare at him. "Patrick, I am dumbfounded at this side of your personality."

He shrugs. "What? I'm just stating the facts. The way I see it, there are no victims here. And also—look at it this way—you've now freed him up to find the true love of his life. *And* he'll always have a great story to tell about Thanksgiving in Brooklyn. How many people get such a good breakup story?"

"I hope he'll be all right. It's like he's a person who has his emotions in a safety-deposit box somewhere, and he forgot where he put the key." I realize with some surprise that this really *is* what makes him boring. He's protected himself with layers of emotional padding, tamping down every single true feeling that might cross his mind. Maybe it's because of losing his father at an early age and having that anxious mother he had to take care of. Emotion was a luxury item on the menu, and he couldn't afford it.

"Even when he asked me to marry him, he wasn't overjoyed," I say slowly. "When I said yes, he looked absolutely shocked. Happy, maybe, but mostly shocked. And even when we had sex, it was—"

"Okay. I'm willing to listen to most things, but I draw the line here. Your sex life. I used to have to put on headphones when you and—oh, never mind."

"Sorry." I look over at him and think about him listening to Noah and me making love. Fighting. Crabbing about things. Making up again. And him knowing all along how Blix hadn't wanted Noah there.

Then his phone rings, and he picks it up and says, "Hi, Elizabeth."

He takes the phone into the kitchen.

"Yeah, I'm thinking the second week in December most likely," I hear him say as he paces the kitchen. "No, no. I'm renting a U-Haul. Sure . . . No, people do drive in winter. I've heard it can be done . . . I think the drive will do me good."

Ah, his sister. He really is going to Wyoming. With a U-Haul.

I slump down into the couch even farther. I feel exhausted to my very core. My head is throbbing and now my leg aches where I knocked it when I slipped, and I just want to close my eyes and disappear.

And I'm so tired, so paralyzingly tired, and everything I've thought and believed here has been wrong. I don't know what Blix saw in me, but I didn't help *anybody*. And I'm certainly not a matchmaker. I've lost the one guy who, boring or not, actually *wanted* to marry me, all because I cheated with the guy who had *left* me! And I've made a mess of things with Lola, whom I like so much, and somehow I feel like I've even betrayed Blix, by not protecting her papers. And because of that, her stupid grandnephew and his unscrupulous family are now going to try to get the will changed.

And Patrick, the one person here that I can talk to, who makes me laugh—though he thinks I pity him—is going to move far away. Retreating even farther away from people. So much for Blix's plan.

"I'm going to drive straight through," he is saying. He laughs. "Right. It's not like me to stop. In public."

And what am *I* going to do, now that I'm not heading home to marry Jeremy?

Am I just to go back home and face my family's exasperation? They'll hear tomorrow from Jeremy what happened. They may even be hearing about it right this minute! He will, of course, move on with his life—so much for the fun little team we were going to create. Working in his office together and being all happily married and going to Cancun when we retire. Why couldn't I have just done that? What the hell is wrong with me, anyway? I'll be back in my childhood bedroom once again, seeing the consternation on everybody's faces as they try to figure out *once again* what I should do with my life.

Ohhh, Marnie!

What are we going to do about Marnie?

And Natalie—*sorry, sis, but I won't be having a baby and raising it right alongside yours. No barbecues by the pool with our tanned, relaxed husbands. I screwed everything up.*

Of course I don't *have* to go back there. Once I leave here, having disrupted and/or ruined everyone's lives, I can pick somewhere else to go. Look on the map and select a new location where no one knows the havoc I can wreak. Honestly, I should be required to have a sign on me: MENACE! THINKS SHE'S GOT MATCHMAKING SKILLS. STAY AWAY!

I close my eyes.

Patrick, as if speaking from a great distance: "Well, yeah. Myself, yes. No—well, not much furniture, of course, but I have the computers." He laughs. "No, of course I *need* them! I'm not exactly going to leave them behind."

I open one eye and see the computers across the room, blinking approvingly as I slide away, down into the darkness.

Later I feel something being placed over me, and I struggle to open my eyes. Patrick says, "Let me make sure your pupils aren't dilated." He lifts my lids, one at a time, and says, "Hmmm."

"Patrick," I say through a thickness in my mouth. "I don't believe in magic anymore."

"Bullshit," he says.

"No, it's *not* bullshit. And I have to go home." I struggle to sit up. Roy has been sleeping in the crook of my arm, and he jumps off the couch. My head is throbbing like there are a million tiny hammers inside my brain. My eyes don't seem to be operational in the usual way.

"Absolutely not," says Patrick. "You need to stay here. You shouldn't be alone with a possible head thing. Come on. You can sleep in my bed. I'll get you settled."

He gently helps me up and leads me to his room, which, even in my sleepy state, I can tell is so spare it's almost monkish. Hardly any lights. And he draws back the covers, and then he puts his hands on my shoulders and sits me down on the side of the bed and takes off my shoes. Then he sits back on his heels. I feel his eyes on me.

"Hmmm. Your clothes still have turkey stains all over them. Shall I go upstairs and get your pajamas?"

I don't answer. I just plop down on the bed on my back.

"Right. I know. You can wear one of my sweatshirts."

"Too hot."

"Okay, then a T-shirt." There's the sound of drawers opening and closing, and then he's back—I smell his presence more than see him—and he puts something in my hands: a shirt, I realize. "Do you need help? Oh, dear. I hadn't thought much about this part."

"I can do it," I mumble. And then sleep overtakes me again; I am thinking about the computers blinking—but they're not here, are they? Not in here. Patrick says, "No, no, sit up. Here. Alllll right. I'll do it for you. Lift your arms. I'm going to slide your sweater up over your head. There."

The air is cold on my skin all of a sudden. Then he's sliding a shirt down over my chest and arms. My bra, I think. No one likes to sleep in a bra. Men probably don't know that. I feel like laughing about that, but I can't.

And anyway now he's eased me back down on the bed and is tugging at my pants, which are so tight that he has to yank them, but then they're off, one leg and then the other is free, and I'm trying not to think of what underpants I have on, that he's *seeing*, and then the covers are over me, and there was something else I wanted to say to him, but I can't think just now of what it is, and anyway, I'm too tired to get the words out. I'll think about Patrick seeing my underpants tomorrow. And oh yes, I want to ask him not to go. I want to tell him that Blix really wants him to stay. That there's other art he could do. I want to try one more last, desperate, begging thing.

And I will, just as soon as I can hold my head up again.

Later—how much later?—I turn over, and the cat jumps down off me. I hear Patrick breathing deeply somewhere, and when I open my eyes, he is right there, next to me in the bed. I command myself: *touch his arm,* but I can't tell if that really happens or if I am just thinking it, and then when I wake up, there is the smell of cinnamon, and Patrick is coming into the room saying, "How's the head? Did you sleep okay?"

The first words out of my mouth are maybe not the best ones. "What time is it? What's that smell?"

Patrick says, "Deep breaths. I made cinnamon buns."

"Cinnamon buns. I thought I was dreaming. You made them?"

"I made them." He's smiling at me. "I also made you some tea, so if you want to get up and come in the kitchen . . . or do you want me to bring it to you here?"

"Wait. Did I *sleep* here?"

"You did sleep here. You bumped your head, remember? So I put you to bed here."

"Of course I remember." And then I remember the rest—how everything blew up, how I don't believe in magic anymore, or matchmaking, or being extraordinary, and that makes me so sad, because I *wanted* to believe in Blix and all the things she said about me. I wanted to believe I was here for a reason, but I'm not. I feel tears just behind my eyes, and then they're rolling down my face, and my nose is running, too, and this is going to be ugly.

"Oh, dear," he says. "Here, come in the kitchen and have some tea and cinnamon buns. Let's get you moving again."

I obediently swing my legs over the side of the bed and look down at myself. Bare legs and a T-shirt I've never seen before. Oh God. I look back up at him.

"Yes. You're wearing my T-shirt. I couldn't let you sleep upstairs with a head injury. And your clothes had a lot of turkey fat on them."

Ah yes. Then I sort of remember. Underpants. Being put to bed. Patrick there in the middle of the night, snoring softly next to me. It's all coming back to me. Oh God God God God. I look around for my clothes, which he hands me, folded neatly in a little pile.

"Well. Thank you," I say primly. I don't want to look at him, and I wish to hell he'd stop looking at me. Maybe if I *don't* look at him for long enough, he'll get the idea and head somewhere else. Go scare somebody about cancer or something.

"Well," he says. "Well. You're welcome." He stands there for what seems like another whole eternity, and then he says, "So, uh, I'll get out of your way and let you get dressed."

"Okay."

"When you get dressed, come into the kitchen, because I have something of a surprise for you. Well, let's not call it a *surprise*, shall we, because that word got ruined yesterday by Jeremy. Let's call it a plan."

Oh, yes, Jeremy. Ugh.

When he leaves, I blow my nose on tissues he has by the bed, and then I get up and struggle into my clothes. There are no mirrors in his apartment—it occurs to me that he probably doesn't like to look at himself, which is another thing that threatens to make me cry again—but I comb my hair as best I can. There may be some dried blood here and there. I wish I had a toothbrush.

Where are my shoes?

Oh my God, I think a real estate agent is coming! And the place is probably a wreck! Please tell me there's not a turkey carcass in the living room anymore.

Patrick slept beside me last night. He took care of me!

Wait . . . so Noah had moved out and yet he came to Thanksgiving, and why was he there, again?

And Jeremy. I have broken Jeremy.

So this is going to be the way life is for a while—thoughts showing up in my brain without notice, each one feeling like an emergency that needed to bump the previous thought out of the way.

I go into the kitchen, blinking from the fluorescent light.

"Hmm," he says. "You may want to work with that jaunty bandage before the real estate agent comes. You look a little like a pirate."

There's a bump from upstairs.

"Noah," I say. "Did I tell you he was taking things off the wall yesterday in the middle of everything? Blix's stuff. I'll bet he's back. Doing it again."

"Well, that," Patrick says. "That's what I wanted to talk to you about last night, but then my sister called. I have to show you something. Can you follow me?"

He steers me over to the back door and unlocks all the bolts and—out on his little stunted terrace—there is a whole stack of cardboard boxes. Three, maybe. Large ones.

I look at him blankly. He smiles.

"Frankly, this is the most unethical thing I have ever done in my life, but I kind of don't feel bad about it."

"But what is it?"

"The stuff Noah's been packing," he says. "Blix's stuff. It's all here."

"But how did you get it?" This is hurting my head even more.

"This is my brand of magic." His eyes are twinkling. I've never seen him look so happy.

"You *magically* got the boxes to get on your terrace?"

"Well. I *magically* overheard Noah asking Paco if the UPS driver stops at his bodega, and if he'd take these boxes, since Noah didn't feel like schlepping them to a post office, God forbid, or to a mailing center. And Paco said sure, no problem. And then *I*—"

"You didn't!"

"I did. I made an arrangement with Paco. He brought the boxes over here—Noah had brought some over to him on Wednesday afternoon, which means they must contain Blix's journal and your letter."

"Oh, Patrick!"

"So we can go through them and take out what we need—or rather what Blix needs us to have. And decide if we want to mail the rest."

"Can I kiss you?"

"No."

He says it so quickly that I laugh. First laugh since the fall.

"Come on. Technically we've slept together, so I think I could give you one kiss on the cheek."

He seems to consider this. "Well. Is it a pity kiss?"

"*No!* It's a legitimate thank-you-for-the-magic kiss," I tell him, and I go over and stand on tiptoes and kiss him on the cheek. "And by the way, just so you know, the other one wasn't a pity kiss either."

But then he says he knows pity kisses; in fact, he is all too familiar with pity kisses, pity looks, pity chocolate chip cookies, pity invitations, pity car rides, pity flowers, pity conversations, pity sandwiches.

I would argue, but I am not in my right mind, and also it's time to go upstairs and see the new real estate agent, the person who might solve everything.

FORTY-TWO
MARNIE

I'm relieved to see that the real estate agent, Anne Tyrone, is not a Brooklyn hipster. She's motherly, bosomy, and comforting. Not the type to expect perfection in a house the day after Thanksgiving.

She's wearing her glasses on a little filigreed chain around her neck, like a proper older lady, and she walks through the house without making a single note, just soaking up the ambiance and looking around.

"Lovely, just lovely," she murmurs.

I am pleased to see that no one would know that a near riot took place in here just hours ago—probably thanks to Patrick cleaning everything up. The only hint that there might have been a disaster is that the kitchen floor has a wonderful gleam to it this morning, the gleam of being well oiled with turkey fat perhaps. Four pumpkin pies are sitting calmly on the counter with plastic wrap over them. There is no turkey carcass in the living room. Bedford isn't even there—he was taken upstairs by Jessica to sleep off his turkey hangover, according to a note I see on the counter.

So then Anne Tyrone goes upstairs and looks at Jessica's apartment and then downstairs to look at Patrick's, and when she comes back up, she says to me, "So, darling, how much work do you want to do here before we put it on the market?"

I explain about my life, Blix, my head injury, the three-month legal agreement, my move back to Florida, and I'm about to launch into a speech about my uncertainty about whether that's the right place for me, when she pats me on the arm and says, "So, basically nothing then? Is that what I'm hearing?"

Yes. I can't. I can't do one single thing.

"Well," she says. "I think you're going to be fighting the market the whole time. This isn't a good time for sales anyway . . . blah blah blah . . . and with so much needing to be done . . . blah blah and additional blah . . ."

"Can't it be a fixer-upper?" I say. I like the concept of the fixer-upper. We're all fixer-uppers in this building, I tell her. Seems like we should be sticking together, in a place that understands us—but we're not. We're scattering like tumbleweeds, and it may be all my fault.

She is polite enough to let all that news go right by her. "I'll try," she says at last. "In the meantime, you may want to do what you can to make it look normal. You know, maybe paint that refrigerator a different color. At least that."

"Sure," I say. "Thank you, thank you."

Whatever.

After she leaves, I go outside. I take down the tattered Tibetan prayer flags and pick up some of the leaves on the stoop. I go down and look at Patrick's door. His curtains are closed, and the leaves are still piled up in the little entryway by the stairs.

Ah, Patrick.

I remember hearing the conversation he was having with his sister—the U-Haul truck, his computers going with him—and I feel like crying again. I am going to miss him so much. How is it that I was able to withstand losing both Jeremy and Noah, and yet the thought of Patrick leaving—Patrick, who won't touch me; Patrick, who is so damaged that he thinks everything is about pity; Patrick, who will never go out in public with me EVER—pierces me almost to my core?

Is this love? Or is it what *he* thinks it is—pity, perhaps mixed with some adoration because he was this tragic superhero, trying to save his girlfriend from the fire? He would say I love his story, not him. Not the reality of a man whose soul and body have been burned beyond his own recognition.

Lola comes outside on her stoop, and she waves to me, a listless wave. Nothing like before.

"That the real estate agent?" she calls.

"Yeah."

"You're going with her then?"

"I guess so. How *are* you?" I ask her, and she says she's fine.

Then she leans over the railing and says, "I'm sorry I got so mad at you yesterday. It's really my old argument with Blix, I realized. I loved her to pieces, but damned if that woman didn't always think she knew best about everybody else's life! I can't stand the feeling of being manipulated—even by magic. *Especially* by magic."

"I know," I say. "I'm sorry. I am so sorry."

"You should feel the same way I do! What she's done with you and Patrick!"

"Well," I say. "But it's not going to work with me and Patrick."

But she waves her hands over her head like she's trying to bat away a bunch of gnats, and then she goes inside.

I head back in, too. The sun is beaming through the windows, making patches of light on the oak floors. I love the bay windows, the brick fireplace, Patrick's graceful sculpture on the mantel. I'm overcome suddenly with the feel of this room, and the high ceilings, the staircase up to the kitchen. The little decorative touches, the wainscoting in the kitchen. The way the stove leans just a bit. The soapstone sink that stopped me in my tracks that very first afternoon, when Noah was showing me around, before he knew.

And, may I just say, I *love* the turquoise hand-painted refrigerator. It speaks to me, this refrigerator.

Ah, this house is a sly one, piling up the memories—Blix's and mine. The scarred table with the star carved into it. The little plants on the windowsill. The view of the park and the busy street below.

The dust motes drift down, ready to coat everything as they always have. The light continues to pour in, making shifting patterns on the floor as the breeze moves the gingko tree outside, shedding the last of its four leaves, pretending we belong together.

Marnie, it's okay to love him.

No, he won't let me.

It's okay to love him.

"Well, my friend, I think we struck out."

I'm at Best Buds the next day, and I look up from deadheading the chrysanthemums, hearing a familiar voice. Sure enough, William Sullivan is standing there smiling and jingling the change in his pocket.

"If we struck out, then what are you doing here?" I ask him. Which isn't the most polite way I've ever spoken to a customer, I admit. But really—he drives up from New Jersey to tell me how Lola turned him down? Has the world gone barking mad?

"Well, I'm here because we've got to try again," he says, his eyes lit up. "I thought I'd visit her this weekend, our usual Saturday outing, and I thought you and I could think up something new. For me to say to her."

"Wait a second. She turned you down, and she was furious at both of us, and yet you still think she's going to be open to your usual Saturday?"

"Yep." He smiles at me. "Well, I hope so, at least. I'm going to give it the old college try."

I want to say, *What is* wrong *with you, William Sullivan? What is it about a woman turning down your proposal of marriage that makes you think she'll be willing to go on an outing with you forty-eight hours later?* Instead I say, wearily but with a fascination at the obtuseness of the human spirit, "So you see this plan involving flowers, do you?"

"Well, sure, involving flowers. You're a flower shop, aren't you?"

"All right," I say. "I have to say, though, I'm not sure we're going to be able to change her mind. She's pretty convinced she doesn't want anything interesting to happen for the rest of her life."

"Ah, I know. That's how she feels now. She's pretty fierce." He chuckles. "She was something else on Thanksgiving, wasn't she?"

"Well, yeah. She was pretty upset."

He wanders around the shop, whistling something. And then he comes over to me at the counter. "What did you say your favorite flowers were?"

What had I said? "Gerbera daisies?"

"Oh, yes. Okay, I'd like a bouquet of those. And while you're fixing them up, I want to tell you my plan. Because I have cooked up a great one. And I am very optimistic that *this* is really going to work."

I shake my head. "William, I'd sort of forgotten that people can even be optimistic sometimes."

"Oh, I'm frightfully optimistic," he says. "Frightfully. Okay, let me tell you what I've realized. I was a basketball coach in my old life, and what happened here is that I misjudged the layup. Simple problem. I thought this was going to be a slam dunk because Lola and I were such good friends from before, and we were both lonely, and we had all this history—*good, good history*—but no! I hadn't prepared for no. I hadn't thought it all through." He grins.

"Well, that can happen."

"So you were right—I sprung it on her. So I'm going to baaaack up and take it sloooow, approach her another way. Today, if she'll have me, I'm going to take her somewhere neutral. No big talks, no heavy scenes. Not even going to hold her hand. And that's my plan. Just keep seeing her. Do what she wants. Never ask for more. No pushing. I'm going to wait it out. Woo her until she's not scared anymore. Not make any big moves. No proposals."

"Well, good luck to you. I wish you the best."

"Yep. That's the right thing. I'm launching a plan—I call it A Year of One Hundred Dates with Lola. We'll go slow, drink a lot of coffee, see some shows, then maybe visit my house, to see my friends. Maybe we'll take a little jaunt up to New Hampshire. Stay in separate hotel rooms, drinks by the fire, go dancing. That sort of thing. Whatever she wants, and at a pace she's comfortable with. My goal is to give her something she can't have in her house all by herself. Laughter. Companionship. Admiration."

"What she says, though, is that she doesn't want to be disloyal to Walter's memory. That's what you're up against." Uh-oh—here I go, being disloyal again. Working behind the scenes. Only somehow I can't help myself. I love this old guy with his optimism!

He smiles widely. "But you know? I knew Walter, too, and *I* think he would have been glad for us. He'd like that she's got someone to love her and look after her. We don't have to shut down his memory."

"Well," I say. "Wow. This is amazing. I wish you the best of luck. I'm rooting for you hard. So you want the flowers to take to her, or do you want them delivered?"

He smiles. "The flowers are for you. Because of the first-rate magic you did."

I stare at him. "The magic? You knew about the magic?"

"Lola told me that you and Blix are matchmakers, and that you work with magic to bring people together."

"But the magic didn't work. It was an epic fail." *So much so that I'm giving up on magic altogether.*

"What? That's what you think? Marnie. *It's still working.* Don't you see? It's taking a new route, that's all. When you're as old as I am, you learn a couple of things about love. And one of the main things is that you can't give up on people you love. When you really believe."

I look into his rheumy old blue eyes, so lit up that they're practically shooting sparks. "But what can you do if the other person has given up?" I say. It's hard to talk through the lump in my throat.

He says, "Well, you just gotta keep trying. That's what you do."

"But what if you're running out of time?"

"Honey, we're *all* running out of time. And"—he lowers his voice like this is going to be momentous—*"we also have all the time in the world."*

"Um, that doesn't really make any sense."

He laughs. "I know; it doesn't. I thought I could make some wise pronouncement here, but I got nothing. Well, okay, except this. Here's my bit of old-man wisdom for you: You gotta have faith in *something,* don't you? And when you pick what that thing is going to be, you don't give up on it. Just don't. It fails, you try another way and then another."

And he takes my hand and kisses it, like a courtly gentleman, and heads out of the store. Then he remembers something and comes back in and pays for the flowers. Once more I think if I ran over to the window, I'd see William Sullivan doing himself a little dance down the street, laughing and snapping his fingers, although nine people out of ten would know that he's got no shot at his plan.

But what do nine out of ten people know?

You know what I miss?

I miss seeing those little sparkles, the ones that meant something good was about to happen. That there was love around. I don't know why, but they've somehow vanished.

That's all. I just miss that.

Natalie texts me the next day while I'm in the kitchen, washing down the turquoise refrigerator in preparation for painting it. The Internet says that a person can actually buy special appliance paint that makes old fridges look like they just came from the showroom. This one could look new again, according to some of the more gung-ho commenters.

And then this text sails in. Which I've been expecting. The big sister weighing in on the disaster that is my life. She Who Knows Best.

I dont trust myself 2 speak w/you. Trying 2 B on ur side, but WTF? U BROKE HIS HEART AGAIN?

I broke his heart again. Yes.

AND U R LIVING WITH YOUR EX-FREAKING-HUSBAND?

No, and stop yelling.

I AM NOT GOING TO STOP YELLING UNTIL U EXPLAIN WHAT U R DOING.

Here's what I am doing: I am right now painting a fridge. Bye.

I CAN'T EVEN.

Then please don't.

You know what I can't even?

I can't paint the refrigerator some cool, professional white. I walk to the hardware store and look at the special white paint, and I even go stand in the checkout line with a can of it, but then something happens in my brain. I try to picture Blix's kitchen with a refrigerator trying to pass itself off as a normal fridge, and I can't.

Anybody who wouldn't buy Blix's house because they have no feeling for her refrigerator—well, they simply shouldn't be allowed to have it, that's all.

I put it back on the shelf and leave.

Things that can't be ordinary:

Me.

Patrick.

The refrigerator.

William Sullivan.

Sorry, that's just how it is.
Sorry/not sorry.
And *where are the sparkles*?

FORTY-THREE
MARNIE

Monday morning is a regular school day, and Jessica and Sammy come banging against the door early, the way they always do. I'm sort of caught off guard, because in my own little mind, everything has changed completely, and nobody but Bedford and William Sullivan—and okay, Patrick—really likes me anymore, and Patrick doesn't count because he's leaving and I won't ever see him again.

But there are the two of them: Sammy with his scooter, and Jessica all harried as usual with her bag over her shoulder and her coffee cup in her hand. As soon as I open the door, she gives me a big smile and starts apologizing for not checking in on me over the weekend.

"Here you had a head injury and everything, and I'm off sorting out my own little life, not even making sure you weren't in the hospital or something," she says. Then she laughs. "Well, I *knew* you weren't in the hospital because that real estate lady on Friday said you were perfectly fine. And also I came to check on you in the middle of the night on Thursday, and found out you were with *Patrick*." She narrows her eyes a little bit when she says his name, the girlfriend body language for *so what was that about*, and I shrug in reply, the body language of *it wasn't anything, believe me.*

Sammy seems distracted, playing with the handle of his scooter and squirming around under his backpack. Every now and then he looks up at me like there's something he wants to say. No doubt he has opinions about how badly our magic project turned out.

Join the club, my boy. Stand in line.

All of a sudden Jessica says, "Listen! I don't really have to be in until noon today. I was just going to go get a haircut, but what if you and I got a little breakfast first? Maybe not at Yolk, of course." She laughs and ruffles Sammy's hair, and he does a comedic googly-eyed look right at me and mouths the word "Yikes" where she can't see.

Marital situations can be so confusing for the little ones. Especially the ones who've tried to mastermind adult lives and found it horrifyingly difficult.

"Sure," I tell her. "Breakfast it is!"

I'd forgotten the main thing about being with Jessica: how much fun it is to have a girlfriend who is also living some version of a possibly chaotic life. Most of the time, I have to say, *I* seem to be the person who can't get it together, the one being left at the altar and then cutting up her wedding dress in the preschool, the one setting out for a strange city and failing at reinventing herself even there.

And yet here is Jessica, linking arms with me, walking down the street, and she's actually laughing about the whole Thanksgiving catastrophe. She said she and Andrew keep referring to it as Fucksgiving. "Like, one thing went wrong, and then it just set off a whole cascade until absolutely everything was shit. Was that basically your take on it, too?"

"From what I can remember. I had a convenient head injury, remember."

"Oh, yes. Although you coped masterfully even after that. As I recall, you took care of pretty much everyone, even through the yelling and screaming. And you solved two of your most pressing romantic problems—both Noah and Jeremy. It was actually kind of epic."

"One of the only Thanksgivings I've had in which nobody ate any turkey."

"Or clam chowder either. Or lobsters. Hence, Fucksgiving."

She smiles at me. By now she's steered us into a little breakfast place, far, far away from Yolk. A waiter has brought us menus and coffees, asking if we want almond milk, soy milk, cream, half-and-half, skim, or regular milk. And after that question is answered, he'd like to know which kind of sweeteners to haul over: pink packets, blue ones, yellow, stevia, Truvia, regular sugar, regular raw sugar, or sugar syrup.

"I'm going to miss this about Brooklyn," I tell her when we've sorted out our order. "It's a place you can't be indecisive. Even about coffee. In Jacksonville, it's so not this way."

She runs her fingers through her long hair, shakes out her waves, and stares off into space, her mouth a closed, straight line. She has the kind of hair that should ensure its owner's perfect lifetime happiness. Too bad her hair is not in charge of negotiating her love life, because then nothing would ever go wrong.

"So, tell me where things stand," I say. "Andrew's out of the picture, I take it. Relegated back to divorced dad status, but I just want to say—"

"Well, no, actually," she says, but I don't take it in because I'm talking at the same time, and what I'm saying is, "want to say that I think that was really a stupid move, for the *waitress*, that *woman* to speak up like that, right in front of everyone, to say *she* was, you know, the one."

Jessica is looking at me with her wide blue eyes. "I know, I know, but you know what else? It made me realize how I am not remotely well enough to love Andrew completely. Which I was in such denial about. I was all like, 'Oh, our kid is so cute, writing that little poem, and he needs us, and why don't we just forget the past and get back together?' when that was *not* even realistic. First fight, and we're done again. Right?"

"I guess . . ."

She leans forward. "So bad as this was, it got us to talking. Which was painful and excruciating, and I'm surprised you didn't hear us. On Friday we took Sammy over to my mother's house just so we could fight and yell and scream and get it all out. I don't normally approve of yelling and screaming, but Andrew said we had to air *everything*, and if voices were raised—then that showed we cared enough to risk it. Or something. Anyway, we did. And at the end of it, hours and hours of talking and pacing and yelling, he said he wanted to keep trying. And I said I did, too. And so we are."

"Wow."

"Because what I realized is that I had something to do with the marriage falling apart, too. Here I was blaming him and everything, but I was really the one who checked out of the marriage first. I was bored and frustrated at my job, and I started criticizing him for everything, and getting so annoyed with him, and ignoring him and doing stuff elsewhere—and he just felt pushed out. Plain and simple. And then she was there—and nobody's saying it was right—but I can see how somebody *fun* and *interesting* might be appealing when your wife is going to bed at eight o'clock just so she won't have to talk to you."

The waiter comes over with our eggs, and we make room at the table for our gigantic plates, filled with eggs and potatoes and whole-grain toast.

"So the bottom line is that we've decided we need to be in a different house, not his, not mine, which is convenient because mine is getting sold—"

"But not yet!" I protest. "You can stay. I'd like it if you stayed, in fact."

She shakes her head sadly. "Nope. No can do. We need a fresh start, symbolically if not for anything else. We'll stay in Brooklyn so that

Sammy can continue to go to a school where kids are allowed to write poems about breakfast foods to embarrass their parents. I want to start my own business at some point, and Andrew wants us to spend every summer at his parents' cabin in the Berkshires, now that they're getting old. So . . . big changes."

On the way home, I fill her in as best as I can on Noah taking Blix's stuff so his parents can challenge the will, and William Sullivan not giving up on Lola. And Jeremy getting furious with me and believing that I'd somehow known all along I didn't want to marry him.

She wrinkles her nose. "Well, I have to say that I've never been quite convinced of your supposed love for this guy."

"My family is probably never going to speak to me again. They're all so sure he's the guy I'm supposed to be with."

"Sorry. Nope, nope, nope. You couldn't have settled for him. I wouldn't have allowed it. And now—I don't care what your family says—you've got other people looking out for you. We're your posse now."

"I have a posse?"

"Yes. And as a spokeswoman for the posse, I say you shouldn't go back to Florida. There's nothing for you there. You may have to face the fact that, despite all your best efforts, you actually do belong to Brooklyn."

"But it's *dirty* here, and cold, and there's trash in the streets, and the subways don't run on time, and you have to go grocery shopping every single day because nobody has a car . . ."

"Yeah," she says, punching me in the arm. "We're not perfect, by any means, but we're your city. You might as well save yourself some trouble and accept it now."

But Patrick, I think. I can't tell her that part, that there's a hole in my heart.

FORTY-FOUR
MARNIE

As soon as I unlock the front door and walk into the house, I nearly have four kinds of heart attacks. There's Noah standing there in the entry hall, holding a cardboard box. I let out a blood-curdling scream, and he jumps in the air.

"WHAT THE HELL ARE YOU DOING?" (That's me.)

"WHAT THE HELL ARE *YOU* DOING?" (Not his most original moment.)

We stare at each other. Then he says, "I came to get the rest of my great-aunt's possessions. Now if you'll just move out of my way, I have to take these to Paco's before the UPS guy comes."

"Wait. Wait just a minute here. What makes you think it's okay for you to do this?"

He sighs. "My mother wants Blix's clothes."

"Why? Why? What is she going to do with all this stuff? You're just doing this to get back at me, is all. I did not talk your aunt into leaving me this building, I did not interfere with her will in any way, shape, or form—and why do you have to be instrumental in contesting a will that you know from Blix's lawyer is legitimate—"

He sighs again. "Listen. My family is freaked out. Okay? They know that you asked her for a spell, and they think that was tampering with the will. Or something. I actually can't bring myself to pay attention."

"So what, I asked her for a spell? I missed you. I wanted you back. What does that prove?"

He looks confused for a moment. "Fuck. I don't know. Maybe she felt sorry for you and mad at me, and so she changed her whole will."

"That was her choice, not mine."

"Well, my mother wants the building, and my father has called his attorneys, and now they want all the evidence they can find, and also the contents of the house."

"No," I say. "No. The contents of the house go with the house. You are not removing another thing."

"Look," he says. "This is weird, okay? I couldn't give a crap about this house or the will or any of it. I don't even care if my parents get it, or you get it, or it falls into the sea, frankly. But my mom is on her high horse. She—well, if we had all day, I could tell you the whole story, but it's pointless and stupid, and—"

"I happen to have all day."

He lets out one of his huge sighs again, and gives me one of his guilty-conscience looks, and we go into the kitchen. I get the feeling somehow that he wants to tell me the whole story, to get it off his chest.

He grabs a beer from the fridge and admires the shininess of the turkey-fat–sparkling floor, and he actually laughs about that a little. *Ha ha—wasn't that something—you and your fiancé, and the way the turkey skidded across the room just at the moment Jeremy realized you'd been living with me!*

"Hilarious," I say.

I'm still so mad at him, but fascinated by him, too, in the way that I always have been and probably always will be—and we sit down at the scarred old table, and he drums his fingers on the table and then he begins, "So Blix was the one who was supposed to get my family's mansion, the one that got passed down through the generations, oldest daughter to oldest daughter. But she got cut out of the will after what were probably high-level shenanigans, knowing my parents, and—well, whatever. My mom's mom ended up with the house instead."

After that start, he has to get up and pace around, and the story is like something from some Southern Gothic network TV miniseries. It all started back with robber barons and war heroes and wills and pistols at dawn—but basically the part that meant something was that Blix got cheated out of the family mansion, and Noah knows that his mother has always been *squirrelly* (his word) about Blix, maybe because she feels guilty for what they did. She was always proclaiming how, in her own defense, she took much better care of the house than Blix would have—and how *she* was so much more connected to the community, and had so many *charitable* causes.

But meanwhile Blix traveled around the world and then went off to Brooklyn, of course, and the family watched with consternation as she took up with all those alternative things: "magic and mayhem," Wendy called it.

"She would never admit this, but I think she was kind of worried that Blix was going to do voodoo on her or something. Get the house back, or expose her. And so now that Blix has died—and this is strictly my theory—my mom is desperate to get Blix's papers and find out what she was up to all those years. And if she has to, she'll prove that Blix was never in her right mind, and therefore, for that to happen, *you* should be cut out of the will."

"Speechless," I say. "I am utterly speechless."

"Yeah. It's ugly. This is why I never wanted to have much to do with my parents. My dad wanted me to go into business, learn all the ropes of his firm—but nope. I picked teaching school. And going to Africa. And now I just want to do more of that. I'm scheduled to leave the country next week. Going to Bali this time."

"To Bali? Aren't you in school?"

He grins. "Actually . . . ah . . . that would be a no."

"But you said that was why you wanted to stay here—" I see his face. "No? You were never taking classes?"

"No. I told you that so I could stay. I didn't have anything else going, and besides, I kind of was intrigued by you. You know. You're hot. Aaaand . . . well, my mom wanted me to keep an eye on what was going on here."

"Wow." I sit back in my chair. "Okay, so let me get this straight. So basically you're dismantling this house to help your mom get it away from me, then? You have no stake in it."

"Pretty much." He ducks his head. "Sorry."

"Well, then why don't you stop? Why don't you right now just this minute stop it?"

"I would. I really would. But you don't know my mom. She's relentless. She talks to me every day, getting more and more worked up." He gives me a guilty little smile. "Also, I've already sent her a whole bunch of boxes of Blix's stuff. Including—and I'm sorry about this, Marnie, I really am—I sent her that letter Blix wrote to you. And her book of spells."

I think for a moment of telling him the truth, that those things are never, ever going to make it to Virginia. But I decide not to.

Noah is, among other things, an ex-husband. An opportunist. A havoc wreaker. A double agent. The best lover I've ever had. And I am so ready to be rid of him forever.

I decide right that minute that if he heads out to Bali, Wendy Spinnaker can always just wonder what exactly her aunt's wacky career in magic consisted of, and why nothing ever turned up in those boxes. She can text him over and over again while he's lying on the beach somewhere, and he can turn over on his towel, adjust his sunglasses, take another sip of his mai tai or whatever, and gaze out at the azure sky.

But he'll never be able to tell her for sure what happened, because he'll never know.

FORTY-FIVE
MARNIE

Blix's nefarious magic career is still on my back patio. Just so you know.

Shall I put on the tinfoil hat and come down and tackle it?

Ahem. I believe, if you will check your popular culture references, tinfoil hats only protect you from electromagnetic waves and therefore cannot have any effect on magic spells.

Oh.

Still, if you have one, bring it. It might look cute.

Should I bring dinner? I bet Roy would like a chicken.

I'm making popovers. I've decided to be the Reigning Prince of Popovers.

A tinfoil crown is definitely in order then.

Oh, we are so clever, aren't we? Tinfoil hats and well-punctuated text messages—that's us. So funny and chaste and clever and innocent. And it is December second, and he is leaving on December fifteenth, and that will be that.

I sit at my table with aluminum foil and a pair of scissors and a cardboard cutout of a crown. What am I doing? Why, making him a crown, of course. To make him smile. To keep up the joke, to make one of our last evenings together *fun* and *companionable*.

So he'll think as he's driving cross-country: *Yes, we had such fun, she and I.*

Fun, fun, fun.

I slam the scissors down on the table and stand up. Oh my God. I want him. I want to unwrap him, press my head against his chest. I want his mouth grazing my nipple. I want to be in his bed with him again, but I want to be on top of him. I want him to kiss me and not look at me like I'm some kind of monster that he can't give in to.

I want Patrick. I want him, I want him, I want him, I want him.

I look around the kitchen. The sky is darkening outside already, the lights of the skyline shining against the thick gray clouds of night. I walk around the room, my arms folded tight across my chest, my heart beating so fast.

I want him.

When I squint, I see them. The sparkles.

Oh my goodness, I see the sparkles again. They're back.

If I had the spell book from his patio, maybe I could figure out if there's a little bit of magic that might work on him. On us, before the time runs out.

Then I remember something. The first night I met her, she gave me a scarf when I was leaving. And it's hanging in the closet. I saw it the other day when I was looking at everything. Somehow it's always seemed too fancy for me.

Like it would have been cheating to wear Blix's essence around my neck that way. But now tonight, we need the big guns.

It goes all wrong from the moment I get there. I'm too shy or too forward or too tense. I forget to bring the chicken, and when I offer to go get one at Paco's, Patrick says not to bother. And I'm wearing a dress, which I see is ridiculous, because you can't unpack boxes in a dress—you can't search through magical artifacts when you're dressed like you wanted to be out at dinner or at a movie instead.

And why did you do it? Because you wanted to look beautiful.

I'm wearing the best thing in my closet, the black-striped dress with the leggings. The dress that shows a bit of cleavage. Patrick might appreciate the cleavage, and he could peel off the leggings—that's what I was thinking, Your Honor. I plead guilty to lustful thoughts while getting dressed.

But now I am here, and there is no chicken, and the popovers are just popovers—flour and milk and eggs and air. And he is in a mood—too jokey, too *something*. Brittle, somehow. Guarded.

I tell him about Noah and the story of Blix being in line to inherit the family mansion but then having it stolen from her, and I make it all dramatic—too dramatic—and he asks questions I can't answer. And I'm acting all flustered and he looks at me funny, and it's probably written all over my face: *Dude, I want you.*

But we can't. He won't.

We sit on the floor and go through the boxes, and there's really nothing to it. The book of spells is at the bottom of a box that contains Blix's muumuus and caftans, the dress she wore to my wedding, some fabulous scarves and coats. I take out the book and open it, and I say, "Look at all this magic! It makes me feel like she's right here when I see it."

He suddenly gets up and goes over to the sink and starts washing dishes.

"What's wrong?" I say.

"Nothing."

"Is it the Blix stuff?"

He hesitates, bites his lip. Puts a cup in the dish drainer. "It's the anniversary of the fire."

"Oh. Oh, I'm so sorry."

"Yeah, I'm not fit for company. I'm sorry. I should be by myself."

I go over to the sink and I reach over and touch him, and to my surprise, he doesn't pull away. I touch his arm and then his hand, where the scars are. I take his hand out of the soapy water. Slowly I run my finger along a ridge of scar tissue. He lets me.

"It wasn't your fault, you know," I say. "You couldn't have changed it."

When he speaks, his voice is ragged, and he pulls his arm away from me. "Yeah, well. If it hadn't been for those ten seconds . . . do you see that if somehow those ten seconds didn't happen, everything would have been different? Ten seconds, and the world doesn't have any oxygen left for me. It's like the color blue is missing or something, everything good drained away. I can't—I don't feel *anything*."

"Oh, Patrick."

"My life—you really don't know me. You don't see that my life is a before and after, and that I have to live in the shadows."

"Wait a minute," I say. "I know what's going on here."

"And what is that?" He closes his eyes. "Not enough *magic*?"

"No. You *are* feeling again. You're seeing there's a bridge to healing, and you're not sure you want to cross it. You might get hurt again. You can stay on the planet of My Lover Died in the Fire as long as you want, but eventually I think you're going to want some company there. Because you survived the fire. And you can heal from this. I think—and I could be wrong about this, so don't get mad—but I think you really can do art again."

He's staring at me. Now I have done it. I've gone too far. "Did you really say that? That I'm on the planet of My Lover Died in the Fire?"

"I believe I did."

"Well, thank you very much for that image, but I'm not going to do art again. I'm going to planet Leave Me the Fuck Alone, Wyoming, and I'm going to walk along the plains by myself and watch television with my sister."

"Um, giving up."

"Call it whatever you like."

"I do call it giving up, because, Patrick, I have this unshakable idea about you, which is based on knowing that when the worst thing that ever happened to you happened, you didn't run away from it. You ran toward that fire. And that man isn't going to get away with walking alone on the plains and watching television with his sister. You're healing right now. Don't you see that? This is probably like when those horrible burn wounds were healing, and they hurt like hell. This is what your spirit is doing right now, too. But then maybe things will get better, one angstrom unit at a time. You can get your life back."

He turns off the water. "Shut the fuck up," he says. But he is smiling in a weird way.

"I honestly think you do not want to give up."

He closes his eyes then, like everything just hurts too much. I go over and take Blix's journal and books and my letter out of the boxes, and then I seal them back up with the packing tape. And then I do the bravest/stupidest thing I've ever done, which is tell Patrick that I love him, and that no matter what he thinks, it's not pity and it's not any of those other lesser values. It's love, love, love.

I even say it loudly: *"Love, love, love."*

And he does not respond, because he is lost beyond my reach. He has traveled as far as he can go, and he didn't get to where I'm standing.

I've watched enough dramatic movies to know that there's nothing to be done. Taking off my clothes wouldn't help, begging won't help, even throwing plates or singing or starting to make out with him.

Nothing I can think of will help. Not magic, not making him laugh, not feeding him a popover one morsel at a time.

So, while I still have one shred of pride left, I go home.

Because the wisdom that William Sullivan *doesn't* know is the thing I remember best: When all is lost, the Law of Giving Up will save you every time. But it only works if you're really, really giving up.

And I am.

Anne Tyrone calls me later that night and says she has somebody who wants to come look at the building tomorrow, and I say *bring it on*.

I have officially given up, and now Blix's place will sell, and I will leave.

FORTY-SIX
MARNIE

Brooklyn, in a show-offy mood, has its first snowfall on the fifteenth. It starts snowing before the sun comes up, and by the time I get up, the world has turned white outside. Five inches have already fallen, and the schools are closed, much to Sammy's delight. The mayor thinks that people should stay home if they possibly can, because this isn't going to stop anytime soon.

"The mayor never says that!" Sammy tells me. "Well, maybe two times in my lifetime is all. Or three times. Maybe five. Or one. But it is a big deal. Trust me on that." He is following me around the kitchen while his parents sleep. "I mean, we have snow days. Sometimes. Not often, but we have them. But a snow day when my mom and dad don't have to work—that never happens. Hardly ever."

"Sammy, do you think you'd like some oatmeal, or would you like pancakes?"

"Oooh, pancakes," he says. "Can we really have pancakes? I never get pancakes on a weekday. That's because there's never enough time. I should call my mom to come over. She loves pancakes. I wonder why my parents are sleeping so late."

"It's not late. It's only eight o'clock," I say.

"Maybe I'll go tell them we're having a great breakfast over here."

"No, let's let them sleep," I say.

"But why are they so tired?"

"I don't know. But I have a firm belief in letting tired parents sleep. My own parents used to take naps sometimes. In the middle of the day. My sister and I had to leave them alone."

"Well, you know what *that* probably was, don't you?" he says.

"Do you like butter and syrup or butter and powdered sugar?" I say.

"They were doing their taxes, I bet," he says. "My parents told me that they need a lot of peace and quiet to do their taxes. So when they would take naps in the middle of the day, that's what they were doing." Then his face breaks out in a big grin. "Can I tell you something? Promise you won't tell anybody?"

"Okay," I say.

"Two things, really. The first is that I know about sex," he whispers. "My mom told me all about it."

"Oh," I say. I love Sammy's non sequiturs, and I have decided to assume that this is simply one of those. "Well, then. What's the second thing?"

"I heard my mom ask my dad if they should have a whole wedding when they get back together officially, or just go down to the courthouse and sign the papers."

"Really! And what did he say?"

"He said he wants a wedding, and he wants me to walk with them down the aisle and have everybody there cheering for all of us. He wants me to hold both their hands."

"That's so nice," I say. "Are you up for that? I bet you are."

"I'm up for it," he says.

I don't tell him the secret that I know—that Jessica is already pregnant. There's a baby coming in about eight and a half months. Yeah, she knew early. She's one of those women who knows she's conceived the moment she gets up from the bed, she told me. She's keeping it from Sammy, she says, until she's absolutely sure everything's okay.

And I have another secret, too. Andrew's already gone out and bought her a new ring. He says the old wedding ring might have to be put down, like a sick animal. It didn't do its job so great.

The new ring is going to be one you can count on for life.

Will that work? What do I know? All I know is that sometimes miracles simply show up, and you have to take them at face value. What really happened is probably something that Jessica can't put into words: she just made up her mind to love him again.

Maybe it was timing, or, in some weird way, it could have even been the waitress showing up at Thanksgiving. But I can't rule out that it was the spell I did.

I wonder if Blix had these doubts. Or if she just cast the spells and asked for the miracles, and then sat back and welcomed anything that came. Maybe this is how the whole system works. You put the wish out there, and then it takes the entire universe operating on your behalf to get it to come true.

If Blix's idea was to put Patrick and me together, though, she's not done so well. I'm awaiting an offer on the house, and right now there's a U-Haul truck parked out in front of the building that's saying that sometimes things simply don't work out.

Patrick is getting ready to leave.

Around one o'clock, Sammy and I are bored with playing checkers, doing puzzles, and baking cookies, and I can no longer stand to see that truck sitting there, so we take Bedford out to the park. It's still snowing, but we bundle up. Jessica lends me her snow pants and a parka and a scarf. She's decided she'll stay home and do the lie-about-the-house-napping-and-gestating routine. Sammy gets his gear all together, his snow saucer and his mittens and hat and scarf. Winter requires so much *stuff*. I don't know how these Northerners keep track of it all.

We walk over to Prospect Park with Bedford on his leash. He's fascinated by snow. He wants to run around in circles and bark at the snowflakes. He's really lost his little doggie mind, such as it is, and he's dragging me along, trying to make me go into the street so he can chase more flakes. As for me, I may be just as bad. I can't get over the way the snow feels landing on my nose and face. These are big, fat flakes, drifting down to earth looking like jagged pieces of lace, all clumped together. Soft and delicate, melting on impact.

"The world looks so different," I keep exclaiming. "It's like it got all cleaned up."

Sammy shows me where the best sledding hill is, and we take turns, one of us holding the leash while the other rides the saucer down the slope. Every time I get myself on the saucer, tucking in my legs and arms and holding on for dear life, the pan spins me around, and I always seem to go down the hill backward, screaming and laughing and closing my eyes.

"If you lean the other way, you won't go backward!" Sammy calls. "Here, lean!"

"I don't know what you meeeeeeeeean!" I scream, because I've hit an icy patch and I'm careening across the whole length of the park. "Heellllllllp!"

He comes running alongside me, laughing and saying, "Lean left, Marnie! Lean to the left! I mean, the other left! Lean to the other left!"

I wipe out on the path, and I'm lying there, glad to finally be at a stop, sprawled out on my back staring up at the sky, feeling the snow coming down right in my face, landing on my mouth and nose and eyes. I can't stop laughing.

"Get out of the way! MARNIE! Here comes somebody!" Sammy is yelling, and I jump up just in time to avoid being hit by a demon in a red snowsuit screeching as she barely misses me, going hundreds of miles per hour. The wind whistles past me as she breaks the sound barrier.

"Oh my God! How am I ever going to not want to do this every day? This is what *winter* is about? Why didn't anybody ever tell me the good parts?" I ask him. We link arms and go trudging up the hill, back to the line again.

We're standing in line—*on* line—and suddenly I look around. "Wait! Where's Bedford?"

"Oh, no!" says Sammy. "Where did he go? I went to help you, and I—"

"It's okay," I say. "I'll go find him. You stay on the snow pan."

"No, I'm coming with you," he says. His face has gone pale.

We thread our way through the crowds of people all coming to sled and play, calling his name. There's a German shepherd roaming free, and a golden retriever who's walking along between some twins like he's their supervisor. No Bedford. A poodle comes by in a fussy sweater. And two dachshunds in down jackets.

"Bedford! BEDFORD! Here, boy!" I call. It's snowing harder now, and I can't see quite as far as I want to.

Sammy looks like he's about to cry. "This is my fault. I lost him. I lost your dog."

"It's fine. We'll find him. Let's go down this other street. Maybe he left the park and started for home."

"Yeah, dogs always know the way home," he says. "I heard that somewhere."

I don't want to say that I'm not so sure that's true of Bedford. He's been a freelance dog since long before he belonged to me. He may not really know for sure where his home is, or even that he belongs with me. Maybe he met some nice people at the park and trotted off with them because they had fried chicken or something. I may never see him again, and I won't know if he left me for a ham sandwich, or if he got taken to the pound.

I get out my cell phone and call Jessica. "Are you feeling okay?" I ask when she answers.

"I'm now lying about, being lazy," she says. "What are you doing?"

"Well, we're having a fine old time, but Bedford seems to have gone missing. Would you mind looking outside and seeing if you can spot his lovely countenance? Sammy has a theory that dogs know to go home when they're lost."

After a while, she comes back to the phone. "No sign of him. I'll ask Patrick if he's seen him and I'll call you back."

"Oh, don't bother Patrick. He doesn't even like Bedford. I'm sure he hasn't seen him."

"Well," she says. "Okay."

"I'll keep looking around here for a while, and then Sammy and I will come back. The wind's coming up, and it's getting kind of cold."

"I can barely hear you, there's so much noise from the wind," she says.

"I know. But listen, my battery is about to die, so we're going to keep searching and then we'll come back . . ."

"Shall I send Andrew? Are you near the pond?"

"Maybe. I'm not sure exactly. But give me a little while to look before you send him."

The phone goes dead.

"She hasn't seen him?" asks Sammy. His shoulders slump, but then he gathers himself up and starts calling again, "BEDFORD! BEDFORD!"

We walk along. My hands and ears are freezing. And even though the snow has stopped falling, it's even harder to see. By the time it's four thirty, we've walked blocks and blocks, and there's the feeling of twilight. People packing up to go. I think I have possibly lost a couple of toes by now.

"I think we have to give up, Sammy boy," I say. "I'm sure he'll show up at home."

"But what if he doesn't?"

"He will. Dogs are smart creatures."

"But what if a car hit him or something? What if somebody took him and stole him?"

"Sssh. Let's think positive. He's probably just fine somewhere. Probably he's gone to a bodega and is enjoying a meatball sub in the back. Let's go home and warm up. Get some hot chocolate. Maybe we'll go out later and look again, with your dad."

We walk along the sidewalk. I keep peering down the street, trying to see. And then I see two men coming toward us, and one of them is Andrew—and the other one is Patrick, and my stomach feels like it slides down to my toes.

Patrick. Outside, in a flimsy parka and sweatpants. Running toward me. He's outside and he's running to me, and I put my hand over my mouth because this is clearly not good. I freeze in position, but Sammy says, "Dad!" and starts galloping to Andrew's side, blubbering now, talking about the dog and how he's sorry. Andrew leans down and scoops him into a hug, but Patrick keeps coming toward me.

"Bedford—" he says, and I start to cry.

"Oh my God. Is he dead?"

"No, but a car hit him. In front of our house. I've been trying to call you." He stops talking, panting so hard he can't make words right.

"Oh, no! Where is he? Oh my God. Is he going to be okay?"

He bends down, puts his hands on his knees, tries to catch his breath. "No . . . it's okay . . . going to be okay . . . I took him to the vet . . ."

"The vet? You took him—? Wait. Patrick, take a deep breath. Breathe." I put my hand on his arm. "Just nod—you saved him, didn't you?"

He takes a deep, deep breath, and another and then nods. "He's going to be okay. A broken leg, they said. They fixed it up. I've been looking for you. Jessica said you and Sammy were sledding . . ."

"Where is he?"

"The animal hospital four blocks from here. They're setting it now." Another deep breath. "So he'll stay there tonight. Make sure there are no further complications."

"You saw it happen? Was it awful?"

He straightens up and looks at me. "I saw it right afterward. He was in the street, and he was lying down crying and I picked him up and moved him. I probably shouldn't have moved him, but I needed to get him out of the road."

"You picked him up?"

"I did. Well, I had to. He's *your* dog."

"Oh, Patrick! Thank you so much. I'm so glad you did. Oh my God. I get a dog, and already I've wrecked him." I can't help it; I grab him in a hug, and he lets me. He even puts his arm around me. "How did you know it had happened?"

"I heard it happen. Heard him yelp. So I went out, and the driver of the car was there. He'd pulled over and he came and talked to me. He said he never even saw him dart out."

"No. He chases snowflakes and loses his mind. Do you think—I mean, can I see him? Oh, that poor dumb mutt!"

"Yes, we can see him. They do magical things with dog legs these days, I've heard."

Andrew and Sammy are coming toward us now, and Sammy is holding back tears. Andrew has his arm around his son's shoulders. I've never noticed how alike the two of them look.

"It's my fault, Marnie," Sammy says.

"No, it isn't. Not at all. Bedford is his own free dog, and he should have followed you. He just got distracted in that doggie way. And you were right; he went home. He probably was chasing some snowflakes and went out into the road, because—well, I hate to say it, but he's kind of an idiot dog. You know? Doesn't know much about sidewalks and cars." I hug him, too.

"I'm sorry!"

"It's okay, sport," says Patrick. "They're fixing him up." He looks at me. "Shall we go over to the animal hospital and see how they're doing with him?"

"Yes, I'd like that," I say. "Wait. You'll really come with me?"

He closes his eyes for a moment. "Yes, of course I'm coming."

Andrew says he and Sammy are going to head home, if that's okay. "I've gotta get this guy into some dry clothes."

I kiss and hug them both good-bye, and then I turn back to Patrick. "Why are you doing this? What in the name of God happened to you since I last talked to you?"

"Do you want to walk or take my truck?"

"Wait. You have a truck?"

"I have the U-Haul. That's how I got the dog to the vet."

"You're so full of surprises."

"I thought we had a moratorium on the word *surprise*."

"Sometimes it's a good word."

We walk for a long time in silence. I keep stealing little looks at him.

"You don't even really like him. You said you don't have any time for dogs."

"Yeah, well, he licked my hand. So that may mean we're bonded for life now."

"Patrick."

"Yes?"

"This means more than I can say. Really."

"I know."

"This is like the most amazing thing anyone's ever done for me."

"Listen, I'm not prepared to make a big speech or anything," he says. "I'm still a wreck. Still me. But I thought about what you said."

"Oh my God, Patrick, you're outside. For me."

"Yeah, well, I want to go see how this dog of yours is doing. And I want—well, then I want to start the process where Roy and Bedford get to be friends."

"You do? Aren't you moving, like, in twenty minutes? Going to Wyoming?"

"And then maybe if you want we could have an exploratory preliminary talk about how ridiculous it would be if one of us is walking on the plains of Wyoming alone while the other one is in Florida. *Flah-rida,* as you say it. You know, as a long-term plan." He stops walking and faces me and takes both of my hands in his leathery, stitched-together, wonderful hands, the medical miracle hands.

His eyes are luminous in the half darkness. "I probably can't be fixed all the way, you know. There's always going to be some . . . pain . . . and maybe some visits to that planet. The My Lover Died planet. I may have a permanent parking space there for my spaceship. But I . . . well, I need you. I don't want to live without you."

"Patrick . . ."

"Please. You don't have to do this. You're going to have to think very hard about what you want. I'm no bargain, believe me. Just tell me this. Is this—*am I*—I mean, could this ever be something you even want?"

I close my eyes. "So much."

He pulls me to him and kisses me so softly. "Is that really true?" he whispers. "You want this?"

I nod. I'm about to burst into tears, so I can't trust myself to speak.

"Okay," he says, "so we'll go visit Bedford. Then we have to go home and tell Roy the news. That he's now a dog owner. He's not going to be happy, believe me."

We start walking again, and the sky gets dark, and yes, there may be sparkles everywhere I look, or maybe it's just the streetlights coming on and shining on the snow. We can't stop smiling. Smiling and walking and holding hands.

"You do know there are going to be piles of problems, right?" he says about half a block later. "This isn't going to be like—"

"Patrick," I say.

"What?"

"I may need you to be quiet just now so I can love on you better. I'm thinking how it's going to be so amazing, unwrapping you."

"Unwrapping me, did you say? You are?"

"Yes," I say. "Yes! Yes! Yes! I've been thinking of nothing else."

"If you'd been texting that, would there have been periods or commas between all those yeses?"

I stop walking then and put my arms around him, and he kisses me again and again. And it's the best, really—kisses that have exclamation points between them. Like all the yeses from now on.

FORTY-SEVEN
MARNIE

On the day that the three months are up, Charles Sanford gives me the papers to sign, now fully accepting the terms of the will—and then he hands me the last letter from Blix, the letter he'd explained would be mine once I'd fulfilled the terms of the will.

"Just out of curiosity," I ask him, "did she really write me two letters—one if I was staying and one if I was going?"

He laughs a little bit. "Well. No. Not really."

"Oh, because she would have been too disappointed in me if I'd gone back to my regular life," I say.

"That's one way to look at it. But probably, it was more that she always was sure you wouldn't."

"But I almost did," I say. "I even had a real estate agent showing the house! I had a plane ticket home."

And he smiles. "Yes, but no offers ever materialized, did they? And you decided to stay. You see, Blix didn't deal in almosts. She knew what she was doing."

I go to the Starbucks where I had read her first letter, three months ago. And then I open up this letter, my heart beating fast.

> Marnie, my love, welcome to your big, big life. Sweetheart, it worked out just as I knew it would. For the good of all.
>
> As you look around you, I know you're seeing all the nonstop, everyday, and everywhere miracles. They are everywhere.
>
> And, sweetheart, keep loving him. He's a good man—damaged and broken, but as someone wiser than me said, it's in the broken places where the light gets in.
>
> And as you and I both know, he is LUMINOUS. Filled with trapped light. It beams out of his eyes, doesn't it, darling? I also want you to know that he has a Hawaiian shirt and he has straw hats—and when he puts those on and dances, you are not going to believe the transformation that takes place. I am there with you, loving every minute. So live your little hearts out. Love is everything there is. Never forget who you are.
>
> Love,
>
> Blix

I put down the letter and smile off into the distance.

So she did know. She fixed it so it would happen just this way.

I feel like if I turned around fast enough, if the principles of time and space could somehow allow it, I'd see her there, dancing in the street, twirling, with her hands in the air, just the way she danced at my wedding.

And I wonder if she knew even way back then that I was meant for Patrick. Someday I hope I can ask her.

Oh yeah. It's now a year later, and here are some other things that have happened.

My parents were upset at first about me staying in Brooklyn, and could barely stand that I broke Jeremy's heart two times. But they came around. Parents always do when they see you are truly happy. My mother said she just knew, with a mother's intuition, that when I went to Brooklyn my whole life was going to change. And she's resigned to the fact that I'll turn into a Northerner and that my children, when Patrick and I get around to having them, will speak Northern instead of Southern.

Natalie has visited me and met Patrick. She said she needed to see my life here, to figure out what in the world Brooklyn offered. She left still perplexed, I'm afraid. She'll always prefer big green lawns, swimming pools, and the quiet certainty of a suburban boulevard at midday. Me, I love how the city wakes up merely two hours after it went to sleep, and the way the 6:43 bus roars around the corner and hits the pothole—the same pothole—every single morning. And how the dance of the city means you never know who's going to show up next on your street, in your life.

Jeremy—well now, Jeremy is really the casualty of the whole situation. No getting around that. What can I say? Such a nice guy, and I know he's telling himself the story of how nice guys always finish last, never get the girl. He joked that maybe he and I will try again when I'm between husbands number two and number three. I told him that wasn't funny at all, but actually I was happy to hear him say that. Maybe it means that his snarkiness is coming back.

William Sullivan is on number ninety-two of A Year of One Hundred Dates with Lola. He says he has the patience of a mule. And

I happen to know that she's been to the drugstore. For products that make things easier, you know. On their one-hundredth date, he tells me, not only is he going to propose, but they're going to figure out whether to move to New Jersey or stay in Brooklyn. (Lola told me they're staying, and she thinks Walter will be fine with that.)

Andrew and Jessica, now members of a family of four, bought a house in Ditmas Park (a much more residential section of Brooklyn). They're planning a spring wedding. Best man: Sammy. The maid of honor will only be nine months old, so her mother plans to carry her up the aisle.

Sammy's school bus brings him to me after school twice a week, and we sit in the kitchen while he works on the poem he's going to read for the wedding toast. (It's a pretty good bet we'll be hearing about the further adventures of the egg and the toast.)

And some new tenants moved into Jessica's apartment: Leila and Amanda, who will forever after be known as the lesbian moms, a title they love, by the way. Their baby is adorable. And their sperm donor, the one they were writing the note to when I first met them at Best Buds—well, I have to say he's around a fair amount, too. I've been asked if I can think of a spell that might bring him his own woman and baby.

Oh, and then there's Patrick—and, well, Patrick is still Patrick. Wonderful and generous, startled by life and all it can hold. I talked him into quitting his depressing job when he moved in with me upstairs. Now at night I'll see a wistful look come to his face, and he'll get his watercolors out and take my hand, and we go up on the roof, where he paints the Brooklyn sunsets and the skyline while Bedford and Roy and I keep him company. He's taking photographs, too—going outside and taking pictures of everything that Brooklyn holds for both of us.

Here's something. The other day we were in a store buying art supplies, and there was a little girl, about four years old, who was staring at him curiously. Normally Patrick would have tightened up, scowling and turning away. But this time I watched as he bent down there to her level, and then she reached her little hands up and lightly touched his skin, ran her fingers slowly along the scars and the places where the skin is pulled tight. I could hardly breathe. I saw them look into each other's eyes, and then she said, in barely a whisper, "Does it hurt?" And he smiled at her, closed his eyes for just a moment, and then he said, "No. No more hurt. Not anymore."

You don't know, until there's a moment like that, how much more space there can be in your heart. How much breathing room there is out in the world just for you. That's when you learn for sure that love will win in the end. It just will.

As for me, I'm still working at Best Buds. And I keep the book of spells right there with me—with all its vines and flowers on the cover—because sometimes I add in one of Blix's little blessings when a customer needs some magic along with their bouquet.

Oh! And Patrick and I are working together on baking cupcakes with the little messages in them. We've figured it out, I think. Just last night I told him that all the messages should say the same thing: WHATEVER HAPPENS, LOVE THAT.

Because, as Blix told me at the wedding, if you need a mantra, that's one of the best.

ACKNOWLEDGMENTS

If it takes a village to raise a child, it takes at least a spark of magic, a whole lot of luck, and the patience and intelligence of countless good friends to get a book out there in the world. I've been fortunate enough to have all these things in my corner while writing *Matchmaking for Beginners*.

I particularly want to thank Kim Caldwell Steffen, who walks with me nearly every day and knows my characters at least as well as I do; and Alice Mattison, my longtime writing friend, who knows everything about storytelling and is always willing to help me get my book unstuck; and Leslie Connor, who listened to many, many early drafts and shared her best ideas and opinions. Nancy Antle read a very early draft and has encouraged this book every step of the way, as have Susanne Davis, Holly Robinson, and Nancy Hall. Karen and Terry Bergantino gave me a week at their friendly, warm condo in Newport, where I wrote without stopping.

I have so much gratitude for my wonderful, insightful, and brilliant editor, Jodi Warshaw, who loves talking about books and plots and always helps me figure out the story I'm trying to tell. She and Amara

Holstein are both editing geniuses. My agent, Nancy Yost, is a treasure who makes me laugh and who always believes I'll be able to finish the book.

Many thanks to my children—Ben, Allie, and Stephanie—who have taught me everything I know about love and patience, and also to the wonderful people they've brought into my life: Amy, Mike, Alex, Charlie, Josh, Miles, and Emma.

I also want to thank the "Blix" in my own life—my outrageous, hell-raising, spirited grandmother, Virginia Reeves, who taught me that love is the only thing that really matters.

And as always, my undying love to Jim, who shares my life and makes everything fun.

ABOUT THE AUTHOR

Photo © 2015 Peter Casolino

Maddie Dawson grew up in the South, born into a family of outrageous storytellers. Her various careers as a substitute English teacher, department-store clerk, medical-records typist, waitress, cat sitter, wedding-invitation-company receptionist, nanny, day care worker, electrocardiogram technician, and Taco Bell taco maker were made bearable by thinking up stories as she worked. Today she lives in Guilford, Connecticut, with her husband. She's the bestselling author of five previous novels: *The Survivor's Guide to Family Happiness*, *The Opposite of Maybe*, *The Stuff That Never Happened*, *Kissing Games of the World*, and *A Piece of Normal.*